## Danville Public Librar
## Outreach Department

| FEB 1 5 2013 | | |
|---|---|---|
| Dmm | | |
| Way | | |
| | | |
| | | |
| | | |
| | | |
| | | |
| | | |
| | | |
| | | |
| | | |
| | | |
| | | |
| | | |

**Comments:**

# FAITHFUL UNTO DEATH

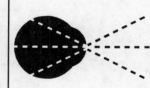

This Large Print Book carries the
Seal of Approval of N.A.V.H.

# FAITHFUL UNTO DEATH

## STEPHANIE JAYE EVANS

**THORNDIKE PRESS**
*A part of Gale, Cengage Learning*

Detroit • New York • San Francisco • New Haven, Conn • Waterville, Maine • London

# GALE
## CENGAGE Learning®

LIBRARY OF CONGRESS CATALOGING-IN-PUBLICATION DATA

Evans, Stephanie Jaye.
    Faithful unto death / by Stephanie Jaye Evans.
        pages ; cm. — (Thorndike Press large print mystery) (A Sugar Land mystery)
    ISBN 978-1-4104-5263-4 (hardcover) — ISBN 1-4104-5263-8 (hardcover)
    1. Clergy—Fiction. 2. Murder—Investigation—Fiction. 3. Family secrets—Fiction. 4. Sugar Land (Tex.)—Fiction. 5. Large type books. I. Title.
    PS3605.V3767F35 2012b
    813'.6—dc23                                                        2012034539

Published in 2012 by arrangement with The Berkley Publishing Group, a member of Penguin Group (USA) Inc.

Printed in the United States of America
1 2 3 4 5 6 7 16 15 14 13 12

To Dwain and Barbara Evans,
who, for more than fifty-seven years,
have kept their promises.

# PROLOGUE

The moon was low in the sky, as bright and weightless as a lover's promise, when the first of the joggers passed by the body on the golf course. In the March predawn, the Gulf Coast air was thick and humid, and the early, dedicated joggers were focused on keeping their breathing regular and their heart rates steady. They weren't looking around for stray corpses. In any case, they wouldn't have seen Graham Garcia even in full light. He lay on the grassy incline where the cart path dipped down to tunnel under Alcorn Oaks Boulevard. He couldn't be seen from street level, not unless someone stepped out onto the grassy overhang, lay down, and peered between the leafy trees lining the entrance to the tunnel. And no one did that, not even the jogger whose life had been completely overturned last night.

Half an hour later the sun was rising when Rebecca Rutland passed by with her two pug dogs. She was dressed in serious work-out clothes for the not-so-serious workout she would get airing the two overweight dogs. She had makeup on. Exercise makeup. She would shower soon and then put on her going-to-work makeup.

When her dogs drew close to where the road ran over the golf course tunnel, they broke into gasping, snorting barks. They pulled so hard on their halters that their fat, fawn shoulders bulged over the leather straps like plump backs in too-tight bras. Rebecca thought a turtle must have climbed out of a water hazard, turtles being one of the few animals a pug could chase down.

But she was in a hurry.

She said, "Who wants a cookie?" There was a short, still silence while the pugs internalized this new option.

Pugs are not Rin-Tin-Tin dogs; they don't rescue small children and they can't balance checkbooks, but they can master a large variety of food terms and "cookie" was a familiar and favorite word. The fact that cookies were no rarity in Rebecca's house had not diminished their appeal one jot. The hysteria changed in timbre, and the pugs leaned their weight against the leash, heading for home. The only thing stronger than a pug's curiosity is a pug's appetite.

At seven, the street was full of school traffic. In the master-planned communities of Sugar Land, the multiplicity of elementary, middle, and high schools meant that school traffic had to be staggered. Consequently, the high school students, those least able to rise early in the morning, had to be in their classes before seven thirty. Elementary school started at seven fifty. It wasn't until eight thirty-six, twenty-four minutes before the middle school tardy bell would ring, that thirteen-year-old Jessica Min found Graham Garcia's body. If it had been any day but Monday, golfers would have found him earlier. On Monday, the Bridgewater Country Club golf course was closed for grass maintenance.

Every school day Mrs. Min would hand Jessica her lunch bag and backpack, and Jessica would go through her backyard to the gate that opened onto the golf course. She did that today with her iPod headphones curled around her ears, a boy band pleading with her to be, be, be their baby.

Jessica followed the cart path down to the tunnel where she could cross beneath the road. That was so Mrs. Min wouldn't worry about some sophomore in a sports car, late for his second period, tearing around a corner and knocking to kingdom come all the hopes and dreams and love she had placed in the fragile vessel that was Jessica Min.

Because the cart path turned and twisted among the Arnold Palmer–designed mounds before it dipped to the mouth of the tunnel, and because the landscape trees camouflaged the tunnel opening, Jessica was almost upon Graham Garcia's body before she saw him. The sight stopped her toile ballet flats midstride.

A pop princess was now singing in her ear, "I don't think so, no, no. I don't think so . . ." but Jessica wasn't listening. She dropped her iced cherry Pop Tart when she saw Mr. Garcia and stopped chewing the bite in her mouth. She tried to swallow but her mouth had gone dry. Her heart was pounding so hard she couldn't hear the diva's crooning, and Jessica's hands, unlike her mouth, had gone wet. She dipped into her skirt pocket and found the pressed cotton handkerchief her mother made sure she carried.

Graham Garcia lay sprawled on the slope, the heel of one foot dug into the soft ground so that the toe of his shoe pointed straight down to the cart path. *Sur la pointe*, Jessica thought. Ballet was one of her many enrichment classes. His pale blue eyes looked up past the treetops.

Since Graham Garcia's head was higher on the slope than his feet, his blood had not pooled in his face and he looked peaceful for a dead guy. If some weird karma had deemed that Jessica Min had to come across a dead body, she could have done a whole lot worse than Graham Garcia.

The blond man Jessica saw was tall and slim and not young anymore. Some part of her brain told her that, if he wasn't young, he was never going to be old, either, and she nodded her head in agreement.

Graham Garcia was wearing a white golf shirt, open at the neck — Jessica could see a gold James Avery crucifix visible in the vee of his collar. His khaki trousers were hiked up on one leg and his blond leg hair curled over white golf socks, the low kind that you could barely see above the rubber-spiked golf shoe. Jessica's father wore that kind of golf sock.

Jessica didn't call out to him or touch him. She read mysteries and she watched *CSI* when her parents weren't there to stop her, and she knew all about forensics. She couldn't pick up her Pop Tart. She had taken a bite out of it, and seeing it on the ground a few feet from Graham Garcia's hand, she was reminded of the Walt Disney scene where Snow White has bitten the poisoned apple and fallen senseless, the bitten apple rolling from her grasp.

For such an overprotected child, Jessica was mature and stoic, so she was surprised by the tears that started up in her eyes.

Jessica switched her iPod off but left the headphones on. She looked all around. She turned back toward her house and began walking very quickly, her long, black ponytail swinging from side to side keeping perfect time with her short black skirt. Though she had a spooky, creepy feeling that something might be following her, she didn't run. Cool middle school girls don't run — Jessica was cooler than anyone knew.

But she couldn't help feeling that someone was behind her, watching.

# ONE

"I'm a preacher, I'm a teacher, and I'm a fellow human creature so don't worry about minding your p's and q's when we're together, we'll both be judged, but it won't be by me." That's what Daniel Brotherton had liked to say, and it had sounded corny to me even five hundred years ago when I was a five-year-old boy. Or maybe I just picked up on the corniness from my dad; certainly I always knew that he had to gird himself for his encounters with Mr. Brotherton, who was an emotional man, easily moved to tears by a touching story, always laughing too hard at anyone's attempt at a joke.

But as corny as the "preacher, teacher, creature" line was, I can relate to it now in a way I couldn't then. It's how I felt when Detective James Wanderley strode into my office, ignored my offer of a chair, and walked around, his hands jammed into the pockets of a navy linen jacket so faded it was almost gray. Not that he was minding his p's and q's.

I knew what he'd come about. He wanted to ask me "a few general questions about a member of the congregation." That's the way he'd put it. Rebecca had filled me in on the phone before she let him in my office. Rebecca Rutland is the church CEO who pretends to be my secretary.

Wanderley was a good-looking guy, not that I notice that kind of thing, but I knew my wife, Annie Laurie, would think he was handsome. He wore his longish dark hair brushed straight back off his forehead. His brows were thick and dark, and so close together he only just missed having what my daughters would call a unibrow. He would have been a little over six feet tall in his socks; the cowboy boots probably added another two inches.

It's hard to tell about cowboy boots. This is Texas, after all, so when a guy wears them, they might be an affectation, or they might be the most comfortable footwear he's got in his closet. These boots looked old enough that I was willing to give Wanderley the benefit of a doubt. They were worn but immaculate, polished and buffed to a soft glow. He wore jeans with that faded linen blazer — the blazer had me stymied. It was good-quality stuff, but at least a generation older than he was. You could tell by the cut. That and the fact that it was faded past ignoring.

He gave my beige, brown, standard-issue preacher's office a focused scrutiny it had never before been accorded. He stopped at my bookshelves, ran his eyes over the spines, pulling books out, riffling the pages. He held up Bertrand Russell's *Why I Am Not a Christian*, a paperback copy from Half Price Books.

"Funny book for a minister to have, don't you think?"

"Oh, I don't know," I said. He was getting on my nerves, the familiar way he was touching my things. "It's a good idea to know the opposition's position, don't you think?" As soon as I'd said it, I was sorry I'd echoed that "don't you think?" He wavered in front of the bookcase, looking for the space he'd pulled the paperback from, couldn't find it, and wedged the book in sideways, spine turned in.

I flinched when his hand moved over my own slim volumes, my name clearly printed on the spines. Lots of people have been happy to share with me their opinions about my writing skills, and over the six years it took me to write, and rewrite, and finally publish each of the commentaries, I've had time to grow a shell to the criticism. But I haven't.

He pulled out my latest effort, *Grace and the Book of Romans*, and turned it on its back to read the blurbs. I'd gotten some good ones. Not from James Patterson, you understand, but then it is a book of theology.

"Is it funny?" he asked.

"Not intentionally."

"Umm." He put it back. The right way.

Wanderley next stopped in front of my diplomas. Annie Laurie had had them matted and framed for our fifth anniversary. I'd been horrified when I found out how much she spent; they do look good, though.

"Walker Wells? That your real name?"

I said it was. I'm not sure I could imagine the circumstances under which a preacher might have diplomas made out in a fake name.

"Some crazy names people give their kids. University of Texas, huh? Class of 1985 . . . that'd make you, what?"

"Old," I said. This guy didn't even look thirty. Maybe twenty-eight? Certainly he was young to be a detective.

He smiled up at me. I may be old, but I was a good three inches taller, and glad for every one of those inches right then. I'm not sure how it happened, but the minute James Wanderley walked into my office, we were engaged in a competition — over what, I couldn't have said, but I always play to win.

"Way back then, UT took just about everybody, didn't they? None of that top ten percent of the class business?"

I drew in air to tell him that yes, way back then before the combustion engine was invented, University of Texas did take a goodly number of C students, but I had been offered an athletic *and* an academic scholarship. Naturally I took the athletic scholarship as it was a full ride. I'd been a starting tight guard, too, no small accomplishment at UT no matter what decade you played in. But I didn't say it. I shut my mouth and smiled as best I could. Annie Laurie would have been proud of me. Maybe He would have been, too. Then again, maybe not. He would have heard the snap of my teeth when I shut my mouth.

"Whoa! Master of Divinity from freaking Princeton University! And a Doctorate in Theology from Rice! Well, you are a very learned man, Brother Wells. I'm impressed."

"Oh, good. I had so hoped you would be." I couldn't help it; it slipped out. Wanderley

17

laughed out loud. It was a good-natured laugh. That surprised me.

A family picture on my desk caught his eye, and he strolled over to get a better look. As he passed a window, he drew his finger across the sill and checked it for dust. I swear I'm not making that up. He was real open about it, too. Wanderley picked up the framed portrait and held it close to his face.

"Nice-looking family. Pretty girls. Is it a recent picture?"

I nodded yes. It had been taken about six months ago, one of those pictures we get every three or four years for the new church pictorial directory. I'm in a houndstooth blazer, and Annie and the girls are in red. Red goes great with Annie and Merrie's blond hair but it was maybe the wrong shade for Jo. Made her look pale.

Wanderley tapped the photo under Jo's face. "You've got a changeling."

Jo's hair is dark brown, and wavy, and she's built smaller than Merrie, but if you look at their eyes, well, not the eyes so much, but their mouths are shaped just the . . . "She looks like my mother. At that age."

He glanced over at me, nodded, and then back to the picture. "I guess it's that dark-haired delicacy with the rest of you being so blond and athletic. You were a blond, weren't you?"

I drew my hand over my hair without thinking. I'm still a blond, a little gray on the sides . . . at least I have plenty on top. Wanderley looked to me to be the type to go bald early.

He held on to the photo.

"Let me guess. No, let me deduce. You're easy; with that bulk, you had to have been a football player."

Did you catch that? *Bulk*. I nodded.

"You married a pretty woman, Mr. Wells. You're a lucky man."

I am. I know it.

"The statuesque blonde, she's, what? Eighteen? Nineteen?"

I nodded. Merrie would be nineteen this summer.

"Okay, she's a volleyball player. Could be track, she's got the long, lean build you need for track, but the cool girls, they all play volleyball and this one, yeah, she'd be with the cool girls. Am I right?" He looked up at me with a cocky grin.

I'd had enough. "I'd appreciate it," I said tersely, "if you stopped looking at my girls like that."

Wanderley's mouth dropped, and he flushed up to his hairline. "Stopped loo—

oh. Damn. I beg your pardon. And I mean that sincerely. I think I'd shoot a man who laid a leering eye on my own daughter's picture."

"You've got a daughter?" I felt better. If a man has daughters of his own, he's going to understand.

"She's two. Molly."

"Molly Wanderley. Nice name."

"Not Wanderley. It's . . . complicated."

I had a tug of sympathy. Life is often so much more complicated now.

Wanderley stood and pulled his cell phone from his jeans pocket. He scrolled to a photo and passed it over. A dark-haired beauty gazed at me with saucer-sized eyes, her baby mouth not quite smiling. Her café au lait skin and loose curls told me something about Molly's mother, and something about Wanderley, too.

I handed it back.

"She's lovely," I said.

Wanderley looked into the little face for a moment, nodding gravely. He tucked the phone away.

"She is, yes."

"So was that your Sherlock Holmes act?"

Wanderley tilted his head. "Depends. How'd I do?"

I relented. "Merrie is at Texas Tech on a

track scholarship, but she doesn't compete because it's the cool thing to do, Merrie competes because she loves it. She did volleyball, too. In high school."

He gave a small smile and turned back to the photo. I don't think I've ever looked as closely at the picture as this guy did.

"It's your little changeling who's interesting," he continued. "She's what, fourteen?"

If Wanderley ever lost his job with the department, he could always be the "Guess Your Age" guy at the carnival.

"She's too small for volleyball. And I'm going to guess this one is not a team player; you can see it in her eyes. Way she holds her head, yeah, that's the tell, the way she holds her head, the way she holds her whole body; this one is a dancer."

He looked up. "So?" he asked. "Am I right?"

"Jo is a dancer," I admitted, "but dancing, ballet dancing at least, is a team sport." At least that's the way Jo had sold me on it.

"Oh, not for this one, I'm betting. She looks like a star, doesn't she?"

He held the photo out for me to see and I took it from him. You know, Jo does have a regal tilt to her chin. She has spent her time in the corps, the chorus line of a ballet company, but even then, she stood out.

"She does. Mr. Wanderley . . ."

"Detective. And your title is . . ."

"Mister. Mr. Wells."

"Not Reverend Wells? Not Doctor Wells? Not your holiness?"

"Mr. Wells will do fine."

Again the grin.

"And you can call me Detective Wanderley."

"Detective Wanderley, Rebecca said you needed to see me urgently, and I'm a little lost right now about where the urgency lies because . . ."

Wanderley took the picture from my hand and set it back on my desk, facing toward him. I turned the frame around to face me. He finally took the swivel chair across from my desk and sat in it or rode it, I don't know which. He rocked it back and forth and swung it from side to side the whole time we talked. I thought he was going to bust the spring.

Wanderley leaned forward. He'd fished something out of one of his pockets and was turning it over and over between his finger and thumb. "Let me tell you what I've come about."

Which would be good, since I had about a hundred things I needed to get done. I sat down at my desk and gave him my patient, expectant smile, the one I use for elders' meetings.

"There's a member of your congregation," Wanderley said. "His name is Graham Garcia."

My heart grew still inside me. *Something bad is coming. It's not my fault. It's on you now.* Graham's voice.

I took a careful breath. Whatever it was Wanderley had come to tell me, it wasn't going to be good news. It would be nothing I wanted to hear.

"Well," I said, "Graham Garcia isn't a member, but his wife, Honey, is. And their son, Alex. I think Graham goes to St. Laurence; he's Catholic, their daughter, too, I think. Jenasy. She's at Southwestern in Georgetown. You've got the wrong church, Mr. Wanderley —"

"Detective," he interrupted.

" 'Detective,' you'll want to talk to one of the priests over at St. Laurence. Probably Father Fontana. You want me to call him for you?" I had my cell in my hand, waiting for the word. I'd be glad to turn this fellow over to my comrades down the street. I needed this to be the wrong church for whatever bad news was going to come out of his mouth.

Wanderley shook his head no and I put

23

my cell down and picked up a pencil instead. Put that down and picked up a pen. No more use to me than the pencil was. I was about to hear bad news and busywork wasn't going to make it go away.

"I'll talk to Father Fontana later. It's you I want right now. From talking to Mrs. Garcia, I think you might have some information Father Fontana won't."

Whatever it was Wanderley had been turning in his fingers, he popped it into his mouth. I could see little glints of red when he talked.

"What's this about, Detective Wanderley? Is Graham joining Homeland Security or the FBI? You doing background checks? Is that a guitar pick in your mouth?"

He did some maneuvering with his tongue and smiled, the bit of red plastic held between his front teeth for me to see. It was indeed a guitar pick.

"How did Graham Garcia get to be a Garcia?" he asked, paying no mind to my questions. "I've never in my life seen such an Aryan-looking Garcia."

I wanted to tell Wanderley that the word "Aryan" had been misappropriated by the Nazis, that "Aryan" didn't originally mean anything like a blond-haired, blue-eyed Northern European, but instead referred to the ancient Indo-Iranian peoples, whose descendants now occupy Iran, Afghanistan, and India, but I gave Wanderley the short answer.

"His mother married Dr. Garcia."

I put the pen down and straightened my papers. If this was all on account of Homeland Security or such, I was going to be sending Pete Olson, my representative, another e-mail, and this one wouldn't be on behalf of PBS and NPR. I would be relieved, too.

Wanderley nodded his head like he had it all figured out now. He was in my office, head nodding, chair rocking, fingers drumming, and tongue working that red plastic pick around in his mouth so I could hear it click against his teeth.

"Detective Wanderley, are you going to tell me why you're asking about Honey's husband, or are you the only one who gets to ask questions?"

"He had a meeting with you last Friday." Wanderley lifted his butt, fished a notebook out of the back pocket of his jeans, and flipped it open one-handed, pretended to consult it. He kicked out one long, skinny, jean-clad leg and rested the ankle on his knee. Gave me a look at those boots. They were good-quality cowboy boots, possibly from the same era as the jacket. They had the "cowboy heel" — angled and two inches high, so either Wanderley was a rider, or whoever first wore those boots was a rider, or Wanderley was a poseur. I'm not judging, I'm just saying.

"At three o'clock," he added, in case I'd forgotten, me being of advanced age and all.

"He did, yes."

"Even though he's not a member of your congregation; doesn't even belong to your religion." He gave me a bland, inquisitive look that he stole from Fox Mulder. Totally over the top, this guy.

"Broadly speaking, we're both Christians, but yes, we come from different religious traditions."

He stopped rocking in the chair and got still. The stillness was a relief. "Do you mind telling me what you talked about, the reason for the meeting?"

I leaned back in my chair and pushed it until it leaned against the window. The air was noticeably warmer close to the window. This visit was making me feel increasingly anxious; my system was on that "high alert" setting that gets you ready for that whole fight-or-flight thing. "I do mind. Enormously. If this information is important to you, and I can't see how it could be, I believe I'd be more comfortable letting Graham share it with you."

Wanderley was shaking his head before I stopped speaking, and he pulled his own chair up until his knees were against my desk.

"No, nope, that's not going to work, and I'll tell you why. Somebody murdered Mr. Garcia early this morning. Graham Garcia is dead."

So there was the bad news. And it was so much worse than I had been preparing for. Dead. Finished. Final. Over. Time's up. *Something bad is coming. It's not my fault. It's on you now.* Ohhh. I did not want this to be on me.

Two heartbeats later I scooted my chair over to the intercom, pressed the button that gave me Rebecca's desk. I said, "Rebecca, please call Annie Laurie, try her cell if you don't catch her at home; tell her I'm going to need to pick her up in ten minutes if she can get free, we've got an emergency in the church family. Make sure she knows it's not Merrie or Jo."

I buzzed off and buzzed right back on.

"Tell her if she's got one of her pound cakes in the freezer, this would be a good time to haul one out."

27

Rebecca's voice from the speaker said, "Bear, is there any chance you're going to let me know what this emergency is?"

I grabbed my Bible, didn't bother with my jacket, this was shirtsleeves work anyway, and opened the office door so I was talking to the back of Rebecca's head while she was talking to the speaker.

"There is. I'll call you from the car. No, you call me after you get Annie."

Rebecca nodded, already dialing my home number. I bypassed the elevator and took the stairs two at a time, noticing that Wanderley wasn't having any trouble keeping up with me even though I had to have the longer stride, what with me having those three inches on him.

"Wells, we weren't done in there."

"We're done for right now."

"Listen, there's some questions I'd like answered. I've got a job to do."

He was the one irritated now; I could hear it in his voice. Not that I cared. The guy ran his fingers over the balusters like he was twelve. The air filled with the thrum.

The soft, wet air closed around me when I stepped out of the air-conditioned building. My keys were in my hand and I beeped the door locks open. I shut the door harder than I needed to, but lowered the window

28

as I pulled out of the space marked OFFICE STAFF ONLY, PLEASE and looked back at the young man standing there, nearer Merrie's age than mine.

"Mr. Wanderley —"

"Detective."

"Right. I've got a job, too. And I'm going to go do it now. If you still want to talk later, we'll talk later." I didn't wait to see if this was agreeable with him.

# Two

Ten minutes' notice and my wife was on our front porch, neat as a new dime in khaki slacks and white leather Keds, clasping a tote bag that I could be pretty sure held a foil-wrapped pound cake in a ziplock freezer bag. I am a lucky man and I know it. That makes me twice blessed.

Annie Laurie slid in beside me nearly before the car came to a complete stop, and I drove back the way I came. The Garcias live the other side of the church from us. I keep a church directory in the car, and on the way over I tried to get through to Honey, but I kept getting a busy signal. I put my cell on speaker phone, and as I dialed Rebecca, I said to Annie Laurie, "Let me call Rebecca and you listen in. I'll do the telling once, not that I know much of anything yet."

Rebecca picked up on the first ring, saying straight off, "I did call you the way you

30

said to, but your line was busy."

"I was trying to get through to Honey Garcia, but I couldn't get her. That young police officer, detective, whatever, that Wanderley fellow says Graham Garcia is dead. He says Graham was murdered this morning."

There was a gasp from Annie Laurie next to me and from Rebecca on the phone. Annie put her hand on my knee.

Rebecca said, "Oh, my good Lord. I'll call whoever is heading the prayer team right now. She's got one child still at home, doesn't she? A sixteen-year-old boy, right? What's his name?"

"Alex. Alejandro, but he goes by Alex."

"You know which youth minister he's closer to — Jason or Brick?"

I didn't.

"I'll buzz them, see what they can do. You think it's too early to call the women's association to start making some meals for the family?"

I told Rebecca to do whatever she thought was best, which was what she was going to do anyway no matter what I said. I told her that I'd keep my cell phone on but to try not to call unless she had to.

"And if you don't hear from me before two thirty, would you pick up Jo? I may not be able to get Annie back in time."

"I'll pick her up and feed her, too, assuming I can get your child to eat anything. She have ballet class this afternoon?"

I said Jo had ballet class every afternoon, eight days a week.

"Well, I'll take her on to ballet, don't worry, I've got you covered."

Rebecca is Southern Baptist, not Church of Christ, and it was the Baptists' loss when she came to work for me. That woman makes my life run smoother, and if she critiques my sermons as she takes dictation, well, it's worth it to have her handle the myriad organizational difficulties that would otherwise consume my day. I have taken to telling Baptist preacher jokes, which is some retaliation.

The Garcias don't live in any of the new subdivisions that surround the church. They have one of the older homes on Oyster Creek. These are expensive homes, most of them on two- or three-acre lots that back up to a small lake that's really an overgrown retention pond. The neighborhood was built thirty or forty years back by oilmen who wanted their kids to be able to keep horses and boats and who didn't mind the half-hour drive into downtown Houston. Of course, since then Houston had sprawled all the way out to lap up against Sugar Land — that same drive would take you an hour or more today, what with traffic.

Honey and Graham lived in Honey's childhood home. Her dad is HD Parker, one of the big ones in Houston's oil heyday. HD's own father had been a West Texas dirt farmer, yet with equal parts hard work, recklessness, ruthlessness, and good luck, HD eventually scratched out for himself a tidy piece of the Houston oil scene, and the money and notoriety that went with it. I've read a couple of books about the wildcatters and their years of excess, and though HD didn't warrant a whole chapter in either book, he was the subject of some pretty lively paragraphs.

Honey had been HD's only daughter. His first wife had given him a horde of sons, and had worked and worried herself into an early grave as she dealt with the initial ups and downs of HD's fortunes. HD was in his forties and his ascent assured when he and his new bride, Belinda — known as Beanie — had Honey. He had named the child "Honey" over Beanie's objections because she was "the sweetest gift life had given him." It would be fair to say that HD Parker was a doting father.

When Honey got engaged to Graham

Garcia, her father was putting the final touches on the new swankienda he'd built in River Oaks, Houston's most exclusive neighborhood, so he made a gift of his old home to the new couple. He took care to give it to Honey before she got married, however, to make sure the house would always remain her separate property.

Texas is both a community property state and a homestead state. By giving Honey the house before she married, HD had assured that the house would never fall under the community property law and become half Graham's. And because Texas is a homestead state, a house offers a significant margin of financial protection. Houston had a bankrupt millionaire try to claim homestead protection over a thirty-story office building. He had made his home in the penthouse. I don't think the argument prevailed, but it kept a number of lawyers busy for several years.

Over the years, Graham and Honey had made the house their own, and it was a lovely, welcoming home, one they frequently opened up for church and community affairs. It was a long, low, late-sixties ranch that didn't look like all that much from out front, but inside had been expanded and restored and was a beautiful, glowing example of what good taste and a truckload of money can do.

The gate to the Garcias' home stood open — I've never seen it closed. The house wasn't visible from the road. Thick hedges surrounded the property. You drove up a gravel drive past rows of mature crepe myrtle, currently covered with little green buds. It was only March, and crepe myrtle doesn't bloom till June. Mainly what you noticed, especially this time of year, were the huge five-foot-high shrubs of blooming azaleas, lilac and white and pink and coral. Your landscaping has to be in place a long time to achieve that lush look.

Honey's black Escalade was parked in the circle drive. It was dusty and spotted with water drops. There were two police cars parked to the side and a sedan I didn't recognize. I didn't see Alex's F-150. He'd had the fire-engine-red truck jacked up, those great big tires like you see on monster trucks, so there wasn't any missing it.

I parked next to the Escalade. I took a big breath, let it out, and opened the door. Annie Laurie caught my sleeve.

"Bear, you want to say a prayer first?"

I kind of had been, all the drive over, though it hadn't been anything more specific than "Please, God, please, God, please,

God." I was counting on God to fill in the missing parts, but Annie was right, I needed to take a moment before I rushed in like a lineman opening a hole for my running back. Following that simile through, I guess that would make Jesus my running back. Sounds like a country-western song. My sister-in-law, Stacy, says if I use one more football simile in a sermon, she's going to get up and walk out and she's going to use the center aisle, too.

Annie and I held hands and I asked God to give me the right words to comfort this family, asked Him to send them the peace that passes understanding. I was trying to keep my mind on praying and not think about the heartbreak we were going to walk into.

We didn't have to knock; a pretty young woman in a police uniform opened the door as we walked up the steps.

"Ya'll the Wellses? Detective Wanderley called, said to expect you, so ya'll come on in."

She was keeping her voice subdued, but her eyes were alight. We don't usually get this kind of excitement in Sugar Land.

"Mrs. Garcia is out on the sunporch," she said. "Don't worry about touching things, everything's already been dusted."

The brick-floored foyer opened onto a large, comfortable family room and on past the kitchen, where I could see Cruz Valtierra, who'd worked for the Garcias as long as I'd known them, standing at the kitchen sink, her back to us, peeling something with a potato peeler. Potatoes, probably. The kitchen had that same polished brick floor, which was probably easy to clean but must have been hard on Cruz's back.

The glassed-in sunroom was bright with morning light. The wrought-iron furniture had been stacked high with floral cushions and pillows, and there was a deep-pile flower-patterned rug on the brick floor. Fresh daffodils stood in vases on the side tables, and on the small glass breakfast table was a woven basket filled with bright orange clementines. The room seemed like an extension of the backyard, flower-filled and sunny. The lake looked blue and cool, and if it wasn't big enough for sailboats, it was just the right size for the white canoe pulled up to the Garcias' dock.

Honey sat alone in the corner of the love seat, her knees drawn up to her chin and her hands clasped around her ankles. A roll of toilet paper next to her was trailing its sheets on the floor. A scattering of damp tissue wads littered the cushion around her. On the table to her left, there was a part-full glass of lemonade almost the same color as the slacks she wore.

Annie Laurie dropped her purse and tote bag on the floor and went over to Honey, brushed aside the tissues, sat down, and put her arms about her. Honey's face was puffy and streaked with weeping; now she laid her head on Annie's breast and let the tears fall. She didn't let go of her ankles, didn't make any effort to wipe the tears away, hardly made a sound as her shoulders heaved. Her tears left a wet patch on Annie's blue cotton shirt.

Looking at the two women together, I was taken aback by how much Honey had changed. Annie has always been a slim woman; after our girls were born, she rounded out some, but for a woman over forty, she looked good. Shoot, Annie would look good for thirty.

Honey, on the other hand, had battled her weight for as long as I'd known her. She hadn't ever been less than plump, and there had been times when she had veered off into, well, if I were an unkind man, I'd say she'd gotten a little fat sometimes. The thing is, Honey looked good plump. She's a peachy-skinned redhead, and full-bodied, she looks ripe and luscious and more than one man has been surprised that her unfashionably fleshy curves have caused such a stirring in his loins. I'd be a liar if I said it hadn't ever happened to me.

But the Honey who sat in front of me, eyes squeezed shut, leaking tears all over my wife, was not plump. I'd say she was skinny, but the word that came to mind was "deflated." She must have dropped a good thirty pounds. That's a lot of weight to lose, even for someone as big as I am. Honey was maybe five feet nine. And I'll tell you something else: Honey's probably a bit over forty, but I'd never before noticed. Now those years clung to her. Looking at her made me feel sad, and old.

Annie Laurie did that comforting murmur thing women who care for each other do when one is in terrible pain. I took a handful of clementines before I sat down on the chair closest to the love seat and I peeled and sectioned four or five just to give my hands something to do. There wasn't a trash can anywhere I could see, so I mixed the torn pieces of peel in with a bowl of potpourri. Then I lined the miniature orange sections up on top of one of the magazines stacked on the coffee table. In case someone might want one. The phone rang somewhere in the house; there was talk and then a definitive click as the receiver was replaced in the cradle.

Cruz came in with a coffee tray and I jumped up to take it from her, but she wouldn't let me. She put it down on the glass table with a thump that brought Honey's head up, and before she could go back to crying, Cruz handed her a folded, damp washcloth and said, "Wipe your face. You're all splotches. That was your father on the phone again. I told him what you told me to tell him."

Honey patted her face with the washcloth and said through the cloth, "Thank you, Cruz."

"Yeah, he's coming out anyway. He'll be here in a little bit, so you want to pull yourself together."

Honey threw the washcloth across the room.

Cruz was unperturbed. "I told him what you said, he said he's coming out. *You* can't stop that old man. I don't know why you think I can. Your momma is coming, too. You should have called her first thing, Honey. How you think that's gonna make her feel, getting that call from me? Should have called her yourself with the news. And you gonna pick that cloth up yourself."

Honey unfolded herself and crossed the room to fetch the wet cloth. Cruz poured out four cups of coffee, fixing each the way she knew we drank it; she put three sugars and milk in mine, four sugars, no milk in hers. She sat down in the chair opposite me, smoothed the straight, navy blue skirt of her dress over her knees, and said without preamble, "Alex isn't home."

"Hasn't anyone called the school yet?"

Cruz gave me a look. She's really good at that, giving meaningful looks.

"Of course we did, Bear. What you thinking? He's not at school. He didn't come home last night. He's not answering his cell. Jenasy's roommate is bringing her home later today. You know what happened?"

Annie said, "No, we just heard . . ."

"You gonna tell them what the police say or you want me to?"

Honey shook her head. Her hair was clean and brushed, but she needed a color touch-up. I could see a dark line at the roots of her curls. She got one of Cruz's pointed looks as she curled back onto the love seat. The coffee in front of her was black. She used to prefer coffee with cream. Lots of cream.

Cruz drank her cup halfway down and set it in the saucer.

41

"Okay. This is what they're telling us. You know the Bridgewater golf course? I'm talking about that piece of it at the corner of Alcorn Oaks and Elkins Road; you know where I'm talking about?"

I said, yes, I knew it. I'd played the course at least once a month since we'd moved to Sugar Land. It was easy walking distance from our house.

"So that's where she found him. Some little Chinese girl on her way to school."

"Cruz, she's Korean, or her parents are Korean, she's American . . ." Honey trailed off under Cruz's gaze.

"Is that important to what I'm saying?"

Honey shook her head. Cruz took the story up again.

"No. So anyway, this little girl, her house backs up to the golf course, and she crosses the golf course each day to get to Fort Settlement, that's the middle school, you know."

We knew. Jo had been in school at Fort Settlement last year. She was a freshman at Clements High School this year.

"So that's where she found him." Cruz drank from her coffee cup and put it down with a clink that said "There, now."

We had come full circle in the story and I

42

still didn't know how or why Graham had died.

I asked. "Cruz, how did Graham die?"

"Somebody hit him on the head. Hard."

In my mind's eye I could see a golf ball ricocheting off a pine tree and beaning Graham.

"Are they certain it wasn't an accident?"

"Yeah, they're pretty sure." Her tone of voice meant they were positive. Cruz shook her head firmly, finished off her cup, and turned it upside down in the saucer. Cruz Valtierra is the only person I've ever seen do this.

"Probably not an accident unless he could manage to whack himself in the head with a Big Bertha. Graham has got a dent in his head that fits a Big Bertha."

I ran through the mechanics in my mind's eye. A Big Bertha golf club has a great big head, hence the name. There wasn't any way on earth I could accidentally brain myself with one. But a Big Bertha seemed an unlikely murder weapon. Still, I could see how someone else could accidentally hit you with a Big Bertha. I've played with guys who made me feel like golf could develop into a contact sport. Say, if they stepped back when they were swinging, not that you're supposed to step back in the middle of a swing, but say they stepped into your space . . .

Cruz said, "Then we got the problem of what Graham was doing on the golf course in the middle of the night. Not playing golf, I'm thinking. Not in the dark."

It wasn't all that dark last night. There was a full moon. With a glow-in-the-dark ball, a really good golfer like Graham might be able to play — you shouldn't, the course closes an hour after full dark, but . . .

"Was he robbed? Do the police have any idea who did this?"

At this, Honey lifted her head. She wore a bright, tight smile.

"Do *you* have any idea, Bear? You may have been the last person to have a real conversation with Graham. Did he tell you anything? Because when he got home after talking to you, he locked himself up in his study for three or four hours and then went out. He didn't say more than a sentence or two to me. So of course, I'm wondering what went on between the two of you. Did you learn anything I should know about?"

I said no, which maybe wasn't entirely true. She might need to know about some of it. But not now. Maybe not ever.

"Did you get one of Graham's staring sessions? You doing all the talking and him looking at the ceiling, giving back a whole lot of quiet?"

I didn't say anything and Honey took that for assent.

She sighed and pushed her hair back off her face, holding it high at the crown and then releasing her hair to fall limply back down.

"If you want to know what the police think," Honey said, "their idea is that he was living with the enemy. Their idea is that *I* picked up that golf club and swung it at my husband's head as hard as I could and smashed his brain to a jelly."

She stood up and slid her hands down her newly sleek hips. Her waistband slipped an inch and exposed some tummy. Not plump, but not tight, either. Honey picked up her glass of diluted lemonade and drank it down. She hadn't touched her coffee.

"That's their favorite idea numero uno. Ideao favorito numero two-o . . ."

I wasn't sure where the cartoon Spanish had come from; I didn't like it. Honey put her empty glass on the floor, and rested her hand on the back of my chair, leaning in close to me and breathing gin in my face. Now I knew where the cartoon Spanish had come from, and I didn't like that, either.

"Um . . . *numero duo*, I mean, that would

be Alex, Bear. My baby boy is their number two suspect. The police have just given my boy's room the kind of tweezers and Baggie search no sixteen-year-old boy should have to go through. Do you know what I mean, Bear?"

Honey was upright now, swaying a little, hands on her hips, as much to keep her pants up as to demonstrate her outrage. Annie Laurie looked bewildered. Cruz was stacking coffee cups on the tray, making a lot of clatter. The clatter distracted Honey and she turned to Cruz.

"Cruz, sugar, could you get me some more" — there was a hesitation — "lemonade?"

Cruz walked out of the sunroom with the tray. She called back over her shoulder, "No, Honey, I got work to do. Better you drink your coffee instead. And did you hear me say your daddy is on his way? You want to lay off that 'lemonade,' Honey. Your daddy ain't going to like that."

Honey wavered, looking uncertain. She noticed the orange segments on the magazine and sat back down.

"Why, look here, Annie Laurie, here's someone gone and peeled these oranges for me. I love these little clementines, don't you, too? Little California Cuties, that's what they call them. They're so sweet, and no pits! I love that there's no pits, don't you, Annie Laurie?" Honey was working her way through the orange segments, chewing and swallowing, big tears running down her face. Annie Laurie slipped over to my side.

"Bear, I think —"

"Uh-huh, Annie. Let me talk to her. See if you can help Cruz, see if she knows where Alex might be. I know that boy didn't do anything" — I didn't know; that's what I was praying — "but it doesn't look good for him to be gone, and anyway, I'd rather he be here at home when he gets this news. Would you take that cake with you before somebody steps on it?"

Annie Laurie nearly stepped on the pound cake herself as she backed out the door.

I sat back down in the chair, noting that I could feel the cast iron beneath the cushion and all those pillows. Honey patted the seat next to her. Her rings slid stone side down; they were loose, too. Dang. Did she have some wasting disease?

"No, Honey, I'm fine over here. Let's go ahead and get this over with. I know you're a good woman, and you know Annie Laurie and I love you, but good people do bad things sometimes; you and I know that's the truth. So, did you kill Graham? Maybe

47

not meaning to kill him, but are you the one who hit him with the golf club?"

Honey looked at me and her eyes cleared; I could see the Honey I used to know looking out of that haggard face. Cruz ought to bring a plate of cookies, or something. I wanted Honey back to herself again.

"Walker, I guess you know I had a drink this morning." When people get serious, they often call me by my given name.

I said, "I know you've had more than one, Honey."

She tried to smile but gave it up. "I'm just trying to 'stablish that even though I had a drink this morning" — a pause — "maybe two, that I am stone-cold sober when I tell you that I didn't kill Graham, not accidentally, not on purpose.

"I did hate him sometimes, Bear. There were times when I wished he would die. I suppose that's kind of a 'Jimmy Carter murder.' " She looked down at her hands, stretching them out. They were good strong hands, long-fingered, the nails manicured that way where the tips were white.

"If I did any fantasizing about someone dying, it was more often me. Preferably like Camille, slow and easy and not disfiguring, so that Graham would have plenty of time to feel guilty and fall back in love with me.

"See, what it means, Bear, Graham dying, what it means, is that God isn't ever going to fix us. Graham isn't ever going to find his way back to me. He's not going to love me again. All those nights on my knees, praying, and the extra highlights in my hair, the Botox, the personal trainer. Me being so careful what I put in my mouth that I went to bed hungry every night for the last year."

She shook her head, picked up the cup of now-tepid coffee, and sipped it.

"When I was in high school, I dated, I dated all the time! And I was a fatty, then, too. Well, I was chubby. But boys liked me, thought I was pretty. *I* thought I was pretty. Graham wasn't the only fellow to ask me to marry him. Two boys bought me rings outright, before they even asked."

I didn't doubt that, and it might have been true even without HD Parker's millions.

"But once I met Graham, there wasn't anyone else. I was drawn to that boy like a beetle to the bug zapper. And he burnt me to cinders. He'll be getting buried in a couple of days, but when they put him in the dirt, a whole lot of who I used to be, who I ought to have been . . ."

Honey's face was so contorted with anger and grief it was hard not to turn away. She saw it in my eyes and her hands flew to her face. She covered her face with her hands, and then, with her fingers, she smoothed out the wrinkles on her forehead, drew her palms up along her cheekbones, briefly lifting her face. When her hands dropped, her face was calm.

"A whole lot of Honey will be down there with him. That part is going to be every bit as dead as Graham.

"Let me tell you about Graham, Bear, the Graham you didn't get to know. The Graham hardly anybody knew. He didn't let many people know who he was.

"You know how I met Graham? Momma and I were flying up to New York to hit the after-Christmas sales. The flight was delayed, and Momma was engrossed in some book, and I've never been much of a reader. There was this handsome young man, already looking like the big-time lawyer he would come to be, waiting for the same flight. He was talking to these three women, they're dressed just as plain as mud, and I'm thinking what do they have that can attract someone as sharp as Graham, because that's who that was, that was Graham. And come to find out, they were nuns.

"I know that because after a little bit, Graham comes over to Momma and me and wants to know do we want some coffee or anything since he was going to get some for himself and it would be his pleasure to get some for us, too. I'm not the dummy I look like and I said I'd go with him, help him carry it all back. So this nice-looking man tells me those three women are nuns on their way to New York, and the place they were staying was in Harlem. Those nuns were planning on taking the subway to Harlem. Because the flight was delayed, those poor women were going to be heading off to Harlem on the subway at, like, one in the morning. I learn all this walking the concourse drinking coffee, which I didn't even like back then, and talking to Graham.

"Only when we finally got to JFK, there was a limo driver holding a sign, SISTERS MARY ALICE, THERESA, AND DOLORES. I don't really remember their names, but, you know. What I do remember is, Graham had called ahead to get those poor women a limo to take them right to the door of their school or whatever it was. He didn't have much money then, either."

Honey's face went soft and dreamy.

"I loved him for that. I fell in love with Graham right there and then, with my matching luggage all piled at my feet, the nuns flustered and surprised, kissing Graham on the cheek and blessing him, and I see Graham slip them money to tip the driver."

Honey pleated the bottom of her blouse and her eyes filled again.

"Graham used to make word problems for me, you know that? No. No one knows that but me. He'd leave them on the kitchen table for me to find when I got up. Once I had the puzzle worked out, it would be a love message, or maybe a funny poem he made up about how sweet 'honey' was. Every once in a while it was to tell me to look someplace — I'd find a piece of jewelry wrapped up in that pale blue box that makes every girl's heart flutter."

I had no idea what that pale blue box was and made a mental note to ask Annie.

Honey held a slim hand out to display a ring with a large sapphire. She straightened it on her hand, but the heavy rock slipped down to hide in her palm and she sighed.

"There are one hundred stories I could tell you. One thousand reasons why I chose Graham and was never sorry I did. I love those stories."

I wondered if Honey had loved the stories, but had stopped loving the man.

"With Graham gone, I don't know who I am."

Her face crumpled and she flung her head

back dramatically and bumped it hard on the wrought-iron frame that surrounded the cushions.

"Oh! Dang it!" She put her hands up to rub the back of her head and giggled a little, unnervingly. "You see what I get for being a drama queen." There was a big sigh and she picked up the toilet paper roll and held it close to her flattened bosom. "So, you see, it's true. I did not kill Graham."

She looked at me from under her lashes.

"Not that I'd tell you if I had." She gave that giggle again.

The pretty police officer stuck her head in the door. "Mrs. Garcia? Detective Wanderley is back and he'd like a few words."

I stood up and put my hand under Honey's arm to steady her, the way you do with an old person. I could feel the toned muscles, yet her skin felt loose over the muscle.

Detective James Wanderley was squatting near the mail flap in the front door, shuffling through the mail on the floor. He gave us a glance when he heard us, then went back to the mail in his hand. He didn't seem the least bit embarrassed to be caught going through someone else's mail. He rose up and was about to put the mail on the foyer table. Cruz came in and snatched the mail from his hand. Annie Laurie was right behind her. Annie, ever friendly and welcoming, something I normally like about her, put her hand out to the young man.

"Hi, I'm Annie Laurie, Bear's wife."

Wanderley took her hand and held it longer than I felt courtesy required.

"Bear?"

"Oh, you know, Walker here. Only strangers call him Walker. Everybody else calls him Bear."

I didn't need to see Wanderley's pie-eating grin to see where this was going to end up.

"I hope you won't mind, then, if I call you 'Bear'? Since we'll be seeing so much of each other."

I nearly answered back in a way I would have had to repent for, but Annie, all unaware, saved me.

She slapped Wanderley on the arm and said, "Course he doesn't mind. Bear's the friendliest man you'll find in Sugar Land. He hates to stand on formality."

Sometimes that woman is way too familiar.

I said, "If you're going to be questioning Mrs. Garcia, I'd like her to have legal counsel present. That all right with you, Honey? I'll give Glenn Carter a call."

Honey had the waistband of her pants

54

gathered in one hand. Surely she had some clothes to fit her. Or a belt. Or a safety pin. Since Honey had plenty of money to buy clothes after her weight loss, I wondered if she was wearing her old clothes to emphasize her new slimness. Bad decision.

Honey looked startled at the mention of calling a lawyer. "Why, Glenn's not that kind of lawyer, Bear, Glenn does, like, I don't know, land things, oil —"

I cut her off. "I know that, but he'll know someone to call —"

Wanderley said, "It really isn't necessary, I only —"

"It is necessary. Mrs. Garcia is upset and worn out; she's had a terrible tragedy. I want her to have someone who's familiar with the system sitting —"

"I'm familiar with the system and I'll be sitting —"

"Someone who's on her side sitting —"

"Mr. Wells, I'm on her side. I'm trying to find out who killed her husband this morning. That's what she wants, too, isn't that right, Mrs. Garcia? Now she and I are going to —"

"Honey isn't going into a closed room with you; she is not going to say one word to you!"

We were in each other's faces at this point,

and if we weren't exactly yelling at each other, we had certainly passed the point of raised voices. Honey and Annie were staring. Cruz had come back after depositing the mail someplace and looked ready to forcibly eject us both. Then a red Ford F-150 on monster tires took the circular drive at a speed that sent a spray of gravel pinging against my car.

Alex Garcia jumped out of the cab and hooked a bulky backpack over his shoulders. He had his father's sharp good looks, not yet fully developed. His dark blond hair was in his eyes and past his shoulders, unfashionably long. I was surprised the Garcias allowed that hair.

Through the beveled glass front door, the five of us watched him. He took a step and stopped, taking in the police cars. One hand went to his chest like he was feeling for a heartbeat. He rubbed at something under his shirt. Alex looked at the police cars, looked at my car, and turned and looked at his own truck. I'd have wanted to get in and drive off, too.

"Alex is home," said Cruz.

Indeed he was. All five feet eleven inches of skinny, gangly, sixteen-year-old angst shuffled toward the front door. His huge sneakers kicked up nearly as much gravel as his truck had.

It looked to me that he was having the same wardrobe problem his mother had; his pants rode low, displaying sea-blue boxers with hula girls printed all over them. His head was lowered and that hair was fanned across his face, but he had to be aware of the faces behind the glass door.

Wanderley opened the door and everyone but Cruz spilled out to meet him. Without a glance, Alex walked past us, his mother, too, and said to Cruz as he passed her, "I skip one lousy day of school and she calls the cops?"

Alex was in the kitchen pulling food out of the refrigerator before we got back inside and shut the front door.

Honey was in tears. I went into the kitchen and put my arm around Alex's shoulders, leading him back toward the living room; he didn't let go of the ziplock of deli meat and carton of coconut water he was clutching.

I was saying, "Alex, let's bring your mother in here for a moment . . ."

Alex rolled his eyes and sighed, "One lousy day."

I saw Wanderley following and I let go of Alex to face him. "This is going to be private, Wanderley, so why don't you —"

He grabbed me by the elbow and pulled me over to the dining room. I was surprised by how strong his grip was.

That fellow put his nose about two inches from mine and hissed at me, "You listen here, *Bear*" — he put unnecessary emphasis on the nickname — "I'm going to be in there when you tell that boy his father is dead, see. He's a suspect. I don't care how many youth group meetings he's attended, or if he passes the collection plate on Sundays or if God gave him a free pass saying he can skip Judgment Day and go right on up to Heaven.

"Now I plan to sit there quiet and observe, but if you give me one quarter-cup's worth of trouble over this, then I'm going to call three of my officers in here, including the pretty little miss with the bouncy ponytail, you try to imagine how embarrassing that would be, and I'm going to have them escort your own high holiness right down to the station on the grounds that you are interfering with my investigation. And I'm going to call a reporter I know at the *Chronicle* and make sure she's there to see you get booked, because it will make exactly the kind of human interest story she specializes in. Won't all that publicity make this mess that much easier for the grieving widow and son? You hear what I'm saying, preacher?"

I heard what he was saying and I was about two seconds away from decking him when Cruz appeared in front of us in the dining room, her arms crossed over the white apron that stretched across her abundant bosom.

"Bear. That boy's daddy died this morning," she said. "You going to get your bottom in there and break the news to him, or you going to make his momma do it? You" — she pointed her chin at Wanderley — "probably you need to be there, too. Alex is going to have questions for you. Maybe you have some for him."

We stood there breathing hard for a minute. Wanderley shot his cuffs and walked away. He really did. Shoot his cuffs, I mean. Never did know what that meant until I saw Wanderley do it. I went after him but Cruz caught me by the sleeve. My rolled-up shirtsleeve, so there was no way I could shoot my cuffs right back.

"You a man of God, Bear. Who the hell you fighting for right now? Your God come into any of this? I have to tell you, I don't see Him."

She left me there. She was right. It was all me and none of Him. I leaned my head against the wall and said a prayer. I didn't do much better than, "Please, God, please, God, please, God," but I knew He understood. I waited to feel His peace. I'm not sure I got it. But I gathered myself and walked into the living room.

# THREE

Detective James Wanderley stood by the fireplace, one elbow on the mantel. Honey Garcia was trying to get Alex to sit down, but Alex was having none of it and shook her off, dropping the bag of lunch meat and the empty crushed drink carton on a side table.

"What, Mom? Just say whatever psycho-crazy plan you've come up with, right? I'm sick of this shit. My grades are better than yours ever were, and something else" — Alex's eyes got mean — "*I* don't drink in the morning."

Honey's hand went to Alex's face, and hovered for a second, poised between a slap and a caress. She put her palm against his cheek and breathed out his name.

"Oh, Alex." There was shame and grief and shock in those two words.

Alex stepped out of her touch, his hands up and out.

"No. Look. I'm sorry. Did you think it was a secret? Did you think I didn't know? Just . . . Look. Don't make it such a drama. Everything's always such a big freaking drama with you."

Alex looked over, noticing me in the door of the room. He moved closer to his mom and his voice dropped. "I'm sorry I said that in front of Mr. Wells. I'm not the one who got him involved, though. I mean, for real? You've got a cop and the preacher over here because I cut school?"

I came forward and again put my arm around his shoulders. I said, "Alex, would you sit down for a minute? I want —"

He shook his head and slipped out from under my arm. "You want to say something? Just say it, okay? Could we just be done with this?"

The kid looked like a cornered raccoon, desperate and ready to fight back. His eyes were dark-circled. His face was tight. And he didn't yet know that his father was dead. At least I didn't think he knew.

I said, "Alex, Detective Wanderley and I are here because your father died this morning. The police think it's murder. I'm so sorry, son."

He cocked his head at me, and those big eyes got bigger. "What?"

I started to say it again but Alex put out a hand to stop me. He turned to his mother, all the near-adult mannerisms gone. His face was a child's, looking to his mom to ward off disaster.

He said, "Mom?"

Honey's face was confirmation. She went to him, her arms open, but before she reached the boy, his eyes rolled up and Alex dropped to the ground. His head hit the hardwood floor with a thunk.

Honey started screaming and I began to have some sympathy for Alex's charge that his mother got too dramatic. Wanderley was beside the boy before I could react, calling to his sergeant to get an ambulance. He put his fingers against Alex's throat, hand against his chest, lifted an eyelid. He turned Alex's head to the side. The boy's face was the color of celery.

Wanderley said, "Wells, see if you can get a cushion under his butt and another under his feet."

I pulled at a seat cushion but it wouldn't budge. It was hooked on to the back of the chair somehow so I gave it up and tucked Alex's backpack under his butt and lifted his heels onto the sofa seat.

I got on my knees and checked the back of the kid's head. No blood.

Honey was still screaming, so I said, "Honey, shut that up now and get me a cold cloth for his face."

She kept screaming and now Cruz and Annie Laurie were in the room, adding to the melee.

Wanderley shouted out an order to his sergeant and dragged Honey over to a chair. He put both hands on her shoulders and got his face right up into hers.

He said, in a calm, loud voice, "Mrs. Garcia. I need you to look at me. Please stop screaming right *now*." The "now" came out sharp and hard and it was like flipping a switch. She stopped.

"Alex is going to be okay. He fainted. He's had a shock."

We heard the front door burst open and an old man's voice.

"Honey! Honey! It's gonna be all right, Daddy's here!"

Alex stirred and bolted up. His blue eyes were wide and staring and blank.

He said, "Mom! I can't see!"

Honey started screaming again.

It's not more than a twelve-minute drive from the Garcias' to Methodist Sugar Land, less if you have a siren on the roof. The ambulance beat us there. HD Parker's chauffer-driven 1980s Bentley beat us there. By the time Annie Laurie and I hit the emergency room, Alex had been admitted and was already being seen by a doctor.

We were ushered to the room and found Alex prostrate, the doctor bending over him and murmuring softly. Honey was rocking back and forth in a plastic chair, moaning like the Water Ghost of Harrowby Hall while Cruz exhorted her to get a hold of herself and act like a grown-up. Beanie, Honey's willowy, wilted-looking mother, stood close to Alex and kept a hand on his ankle as if she could tether him to this earth with her frail fingers.

HD Parker, however, had no interest in acting like a grown-up and instead was acting like a Grand Pooh-Bah — barking orders at the nurses and demanding that Dr. Michael DeBakey be brought in for his grandson. That was going to be a problem not only because the great DeBakey was a cardiologist and not a neurologist or whatever was needed here, but also had died in 2008. Maybe HD could get ninety-year-old Denton Cooley to come in and check out the head bump instead.

The doctor with Alex straightened up and turned, and Annie Laurie and I both exclaimed, Annie with a little more enthusiasm than me.

"Dr. Fallon!"

Dr. Malcolm Fallon was a relatively new member of our church — I knew he was a medical doctor, but hadn't put together that he was still practicing. He had to be, well, old. He'd moved to Sugar Land a couple of years ago to be close to his son and grandchildren and had tried out a number of churches before coming to ours. I think our church was still in the probationary period for Fallon, and I wasn't sure we were going to pass. He'd had some criticism for several of my sermons — for instance, he thought I put way too much emphasis on grace and not nearly enough on law.

Fallon had really let me have it after I'd had the temerity to give a Memorial Day service last year. Evidently he didn't think anyone but a veteran had the right to speak on the subject. After services, Fallon wanted to know if I'd ever served my country and I asked him if being an Eagle Scout counted. He didn't think that was funny. Fallon wanted to know *why* I'd never served my country, and I replied that the draft had ended some ten or so years before my eligibility. That was the wrong answer. Fallon found it even more offensive that I would have to be "compelled" to serve.

I've never been the biggest George W. fan, but I had some real sympathy for the man about then — I don't think of myself as a draft dodger; the military simply hadn't ever occurred to me as a career path. Fallon made me feel ashamed. Every time I ran into the man, I felt a little ashamed.

Fallon himself, as he'd let me know, had served as an Air Force doctor during the Vietnam War, and even if "the U.S.A." had betrayed that tiny nation, he, at least, had kept his promises. As he'd spoken, he'd drawn himself up stiff and straight, and honest to goodness, if I'd had a medal in my pocket, I'd have pinned it to his lapel, because the moment seemed to call for something like that.

I'd been at a total loss as to what to say afterward, and I've never quite lost my awkwardness with Fallon, which was inconvenient seeing as I frequently ran into him around the neighborhood. Plus somehow Fallon got put on the building committee in addition to the new members class he led, and I had to go to building committee meetings.

So on top of having had a pretty harrowing morning so far, now I had to deal with a man who didn't much approve of me. He did like Annie Laurie. Everyone likes Annie

67

Laurie. Not that she ever served in the military, either.

I put my hand out to shake, but Fallon put a finger up to tell me to wait. He leaned over to whisper something to Alex, who shook his head and covered his eyes with the crook of his elbow. Alex was crying. Dr. Fallon patted the boy's shoulder and walked over to the counter.

He filled a paper cup with water and brought it to Honey. Fallon had an orange tablet on his open hand and he squatted next to her chair.

The door burst open and HD entered the room. I had never met Honey's father before today. Honey must have gotten her height from her mother, because a bantam rooster stood in front of me. Parker was five foot six with a Sam Spade chest and a jaw that stuck out a good twelve inches farther than the rest of his face. Okay, not twelve inches. But yes, that old man had a jutting jaw. He could have been the caricature of a Marine sergeant were it not for his height and his immaculately tailored suit.

"Honey! Don't you dare take those filthy drugs! Don't you pollute the temple of your body! Doctor, my daughter will not be taking any mind-altering, hoodoo pills, and you aren't needed here anymore. Alex, don't you worry, HD has everything under control. I've got a neurologist, he's the best in the whole wide world, and he doesn't ever leave the loop, but he's coming all the way out here to Sugar Land to see you just because your granddaddy told him to. No one but the best is going to lay hands on HD Parker's grandson, so sit tight. I'll take care of it."

Mrs. Parker said, "Now, HD," in a tone of voice that made it clear that nothing she said was going to make a lick of difference in HD's behavior.

Dr. Fallon stood up, his knees creaking. He looked down on Parker without expression.

"You need to leave my examination room."

Parker's eyebrows rose as his jaw dropped. He caught it and snapped his mouth shut.

"That's my grandson you have on that table! Honey is my daughter! Honey's preacher boy is over there in the corner with his little bit of fluff and you want *me* to leave?"

Wait. "Preacher boy"? Really? And did he just call my wife a "little bit of fluff"?

I said, "Now, Mr. Parker —"

Dr. Fallon pressed an intercom on the wall.

"Catherine, I need some orderlies to come escort an unruly guest from my examination room."

Parker looked like he was having apoplexy. "Are you joking? Do you know who I am? I am HD goddamn Parker, that's who I am. I will buy this hospital tomorrow and put you on the street. You will be disbarred. I'll have your stripes! I can have that done. I can have that done by six p.m. this evening, you see if I can't. You'll be working in the USS of R in the space of a week."

Mentally ticking off the errors in that one outburst, I came up with at least three and wondered if Parker's education had extended much outside of the oil field. Or if the man was beginning to lose it.

The door pushed open quietly and two large gentlemen in scrubs came in and very gently herded out an increasingly indignant Parker. He continued to sputter, his voice growing less distinct as he was moved down the corridor. I heard the orderlies saying, "That's right, you say it, sir, we hear you," and other calming things.

Honey had her hands over her face. She lowered them and said to Fallon, "He can't buy the hospital. Not anymore. And I don't think he can really get your license revoked."

Dr. Fallon said, "Imagine my relief."

70

I gave a snort. I couldn't help it but it stopped with Annie's elbow reminder. I had never liked Dr. Fallon so well as I did at that moment. Right then, Dr. Fallon was my hero.

Dr. Fallon knelt next to Honey. He went on like HD Parker had never interrupted.

"Mrs. Garcia, Alex isn't blind and he doesn't have a brain tumor. He can see perfectly well now. He will be up and about in a few minutes. I'll explain what happened. But first, take this, please. It's Xanax."

He nodded his head at her look of alarm. "I know you've heard things, but you aren't going to get addicted from one pill. This is a low dosage. It's to help you pull yourself together so you can be there for Alex."

Those were magic words.

Honey took the pill from Dr. Fallon, swallowed it, and then held on to his hand tightly.

Dr. Fallon cleared his throat wetly and said, "I'm so very sorry for your loss." He paused for a moment before going on. "What Alex has experienced is called a vasovagal attack. That sounds scarier than it is. It's a kind of shock. Lots of things can bring it on. If you ever had to stand at attention for a long period of time, your commanding officer would be sure to tell you not to lock your knees. That can bring on a vasovagal attack, too, so you see, it isn't that serious, despite the temporary bout of blindness.

"In Alex's case, he hadn't slept last night, hasn't had much to eat today, and he got some terrible news when he came home. I don't know who delivered the news, but it might have been a good idea if they had asked Alex to sit down before they laid that burden on the child."

Dr. Fallon, Cruz, Honey, and Annie Laurie all looked at me. I *had* asked the kid to sit down. I had.

"I'm going to ask you to stay a little longer so that I can run some blood tests, but I want to assure you that the tests are to rule out some extremely unlikely scenarios. You have a fine, healthy boy there."

All this was pretty much what Detective Wanderley had said as Alex was being trussed up and hoisted into the ambulance, but I could see why Honey took more store in it coming from a doctor, especially one who looked like the wise old family doctor from a Norman Rockwell picture.

Dr. Fallon stood up, using the arm of Honey's chair for support. His eyes went to Alex and he put a hand on the boy's huge sneakered foot.

"It's hard to lose a father when you're still so young, son, but you'll get through this. You'll find that God will work good through even this."

Alex uncovered his eyes and sat up. His big feet dangled, as disproportionate as a puppy's. Honey stood up and wrapped her arms around her son. He looked at us over her shoulder, his face a bleak and barren desert. He gave me a chin tilt.

"Do you believe that, Mr. Wells? That this was God's will?"

Annie started forward, answering for me, "That's not what Dr. Fallon said, Alex. He said God could use even this terrible death to the good of those who love Him. I do believe that. It may take years to see the good; we may not be privileged to recognize the good, but it will come." My lovely, precious wife.

Alex still stared at me and I nodded. I thought Annie Laurie had said all there was to say.

# FOUR

I dropped Annie Laurie, my "little bit of fluff," off at home to get her car; she had her own work to do. She designs educational computer programs for homeschoolers, so she spends a lot of time doing research at the University of Houston's main campus and at the big downtown Houston Library. I drove to the golf course, to the corner where a man was murdered in the early hours of the morning.

Sugar Land doesn't make a good setting for a murder. The name is all wrong, for one thing. Sugar Land. Sounds like a kid's game I played a hundred years ago. The name comes from Imperial, one of the country's oldest sugar factories, which still stands across the freeway and was in operation until a few years back. Although even that had a dark side, since for years the sugar company had used slave labor, then convict labor. Not so sweet.

Now Sugar Land has been developed into a number of master-planned communities. In fact, Fort Bend County has more master-planned communities than any other county in America — I know that because it's used as a promotional tag. Why, I'm not sure. Are master-planned communities what everybody's looking for now?

What it amounts to in Sugar Land are lots of cleverly designed playgrounds, community centers, neighborhood pools, and schools. Schools all over the place, with their accompanying school zones to accommodate the thousands of families living in the bland two-story redbrick homes all up and down the live oak–lined streets.

Even the fast-food restaurants have to have discreet, redbrick-bordered signs. So as to be tasteful and unoffending.

I'm pretty sure that murder isn't just against the law in Sugar Land; it's a violation of the Neighborhood Association Guidelines. Nearly everything else is. I can't even paint my front door without written Neighborhood Association permission, and you can bet permission will be denied — front doors in my neighborhood have to be stained and polished.

It's not that we don't get some excitement. We get a lot of professional sports players out here. I've seen Mercedes and Porsches modified with the backseats removed so that the front seats can be pushed back practically to the trunk, to allow room for impossibly long basketball-playing legs. Shaquille O'Neal owns a home out here in the Sweetwater neighborhood, where the homes all have media rooms with theater seating and five-car garages. Friend of mine saw him checking out at Randalls grocery store with a twelve-pack of beer and she said he palmed it. No lie. That's a big hand.

You go to school auctions and see autographed footballs, baseballs, basketballs, and golf balls that would sell for hundreds on eBay. I've got a professional baseball player and golfer in my very own congregation. When I see the golfer on Sunday, I know it was a bad weekend for him; he didn't make the cut.

In our subdivision there are people who were born in Vietnam, the Ukraine, China, Spain, Korea, Africa, India, Japan, all over the Middle East . . . that's off the top of my head. My girls may be growing up in a small Texas community, but they're brought into contact with as many different cultures as any kid in Manhattan could boast.

Merrie and Jo have lit Shabbat candles, gone to Mormon dances where Coke couldn't be served, been invited to the Hindu engagement parties of the older siblings of friends. When my girls have pizza parties, the pizza is all cheese or veggie. Some of their friends can't eat beef; some can't eat pork. Jo won't eat meat, period.

All different. All the same. We all live out here in the hinterlands of Houston because of the incredibly affordable housing, the superb safety record, and — the number one draw — the award-winning schools.

We have all kinds of people here in Sugar Land.

Apparently, even a murderer.

The Bridgewater golf course was green and smooth, and I could see touches of color burgeoning out through the required iron fencing around the houses bordering the golf course. Azaleas, mostly; they give such a lot of show for the little effort you have to put into it. But pansies, too, they do fine till it gets too hot.

I stood there, watching greens keepers walk past the spot where a man had died only hours before, and wondered what Graham Garcia had done to get himself killed.

Assuming it wasn't Honey who killed him.

Because if it was Honey, then I knew exactly why she'd killed him.

# FIVE

**From**: Walker Wells
**To**: Merrie Wells
**Subject**: Jenasy Garcia

Didn't you spend some time with Jenasy Garcia through volleyball? Sad news, her father died. You might want to send her a note or call her.

**From**: Merrie Wells
**To**: Walker Wells
**Re**: Jenasy Garcia

Never competed — J went to St. John's. Met her at volleyball camp. Not sure I know her well enough to contact. We're only Facebook friends.

**From**: Walker Wells
**To**: Merrie Wells

**Re**: Jenasy Garcia

It would be a kindness.

**From**: Merrie Wells
**To**: Walker Wells
**Re**: Jenasy Garcia

Okaaaaaay Dad.

# Six

Graham Garcia had arrived at my office the previous Friday at three o'clock on the dot. It was Honey, not Graham, who'd made the appointment.

I hadn't seen much of her lately but hadn't really noticed until she called. The church draws one thousand plus most Sundays and we have three services. I'm hard put to tell when someone goes AWOL for a while. I rely on getting a heads-up from the attendance committee; they're the ones who collect the attendance cards we ask people to fill out each Sunday. I'm not totally satisfied with the system, but I haven't come up with a better one.

When Honey called on Friday to make the appointment, she said, "Bear, it's Honey and I want you to talk to Graham. He's got a problem."

I said I'd be glad to and what was the problem.

"If I knew what the problem was, I wouldn't need you, I'd take care of this on my own. But I can't get it out of him, and if we don't get this solved in a hurry, it's going to kill me. Or him. I don't know, Bear, I feel like I'm dying."

This didn't send me reeling back in my chair. Honey tends to be a tad over-emphatic, and it was nothing new to hear that something was going to "just kill" her.

I asked Honey if it might not be a good idea for her to come in at the same time, but that wasn't what she wanted, and she didn't want to see me on her own, either.

"No offense, Bear, but I'm seeing a real therapist. The only reason I'm sending you Graham is because you're the only one I could get him to agree to see."

I reminded Honey that I had a degree in pastoral counseling and she said, "Well, whatever." So I gave her a time for the appointment and she hung up.

I didn't know why Graham had agreed to see me. Graham wasn't a parishioner of mine; he was Catholic, and went to St. Laurence. I know a number of the priests at St. Laurence, and I count Father Nat Fontana as a good friend. He's also a fully accredited family therapist. Like me. I mean, I am, too. Accredited.

In the years I've known the Garcias, Graham and I hadn't spent much time together alone. Honey was all over the place — heading committees, hosting showers, planning the seniors' high school graduation dinner in May each year — but my time with Graham was limited to a few rounds of golf when the church would have a charity tournament, or dinner parties where he played with his wineglass and let Honey do most of the talking. Great food at those parties. Cruz is a wicked good cook and Honey is fun.

On Friday afternoon, Graham came in wearing a business suit. Not a Joseph Banks sales suit, but something that looked fluid and Italian. I tried on an Armani once, for kicks; I looked like a gangster, a made man, the kind that breaks knees, not the kind that sits behind a desk and makes offers you can't refuse. Annie Laurie started laughing and that was the day I discovered that she could recite almost all the dialogue from the first *Godfather* movie. Who knew?

Graham, however, looked like a model for *GQ*. He gave me his hand, sat in a chair in my "conversation nook" (that's what the designer called my coffee table, love seat, and two easy chairs arrangement), and crossed his legs. His arms were relaxed, his hands loose. His face was a still mask.

I said, "Honey tells me you wanted to talk to me about a problem."

He smiled. "Is that what she told you? Did she tell you I wanted to talk to you about a problem?" There was an emphasis on the "I."

I thought back. "No. She said she wanted me to talk to you. Is there something I can help you with, Graham? Is there a problem?"

Graham smiled again. It was a dry smile, not sarcastic, not sardonic. It was bleak. He leaned his head back in the chair, eyes on the ceiling. There wasn't anything to see up there. He wasn't looking.

"There isn't anything you can help me with."

Alrighty, then.

"So why'd you come see me? Drive all the way out from downtown on a workday? You're wasting billable hours on me," I said.

He let a good ten seconds pass, a long time in a conversation. "Because it was the only way I could get her to shut up. For a while, at least. Nothing works for long."

He snapped his chair forward. "I can't get Honey to shut up. She won't shut her mouth. She thinks if she understands, she can make it better. She can't. She follows me around when I'm home. 'Can we talk? What is it? We can work it out. Whatever's wrong, I'll change. Whatever you've done, I can forgive.' Of course, it has to be something that *I've* done."

He stood up and walked to the windows. "I don't want Honey to forgive me. There's nothing to forgive. This isn't my fault."

He didn't raise his voice; his movements were smooth and controlled, a little too precise. I don't think I've ever in my life seen a man so tightly controlled.

Graham leaned against the window, his hands grasping the sill. I could see, on one white French cuff, a black embroidered monogram, "GVG." The cuff links were gold scales of justice.

"I don't need her to forgive me," Graham repeated, "I need her to let me go." His voice was low, uninflected, but it didn't lose any of its power.

There wasn't a whole lot for me to say at this point. This wasn't a man who was trying to find his way back to loving his wife. This was a man who was done.

Some ministers believe that any marriage can be saved. You get the couple together, get on your knees and pray with them, enlist the help of a good Christian counselor, have elders drop by, make some phone calls.

Theoretically, I agree. But it only works if both partners want that marriage to last, want it enough to give up a lot, even give up part of who they are.

Sometimes, when the couple comes to see me, the marriage is dead. All they really want from me is to help them get it decently buried.

Honey didn't know it, but her marriage was dead.

There was a time when I would have pushed with everything I had to save a marriage. I wasn't interested in the couple's happiness. I was interested in their salvation. I've come to see that single-mindedness as a kind of arrogance.

I tried to listen, see if Graham had anything to tell me, something that could help them stay together, but I didn't hear anything.

"Why don't you divorce her?" I said. "If you want out so bad. You're a lawyer; you know it only takes one to end a marriage. You don't have to have any reason except you don't want to be married to her anymore."

Graham shook his head, pushed back from the window. He was looking out the window, not seeing anything more out there than he had on my ceiling. Those long fingers laced together and then did an inside-out motion, cracking the knuckles. He looked at me a moment, his face a blank, then his gaze turned toward the window again. He put his hands in his trouser pockets and I could hear him jingling coins.

"Is there someone else?"

He didn't say anything, so of course there was.

"If you tell Honey, I'm pretty sure she'll let you go. Adultery is the magic key for most of us Church of Christers. Your kids are too old to be fought over. You have plenty of money. You do, don't you? You'd take care of Honey and the kids, wouldn't you?"

Texas is notoriously hard on a nonworking wife in a divorce. There's no alimony in Texas. A lawyer at the church once joked, "You want to divorce your wife, do it in Texas. You want to kill her, do it in California." He said California punishes a man for marrying a woman; Texas punishes him for killing her.

We're a community property state, so no matter what, assets are split fifty-fifty. For the Garcias, that might mean something — but in lots of situations, the couple's real financial investment was in the husband's education and career. Then, just when he's starting to make really good money but long before there's been time to build up savings, he divorces his wife, they sell the house and split the profits (if there are any). She might get a nominal spousal support payment — for a maximum of two years — *if* they have been married for at least ten years and she is a stay-home mother. Yes, there is child support — until the child is eighteen, but no assurance of financial assistance with college, no matter what the father's income is. The husband may go on to enjoy three or four hundred thousand a year, and if the wife has been out of the workforce for fifteen or twenty years, she may find herself clerking at the Gap. It's hard to start over under those circumstances if the husband doesn't make a good settlement. A decent man does. I've almost never seen it happen.

Graham shook his head at me as if he couldn't understand how I might think he wouldn't.

I can't tell you how many people I get in my office, men and women, who let me know they've broken one of the most sacred vows we ever make, and then are surprised when I'm not certain they'll do the right thing in other areas. It makes me want to give them a smack on the side of the head.

"She wouldn't suffer financially. Are you kidding? Even if I gave her nothing — which I won't — HD made damn certain Honey never had to rely on me for a penny. She's got a trust fund of old Houston money. She's got more money than me, and she always will. We could be living the high life off Honey's money alone."

I thought they kind of already did live the high life.

"She owns the house. It's in her name. Plus, Honey will get half our savings and that's a significant amount. At least I think it is, though HD probably wouldn't. I've set money away for all the college expenses. Again, not needed since HD set up trust funds for the kids, too. But that's my job and I've done it. And she'll get twenty percent of my income for the rest of my working career." He gave a bark of a laugh. "However much that might be, for however long it might last. These are uncertain times, you know."

What "uncertain times" might mean, I didn't know. A partner in a major firm in Houston had about as secure an income as a person could hope for. Twenty percent of what Graham Garcia made would be more than my salary and then some. And I'm making house payments, car payments, putting one daughter through college, and getting ready to put another one through, if I can get Jo to focus more on her academics and less on her arabesque. If Graham followed through on those terms, that would be, by Texas standards, an extraordinarily generous settlement.

Still, Graham could easily afford to walk away from everything, not even taking into account the money Honey had on her own, and the money *that* money had made over the years. Because half of that would be Graham's. The butter is spread on both sides of the bread.

I said, "Sooooo . . ." Drawing it out, so he'd understand I was asking why he didn't go ahead and get it over with. My grandmother used to say, "If you're going to cut the puppy dog's tail off, don't do it an inch at a time." There wasn't any point in putting Honey through more hope and despair if she didn't really have a chance.

Graham sat down in the chair again and made a tent with his fingers. I could imagine him making that gesture at the negotiation table.

He said, "Could you get her to divorce me?"

I looked at him. Kind of a Cruz look.

"Okay, wait. You don't want to divorce

Honey, but you want Honey to divorce you?"

He nodded.

"And you want me to talk her into this?"

Another nod.

"You mean, without telling Honey about the someone else you'd rather not talk about?"

He nodded again, dead serious. He leaned forward.

I shut him down fast. "No, Graham, I'm not going to do that. I couldn't. First of all, Honey would never believe it coming from me. She'd look at me like I'd lost my mind, ask me had I lost my conviction in the power of prayer — which I haven't, though I don't think God always answers the way we're expecting. So if Honey is praying that God will heal the two of you, He may be doing just that; He may heal you apart from each other. But there's no way I'm going to be able to convince Honey that the best thing she can do for you is to divorce you.

"She's going to be reading First Corinthians thirteen over and over again. 'Love always trusts, always hopes, always perseveres.' What she's going to be believing, coming from where I know Honey comes from, is that if she's faithful and keeps on loving you, if she prays, if she trusts and hopes and endures, you'll turn your heart back to her and love her again."

Graham sat straight in the chair, his shoulders back, his head bowed so low his chin was touching his chest. His hands were now gripping the arms of the chair and the tips of his fingers were white.

I leaned forward on my elbows, looking at him hard, trying to get him to look at me. He wouldn't do it.

"But you're not going to, are you?" I said. "Love her again, I mean."

Chin still down, he shook his head. No. Then he looked up at me, looked me full in the eyes, no flinching. I saw dark pain in those eyes.

"What she wants from me, what she needs from me . . . I think it's a genuine need, I'll give her that . . . I don't have it to give her. Do you understand? It's not my fault."

Graham pushed himself up from the chair and, as he spoke, walked back and forth across my office, his steps measured and unhurried.

"It is not within me. And I can't manufacture the pretense anymore. But there she is, following me, dogging my heels, trying to make things right, trying to find the magic button. And there is no magic button.

"This is what it's like, living in that house

with her. It's like living with a starving child.
You don't have any food to give the child,
but the child doesn't know that, can't
understand, and their eyes follow you all
the time, hoping, begging, pleading. Starving. The child is always either losing it
completely, and screaming like a mad thing,
or doing things, trying to please you, as
though if only they're good enough, you'll
give them some food.

"But you don't have any goddamn food."

He stopped in front of me and leaned
over. His blue eyes were unblinking. I
pushed my chair back.

"If I stay with her, it's going to kill me,
Bear."

"Have you prayed about this, Graham?" I
was shaken by how strong he was coming
on.

He made a sharp chopping movement
with his hand, dismissing my suggestion.
The look he gave me was of cynical complic-
ity.

"I don't talk that talk, Bear." He flung
himself back into the chair.

Evidently he didn't think I walked that
talk, either. That shook me, too. I went back
to my previous question.

"So why don't you just divorce her? I
don't understand."

It obviously wasn't the money. If Graham had been old-time Church of Christ, I might have understood. There was a time in the Church when the only permissible reason to leave a spouse was for "the sin of infidelity." In my parents' day, there were couples who lived together separately, furiously feuding and secretly praying that the other would slip into an affair, leaving the "righteous" partner free. I knew of wives who had stayed in physically abusive marriages rather than challenge that injunction. God preserve us from that kind of sick thinking.

He shut his eyes tight, his mouth thin and bitter. He stood up. Touched the knot in his tie. Reached into his pants pocket and pulled out an iPhone and turned it on. He started walking, stopped, and faced me again.

"I know you don't understand. But I need you to get her to divorce me, Bear. Talk to her, not to me. And you get her to do it soon. That's something you better understand. Time is of the essence. Something bad is coming. It's not my fault. It's on you now."

"Your saying so doesn't make it so, Graham."

He reached the door and looked at me,

his hand on the doorknob.

"It's on you." And he left.

I looked around me at the Bridgewater golf course. Everything green and clean. Everything so ordered and affluent. But Graham Garcia had died out there just hours ago, when the moon was pouring its milky light down. And it was on me now.

# SEVEN

My cell phone rang as I headed for my car — the first four notes of "Onward, Christian Soldiers." Merrie made that custom ringtone for me. She'd gotten hold of my phone when I left it at home one day and downloaded Handel's "Hallelujah Chorus," the whole thing. It was embarrassing. I asked her to instead change it to play the first four notes of "Onward, Christian Soldiers," because it had special meaning for me (those four notes coinciding with the words "Onward, Christian," a good message any time of any day). Also, those four notes are the same note, G, so when my phone rings, it just beeps. And that suits me.

It was Wanderley.

"Mr. Wells!"

"Who is this, please?"

"You don't recognize my voice?"

I was pretty sure I did. "Detective Wanderley?"

"Yep. What can you tell me about Mr. HD Parker?"

"Besides his being Honey's father?"

"I'm all clear on the family relationship."

"Did you try Googling him?"

There was a prolonged pause meant to convey Wanderley's extraordinary patience with a dense and uncooperative man.

"I did my research on the Web, Mr. Wells. I was hoping you could fill me in on the intangibles."

There wasn't all that much I knew, but I shared what I had. I couldn't see that it would be any help. When I'd finished, there was another pause, this one communicating that I hadn't given Wanderley all the information he was looking for.

"Was there something else?" I asked and leaned my butt against the car.

"Yes."

I waited.

"You raised those girls out here in the 'burbs? Did they go to preschool?"

I said they had.

"Can you tell me where you sent them?"

Now I paused.

"Detective Wanderley, are you looking for a preschool for your daughter?"

It came in a rush.

"Clotilde wants to put Molly in preschool starting in the fall."

"Clotilde?"

"Molly's mom. She goes by Chloe."

"I don't blame her. Will Molly be three by September?"

"Three in October."

I thought back. "It's going to be a Mother's Day Out program then. I think. Chloe and Molly live in Sugar Land?"

"In the Heights. But I told Chloe I'd pick Molly up and take her every day if she would let me pick the school."

This was a completely impractical idea. Wanderley would be traveling with traffic to pick up his toddler daughter, and even in the best scenario, the child would be spending an hour and a half in the car each day. Add in a detective's irregular hours — my phone beeped to let me know I had another call. I ignored it.

"Chloe can't find a program she likes in the Heights?"

"She's found one. It's some hippy Greenpeace-type thing. There's no math, no alphabet, all they do is garden and sing songs and play with a baby pet pig."

I snorted.

"What?"

"Wanderley."

"Detective."

"Right. Listen, your daughter won't be taking the SATs for another fourteen years. Maybe it wouldn't be a terrible thing if your baby had a few years digging in the dirt and playing with a baby pig."

A long, thoughtful pause.

"You don't think she'll get behind?"

"I don't, no. I think it's important to let a baby be a baby."

"You didn't push your girls?"

"Not when they were two. And I'll tell you, I don't think the pushing made any difference when I started it."

"I don't want to make a mistake."

This time I laughed out loud. "Good luck on that one, son. You're going to make mistakes. Love her and don't drop her on her head. Everything else, I don't know. Maybe it's luck and genes." My phone beeped again. "Sorry, Detective, I've got to go now; someone's trying to get through."

It was Rebecca. I could hear her pugs yapping their fool heads off in the background as I got in my car. Which meant that Rebecca had swung by her house and picked up her dogs before going to get Jo. Jo would come home covered in pug hair and our dog would go into olfactory overdrive. Rebecca is still miffed that I won't let her bring the pugs up to the office. The pugs don't drool, yeah, but they shed like an old rabbit coat.

"All right, Bear, Jo is at ballet class now and she'll need to be picked up at seven thirty," Rebecca informed me.

"That's a little late, isn't it? We usually pick her up around five thirty or six." I strapped myself in my seat and made a U-turn back toward the church.

"She says she's working on a new routine and she needs the practice. And you tell Annie Laurie to put a spoonful of butter on Jo's tofu and sprouts, or whatever veggie glop that girl is having for dinner. Your girl is getting too skinny."

"She's not anorexic, Rebecca, she's a vegetarian. Can you get those dogs to stop? It's hard to hear you."

I heard paper rustling and there was a snuffling frenzy. Which meant that after Rebecca had dropped Jo off, she had gone through the McDonald's drive-thru across the street and gotten those overfed little pests cheeseburgers, plain and dry.

Rebecca said, "I'm not saying she's anorexic, I'm saying if your shoulder blades stick out farther than your boobs do, you need more padding. Anyway, to my way of thinking."

"Well, thanks for picking her up from

school; it was a help."

There was a small silence. "I picked her up *at* school."

Silence on my part now, while I tried to decipher her pause and the change in prepositions. I couldn't.

"Could you please tell me what you're trying to tell me, Rebecca?"

Another pause. That woman's mind is as complex as a Pharisee's. More benign, mind you.

"She wasn't coming from school," Rebecca said, "not when I picked her up. Some boy pulled up in front and let her out. I was interested in the kids pouring out of the school and I was watching, or I never would have noticed how she joined right in the flow and made her way over to where I was waiting."

I was so stunned I ran a stop sign. Bad idea in Sugar Land. A kid in my church got arrested for playing his car stereo too loud. Well, that, and for mouthing off when he got pulled over.

"Did you ask her what she thought she was doing?"

"No, I did not. I'm not her momma and it's not any of my business and I'm not even certain I've done right in telling you about it. I know I'm supposed to do unto others

100

as I'd have them do to me, but when He's talking about the others, does He mean you and Annie Laurie? Or does He mean Jo? 'Cause if I were Jo, I wouldn't want my dad's secretary telling tales on me. But if I were you and Annie, I would want to know."

My anger rose like scalded milk in a saucepan. I was going to get the truth from that girl, fourteen years old and cutting school to be with a boy. Not like her grades were so stellar she could afford to miss classes. She had improved them lately, but not anywhere near enough to slack off school. Without much thinking about it, I turned my car around yet again and headed toward the storefront studio where Jo has been taking ballet like a religious acolyte for nearly ten years.

"Doesn't a parent's need to know what's going on with their kid trump the kid's desire to keep secrets? In God's eyes?" I said.

"I'm not sure it does, not in my eyes, and it's too scary to presume to see out of God's eyes, don't you think so, Bear?"

"Who was the boy?"

"I don't know who he was, I know very few teenagers. If they don't live on my street, or go to my church, I'm not likely to know them." Despite working for me, Rebecca attends Williams Trace Baptist. "He was a nice-looking fellow."

"I don't give a dang what he looks like." I had a sudden unpleasant thought. "He wasn't a lot older than Jo, was he? He wasn't some predator . . ."

"He looked like a high school kid; he couldn't be all that much older than Jo, though he had to be some older, to be driving. Course, since he's a teenage boy, I think you have to assume he is a predator, same as you were at that age."

I pulled off the road, into the parking lot for the Fort Bend Independent Schools Administration Annex. Kept my foot on the brake while I asked my next question.

"What about drinking? She didn't smell like she'd —"

"Oh, for Heaven's sake, Bear, you do borrow trouble. No, she didn't smell like she'd been drinking. You're not ever going to have to worry about Jo drinking, because booze has calories, and that girl isn't going to put one unnecessary calorie in her system. Evidently ballet dancers survive off spring water and bean sprouts."

I didn't say anything. I was trying to think.

"Are you there, Bear?"

"Yeah."

"You're not going to go tearing over to

that studio and yank Jo out of ballet, are you?"

That was exactly what I was about to do.

"That's a stupid question for me to ask," Rebecca said. "Wait a minute, Bear. Don't eat the paper, Mr. Wiggles, give it here. Okay, I'm back with you. I know you wouldn't do anything so foolish as to go publicly shaming a teenage girl in front of all her friends and ballet teachers. All something like that would do is make her furious and humiliated. She'd be so focused on the awful thing you'd done to her, you wouldn't have a chance of getting her to see that her own deception was wrong and hurtful. I know you and Annie are too wise to fly off the handle and react in the moment. Ya'll will probably sit down together and talk all this out before Jo gets home tonight, have a plan in hand ya'll are both comfortable with."

You see what I mean about Rebecca having the mind of a Pharisee?

"Bear?"

"I heard you, Rebecca." I revved the engine a couple of times to burn off some anger. It just burned gas. At $3.69 a gallon.

"So, are you going back to the office?"

"I believe I'll go on home and have a talk with Annie."

# EIGHT

**From**: Walker Wells
**To**: Merrie Wells
**Subject**: touching base

Hello, sweet Merrie,

Did you get hold of Jenasy?

How's track? How's volleyball? How's Latin coming along? Zarzecki gave you a pretty good foundation; you'll be able to talk to all the dead Romans you want to when you finally get to Venice. :).

Mom and I enjoyed meeting Jackson over spring break. He seems real nice. I don't know how practical it is for a young man to major in education as it would be impossible to support a family on a teacher's salary, but naturally that's his business since you aren't serious about him. You aren't, are you?

Are you and Jo keeping in touch? Do you know who she's seeing? Is there anything Mom and I should know about and if there is and you won't tell me or Mom would you tell Aunt Stacy?

You are in my prayers nightly and on my heart always. I hope you're being faithful about church attendance, it's so important not to drift.

Love you,
Dad

**From**: Merrie Wells
**To**: Walker Wells
**Subject**: re: touching base

Hey dad good to hear from ya :). Yes, texted Jenasy no haven't heard from jo lately im sure everything is fine you can access my grades via the tx tech website get mom to show you how — do c of c preachers make real $$ if they don't get a book published? just asking ;).

merrie

# NINE

Our talk with Jo didn't go all that well, even though Annie and I did have a plan. We'd prayed, too. It might have been partly my fault. After Rebecca's comments concerning Jo's shoulder blades, I paid more attention at dinner to what was actually making its way into Jo's stomach — not all that much, as it turned out. She fed more to Baby Bear, our Newfoundland, a horse masquerading as a dog. Baby Bear (yeah, great name) was sending Jo psychic-dog-brain-waves to get her to sneak him food. That mutt has terrible manners, but no one except me seems to notice.

Annie Laurie had been right when she said I had to let Jo have the Newfoundland puppy that had grown into Baby Bear. Five years ago, we had gone over to Bobbie and Bill Woodruff's for dinner and brought nine-year-old Jo with us because Merrie had plans for the evening and we couldn't find a sitter. Jo had grumbled but that had all changed when we got to the Woodruffs' and discovered that their Newfoundland bitch had nine fat little puppies, just a month old.

I'm not a dog person, but even I was charmed by the tumbling, nipping, silky-coated jet babies. Jo climbed into the pen and Hermione, the Newfie mom, raised her massive head. I thought she was going to eat Jo for violating her space. Instead, Hermione thrust a huge wet nose into Jo's crotch and snuffled. Jo didn't scream, which is probably how I would have responded to that inspection. Jo put her hands under Hermione's chin and drew the dog's face level to her own. Hermione's head was the size of a small television — Newfoundlands are big dogs. Then Jo rubbed her face all over Hermione's, chin to cheek and fore-head to forehead. I'd never seen anything like it and neither had the Woodruffs. Jo settled herself down among the litter, her back against Hermione, and spent the rest of the evening puppy-sitting while Her-mione caught up on her sleep.

Annie Laurie and I had thought Jo looked pretty cute, our mite of a daughter sur-rounded by the wriggling mass of puppy-hood, but Bobbie and Bill watched like Jo was being baptized into some sort of sacred puppy club. Turns out, she had been.

Toward the end of the evening, Bobbie asked if we'd like to take Hermione on her evening outing while they cleaned up the kitchen, and while I didn't have any interest at all in taking a one-hundred-and-thirty-pound dog out for a walk, I didn't see how I could say so.

Annie Laurie, Jo, and I led the dog out into the cool night, and in spite of my misgivings, Hermione proved a placid, calm companion. She peed gushingly a number of times, and when she squatted to leave a cowpat-sized dung specimen, I balked at picking it up in the newspaper bag Bill had handed me on the way out. But my fastidious Jo snatched the bag from me, scooped up the steaming stink, and carried it back to the Woodruffs' as though she were delivering a trophy.

Bill and Bobbie beamed at this confirmation of Jo's inherent dogginess and, with great ceremony, sat us down to announce — Bill gravely, and Bobbie tremulously — that they were going to give Jo one of Hermione's puppies, and that she could choose which one. My hair stood up and my jaw dropped down and Annie Laurie got a pincher grip on my knee and applied some pressure, but not enough to keep me from saying that we couldn't possibly, we wouldn't dream, and our yard really wasn't big enough, and Annie increased the pressure and I shut up.

Jo flung herself into Bill and Bobbie's arms and assured them that she loved them better than anyone in the world (yeah, "how sharper than a serpent's tooth" and all that) and that she would be the best puppy mother who had ever lived and then that canny little nine-year-old did something very interesting.

She climbed back into the pen and picked up each puppy in turn. She tickled and stroked each puppy, but all the while, from the corner of her eye, she watched the Woodruffs. I don't know what Jo was looking for there, and I don't know what she saw, but when she got to puppy number five, whatever she was looking for, she found.

"This one!" she said.

Something like relief passed between Bill and Bobbie, but Bill said, "Jo, if that's the puppy you want, you can have him, but I have to tell you that though he's a purebred Newfie, and perfectly healthy, you won't be able to show him."

Bill held out his hands for the puppy and Jo passed over the protesting fur ball.

Bill turned the yowling puppy over on his

back and touched the puppy's scrotum with a finger.

"See this?" Bill asked.

Jo leaned over Bob's shoulder. "It's his wee."

"Yes," Bill said. "Boy puppies are supposed to have two, umm, two . . ." Bill looked at me.

I was not helping Bill out with this. The man had just foisted a puppy on me that would soon grow big enough to leave cowpats all over my yard.

Bill tried again. "Boy puppies should have two danglies with their, um, wee. This fella only has one. The other hasn't dropped. It's tucked up in his tummy."

"Will he miss it?" said Jo. She fondled a pink-lined ear and the puppy reached up and caught a finger in his mouth and started suckling. Jo's eyes grew misty — she was a woman in love.

"He won't, Jo. This puppy isn't going to need his danglies at all. Your momma and dad will take care of it for you when he's older." (No way was I going to be a party to that bit of emasculation; Annie Laurie later had to make that trip to the vet on her own.)

Jo had pitched a fit when she realized she wasn't going to get to take the puppy home with her that minute; she would have to wait two months for the puppy to be weaned. Then she pitched a fit when I told her no, she could not live with the Woodruffs until the puppy was old enough to come home with us.

When the time finally came to pick up the new family member, the puppy weighed sixteen pounds and had paws the size of dessert plates. Jo brought one of her old baby blankets with her. She wrapped the puppy up and held him against her chest, his chin resting on her shoulder. No new mother ever looked prouder.

"What will you call him, Jo?" asked Bobbie.

Jo leaned her new puppy back so she could look in his face. They stared at each other for a long time. A long pink tongue rolled out and slurped her cheek.

"Baby Bear," she said.

Annie Laurie and Bobbie started laughing.

I said, "Jo, you can't call him 'Baby Bear.' Bear is my name."

"He looks like a bear," Jo said. Newfoundlands do look ursine. "And he's a baby." Jo had that implacable look on her face that, even then, portended somebody other than me getting their way.

"Well, but he won't be a baby forever, and

that's *my name*."

Jo rubbed noses with the puppy as she worked this out. Not whether or not to name her dog Baby Bear — that was already decided on — but how to get the name past me. It came to her, and she lifted her sunflower face to me.

"You named me 'Josephine' for Nana. I'm naming him Baby Bear for you. It's a family name."

Big smile. Checkmate.

And so we became the proud (Jo), bemused (me and Annie Laurie), and envious (Merrie) owners of a Newfoundland dog named Baby Bear. After me.

Merrie had wept buckets when she found that the Woodruffs had given Jo — not her — a puppy. I said the dog would be so big, there would be more than enough of him to go around, but she was inconsolable. My genius wife told Merrie that a dog will always love best the person who takes care of him and gives him the most walks. That, no surprise, set up a fierce competition between the girls, and Annie Laurie and I didn't have to walk the dog once until years later when varsity sports for Merrie, and dance classes for Jo, so ate into their schedules that we started taking up the slack. By then I didn't mind.

As ridiculous as it is for a preacher to own a purebred dog that sells for fifteen hundred dollars, as absurd as it is to have a long-haired, pony-sized dog in the hell of a Texas summer, I love the mutt. It's embarrassing, but I do. Baby Bear will choose Jo over me any day of the week, even though she slips him veggies and I give him the fat I trim off my meat, but even though he's not the guy he once was (halfway, at least, there *was* that undescended testicle), still, he's the only other male in the house. We stick together. When he isn't sticking to Jo.

So anyway, tonight we were eating in the kitchen. Annie had given up on serving dinner in the dining room about two years after our second baby was born. This was a huge concession on Annie's part, because in the home she grew up in, there was this social dividing line between people who had their meals in the dining room with an ironed linen napkin in their laps, and people who ate in the kitchen. People who ate in the kitchen were grouped together with people who lived in trailer homes that were periodically repositioned by tornadoes, and who had season tickets to monster truck rallies. I truly love my mother-in-law, Gaither, but there are times . . . I figure maybe Martha Stewart came up to her standards, before the prison stint. Nobody else is likely to.

Anyway, even though we're eating in the kitchen, Annie does things nicely for her family. I mean it. We don't have linen napkins in our laps, but the napkins are cloth, and not polyester, either — a polyester napkin works about as well as a sheet of wax paper. Annie uses cotton napkins. She doesn't iron them or anything. She's not psycho. She just smooths and folds them straight from the dryer, same as she does the girls' jeans. I think little things like this matter, even if Annie's mom thinks I've dragged her baby to new and unimagined depths of depravity.

Jo put plenty of food on her plate, scrupulously avoiding the grilled chicken and anything it might have touched. Annie Laurie has never made a big deal over Jo's deciding to be a vegetarian; she just started adding more vegetable dishes and nearly always had some sort of beans to make sure Jo was getting protein, but contrary to Rebecca's comment, there wasn't ever tofu on the table because Jo won't eat it and neither will I. Even Baby Bear declines tofu. So what went on Jo's plate were kidney beans (bland from being cooked without any bacon or ham), grilled sweet potato slices (Annie cooks the veggies on the top grill because Jo won't eat them if meat juice drips on them), grilled red and green peppers, and that kind of salad they make at Carrabbas' restaurant, where you stack tomato slices, fresh mozzarella, and fresh basil leaves. Annie always makes sure Jo has a big glass of milk, too. That's the only food item she's a real stickler on — Jo can't leave the table until she finishes her milk. My point being that there was plenty of good food on Jo's plate.

But tonight I was watching to see if Jo was really eating what was on her plate. First Jo used her fork and knife like surgical instruments: she peeled the thin skin off the sweet potatoes, slipped it to Baby Bear, then slipped him a whole slice of sweet potato. He kept a guilty eye on me, but he ate it noisily. He doesn't know any other way to eat. Then she peeled the skin off the grilled peppers, not an easy thing to do, and set the skin aside. She pushed the now-skinless peppers to a new location on her plate. Baby Bear won't eat peppers. Jo then pierced two beans with her fork tines and brought the fork up to her mouth. The fork went back to the plate with one bean gone. There was a long, thoughtful chew. Jo unstacked the salad, ate the basil leaves, all four of them, slipped the fresh mozzarella slices back on the lettuce leaf, and started cutting the skin off the tomatoes. I swear, it was like watching an autopsy. I was almost done with my dinner and Jo had eaten a sum total of four basil leaves and one unsalted kidney bean. I nudged Annie Laurie and nodded at Jo's plate, but Annie poured herself another glass of wine and ignored me.

I stayed quiet as long as I could and then very gently pointed out to Jo that she had eaten nothing so far but garnish, whereas I was already finished with my dinner.

She didn't look up from her plate. "It's not a race, Dad. You don't get a prize for finishing first."

Just as cool as you please, still dissecting that perfectly decent tomato. She was removing the tomato seeds with one fork tine.

"It's not only the time you're taking to dismember the good food your mother set in front of you," I said, "it's the fact that you aren't eating any of it."

Baby Bear made a fussy, nervous noise and pushed my leg with his nose. He had a string of drool depending from his jaws that got left on my slacks. Baby Bear readjusted his bulk under the kitchen table to make sure I had no place to put my feet. I pushed back.

"What do you weigh, Dad? Two-fifty? Two-sixty? I'm less than half your size; I don't need the same . . . mass of food that you do."

I suddenly felt like I'd eaten an entire horse. With my fingers. Raw. And I keep my weight right at 235, thank you very much.

I tried to explain. "You keep telling me that ballet is a sport same as track or basketball or volleyball. A healthy, growing girl needs fuel to play sports . . ."

"You mean a healthy, growing girl like Merrie?"

Annie Laurie's sneaker made a restraining tap on my foot.

"Well," I said, "Merrie is a good example of a healthy —"

Still not looking up, Jo flipped her hair back and cut right in while I was speaking.

"Merrie is a moose. If Merrie wanted to do a pas de deux, she'd need Arnold Schwarzenegger for her partner."

Baby Bear groaned.

"The young Arnold Schwarzenegger," Jo clarified.

I stood up so fast I bumped the table, and the plate holding the grilled chicken slid, sloshing some of the chicken juice on Jo's hand. Hardly any at all, but you would have thought I'd scalded her to death. She jumped up screaming like a banshee and rushed over to the kitchen sink, scrubbing at her hand with a soapy dishcloth.

I said, "Your sister is not a moose, Josephine Amelia. She's five foot ten and —"

Jo whirled away from the sink, her hair flying out around her. What with the steam from the sink and all that dark hair and that pinched, furious face, she looked like a little witch. She had tears in her eyes, too. I don't know why, crying over some chicken juice.

"Oh!" She stood in front of me, shaking, she was so angry. "I swear to God I must have been adopted!"

She slapped the sloppy cloth down on the counter and flew out of the kitchen. Baby Bear slunk off and put his head under the couch. The rest of him wouldn't fit.

We don't take the Lord's name in vain in this house, and I wasn't going to stand for that one minute. I was going after her but Annie Laurie barred my way and pushed me back toward the kitchen.

"Sit down, Bear. Well, now, I think dinner went unusually well tonight, don't you? Everybody's going to go to bed with a full stomach and a peaceful heart."

"I sure hope you aren't going to blame her hissy fit on me because —"

"No, Bear, I'm not. I'm not, because I'm

biting my tongue in two to keep from it, but we won't go into that right now. What I want right now is for you to clean the kitchen, and please don't throw the leftovers away just because that's easier than sticking them in Tupperware. Don't give them to Baby Bear, either, or you'll be cleaning up dog mess, from whichever end he expels it, before the evening is over. I'm going to walk Baby Bear and give Jo some time to cool off and then I'm going to have that talk with Jo that you and I had planned to do together. We're going to change plans and make it a mother-daughter talk."

"She's probably got her period, flying off the handle like that."

Annie Laurie shut her eyes for a minute. Then she got the leash off the hook, grabbed a dishcloth for drool emissions, and called to Baby Bear.

"Come on, Baby Bear, let's get out of here before I say something to my husband that I'll have to pretend to be sorry for."

It isn't easy living in a house full of women. Fortunately, God made me a patient man. I went ahead and ate the leftovers myself. Saves time.

I was propped up in bed, reading a Minette Walters thriller — I'd recently discovered her and she's great; doesn't describe every-thing to death — when Annie Laurie came in after talking to Jo. I said, "Well?"

"Let me get my shower, it's been a long day."

Annie Laurie slipped into our clean white sheets fifteen minutes later. No Waverly prints on the beds in our house. White sheets only. That's another thing Annie picked up from her mom, and one she refuses to turn loose of. Not that I care. I think it's interesting, is all.

She smelled of oranges and lavender and peppermint, a combination of shampoo and lotion and toothpaste. Her lips were still stained pink from the lipstick she'd worn during the day; her hair was wet and slicked back. I was kind of thinking we should have some private time with each other before Annie told me what Jo had to say for herself, but Annie Laurie gave my hand a squeeze and pushed it away.

"I'm going to tell you what I've learned. Then, if you still want to get close, at least we'll both be starting from the same place. Otherwise, I'll be playing catch-up the whole time and probably never get there. You want the light on or off?" She looked at me, hand on the switch.

"Is it going to be easier with the light on or off?"

"If we segue into private time, that'll be easier with the lights off." She switched the lamp off and eased into the curve of my arm, her damp shoulder fitting in my armpit. "Do you want to pray before we start this?"

"I've already said my prayers."

"You don't want to say a prayer with me?"

"Okay. Please, God, would you help Annie Laurie go ahead and give me the information she is so uneager to give me. In Jesus' name, amen."

"You know, Bear, even when you're flip, God still hears you."

"I know He does. Are you going to tell me, or what?"

I heard Baby Bear nose open Jo's door, thump down the stairs, pad to the kitchen, his toenails clicking on the wood floor, and drink noisily from his water dish. There was the return pad, pad, pad, Baby Bear snuffling to be let back in, and Jo's decisive click of the door as she shut him in with her for the night.

"All right, I'll tell you what I know, the first thing being that I don't know everything; there's something she's not telling me, and short of hauling the thumbscrews

121

down from the attic, I don't know any way to get it out of her."

"I'll go up in the attic and search them out if you want me to."

She sighed. Her wet hair was cold on my arm. "She says a friend caught up to her in the cafeteria right before her lunch period, and asked her to have lunch with him; there was something he needed to talk about. He said he'd get her a McDonald's salad and they could picnic at Oyster Creek Park and he would have her back at Clements before algebra. She has a study hall right after lunch, so they'd have an hour and a half or so, if she missed study hall, which she clearly didn't mind doing. Only he got to talking and was pretty upset and they stayed there until school was nearly out. She barely got back in time for Rebecca to pick her up."

I asked the obvious question. "Who was the boy?"

"That's one of the things she won't tell."

"And why not?"

"She says it's private."

"Oh. It's private, huh? So what was this young man so upset about that he had to haul my daughter off from school?" I heard Annie snap open a bottle cap and smelled lavender. The bottle made a raspberry noise as she squirted the lotion into her hand.

"That's another thing she won't tell." Annie was smoothing lotion on her long legs. It was distracting.

"Well, you got masses of information, then, didn't you? You know she went off with somebody, something we already knew, but you don't know who or why. What exactly did you find out?"

Annie Laurie pulled away and turned to face me, rubbing her hands together to absorb the last of the lotion. She sat on her heels with her hands on her hips. Nice hips. We should have had our private time first, just the way I'd said.

"One thing I learned is that our daughter can keep a secret. That's a quality I value in a person, don't you? Another thing I learned is that she's willing to give her time and attention to a friend in need; compassion is another quality I value."

"I'd be interested in what exactly this fellow's 'need' was, Annie Laurie, and how 'compassionate' Jo was. For all you know, he was looking for a piece of sugar candy and Jo looked sweetest!"

"Bear, don't be vulgar."

I thought I had been pretty restrained in my phrasing.

"Look, Annie, you weren't ever a teenage —"

"Boy," she finished for me. "I know it, Bear; you've pointed out half a million times how not having a penis has made me completely unsuited to ever understanding the male psyche —"

"Well, I'm glad you don't."

"Don't understand?"

"Don't have a penis." I grabbed her just above the knee and pulled her onto my lap. She resisted a second, trying to decide if she was mad or not, then relaxed in my arms and put her cold wet head against my chest.

"I asked Jo flat out was the problem anything to do with drugs or sex, and she said no. I hope I can still tell when my child is lying."

I felt somewhat relieved, though Annie is naïve if she thinks she can tell when her girls are lying. The CIA can't tell when a teenage girl is lying. Homeland Security can't tell.

But assuming the problem wasn't sex or drugs, that crossed off the big two as far as I was concerned. Who knows why the boy was in a tizzy. Teenagers get crazy over every little thing nowadays. He might have felt the need to have a shoulder to cry on if he got chewed out by a coach. And right now,

I had Annie on my lap and she was warm and cool at the same time and her legs were silky with lotion. There was a creamy smear of unabsorbed lotion on Annie's calf. With the flat of my hand, I rubbed it in.

I said, "I didn't even know she had someone special, did you?"

"No, and I don't know that this boy is special. She called him a friend. Maybe they really are only friends, not romantic."

I gave a snort. I lifted Annie's wet hair off the back of her neck and kissed her nape. That gives her goose bumps. I love that.

"Just because *you* can't have a conversation with a woman between the ages of twenty and sixty and not think about sex, doesn't mean every man is that way," Annie said into the hollow of my shoulder.

It did, too, but I wasn't going to argue about it.

Annie went on. "What with cell phones and with instant messaging and what all, she could easily have relationships with people we've never met."

Even if we'd met them, it didn't mean we knew them. Look at the Garcias. I pushed Annie back so I could look into her face.

"Annie, did you have any idea how bad things were between Honey and Graham?"

"Oh, my gosh. No, I did not, but I'll tell

you what, while you were visiting alone with Honey, and I went in to help Cruz, I said I would change the sheets on the master bed and Cruz said she'd already done that and I said, 'Oh Cruz, don't wash them or anything because, just think, those will be the last sheets they lay in together and Honey might want, you know, she might want to keep them just the way they are because those sheets will have their, like, smell on them.' You won't understand, Bear, but smells are important to women."

Annie Laurie can be very narrow-minded on gender issues. I'm trying to help her with that.

"So Cruz smiles kind of tight-like and she says, 'Oh, the last sheets they shared together, those would have been washed a long time ago, more than a year ago.' And then she tells me how Honey and Graham haven't slept in the same bed for she didn't know how long, but she knew for sure it had been longer than a year. Just think, Bear, a whole year with no sex!"

I said, remembering my conversation with Graham, "Could be someone was having sex with someone else."

"You think Honey was having an affair?"

That hadn't at all occurred to me; it was Graham who was on my mind, of course.

"You think Honey would be capable of having an affair?" I asked.

"Oh sure," she said without a moment's thought. "I mean, I'm not saying she would or anything, but a whole year without sex? Shoot. Lead me not into temptation. I'd be walking around with my teeth on edge, snapping everybody's head off."

I had an alarming picture of my wife roaming the streets of Houston if some calamity were to prevent me from providing the necessary aid and comfort. It put a slight check in the thoughts that had risen there in the dark with my arm around her, one hand cupping her warm breast. Then the thought of an appetite that healthy brought me surging back, and we finished the evening with some mutually satisfying private time.

# TEN

Tuesday morning Rebecca was in the office before me, as always, but I had an excuse — I'd driven straight to the Garcias' that morning to see about funeral arrangements. I guess I'd assumed I'd do the funeral service, that it would be held at our church, but I was wrong. Graham was a parishioner of St. Laurence, after all, and Father Fontana would be presiding over the service. All the other arrangements would be made tomorrow at the Settegast-Koph Funeral Home, and Honey would be grateful for my assistance then. I learned all this from Cruz. Honey was awake but still in bed, and Alex had driven off in his mother's car before Cruz could get him to eat any breakfast.

Rebecca wasn't the only person to beat me to the office. "Honey's father-in-law is waiting for you — Dr. Alejandro Garcia." Rebecca pronounced his name carefully. "He said he didn't have an appointment, which I already knew as I keep your appointment book, but could you see him anyway and I said probably so and for him to go on in and have a seat. He's been here fifteen minutes. I didn't tell him you were going to be late. Evidently you didn't think to call me and let me know."

Not having anything constructive to answer back to that, I opened the door to my office.

Dr. Garcia is something of a philanthropist in our small community, so I had occasionally seen his picture in the neighborhood weekly paper, the *Fort Bend Sun*. He was sitting on the love seat in the corner, holding a copy of my first book. He wasn't reading it; it wasn't open. He held it in his hands as if it was keeping him steady. He looked like his pictures, a slim, spare man, five-ten or thereabouts, his gray hair cut close to his head, large, dark eyes, dark skin. At eighty or so, he was distinctive without being handsome. None of his adopted son's *GQ* looks, but a likeness in the way they held themselves. Still, quiet.

My hand was out as I crossed to greet him, and he stood and shook it gravely. He had large hands with long fingers. They were the kind of hands you associate with a pianist or surgeon.

"Thank you for seeing me; I know you're a busy man."

We both knew my day wouldn't be as busy as his was. He sat back down and I took the easy chair across from him.

"I'm so sorry, Dr. Garcia. I can't imagine the pain you're going through right now. You're in my prayers. I didn't know your son well, but I've played golf with him a few times. Graham was a . . . an impressive man." The word I had almost spoken, "good," hung in the air a second. Dr. Garcia didn't miss it. His eyes never left mine. He was missing nothing.

"Honey tells me you saw Graham on Friday." His voice was low and even, like his son's, a cultured voice.

I nodded.

"I want you to tell me what Graham said at that meeting."

I did not want to tell this sad, grieving man what I had learned from his son. I couldn't see what purpose it would serve.

"Dr. Garcia, I don't think Graham would want me to discuss that conversation with you, or with anyone."

He nodded; that was the answer he had expected.

"He wouldn't. I'm sure you are right. But Graham is dead, and my sixteen-year-old

130

grandson is a suspect in his murder. The police took his truck away yesterday, did you know that?"

I shook my head. I hadn't known, and it wasn't good news, but I wasn't all that surprised.

He nodded. "To have it tested. Forensics. He was out all that night; he won't say where he was. Driving around, he says. Any intelligent person can see that the boy is concealing something terribly painful. Naturally, the police think he is guilty of his father's murder; I don't blame them. He won't be convicted, because he isn't guilty, and I have enough faith in the system to believe that it works, most of the time.

"I also have enough experience with the system to know that the longer my grandson is caught up in it, the more damage will be done to him."

He put my book down on the coffee table and passed a hand across his face, held his chin and mouth, then dropped both hands to his knees.

"I will not allow more injury to that boy. I should have stepped in before, when I realized things were no longer good between Graham and his wife. But a parent hesitates to interfere. You are hoping the couple will work it out on their own. You are afraid of making things worse."

His mouth twisted. "Alex has been suffering. I didn't know how to stop it."

He turned his hands palm up on his knees, demonstrating his helplessness.

"We couldn't speak of it, Graham and I. Alex and I, either."

I shook my head. "Graham didn't talk about Alex when he was with me. I'm not sure if he even mentioned his name."

"We won't pretend, I hope, that because Alex was not specifically referred to, that what was discussed did not affect him."

"Dr. Garcia, I'm not trying to be difficult."

He stood up abruptly, walked to the window, and leaned against it, his hands white-knuckled on the sill. It was so like Graham it was uncanny.

"My good friend, Father Nat Fontana, knows you quite well. He tells me that in your religious tradition, a minister is not bound by the same laws of confidentiality that he is."

He wasn't asking me, he was telling me.

"Yes . . ."

"He tells me that you are a good man, a 'well-meaning' man, when you can be made to see reason."

That was a backhanded compliment at

best. Dr. Garcia turned and faced me.

"He says you have two daughters, and that the youngest is keenly intelligent, very sensitive."

I didn't know how Father Fontana could have known Jo. And Merrie was the smart one; we'd always had trouble with Jo's school performance, but she certainly was touchy, if that's what he meant by "sensitive."

"So I am asking you, Mr. Wells, if you and your wife were destroying each other, quietly, politely, would that affect your daughters?"

I had a sudden memory of me and Annie Laurie, quarreling in our bedroom over some foolish matter, when in came Jo, couldn't have been more than three at the time. She stood between us, holding a nickel for us to see, and when she had our attention, she put it in her mouth and swallowed it. It didn't go all the way down and she started choking, her big brown eyes wide open, staring at us, and Annie was screaming, diving for the phone, and I picked my baby up by the ankles, one-handed, hung her upside down, and whacked her on the back. The nickel went flying across the room.

I spent the rest of the night holding Jo, all

wrapped up in the comforter from our bed, holding her and rocking her in the big recliner my granddad left me. That tiny, fairy face. She never once cried, the whole night. Wouldn't tell us why she'd done it, though she was already a good talker. Only looked at me as if I ought to know why. And I did.

"Graham wanted me to get Honey to divorce him."

Dr. Garcia nodded hard as if he already knew that. As if I was again only confirming what he was already sure of. He walked back to the sofa and sat across from me, leaning forward, elbows on knees, hands clasped.

I kept talking. "He was unhappy. He wanted out of the marriage. There may have been love between Graham and Honey at one time — he never referred to it, never talked about the 'good days' — there didn't seem to be any love now. Not on Graham's part. For whatever reason, it was important to him that Honey end the marriage. He didn't want to be the one to do it. That's what I picked up," I said.

Dr. Garcia's eyes were intent, his face calm; he nodded encouragingly every few seconds.

I went on. "I couldn't understand why he

didn't leave Honey, why it had to be Honey who divorced him."

More nods, looking at me, his eyes filling brimful with tears. Dr. Garcia raised his face up and pinched the bridge of his nose, trying to keep them in. Then he whipped out a white handkerchief and buried his face in it. His shoulders were heaving with sobs. Hardly any noise escaped his cupped hands. He wasn't the sort of man you could go clap on the back, or fling an arm around. I cracked the door open and asked Rebecca could she please bring us some coffee. By the time she came in with a tray, the coffee in this fancy vacuum carafe the Morgans had given me, he had composed himself. His eyes were red-rimmed, his mouth not as firm, but Dr. Garcia had himself back together.

"Do you know the story of how Graham's mother and I met?"

"No, it didn't come up." It's not a guy thing to talk about. Come to think of it, I don't know how my own parents met. I'd have to ask Dad.

"Three days a month I volunteer at one of the free clinics downtown. It's something I've been doing for decades. When I met Victoria, I was a widower. I had a son in graduate school, one in college, Notre

Dame. My first wife died when she was just forty. Cancer. She was ill for the three longest years of my life. It was . . . hard, on all of us. So I had been alone in my house for five years. I had been happily married and I was only beginning to heal after the ordeal of Gloria's death. I was in no hurry to fill her place."

I served him coffee with some trepidation. Rebecca's coffee is so strong it can take the enamel off your teeth. He poured milk into his cup and took a sip. He put the cup back down and poured milk right to the rim of the cup, stirred, and drank again. He didn't spill a drop. When he put the cup back in the saucer, he'd drunk half of it.

He smiled at me. "Delicious. My compliments. So. I am working in the clinic and I call for the next patient. Into my examination room comes a fair-haired boy, twelve years old, I guessed, and I was right. He is clean and neat, and if his clothes are inexpensive and unfashionable, they do fit him, a long-sleeved T-shirt and those crisp, dark jeans the discount stores sell. He is leading his weeping mother, not by the hand — he has his arm around her, like this."

Dr. Garcia mimed the gesture, arm around waist, hand holding her forearm.

"The way a husband would. He was supporting her. She is not much taller than he is. She has on a bathrobe and flip-flops and nothing on under the robe. That's because there wasn't time for anything else. Victoria was running for her life.

"She is crying, sobbing. She has her hands over her face as if she is trying to hold a broken bowl together. All I can see at first is a tangle of blond curls. She hangs her head down to hide her face. She is wearing dark glasses and I know right away what I'm dealing with. Of course, I see it all the time." Dr. Garcia sighed. He drank from his cup and put it carefully in its saucer.

"Not only in the free clinics, you know that, don't you? Being a minister?"

I told Dr. Garcia I knew. Wife beating is not just a poor man's crime.

"That's right, it's not. I see plenty of it in my regular office. In my regular office, though, the women deny it. I can count on one hand the number of women who have told me in my own office that an injury came from their husband. No, it's always, 'Oh, Dr. Garcia, I fell in aerobics,' 'Oh, Dr. Garcia, it was a car accident.' Hands-down favorite from battered women? 'I fell down the stairs.' "

He shook his head, a wry smile on his mouth.

"Such clumsy women we have walking around Fort Bend County, hm? You hear the same things, I'm sure."

I had heard exactly those words from women in my own congregation, and I had almost always taken them at face value. Evidently, I needed to be more attuned to what was going on behind the words.

Dr. Garcia took another careful sip and crossed his legs.

"Back to my story. Graham guides his mother to the chair, not the examination table, and she sits down. Neither of them is saying a word. He smoothes her hair back off her face, and with a gesture so gentle, so achingly tender, he pulls off her sunglasses. Then he looks at me, this child, this young man, and his blue eyes say to me clearly, 'Can you fix this? Can you make her the way she was?'

"Of course, she has been beaten, badly. Her eyes are so swollen she can't open them at all. I learned later that Graham had himself driven her to the clinic. Twelve years old. Can you imagine?

"Except for cleaning the wounds, giving her some painkillers, there wasn't anything I could do. Her husband had beaten her so that the bones of her face, the supra-orbital margin, the frontal process . . ." He was

138

touching his own face as he named the bones, caught my eye, and amended, "These bones that surround the eyes, they were crushed. They are like honeycomb, you know? Delicate. Victoria was extremely lucky she didn't lose an eye. But anyway. She had to have a plastic surgeon. I am not a plastic surgeon. I'm an orthopedic surgeon. I had her admitted into Hermann. A friend of mine, she did the work as a favor to me. I've repaid her many times; her sons played soccer and all of them were accident prone." He smiled again, remembering.

"So I told her son, I told Graham, 'Can you get me a picture of your mother? A good one so that the doctor will know what she looked like before the accident.' We both knew it was no accident but that's what we called it. And he nods and I say, 'You have a grown-up with you? An auntie?' And again, he nods and tells me the auntie is waiting in the car. I write down my contact information and give it to the boy to give to his auntie.

"I don't know there is no auntie. That the boy gets into the car and drives back home, sneaks past his drunken, snoring father to snatch the picture I asked for, and to gather some clothes for his mother. And then gets back in the car, and using the directions I have written out for an adult, navigates the labyrinthine mysteries of the Houston Medical Center, delivers the picture, and is in the waiting room when his mother emerges from the surgery hours later.

"I have come to check on her, something I wouldn't usually do, since she is no longer my patient, and I see Graham, a Randall's plastic grocery bag at his feet, waiting as if he will wait forever. I ask, where is his auntie? He tells me she has run home to check on her children, she will be right back. This story is taking too long?"

I shake my head, no, it's not.

"You don't mind?" he says and pours himself more of Rebecca's horrible coffee. I had poured a cup for myself, to be social, but I never touch the stuff. Not when Rebecca makes it. It eats a hole in my stomach.

"So. I take him down to see his mother, and as we walk through the hall, I see his quick looks at the trolleys holding the dinner trays for the patients, his nose sniffing. That's when I know there is no auntie, because the first thing an auntie does in a crisis is feed the child, am I right?"

I nodded. It's a generalization — some of my aunts, in a crisis, would first blame it on me, then feed me, but I understood what he was saying.

"Yes. And this child is hungry. If hospital food smells good to you, you're hungry. When I pass the nurses' station, I order two dinner trays, whatever is not too awful. And before I left that night, Graham had eaten everything on both those trays. I had them bring me another dessert and he ate that, too, so, three desserts. Have your children ever missed a meal, Mr. Wells?"

I explained that as my children were girls, yes, they had missed meals, but only by choice, and Dr. Garcia nodded.

"That's a different kind of hunger, though. You know?"

I did.

"So anyway. All that food? That was later. After Graham saw his mother. We go into the room together, and when he sees his mother, her face is a mask, all bandages. She is asleep, thoroughly drugged, thank God. Graham stops short at the sight and he starts to tremble. He put the plastic grocery bag up to hide his face and there are these, these mewlings coming out, little smothered cries. I put my arm around his shoulder and I told him that Victoria was going to be all right. I'd already spoken to my friend, the one who did the surgery. She said Victoria would be fine after she healed. There would be no sign of the injury. His mother would look very much as she had before the attack.

"I told Graham all that, and talked to him about how long it would take to heal, and what Victoria would need to do to avoid infection. I talked to Graham as if he were a grown-up, the person in charge of Victoria's recovery, because, you know, he was. Graham was all she had.

"So the cries stop, and the trembling slows, and soon Graham brings his face up, tearstained but clearing. He nods. He asks intelligent questions. He puts the plastic bag on the swing-arm table and opens it and takes out a hairbrush. I wanted to tell him not to bother. It didn't matter about her hair. It was all tucked up in one of those paper shower caps we use. But I didn't. He slipped the cap off and dropped it in the garbage can.

"Graham separated each curl, starting at the end and brushing the tangles out until it lay around her in a shining, golden mass, very beautiful. Victoria had beautiful hair.

"Graham reached back in his bag and pulled out a picture. He laid it on the pillow next to her poor bandaged face. I saw a picture of a very pretty young woman holding a toddler. Forget the dreadful clothes, and the too-much makeup. Victoria was a

142

pleasure to look at. When I looked up, Graham's glowing eyes were on me and the message in them was . . . what? I have pondered that moment so many times.

"Because that was the moment, Mr. Wells. I looked into those eyes and I don't know what he was trying to say, but what my heart heard was 'help me.' I am still torn by the randomness of birth. 'Every night and every morn, / Some to misery are born, / Every morn and every night, / Some are born to sweet delight. / Some are born to sweet delight, / Some are born to endless night.' "

William Blake is one of my favorite poets. I could recite those lines myself.

"So that was the moment, then and there in that hospital room, I fell in love with them. Not with her, you understand, with them. A married woman I didn't know at all and her son who had asked nothing of me, and had asked everything of me. They needed me. Graham needed me. Need is very seductive, do you agree?"

Dr. Garcia stood and stretched his back; I heard joints popping. "Maybe I should serialize the story, come back tomorrow." He smiled that deprecating smile.

I assured him that my time was his. I knew that Rebecca would be scrambling to reschedule my appointments. Dr. Garcia smiled his thanks.

"I did not see Victoria without Graham until shortly before we married. It was not a typical courtship. Graham slept in his mother's hospital room that night, and the next night, I had my sister take him in and keep him until Victoria was released. I'm not an impulsive man, Mr. Wells, and I'm not a stupid one. I did my research. When Victoria was well, I got her a job at the hospital gift shop, and I found an apartment for the two of them. I was subsidizing the rent and her salary, but Victoria didn't know. I put her in touch with the State Bar so she could get some help with the divorce.

"The divorce was quick. Graham's father had abandoned Victoria when she was pregnant with Graham. He only showed up occasionally, long enough to knock her off her feet again. Literally, not romantically.

"There was no property to speak of, nothing of his she wanted except for their son, and he didn't want Graham. He died not too long after," Dr. Garcia said with satisfaction. "A car accident. DUI. None of us shed a tear."

Dr. Garcia walked over to the window and leaned his back up against it, resting his bottom on the windowsill, crossing his arms across his flat stomach.

"I'm telling you all this because I want you to understand Graham. I know you didn't like him."

My protest died when he held a hand up to stop me. "I don't blame you; Graham didn't put himself out to be liked. He wasn't like Honey. Affection is food and drink to Honey — she can't live without it. Graham needed respect, and he needed it from me."

The doctor's hands had begun to tremble. He cupped them around his elbows to still the shaking.

"I'm going to take advantage of your generosity now, and tell you another story," Dr. Garcia said. His voice was much lower now. "When Graham came to live in my home, the first day, when he came into my study, he sees David and William's high school graduation pictures on the wall. And he wants to know where they went to school and I tell him they went to St. John's."

He didn't bother to explain St. John's to me. Everyone in and around Houston recognizes St. John's as Houston's most exclusive college preparatory school. It's extremely difficult to get into, and influence and legacy status alone will not do the trick.

Dr. Garcia continued. "Right away he says, 'Will I go to St. John's, too? Now that I am your son?' "

145

He passed a hand over his face, then pushed up from the windowsill and came back to sit at the couch.

"Of course, I didn't know what to say. It wasn't the money." He waved the money aside as if the more than seventeen-thousand-dollar annual tuition were nothing. "But the academics are rigorous, even for a legacy. Graham would be a legacy as David and William's stepbrother. David and William had gone to private school all their lives, and their mother, Gloria, was a well-educated woman, disciplined in her own life and in her children's schooling. And still it had not been assured that David or William would be admitted to St. John's. We celebrated, I can tell you, when each of the boys received their admittance letter.

"And now I had Graham, who had gone to marginal schools, and missed a good deal of schooling because of what was happening in his home. His mother, Victoria . . . she was a great beauty, and kind and charming and truly a wise woman, but she was not . . . she did not have an intellectual bent."

He looked at me to see if I understood what he was saying. I nodded.

"I had never, ever lied to Graham." He shook his head and opened up his hands as if he were presenting me with a material fact. "I don't lie, period. I'm not pretending to be a saint, but the habit of honesty is strong in me. So. I told Graham what it would take for him to be admitted to St. John's. And I told him that Dulles High School — Dulles was the local high school then, Clements High School hadn't been built — was a very good school, and if he did well there, he could go anywhere he wanted for college. He didn't hear any of what I said about Dulles; Graham said, 'Then I have a year to get ready for St. John's.'

"When I realized he was serious, I said he would have only half a year; he would need to be accepted the spring before his freshman year." He slapped his thighs. "And he was! The boy worked as though his life depended on it."

Dr. Garcia was silent, and I thought he had finished his story, but he started again, quietly, as if he were speaking to himself, "Every A, every honor, every award, he brought it to me, not to Victoria. Because" — he clenched his fists and beat them softly against his chest, punctuating each word as he said it — "it was me he wanted to be. *Me*." Dr. Garcia's voice broke on that last word, but he shook off the tears. His hands relaxed and sank back down to rest on top of his knees. "Not his father. Not the man who had left Graham and Victoria. You understand? Not the man who had left his wife and son."

Dr. Garcia put his head down. The tendons in his face and neck were working, and he gave a sharp sniff, but he didn't reach for his handkerchief.

"That's why he couldn't leave Honey," I said. "He thought that would make him like his father."

Dr. Garcia nodded without looking at me.

"Or," I went on, "he thought he would lose your love, lose your respect. Was it . . ." I trailed off. What I had been about to say would have sounded like an accusation.

He heard the words even though I hadn't spoken them and he was nodding, his hands up in helplessness.

"Yes, yes, for Graham, it was. I couldn't seem to make him believe that it wasn't necessary, the perfect grades, the perfect life. My son William divorced his first wife more than ten years ago. I wasn't happy about it, and what it did to my young granddaughters, but William and I are still close, very close, and I have learned to love his second wife, Phoebe, as I loved, as I still love Liz."

I wanted to stand up and move around. I felt tense and cramped sitting still so long, but I was afraid if I did, I'd break his flow. I didn't think anything Dr. Garcia had said was going to help me work this problem out, but he wanted to tell someone, and I was the one he'd chosen.

"Whatever this need was that Graham had," Dr. Garcia continued, "this need for perfection, it came from inside him. Graham put himself under impossible pressure. He had to be the best at everything. The best grades, the most job offers, the highest paid lawyer at the firm. I know there was some problem at the firm, something he was anxious about, but he wouldn't tell me specifics. Graham said I was not to worry. He could handle it. If it weren't impossible, I would think Graham had killed himself, for the terrible crime of not being perfect, not being the perfect lawyer, the perfect husband he imagined he would be."

I thought about how Graham had kept insisting on his innocence, how it wasn't his fault.

Dr. Garcia hunched his shoulders, stretching the muscles, then he stood up and offered me his hand. We shook and Dr. Garcia held on to my hand, holding it clasped in both of his.

"That was a long story to tell you to get around to this. This is what I want from you, Mr. Wells. I want you to get Alex to tell you where he was that night. He won't tell me. There's something he's ashamed of. Not killing his father," he said sharply. "He didn't kill his father. But I've done what I can and I can't get him to tell me. You see what you can do. It's on you now."

# ELEVEN

Sugar Land is flat, low, and close to the coast. Perfect for flooding. Levees and drainage ditches were first built in the area in 1913. They crisscross the developments now, and they've worked admirably at keeping out unwanted water. You'd still be a fool not to have flood insurance. We haven't had a direct hit from a hurricane in all the time I've lived here, but we will. I believe in the Lord's providence; I believe in insurance, too.

Besides keeping out floodwaters, the levees are a great place to walk your dog or go for a run. That's what I was doing on the levee after Dr. Garcia left my office. Jogging, not walking my dog. Baby Bear would have loved the run, but he was home. Our house backs right up to the levee and so does the church — it's a nearly straight, four-mile jog down the levee.

Rebecca, God bless her, had run downstairs to where the ladies class was having a potluck luncheon and brought me up a plate piled high. It was one of those foam plates and it nearly buckled under the weight.

I scarfed it down in my office, the King Ranch Casserole and the Fumi Salad and something I'm not sure of but it was tasty, everything but the broccoli, which I hate and Rebecca knows it but she put it there anyway because it's good for me and I guess maybe at six-four, two hundred thirty-five pounds, I'm looking nutrition-poor.

I had two hours before my next appointment, rescheduled, thank you again, Rebecca. That would be more than enough time for me to jog home, give Baby Bear a romp, get a shower, and change, maybe have a short visit with Annie Laurie. Annie Laurie could drop me back at the church if she was home. If she wasn't, I could usually prevail upon Rebecca to come get me, though it would mean stopping off at her house to give her own fat pugs a brief airing before we made it back.

I like the jog, and so I've gotten into the habit of keeping shorts and a T-shirt in my office. It's quiet on the levee, except for this one part where they're readying the land for another kazillion new homes. Lots of big machinery moving dirt from here to there and back again to here. The levee is raised up high enough so that I can look down into people's backyards. It's interesting.

Some people, their backyards don't have anything the homebuilder didn't plant. That means not much. Homebuilders spend their landscaping dollars on curb appeal up front.

But some of the backyards, you see half the backyard turned into a kitchen garden, with pots of basil and cilantro, pole beans and tomato cages, hairy zucchini the size of eggplants, Bonnie Bell green peppers as big as softballs and rows and rows of jalapeños, all, I guarantee you, too hot to eat, and it doesn't matter if you plant the TAMU peppers — something about growing them at home makes them *hot*.

One yard I run past has a batting cage, a basketball goal, and a football sled. I figure the dad is a coach or a Boy Scout leader. Lots of yards have pools or trampolines.

I see quite a few where someone is putting in hard work to have a restful, colorful haven to come home to. There are banks of azaleas and jasmine, great spears of daylilies and irises. Rose-wise, in addition to the ubiquitous Abraham Lincoln, there's Climbing Pinkie, a beautiful, unpretentious hybrid rose, and Katy Road pink, a River

Oaks Garden Club favorite. I know the roses from my grandmother, who loved them, but knowing how much work they are in the hot and humid Houston weather, I never cared to have them in my own yard. You have to spray at least twice a month to keep the black spot off, and that always makes me feel like I'm going to get cancer. Annie Laurie and I stick with azaleas and hibiscus. Once you plant them, they do all the growing work on their own.

Jogging on the levee exercises my body and rests my mind. I try not to think about what might go on in the houses sitting in those yards. I leave that to the Lord unless He dumps it on my plate.

The way He had the Garcias.

While I jogged I was trying to think out what to do. I've spent some time with Alex. Honey has attended our church ever since before I came as the new minister. Back then, before the children had chosen sides, toddler Jenasy would be at her side, along with infant Alex on her hip. I remember her showing off Alex as a baby, dressed in these precious little Feltman suits. A tad *too* precious for my taste, but if Annie and I had had a boy, maybe Annie would have dressed him up like Little Lord Fauntleroy, too.

I'd sat in on a good number of Merrie and Jo's youth classes and activities, and because Jo and Alex were in the same age group, I'd had a chance to see how Alex behaved himself. He was a hotheaded kid, quick to lose his temper, impulsive. Alex had thrown a rock through a window at church camp one year, and the youth minister told me that Alex had apologized, truly full of remorse, as he hadn't meant to hit the window, he had meant to hit the Curry kid standing in front of it. Since the Curry kid was a lion of a boy and more than able to take care of himself, I didn't hold that against Alex, though he had to pay for the window. The church met in the old building back then, and during one Vacation Bible School, I caught Alex and three other guys, in their underwear, sitting on the bottom of the baptistery. Seeing how long they could hold their breath. Apparently the question as to who could hold his breath longest had come up, and one of them had the great idea, "Look, here's some water. Why shouldn't . . ." Yeah. I wasn't that happy about that. Long time ago.

I'd gotten into some trouble myself when I was young. If a teen acts too good, I always think there's a problem; if an adolescent boy acts too good, then I *know* there's a problem.

Alex was smart and articulate, so of course he was snarky. That's how you learn to use those skills. I hadn't seen any real meanness, though, so it gave me hope he would probably grow out of the sarcasm. He'd always seemed like a good kid, but I wasn't buddy-buddy with the boy. I wasn't buddy-buddy with any of the kids — I leave that to the youth ministers. In my position, it's better to have a little distance.

So how was I supposed to get that angry, grieving sixteen-year-old to tell me what he wouldn't tell his mother or his granddaddy? Alex didn't need his minister, he needed a lawyer, and I already had Glenn Carter working on that.

I passed some other joggers: a tiny Asian woman with her hair knotted tightly on the top of her head, a spandexed guy so big he made me look small. Guy's privates were getting so much action I thought it might be safer for him if he wore a sports bra down there. Probably an ex-athlete, though I didn't recognize him. Shortly after, I came up to a winded Dr. Fallon.

I stopped to greet him. After our meeting in the hospital the day before, I felt Dr. Fallon and I could get along fine. I would no longer have to dread bumping into him.

Fallon pulled a sports towel from his waist-band and carefully wiped his face and hands before offering me a handshake. I hastily wiped my own hands on my shorts. I told him I hadn't known he was a jogger and he said he hadn't been until a few weeks ago, but that his daughter had finally gotten him out running.

I said, "The daughter in California?" and he answered, "The daughter from California," and started up jogging again, so I waved and picked up my pace. I'd never met Fallon's daughter. One of his sons and a daughter-in-law and grandkids came on Sundays. Either the daughter never made it to Texas to visit, or she declined to join Fallon in church. Seeing how intense Fallon could get, I wouldn't have blamed her if she gave the Sunday morning thing a miss.

I was glad his daughter was looking into her dad's health. Fallon wasn't that old, he was somewhere in his seventies, but he looked awful out there jogging, gray and drawn and generally unwell. You'd think that a doctor, with all the information and all the finances it takes to maintain good health would, well, maintain it.

By the time I had jogged up to my own backyard, I was winded, too, but only enough to know I'd done my body some good. I wondered how many miles a week Wanderley jogged.

It didn't catch my attention that the back gate wasn't latched; I'm not always as careful as I should be, considering the gate opens onto the levee. I did notice that the door that opened off the back of the garage was open. I'm careful to keep that door shut and locked because you can get into the house from the garage. You can, a stranger can, and four-footed guests can, too. So I keep the door shut and usually locked.

When I put my hand on the doorknob, there was a dry crust of mud on it.

Imagine here a long, creaking twenty-five seconds as my body stops cold and my brain ratchets into gear.

Now, only Annie Laurie and I do any work in the garden that's going to get your hands muddy, and we clean up after ourselves, so I didn't think it was likely we had left mud on the doorknob. And the mud wasn't around the knob, the way it would be if a muddy hand had grasped the knob; the mud was on top of the knob, the way it would be, I thought as I stepped back for a better look, if someone had, say, opened the door and swung it wide — put a foot on the knob in order to get a boost up to the top of the door, hung on the gutter to keep balance — and then hoisted themselves onto the roof of my one-story garage.

My eyes traveled up and I saw, sure enough, a trail of muddy footprints, red clay against the black composition roof.

Those footprints went straight to Jo's bedroom window. Jo's window opens onto the conveniently low, one-story garage roof. That garage sits in a yard that backs up to the levee. And that levee, again conveniently, is intersected by Elkins Road. My eyes took all that in in two blinks.

All I saw then was red.

# TWELVE

I may not be the tallest pine tree in the Big Thicket, but I'm no shrub, and those footprints on my roof led me to one inescapable conclusion.

Jo was leaving the house unobserved, and the only time she would need to do that, since Annie and I are reasonable and loving parents, and not the fascist dictators some people would make us out to be, is at night. When a fourteen-year-old should be home. In bed. By herself.

I did, at least, know no one could have been in her room. Baby Bear is a good-natured mutt, but if someone had climbed through Jo's window, Baby Bear would have chewed him to the bone, cracked the bones for the marrow, and left only the buttons, buckle, and zipper. Newfoundlands are ferociously protective. I like that in a dog.

It's a good thing Jo was in school. At least, I assumed she was in school. Evidently, I had been making several unwarranted assumptions recently.

I took those stairs two at a time, Baby Bear at my heels ready for whatever new game this was going to turn out to be, and burst into Jo's room like I was going through the Oklahoma defensive line on homecoming day.

Nothing.

I don't know what I expected to find. Been afraid to find.

I was glad I didn't find it.

Three years after we'd been in this house, Annie Laurie and I took the carpet out of the fourth bedroom, the one we used as a guest room and sewing room, and we installed a wood floor. Both Merrie and Jo were taking ballet, and it seemed like a good investment. Annie Laurie's mother is a big believer in ballet lessons for little girls. She says it gives a "young lady" grace and poise and a good carriage. I didn't know young ladies still had carriages anymore. It sounded as odd as referring to someone's "countenance." But I figured all that stretching and bending would make the girls more limber for sports that could get them college scholarships.

Annie Laurie and I put the floor in ourselves with a how-to book and supplies from the Home Depot on the Southwest Freeway. Along one wall we mounted floor-to-ceiling mirrors and a ballet barre. It took us the better part of a week, and we couldn't have done it if the girls hadn't been away at church camp. As it was, we covered up some uneven plank ends with baseboard and wood filler. You have to be the kind of person who looks for mistakes to notice that.

Both girls were tickled when they got home from camp and saw the transformation. Annie Laurie and I left them to their unpacking, and went downstairs to start dinner.

We heard some strange thumps and bumps and what sounded like a mighty struggle. The commotion grew in intensity until I went upstairs to investigate.

Jo had dismantled the guest room bed, and had wrestled the full mattress out to the hall landing. She was having trouble with the box springs. I mean, she was only eight or so, and the box springs weighed more than she did, no question.

Tall, blond Merrie was leaning against the wall, arms crossed, laughing.

What on earth did she think she was doing, I had asked Jo, though it was perfectly clear what she was doing. Jo was appropriating the new dance room for herself. I told her no, the dance room was to share with Merrie and with any overnight guests we might have, and I took the box springs from Jo to put it back in place. All sixty-five pounds of Jo — and at least five of those pounds were carried in her long dark braids — grabbed hold of the box springs and pulled back so hard she actually pulled it from my grasp. She sat there, eyes brimming, face set and furious, absolutely quivering with defiance.

Naturally I wasn't going to let her get away with that kind of behavior, and I was reasoning with her, kindly but firmly, not making any headway that I could see, but sticking to my course, when Merrie came over, squatted down on the floor next to Jo, and said, "You want the room that bad, Monkey-face?"

Jo nodded, which was more of a response than I'd gotten from her so far, and Merrie said, "Dad, it's no big deal. Let her have the room; you can make her old room into the guest room. Jo will let me use the barre when I want to, won't you, Jo?" Jo nodded again, less convincingly this time.

Merrie gave her little sister's braid a yank and said, "Come on then, I'll help you move." And from that time, it was Jo's room.

■ ■ ■ ■

Jo's room looked the same to me as it always had. Two twin brass beds that had been Annie's grandmother's when she was a girl. Jo's bed wasn't made up, of course. The blankets were helter-skelter and the sheets were every which way, but I don't let myself get worked up over that. I wasn't wild about the clothes flung all over, across the rails of the bed and on doorknobs and lying on the floor. Jeans and T-shirts and little bitty bras and panties so tiny I don't see any point to them at all, but Annie Laurie says to let her worry about the panties, so I do.

Jo's room had a built-in bookcase against one wall with all the horse books Marguerite Henry ever wrote — I mean everything, all fifty-eight books, and that's no small accomplishment even taking into account eBay and Amazon.

Those books were from Jo's horse-crazy days, and I'd read two of them to her, *Misty of Chincoteague*, which was okay, and *King of the Wind*, which I liked a lot. Jo loved all of them — she would trace the Wesley Dennis illustrations with her finger — but she never became much of a reader on her own. Annie took Jo to an educational specialist, who ran a bunch of expensive tests and came up with the idea that Jo had a reading disorder of some sort, but that's a lot of hooey. No one in my family has ever had one of those ubiquitous disorders being marketed all over the place. Jo won't apply herself; that's what her problem is.

Instead of books, the shelves of the bookcase mostly held ballet trophies and worn-out toe shoes and framed pictures of Jo in different ballet costumes. My favorite picture is the one where she got the fairy queen role. That was two years ago — quite an accomplishment because the part usually went to an older girl. It had been a while since I'd really looked at the picture, and I picked it up.

In the picture, Jo is sitting on the stage with her back to the audience, her legs bent under her in kind of a complicated way, the filmy green dress spread out and sprinkled all over with silk daisies.

Usually when Jo dances, her hair is slicked back into a bun on the top of her head, but in this picture, all that long, silky wavy dark hair is down her back. She's looking over her shoulder so that the photographer has caught her in profile, her little chin tilted up, her gaze off on some imaginary world none of the rest of us could see. She looks like a queen. Not a princess. A queen. A little beauty.

I remembered bringing her a big bouquet of long-stem yellow roses, and when she was done dancing, making those elaborate, graceful bows that ballerinas do, I was still so caught up in her performance I nearly forgot to lay them at her feet. Merrie had to put an elbow in my side. What a good night that had been. Magic.

The memory of that night drained all the haste and anger out of me. I couldn't remember the last time Jo and I had had a really good time together. It seemed like she was always angry at me nowadays, like there wasn't anything I could say that didn't get on her nerves or make her downright mad.

Annie Laurie tells me that it's normal, but it never happened between me and Merrie. We never got to a point where we couldn't talk to each other. Merrie tells me everything. Jo and I have to have Annie to play go-between just to get us through dinner.

I felt depressed and anxious, not to mention hot and sweaty and itchy, and I spent a long time in the shower trying to wash away the depression with the sweat. Baby Bear sat right outside the shower and watched with interest while I bathed. I've tried shutting him out. The French doors don't lock and Baby Bear is very interested in watching me shower, so I've given up on privacy.

I wasn't but half dressed when the phone rang.

It was Rebecca.

"Bear, Cruz called. You know who Cruz is? She's that lady who works for Honey Garcia."

I said I knew who she was.

"She called to tell you the police have picked up Alex Garcia. They're holding him for questioning in Richmond. At the juvenile detention center, thank Heaven for that at least."

"Why 'thank Heaven'?"

"Lord, don't you know what goes on in the adult prisons? Why, adult convicts would be lined up at a young boy's cell door and —"

"Okay, Rebecca. You might want to be more careful what you're Netflixing, you know that? Listen, would you call Glenn and alert him to this new development —"

"I already have and he's sending someone over there. A woman; he says don't let her fool you, she's as tough as nails and twice as sharp and all she does is criminal defense."

"Well, we hope it doesn't come to that."

There was a short silence and I grabbed a

sport coat.

"It already has, hasn't it, Bear?" I could hear her other line beeping. "Got to go, Bear, keep me in touch." And she hung up.

# THIRTEEN

By the time I had made the twenty-minute drive past the George Memorial Library to the juvenile detention center in Richmond, Alex was already closeted with his mother, his lawyer, and Detective James Wanderley. The police wouldn't let me in to see Alex until they were through with him, and when they were through, they would let him go home. I could visit with him then. I knew the lawyer Glenn had sent over would be more than capable of handling whatever came up during questioning.

I'd just wasted an hour going to Richmond and I'd missed all my morning appointments because of my unexpected visit from Dr. Garcia. I didn't want to miss my afternoon appointments, too.

Two or three times a week I make hospital visits. I drive into town to the Medical Center; that's where many people go, even though we have an excellent Methodist

Hospital branch here in First Colony. Houston's Medical Center is the most prestigious in the world, so if you have a serious problem, cancer or heart trouble, say, you'll likely end up in the Medical Center, though a lot of the very same doctors have offices in Sugar Land, too.

That's what I had scheduled for this afternoon, and I didn't want to change my plans. I had to, though. Before I could get to my car, HD's Bentley pulled into the lot and the fighting cock himself jumped out.

I tried to look small and anonymous and slink off to my car. HD saw me. You don't make that kind of money if things as big as me slip past you.

HD waved me over, bellowing, "Preacher! Come on with me. I'll get this sorted out. You come on." He strode on past, it never occurring to him that I might not follow.

I followed.

He burst through the door in what I was quickly coming to imagine was his signature entrance. He called out to the nearest officer, who was quietly conferring with a weeping woman.

"Boy! I'm HD Parker and I'm here to get my grandson out of prison!"

The officer lifted his large, dark head and stared at HD.

I said, "He calls me 'boy,' too." I didn't think HD meant it the way it sounded.

"Where you got him locked up? Get your keys and get your supervisor and get him on out here. His name is Alex Garcia, but he's no Mexican."

Maybe HD did mean "boy" the way it sounded.

The officer's face didn't twitch. If he was irritated, he didn't let it show. His voice was even and polite.

"My name is Officer Laplante. And this isn't a prison, sir, it's a juvenile holding facility and my understanding is that your grandson is being questioned. If you would like to have a seat in the waiting room, someone will be with you as soon as there's any information we are permitted to share with you."

HD gave a squawk.

"Permitted? Permitted! You've got my grandson! You're treating him like a murderer! That boy is no murderer. He's in the Honor Society at Clements High School. Kid plays on the golf team, got a negative three handicap."

Ummm, I was going to have to check up on that one. Negative three? For sure? That would make him competitive with Tiger Woods. Clements High School has a good golf team, but give me a break. HD was partial to hyperbole. That or he was delusional.

"Sir." Officer Laplante spoke louder this time, and let some of his authority show in his straight bearing. "I need you to calm yourself down and take a seat in the waiting room. No one is treating your grandson like a murderer. We're holding him until —"

"How long? How long you holding my grandson? I'd like you to come right on out and tell me to my face, right here, right now, how long you plan on keeping my grandson in this, this hellhole of bestiality and pederasty . . ."

Officer Laplante looked at me. "Are you with him?"

Oh, thank you, Mr. HD Parker.

"No. I mean, I know his daughter and I've met Mr. Par—"

"I recommend to you that you remove this gentleman from the premises. Now would be a good time."

If HD had tail feathers, they would have gone on full display at that.

Another squawk. A Mel Blanc squawk. "I am *not* with this boy" — see, I did say he called me "boy," too — "that is Honey's pantywaist Preacher Boy and" — HD faced me — "I do not believe for one second you played ball for the U of T."

What that had to do with anything I don't know. And I did, too, play for UT.

A female officer, looking big and mad, pushed through the swinging doors in the back and came to stand next to HD and me. She gave me a hard stare, hands on impressive hips. Her badge identified her as Officer Jambulapati.

"What is this racket going on in my waiting room? Do you see there are other people in this room with troubles of their own? Are you under the impression that you happen to be the axis the world spins around? Because I don't think so."

I looked around. Three or four clusters of people were watching us openmouthed. I overheard the soft murmur of Spanish. A daughter translating the drama for the rest of her family.

HD put his hands on his own hips and jutted that chin out an inch farther.

"Are you talking to me?" Instead of meeting the newcomer's eyes, HD's focus was on her boobs. The ones that matched her hips.

"Are you the one making all the noise?"

"My name —" HD paused for full dramatic effect, but it was spoiled when she interrupted.

173

"Did I ask you what your name was?"

"— is HD Parker, and I am —"

"Am I supposed to know who that is? Am I supposed to care? And you would maybe like to move those beady little bird eyes up about fourteen inches before I start to think you are being deliberately impertinent."

HD wasn't giving up. But he did move his eyes, thank you, God.

"Who I am is —"

"Am I not being clear? I don't care if you are President Obama's skinny white grandfather, you have demonstrated a lack of manners to an officer of the law and you will get that skinny white heinie of yours out of my waiting room post-haste. Go wait outside, you can't keep your voice down. We've got work to do here."

"HD Parker! I am HD Parker!"

Officer Jambulapati slued her eyes at me.

"If that's your daddy, you get him out of here before I lock him up."

I said, "He's *not* my dad," exactly the same time HD said, "That's *not* my son," and with the same amount of indignation. For all the perks that money can buy, I would not trade places with Honey Garcia. Mercy.

Officer Laplante intervened. "The situation is this, Mr. . . . Parker, is it? Your grandson, Alex Garcia, is being questioned because he may have information that could be important to an investigation. Because he is a minor, his mother is with him, and I understand a lawyer is representing him as well. There isn't anything to be done right now but wait. If you can take a seat, and behave quietly, the way everyone else in this waiting room is, then you are welcome to stay."

This last was said with a cough as though Laplante were choking on a cherry pit. "Otherwise," he continued, "you may be more comfortable waiting at home. In my experience, these interviews can take quite a time."

A long hard stare from HD, then he drew out his cell phone like a gunslinger. He turned his back on us and barked into the phone.

"Fredrick! We're gonna be here a while. Go get me an Antoine's sandwich, some jalapeño potato chips, a Shiner Bock, and two of those little balaclava pastries. Tell them to go heavy on the relish but not too sloppy with the mayonnaise. Get yourself whatever you want."

His phone went back in his jacket pocket and HD stalked over to a seat.

"No alcohol allowed," said Officer Jambulapati. "And it's baklava. If you're going to eat it and not wear it on your head."

HD's shoulders stiffened. The phone came out again.

"Fredrick. Forget the Shiner. Get me a sugar Dr Pepper. In the bottle. Make sure it's not one of those corn syrup ones. Green label."

He sat, folded his arms, and crossed his legs.

I made hushed apologies to everyone, and got out of Dodge.

I was late, but my hospital visits would be counting on seeing me. Miss Lily, for one.

A hundred years ago, Miss Lily was my Sunday School teacher, one of my two favorites. Mrs. Grant was my other favorite, but I don't get to see her as often; she goes to church at Southwest Central in Houston.

Fate or God had decreed that Miss Lily's daughter, Brenda, a fine, Godly woman somewhere in her early sixties, would buy a house in First Colony, and when Miss Lily got too old to take care of herself, she came to live with Brenda and her husband, and I found myself preaching to my teacher.

It was hard when Miss Lily was diagnosed with cancer. I couldn't understand why God didn't let her slip on away; Lord knows she had fought the good fight, and she was so close to finishing her race. Now she had this new trial upon her, and let me tell you, stomach cancer is a real trial. There isn't much the doctors can do for the pain except dope you into oblivion, but Miss Lily wasn't having that.

"I want to be awake when I get home, Bear," she told me in explanation when I got there, releasing Brenda for a badly needed break. I was trying to breathe through my mouth. I hate the way hospital rooms smell, the disinfectant and lousy food and that weird, sweetish smell I always associate with cancer.

"I think you'll be awake, Lily."

She patted my hand briskly.

"Smart as you are, Bear, you haven't made this trip, so you don't really know, do you, son?"

Then she had a spasm of pain so bad I could hear her teeth grinding and she let a moan escape her. I didn't let go her hand, but I turned my face away, even though I could feel her eyes on me. The pain passed, and she lay there panting, getting her strength back.

Her eyelids drooped and I thought she was maybe falling asleep, but she squeezed my hand, her eyes closed now, and she said, "Bear, God has put it on me to tell you a hard truth."

It always makes me nervous when people feel like God tells them to do something. I never get those crystal-clear-in-your-ear messages from God. And why is it God only sends out messengers with hard truths, never the nice, soft truths?

"I can do that, because I know that you know how much I love you."

That's another thing. Seems like love gives people permission to do so many hurtful things.

"So you aren't going to take this as criticism."

I might, too.

"Bear, part of the reason you want me to take all those painkillers, it's not because of the pain I'm in, it's because of the pain you're in, watching me."

Okay, maybe God did tell her to give me that message. I felt convicted. What she said was true.

"You always wanted to be saving people, even as a boy. I don't mean saving them for the Lord. That came, too, but later. You wanted to save them from themselves and from the consequences of their own actions and . . ." She took some time to catch her breath and gather her energy. I couldn't help noticing that her scalp was bright pink

178

between the strands of her thinning, snowy white hair. Her teeth looked like old ivory. Merrie tells me my generation will be the last to grow old. Something to do with gene manipulation.

"And you tried to save them from the truth. I think that was because you couldn't bear to see them in pain. That made a liar of you sometimes, Bear. I don't mean that harshly. I don't mean to judge you. If I am, then, Jesus, please forgive me." When Miss Lily said "Jesus," it wasn't an exclamation. She was talking to Him.

My eyes were watering. I blinked. I said, "Lily, would you like to pray with me?"

She said, "I get lots of prayers, Bear. Why don't you sing for me?"

"Lily, you know I can't sing."

She opened her eyes wide, the whites clear as a baby's, under lavender, wrinkled lids, and gave a husky chuckle. "I know it's a mercy that Jesus asks you for a joyful noise, not a tuneful one. All the same." She closed her eyes again. She seemed exhausted. "I'd like you to sing for me."

"What do you want me to sing?"

She was silent, thinking. "Sing 'Can You Count the Stars.' When I was a child, my father would put me to bed at night. He'd read a chapter from *Hurlbut's Story of the*

*Bible.* You have that book, Bear?"

I shook my head no.

"You should have a copy. Then he would sing 'Can You Count the Stars.' That was a safe, sweet feeling. Can you sing that song?"

It's a lullaby. My mother sang it to me when I was a baby, too. I sang it through, all three verses.

Can you count the stars of evening
That are shining in the sky?
Can you count the clouds that daily
Over all the world go by?
God the Lord, who doth not slumber
Keepeth all the boundless number
But He careth more for thee
But He careth more for thee.

Miss Lily smiled when I finished, and gave my hand another squeeze, but she didn't open her eyes. I sat there holding her hand until Brenda got back, then I made the rest of my rounds.

It was four thirty when I hit Highway 59 headed south for Sugar Land. Four thirty lands you solidly in rush-hour traffic. I'm deliberately using the word "solidly" — I mean it as opposed to liquid. The traffic seems not to move. There was a taxi-yellow

Hummer in front of me and I could swear it was jouncing from side to side with the boom of the bass. I'll bet you would expect me to be foaming at the mouth, preacher or no preacher, but I wasn't.

Some time ago I was visiting with Carol Thompson after services, and I had expressed the enormous frustration I feel when I'm caught in traffic. If you live in or near Houston, traffic is a fact of life. Carol is a family therapist; the church refers a lot of people to her, so even though I hadn't been looking for advice when I made that offhand comment, I listened to what she had to say.

"For a temperament like yours, I think the frustration stems not so much from the delay, which, intellectually, you can accept as a necessary and unavoidable consequence of living on the outskirts of one of the nation's largest and most sprawling cities, but from the waste of your time. Men like you tend to get their sense of self-worth out of what they accomplish. Sitting in traffic, they aren't getting anything done.

"You might try a couple of tactics. One is to check out The Teaching Company series from your local library. It's an audio series, very good. The professors don't talk down and you could learn a lot on any number of topics — Darwinism, mythology, biography, economics, tons of history — in short, you're feeding your brain, continuing your education even as your engine idles on the freeway. Another tactic my patients have found effective is to learn a new language. You can go to Sam's Warehouse and pick up any of a number of good CD language programs."

I thanked her, trying not to be too conscious of the line backing up behind her; there are always members who want to let you know how well you gave your sermon, or whether they felt it was worth giving at all. Carol noticed my concern and gave my arm a squeeze.

"That consultation was on me, Bear. You won't get a bill in the mail."

Carol had been dead-on with her advice. Since then, I've been alternating between The Teaching Company and the Modern Scholar series and a Spanish language program — it was soothing listening to an educated, well-modulated adult voice confiding to me the intimacies of Winston Churchill's life, or asking me, "*¿Qué te parece?*" — "What do you think?" — about *el restaurante, el libro,* or *los jóvenes.*

I didn't want to puzzle out what Miss Lily had been saying. I'm not a liar; I know that for sure. *Soy un hombre veraz.* I slipped in a Spanish CD and started ordering a make-believe dinner from the make-believe waiter's suggestions. I started with *albondigas. Yo gusto albondigas.*

In spite of the traffic, I spent a relatively pleasant forty minutes chatting with the waiter, the *camarero,* who couldn't hear me. I felt relaxed and collected when I pulled into the church parking lot. That didn't last.

Detective James Wanderley was waiting for me.

# FOURTEEN

Detective Wanderley was sitting cross-legged on the lawn, his back against the edge of the seat of one of the park benches the church had dotted around the lawn. I can't remember the last time I could get my legs in that pretzel configuration.

He was reading a coverless paperback. He glanced up at my car, his hand shielding his eyes from the low sun, and he got up slow and easy, not using his hands, just unfolding. It made my knees hurt to watch him. He stuffed the paperback into his jacket pocket, and strolled over to meet me as I got out of the car.

"Ah. It's the friendliest man in Sugar Land. You have a minute, Bear?"

Probably I was reading into it, but that sounded snarky to me. "Friendliest man." It was one thing coming from Annie Laurie — I was already sorry Annie had given that young man permission to use my nickname.

Wasn't any way I could stop him from using it now without looking like a tight ass.

"Is it going to take a minute?"

He stared at me, his face shadowed now that his back was to the dying sun. I was having trouble reading his expression, with the sun being right in my eyes. I wondered if he had deliberately maneuvered me into that position, some sneaky cop trick he'd learned from TV.

"No. Probably thirty minutes. Maybe more. You might want to ask some questions, too."

I couldn't think of anything I wanted to ask Wanderley, or hear from him, either, unless he was looking for more parenting tips on how to raise a daughter, and I didn't think that was why he was here. Nevertheless, I led the way up to my office, passing Rebecca on her way out. She usually leaves for the day around five because she doesn't think it's good for the "boys" (those would be her pugs) to be on their own too long; I try to work until seven. Normally those two hours after the office has closed are when I write my sermons and work on my next book, but on Tuesdays we had special programs at the building.

Rebecca looked startled to see Wanderley. She didn't say anything, just nodded to him and told me she'd left a pile of messages on my desk.

Wanderley and I had gotten off on the wrong foot at our first meeting. That wasn't my fault, but I felt it was incumbent upon me to start this meeting in a more positive direction, try to talk to Wanderley like Molly's dad, instead of the smart-mouthed detective he had seemed at first. I was praying in my head, over and over, "Let the words of my mouth and the meditation of my heart be acceptable in Your sight, oh Lord, my Rock and my Redeemer." You'd be surprised how many different situations that Psalm covers. Especially the "words of my mouth" part. Rebecca once recommended I quote Psalm 39 instead, and "put a muzzle on my mouth." She was quoting out of context, but I refrained (see?) from pointing that out.

As I passed Rebecca's desk, I pushed a button on her telephone console to make sure we wouldn't be interrupted by calls.

I thought if I didn't put my desk between us, it might help things out some. Maybe make the situation less adversarial. I sat down on the easy chair and gestured to the love seat. It would be interesting to see if Wanderley could turn the love seat into a fun house ride the way he had the swivel chair.

Wanderley plopped down and swung a leg over the arm, knocking askew the lamp shade on the side table lamp. Didn't seem to faze him one bit. He spread his arms out over the back of the love seat, slumped down, and looked as comfortable as a man dressed in briefs on his own living room couch. When his wife was out of town.

I said, "Have you had a chance to check out the preschool Chloe is looking at?"

"Are you ready to tell me what was covered during your Monday meeting with Garcia?"

So it wasn't Molly's dad I would be talking to right now. It was Detective Wanderley.

I went ahead and told him. He had a right to the information; I knew that now. In the Church of Christ, though we hold confidentiality in high regard, if there is a criminal matter being investigated and we have information that might be pertinent, we're going to tell. It's that way in most Protestant churches. Keep that in mind if you decide to go confessing to a minister instead of a priest.

He wanted to know who the other woman was. I told him I didn't have a clue.

187

I said, "Don't you have any suspects besides Alex? I mean, he's a sixteen-year-old kid . . ."

"Lots of sixteen-year-old boys are killers. Hormones are high, they get worked up over nothing; they don't have all the options an adult usually has. They act before they think. But yes, we're looking around. I shouldn't tell you this, but I took notice of the fact that someone from Garcia's law firm showed up at the house yesterday afternoon to 'pick up' Garcia's laptop and 'work-related' papers. He said they were firm property and might hold confidential client information."

"And you let that fellow walk off with that stuff? Don't you watch *Law and Order*?"

Wanderley shook his head reprovingly and grinned.

"No, Bear, I did not let the guy 'walk off' with all that info. I'd had all that packed up before you ever got to the Garcias' yesterday. I wouldn't have even known about the firm's request if the clever Mexican maid hadn't called me to fill me in on it."

I bristled. "Cruz isn't Mexican, she's Colombian, and she's not a maid, she's —"

Wanderley jerked upright and interrupted, "What? She's what? She's wearing a maid's uniform and cleaning the Garcias' house

188

for free because the Pope sent her an edict saying that all the brown-skinned people in the world should do what they can to help their poor, suffering white brothers and sisters?"

"She wears those uniforms because they're cheap and easy to clean. I asked her. She's more like a housekeeper," I finished.

"Right. That's what I said. Don't break my balls, Bear. Cruz is a brown-skinned woman working in the kitchen of a white woman's house in Sugar Land, Texas. I was not out of line to assume Cruz was a maid. And unlike you, I don't think there's anything shameful in being a maid or disrespectful in thinking that's what Cruz is."

I would work on that one later.

"And did you find anything of note on Graham's computer or papers?"

"You mean all of twenty-four hours after we picked them up and less than seven after we've inventoried everything? We're still going through them. I thought the firm trying to pick up 'firm property' on the very day Garcia died was a little hasty, that's all. It caught my attention. I don't know that there's more to it than good fiduciary duty."

"You read John Grisham?"

"I do. With pleasure. I don't use his books to solve crimes."

"Then what did you learn?" I asked.

"Oh, that Honey has a dad who has a textbook case of megalomania."

"Textbooks don't list megalomania anymore."

"But HD Parker fits the definition, doesn't he?"

"Give me your definition."

"Delusional dreams of wealth and power."

"Parker isn't delusional about those things. He's the real thing. Or he was once. But yeah, he's a piece of work. What did you learn from Alex?" I asked him.

"Let's see, more than you might imagine, considering he barely said a word to me, and wouldn't answer most of my questions, and hardly looked at me."

I tried not to smile. "He was taking his cues from his lawyer." God bless Glenn Carter for sending someone sharp.

He shook his head. "I think he saw the lawyer's presence as an insult. He definitely saw his mother's presence as an insult. Alex did his best to ignore them both. And that attitude. Umm. I guess I saw that as a point in his favor. He doesn't seem afraid, not the way I'd expect him to be, not for himself."

"So what did you learn?"

"That he was out all night the night his father was killed. Strictly speaking, Garcia was killed in the morning, but Alex wasn't home when it happened."

"You knew that yesterday."

"That his truck, a very distinctive, eye-catching truck, was seen parked at the Avalon Community Center around two in the morning. You know where that is? Where the tennis courts are?"

That wasn't good news. If it was true, it meant Alex's truck was parked just down from where Graham was killed. A sidewalk led from the parking lot up to the levee and then skirted the golf course right past what I was coming to think of as the murder scene.

I said, "His isn't the only truck of its kind in the whole wide world."

"No, but it may well be the only one of its kind in First Colony; I'm having that checked."

"Did he say the truck was his?"

"He didn't deny it."

"That's not the same as confirming it."

He swung his leg down and leaned forward, elbows on thighs, hands clasped loosely between his knees.

"Not in a court of law it isn't, Mr. Wells. I'm not trying to build a case against Alex Garcia; I'm trying to find out what happened that night. I'm trying to find out the

truth. You know, the truth will set you free."
He smiled at me.

I was afraid the truth might not set Alex
Garcia free.

"It doesn't seem like much to go on, does
it?" I asked. "Lots of teenage boys stay out
overnight, racing their cars, probably smoking pot in the greenbelts," I hesitated. "You
know what a greenbelt is? Those strips of
park the developers use to separate subdivisions?"

I got a look from Wanderley.

"Okay. Just being clear. Anyway, the
Avalon parking lot is a favorite make-out
spot. Or so I've heard. Why would Alex have
killed his dad anyway? Far as I know, father
and son got along fine."

"How far do you know, Mr. Wells?"

And there it was, the great difficulty. How
far did I know? How far did I go on faith?
And where did I place my faith? Not in
men, and certainly not in chariots and
horses, or whatever their modern equivalent
might be.

Beyond the portion that is revealed to me,
I don't have any idea what on earth goes on
behind the members of my congregation's
closed doors. I don't know what tempta-
tions beset them, I don't know what demons
they wrestle, I don't know which of them

cry themselves to sleep, I don't know who is enslaved to addictions that ride them ragged, I don't know who is on their knees all night praying and hearing no answer, I don't know who walks out of church, smile on his face and clap on the back to go home and beat his wife and children bloody or to excoriate coworkers with words sharper than glass shards. I don't know.

I trust in the encompassing love of God, but I know from experience that that love allows horrors on this earth. In short — not that I ever am — I didn't have one clue whether Alex Garcia might have a motive for killing his father. I didn't know but that Alex might feel he had a very good reason for killing his father.

I said, "I don't know."

Wanderley drew something from his pocket and held it concealed in his hand. "The witness who told us about the truck? He told us it looked like there were two people sitting in the cab."

"Really? So Alex might have someone who could alibi him? Obviously, he didn't tell you who it was, or you would have said, but do you have any ideas?"

Wanderley reached his arm out toward me and opened his fingers. A stream of gold slipped out. A heavy rose-gold chain dangled from his finger and at the end of it swung a gold locket, engraved initials twined together. The initials were J.W. for Josephine Wells. It was my mother's locket, until she gave it away. To Jo.

Wanderley said, "I have an idea."

# FIFTEEN

My heart didn't stop, nothing that dramatic, but it did give an extra skip before I could get a hold of myself. My body flooded with adrenaline and I had that high-alert feeling. I took the locket from Detective Wanderley and looked at it, slid my thumbnail in the groove, and popped it open. On the left-hand side was a picture of my dad, taken in his uniform. The picture used to be on the right-hand side. On Jo's thirteenth birthday, Mom made a "now you are a woman" speech and then opened the locket. She had moved Dad's picture to the left-hand side.

"That way, Jo," Mom said, "when you put in your own sweetie's picture, his picture will lie against your heart."

The sweetheart face looking back at me from the right-hand side of the locket was Jo's. And next to hers, Alex Garcia's.

I snapped the locket shut as if I could shut out what I had just seen and closed my fingers around it. I leaned back and rested my elbows on the arms of the chair. It was important to look relaxed and unconcerned even if my mind was whirring like a hamster wheel.

"So you recognize the necklace?" Wanderley said. The jerk.

"How did *you* recognize it?" I asked.

"You mean besides the fact that it's got her initials on it? And that she's in it?" He gave a nod toward the picture I have on the wall. "She's wearing it in the portrait."

"You saw her picture once and you recognized that locket? You must have been damn good at Concentration when you were a kid."

He grinned. "I was."

"Alex had it?" I asked.

"He was wearing it around his neck. Under his shirt, but the chain showed and I asked to see it. It looks better on her."

"He just showed it to you? Handed it over just like that?" Not very gallant.

"He didn't know I wasn't going to give it right back. He was not happy with me when I told him I wanted to keep it awhile. But yeah, he showed it to me. He's proud of it. He's proud of Jo."

Again, I felt my heart do something weird. I'm proud of Jo. I am. I mean, she's not at her best. Her grades have only recently begun to be acceptable, and only barely acceptable, and she quit all her school sports, and Heaven knows she's hard to live with. She's not where Merrie was at the same age, and there's no getting around the fact that that's going to cost her come college application time, but she'll catch up. If she applies herself.

Wanderley said, "I promised him I'd make sure Jo got it."

Then he held out his hand as if he thought I was going to give him the locket. Cretin.

"I'll take care of the locket," I said. I dropped it in the breast pocket of my shirt.

"I told Alex I'd see to it Jo got it back."

He was insisting, still holding out his hand like some Sunday school teacher asking for a pilfered crayon.

I looked at him, not saying anything, and after a moment he withdrew his hand and put it in his jacket pocket like nothing had happened.

"I guess I can tell Alex you'll give it to Jo."

"You can."

And I will, too. When she's thirty.

"I would like to talk to Jo about Monday night; Alex didn't say she was there, but —"

"That's not going to happen, I can tell

you right now."

"Listen, Bear, I'm not saying your daughter was involved —"

I stood up. "You better not be; I'd have a phalanx of lawyers crawling all over you in the time it took you to draw a good breath, and if you make so much as a —"

That sentence remained unfinished because that's when Annie Laurie walked in with a big brown bag under one arm. She stopped when she saw Detective Wanderley.

"I'm so sorry, Bear, I tried to call but I kept getting voice mail so I came on up with dinner. I'll wait out in the reception."

"No, we're done, Annie, go ahead and set up dinner, I'll see Detective Wanderley to his car."

That was as clear a dismissal as anyone could ask for. Wanderley stood up and made a big point of walking over to Annie and taking her hand, saying he was sorry he wasn't going to have a chance to visit.

Annie said, "I've made plenty if you'd like to stay and have dinner with Bear and me. You know you're welcome."

I bit my tongue.

Wanderley turned and looked at me and smiled big. He was still holding Annie's hand. I was starting to perspire and I was saying "Let the words of my mouth" over and over in my head so fast that they weren't words anymore, more like a mantra.

Wanderley gave Annie's hand a final squeeze. "I'll have to take you up on that thoughtful offer another time, Mrs. Wells. Got to get back to the office."

He strolled out of my office and I followed him down the stairs. People were drifting into the building. On Tuesdays, along with the sundry adult meetings in the building, the youth group brings in fast food and they eat together and then have a devotional; that's how Annie and I had gotten into the habit of having dinner together in my office. Wanderley scanned the foyer, noticing everyone: the clusters, the couples, the loners.

Wanderley saw Jo and her friend Ashley Spenser before I did. Ashley was holding a Taco Bell bag. Jo was holding an apple. They were talking. Must have been some pretty important girl stuff; Jo had her mouth about an inch from Ashley's ear and my daughter was incandescent with excitement. Ashley's eyes were as big as duck eggs while she listened, and she squeezed her Taco Bell bag in a way I knew couldn't be good for her burritos.

Maybe Jo was saying, "Hey, Ashley! I got to watch my boyfriend brain his daddy the other night!" I gave myself a shake. A mental shake. At least I hope it was only a mental shake, what with eagle-eyed Detective Wanderley right next to me, taking everything in.

Wanderley slowed when we passed and said, "Hello, Jo." She looked up, not recognizing him, her glance at me a question.

I took him by the elbow to keep him going and called over my shoulder, "Aren't you ladies supposed to be with Brick now? Go on up to your classroom." Jo rolled her eyes but headed up to her class.

"I've never been hustled out of church before, Bear. Do you use that move a lot?" Wanderley said. Then he put the brakes on, near the door where five or six teens were grouped. He shook me loose and walked up to Emma Tilton. I thought he must know her.

Emma is an unhappy sixteen-year-old. She's heavy, and not very pretty. She's gone the Goth route, the way a lot of heavy girls seem to, and the look didn't work any better on her than it does on most of them. She doesn't have a lot of friends, even here. We have failed her that way, all of us at the church.

Wanderley took Emma's hand in his. The

group of teens turned as one to watch the scene.

He said, his voice clear and carrying, "You have eyes like dark purple pansies. I've never seen anything like them."

Then he took her hand and put his mouth close to her ear and whispered something. Wanderley drew back, kissed the knuckles of her hand, and winked at her. He strode out of the church. Emma stared. All the teens stared. I stared, too.

I hurried out after Wanderley and caught him as he was pulling the keys out of his pocket.

I stopped at his car and put my hands on the hood, leaning my weight against the car. It shifted away from me; I was pressing that hard. Right then I felt like I could push his car right over. I could have. I'd abandoned "Let the words" and had resorted to "Please, God, please, God, please, God." I took a moment until I could feel some of His peace calming me.

"Wanderley, are you deliberately trying to get me to lose my temper?"

That surprised him, my being so direct. He pulled himself up straight, looking professional. "Wells, I'm only trying to find out the —"

"What was that in there? With Emma?"

"You're mad because I complimented that girl?"

"I want to know what you were up to — she's all of sixteen, and it's hard for me to believe —"

"Bear. Did you think I was coming on to that girl? What I was doing, Bear, is what someone should have done a long time ago. I *saw* that girl. And I made it possible for all your perfect *High School Musical*-type kids to see — what did you say her name was, Emma? — with new eyes. She was invisible in your church, Bear. No one saw her but me."

I took the time to think before I opened my mouth. I do that sometimes.

"What did you say to her? In her ear? All close and secret?"

Wanderley looked tickled. "Bear, you think I seduce children? I'll tell you what I said." His face got serious. "I said, 'No matter what, don't tell anyone what I'm whispering in your ear. It's our secret, and if you tell, you'll break the magic.'"

Now the detective looked mad. "And if you don't think I worked magic, Bear, wait until you walk back into that building where all you good-looking Christians let a lonely girl stand alone, by herself, with no one to talk to. I don't know if you preach about that sort of thing, preacher, but the God I read about? Don't I remember something like, 'Whatever you don't do for the least of my brothers, you didn't do it for me'?"

He didn't have it exact, but it was close enough. Too close for comfort certainly.

"All right," I said. "You're right. I'll see what I can do about it." That meant I was in a pickle because I sure haven't figured out how to get kids to accept someone they don't want to accept. Another problem to fit on a plate that was overloaded.

"Emma could be Jo, Bear. She could be Molly. I couldn't stand to see Molly in a corner all by herself."

I didn't say anything for a minute. I couldn't. I had a vision of one of my precious girls isolated the way poor Emma was. I made a resolution to find some way to help Emma.

I said, "Listen, Wanderley, I want to help you. I do. I'm not some bleeding heart who thinks cops are bad and murderers are misunderstood. Graham Garcia was a child of God and his blood cries out from the ground. I want you to catch his killer. And I want to be a help to you if I can be."

Wanderley started to say something but I held up my hand.

"Let me finish. Every time we're together,

I feel like you're setting traps for me. But I don't think I'm a suspect, am I?"

Wanderley looked up at me from under those black eyebrows. He was standing head down with his hands on his hips, pinky fingers hooked in his back pockets.

"Not yet, you're not."

My jaw dropped and he grinned that wicked grin. He gave my arm a punch and got in his car, unrolled the window. As he pulled out, he stuck his head through the window and said, "We'll be talking, preacher. I'll try to work on my 'people skills.' "

Cara Phelps, Autumn Flagg, and Becky Bell were all huddled around Emma when I walked back into the church. Her face was glowing. Those pansy eyes were glowing, too. I could see Brandon Ridley and Zachary Zhou watching Emma, too, something appraising in their look. Wanderley was right. He had worked magic. And Emma Tilton did have eyes like pansies. Wanderley made us all see her. She wasn't invisible anymore.

Dr. Fallon stopped me to say a word before I could get back to my office. He leads the New Members class, and to save my life, I couldn't tell you what it was he asked me — I had other things on my mind.

By the time I got back to my office, I had only half an hour to eat before the beginning of the self-help groups, divorce recovery, AA, the church choir practices, that sort of thing. It was a good thing I wasn't leading a group this quarter; I'm not sure I could have talked sense.

Annie had already eaten. She had my dinner set out on the coffee table, on the blue-and-white-checked tablecloth she'd made in junior high. A big roast beef sandwich on French bread, with a Styrofoam cup of spicy broth to dunk it in, plus carrot and celery sticks. There were homemade chocolate chip cookies there, too, lumpy with pecans from my Aunt Sue's farm. I gave Annie a kiss before I started eating. I was starving.

She waited patiently for me to finish my meal and was picking up the mess when she finally asked, "What was that all about?"

I checked my wristwatch. "We need to be in the divorce recovery group in five minutes, sweetie. Can I tell you about it later?"

She smiled. "Just don't forget to fill me in — or you might be in that group for more than moral support."

I pulled her close for a kiss and a squeeze, but when her hands slid up my chest, she felt the lump in my pocket. She pulled Jo's locket out and I didn't get that kiss.

"Why do you have this, Bear?"

"Three minutes, Annie Laurie, let me —"

She sat down and put the paper bag with the thermos and tablecloth at her feet. "I don't believe I'm going to group tonight, Bear. You aren't leading, are you?" She knew I wasn't. "You aren't going to go to hell for missing a group this once; sit down and tell me what's going on."

"I hate to miss Jim's group. He'll be looking for me —"

"It's better you disappoint Jim than you disappoint me. I want to know why Wanderley was here again and I want to know why you have Jo's locket and . . ." Annie Laurie opened the locket with a pink fingernail and stared at Alex's young face. "Oh, my Lord. Do we have a problem, Bear?"

I sat down. I told her I thought maybe we did.

# Sixteen

I'm not going to go into the discussion we had with Jo that night. I'm calling it a discussion; that may be something of a misnomer since an objective observer might be excused for mistaking the exchange for an all-out screaming match. Not that I screamed any. I yelled some, but only after the kind of provocation that would have had the Apostle Paul throwing hissy fits. (I need to think of someone else. The Apostle Paul is known for his hissy fits.)

Let me sum it up. Jo wasn't talking. Okay, that's not quite accurate, either, because she said plenty, mainly to let me know that a suspicious mind was an indication of a guilty conscience, and yeah, she was talking about me there, and that she hadn't broken any rules as we had never specifically forbidden her to use her second-story bedroom window for ingress and egress (and she used those words, too; "ingress" and "egress," I mean).

She wouldn't tell us where she had gone; she wouldn't tell us what she had done; and she wouldn't tell us who she had been with, that last being on the principle that her personal relationships were just that, personal.

I think I started doing some of the yelling right about then, Jo not backing down an inch, grit-toothed and clench-fisted and looking for all the world like a black cat spitting at a dog.

She told us that, furthermore (and she used that word, "furthermore"), "Furthermore, Nana gave that necklace to me and you don't have any right to take it away."

I said I hadn't taken it away from her, I had taken it from a Sugar Land cop, and he had taken it from Alex Garcia in an interview room of the Fort Bend Juvenile Detention Center and would she perhaps care to explain those circumstances to her Nana, because I just happened to know her number by heart and I would be only too happy to dial it for her. And I took her cell phone from her desk. And no, I did not confiscate it. I took it for safekeeping because our rule has always been if you misuse it, you're going to lose it, and the girls understood that from the beginning when I bought them the dang things.

Jo said she hadn't given the locket to Alex, she had loaned it to him because he was so sad, and in any case, she and her Nana had a perfect understanding and she would talk to Nana on her own time, but thank you so very much anyway, and I said had she taken up *Masterpiece Theater* or Jane Austen or something because she sounded like someone in a costume drama. And that's when Annie Laurie, who'd been trying to get a word in edgewise, said, "Why, Bear, she talks just like you." And then I yelled at Annie.

So you can see why I'm not going to go into that night's discussion.

I'd already had a good run but Baby Bear hadn't and he'd missed out on his afternoon romp, too, another thing that was Jo's fault. I stowed Jo's phone in my underwear drawer and left the two women of the house to commiserate with each other for having the terrible fate of being related to me.

My afternoon run on the levee had taken me from the church to the house, north to south. Tonight Baby Bear and I ran south from my house. If you follow the levee this way, you'll eventually end up past Oil Field Drive, which is cow country in some areas and sportscaster megahomes in others. Well, there's one sportscaster out there anyway. Merrie went to his kid's birthday party.

I wouldn't be running that far this evening. I wanted to run off steam, not run away. Had it not been for the full moon, the sidewalk would have been the smarter choice for a jog. The levee is unlit except for the lights shining out of the homes that back up to it.

Elkins Road crosses the levee this way. I would pass right by the golf course, right by the ninth green, where Graham Garcia had died less than forty-eight hours ago. Garcia wasn't much older than me. Correction: He hadn't been much older than me. He was dead now. I've seen a lot of death; ministers do. I haven't seen much unexpected death. Some car accidents. Some heart attacks. Never murder.

I was thinking along those lines, my feet pounding the levee, my head somewhere else, Baby Bear keeping up easily, when the dog gave a low growl and took off like a bullet. Okay, not exactly a bullet, but like a large, hairy dog on a mission.

He left me in the dust and I was hoping it was a nutria he was after and not some poor, lone jogger who was about to get a toothy, slobbery, Hound-of-the-Baskervilles surprise. I heard a cry and a grunt and I knew it wasn't a nutria, and I put on more speed than I thought I had left in me. I came past a bank of trees and saw, to my utter horror, that Baby Bear had some guy on the ground and appeared to be worrying his neck. Baby Bear was making disgusting chewing noises. I had visions of battalions of lawyers descending upon me. I'm not proud of that self-centered thought, but it was my first.

The fellow was struggling to get up, saying, "Baby, get off me. Jo! Call him off! He's getting spit all over me!"

I reached one hand down, grabbed Baby Bear's collar, and hauled him off. With the other hand I grabbed the guy's upper arm and hauled him to his feet. Baby Bear hadn't been tearing the guy's throat out; he'd been showing him the sort of affection he usually reserves for family members.

Alex Garcia was standing in front of me, his long blond hair glistening with dog drool, using the tail of his shirt to wipe dog slobber off his face and neck. He looked stunned to see Jo's dad instead of Jo. I was feeling stunned, too. My mind was putting puzzle pieces together.

I said, "Let's walk a ways, Alex, seeing as you've come all the way out here to meet someone who I'm pretty sure is not going to show. In fact, you better hope she doesn't show."

He said, "Oh, no. Well, I wasn't here to . . . I was only . . ."

I had hold of the back of Alex's shirt and I turned him and sort of propelled him back the way he had come.

I said, "No, you weren't only anything, you were out here to meet Jo. Not for the first time, either. She didn't give you away, you know, in spite of the beatings."

He stopped. "You didn't —"

That made me mad. "Son, can't you take a joke? You have California blood, maybe? I do some hollering sometimes, hardly ever, but I have not laid a hand on a woman in my whole life. Not the way you're thinking."

I gave him a little shove to start him moving in the right direction again. That direction being away from my house. The idea of me hitting one of my girls. Alex thinking I might really have hit Jo, though — it made me pause. Honey had said Graham didn't hit her, but she wouldn't be the first woman to shield her husband.

"Your father," I said, "he wasn't rough with your —"

He pulled away from me.

"I've never even heard him raise his voice to her. So I guess he did better than you, since you 'holler.' From what I hear."

I'm not saying I didn't have that coming. Still, that kid didn't have a clue what kind of restraint it took for me not to do more than yell, what with him sneaking up the levee to entice my fourteen-year-old daughter out to meet him. The thought made me tighten up my grip on his collar. What I really wanted to do was give him a shake and explain to him in no uncertain terms exactly what I was going to do to him if he met Jo behind my back again. I guess I did give him the tiniest shake, a friendly shake, which turned him toward me, and in the blue moonlight I could see his face, his startled eyes looking up at me.

He'd been crying. His face had that thin-skinned look and his eyelids were swollen. He wasn't but a few years older than Jo. There was still a lot more boy in his face than there was man, in spite of the light dusting of beard on his cheeks. So if he'd been crying, well, Alex had a right to those tears. His daddy was dead. Murdered. He'd been treated like a criminal. And he'd had the misfortune to meet up with Jo's dad instead of with Jo. I let go of his collar and put my arm around his shoulder. I got us walking again, Baby Bear snuffling at our feet, pleased as peaches that he'd found a friend to join us. Baby Bear loves company.

I said, "You're right, Alex. It's a bad thing for a man to yell at his wife, and I have yelled at Annie Laurie. Been real sorry afterward, of course."

Partly my conscience and partly because Annie Laurie saw to it that I was real sorry.

Alex breathed in the night air, trying to get a hold of himself. Sounded like he was choking. Baby Bear leaned his weight against Alex's legs as he walked, trying to show support, about to knock him down. I had a strong arm around him, letting him know he could count on me. Between me and Baby Bear, Alex must have felt the teensiest bit squeezed.

"Mr. Wells?" His voice was tight, like he was having trouble breathing.

"Yes, son?" I could tell the boy needed to talk, needed to open up to someone.

"Could you take your arm off me? You're kind of sweaty and —"

"Oh!"

I let him go. I'd slipped on the same workout clothes I'd used to run home from the office earlier, and I must have been ripe.

The kid took a step or two away and bent at the waist, hands on his knees, in the position of a badly winded runner. He was gasping, clearly relieved to be inhaling the warm, humid night instead of warm, humid me and Baby Bear. I should have been offended but I thought it was funny. A serious musking was a good punishment for a boy who had come sneaking around my house, after my daughter.

"Listen," he said, straightening up, "I'm, ah, I was, ah . . ." He started walking backward.

But we'd come to one of those improvised benches the road crews had constructed here and there on top of the levee so they'd have someplace to eat their lunches. A piece of planking nailed between two convenient tree trunks, that's all it was. It was a good place for us to sit and talk on a mild March night like this. If it had been a month or two later, the mosquitoes would have made the night a misery.

"Alex, come sit down here a minute and let's you and me talk."

He was still backing up, his hands in his back pockets, elbows akimbo. "No, I, ah — my mom, she's . . ." Baby Bear kept giving Alex affectionate nudges, sticking his cold wet nose up under the kid's loose shirt and sniffing interestedly.

"You go on and call your mom." I sat

down on the bench, feeling it bend a little. "You've got your cell phone, haven't you? I mean, that's how you were going to let Jo know you were out here waiting for her. I don't guess your generation does anything as low-tech as throw pebbles at the girl's window, do you?"

Alex hesitated, his big white sneakers half-buried in the tractor ruts. Baby Bear stood on one of his sneakers and worried at the other. Baby Bear's favorite game is "Steal the Sneaker." He was having trouble getting Alex's off and he was producing a ton of drool. All Newfies drool. It's part of their charm.

I said, "Son, you don't need to be afraid of me. It's not like I'm going to eat you. Baby Bear might eat you, but I won't."

It was a cheap shot, but with a boy young as Alex, it could have worked. Alex surprised me. He gave me a half-smile, and shook his head like he'd expected better of me.

"Mr. Wells, not wanting to talk to you isn't the same thing as being afraid to talk to you. And Jo's dog loves me. Right, Baby?" Alex grabbed Baby Bear's nape and gave it a rough shake. Baby Bear grinned up at the kid, happy to concur. Alex had been spending a lot of time with my dog. I hadn't known that.

Then he surprised me again. He pulled out his cell phone and dialed a number. Not, it turned out, his mother's.

I said, "If you're calling Jo, she won't answer. I took her phone away."

Alex said, "Jo?"

Which meant Annie Laurie had given Jo her phone back, thank you very much for the unified parental front.

He didn't drop his voice, didn't turn his back. "Listen, I'm out on the levee with your dad — no, don't come — Jo, I'm asking you not to come — I know that, but obviously he doesn't. We're going to talk for ten or fifteen minutes, then I'll call you from the truck. Not more than half an hour, I promise. Okay. I love you. No matter what."

So. All right, then. I felt like he'd made his position pretty plain there, and as far as he was concerned, I could like it or lump it.

Alex snapped the phone shut and slid it in his back pocket. He gave Baby Bear a push and walked over, his sneakers shushing through the weeds and kicking up puffs of gnats. He stopped in front of me and stood feet apart, arms akimbo. That was to make him look more imposing. I saw it on the National Geographic Channel. They were showing frill-neck lizards, but it's the same thing.

Baby Bear sat down in front of Alex and then scooted back until his bottom was on top of Alex's feet. Baby Bear likes lots of physical contact.

"You wanted to talk?"

I scooted aside on the bench, my nylon running shorts picking up some splinters from the unsanded two-by-four. "Sit down, Alex." I patted the bench but he shook his head.

"No, I'll stand — I'm not sure it can hold us both."

Another Clydesdale moment for me, but I smiled anyway.

"They didn't keep you long, up at the station."

"They didn't have any cause."

"That what your lawyer said?"

"She did, but she didn't need to. I could have told them myself. I'm not stupid."

Not stupid, ignorant. There's a difference.

"Your grandfather came to see me today."

"Which one?"

"As it turned out, I saw them both. Your grandfather Parker made an appearance at the juvie jail and caught me up."

Alex gave a snort. "That wasn't an appearance. I heard it was a full-blown scene. I heard HD has been kicked out of the Miss Congeniality contest."

"You always call your granddaddy HD?"

"Everyone does. Everyone but Mom."

"He is a piece of work, your grandfather. Does he always come off like that?"

Alex worked his hands under the collar around Baby Bear's scruff, kneading and pulling the loose skin. Baby Bear made little grunting noises. That's a contented noise for Baby Bear.

"He doesn't. No. He never used to. He's always thrown his weight around, but not like this. He's . . . I don't know. We're kind of worried about him. When I was a kid . . ."

When he was a kid?

"HD is the greatest thing on earth. I've met Muhammad Ali, Yao Ming, Tiger Woods, tons of those guys — HD would make a donation to their favorite charity, and we'd get invited to some function. HD took me to Scotland to play Turnberry and Saint Andrews. It's not like I'm even that good a golfer. I'm about fifth on the team."

So much for the negative three handicap.

"But HD thinks I'm the next Jack Nicklaus." Alex gave a laugh. "He'd pull me out of school in the middle of the day and take me to a business lunch at Tony's. He said listening to negotiations was a better education than anything I could learn in school."

Baby Bear gave a great yowling yawn and

shook his head, making his tags jingle. He settled down in the grass and Alex knelt next to him.

"It made my dad crazy. He wanted Mom to take HD off the safe list at school so he couldn't take me out without their permission. Dad said sitting around watching old men drink martinis and eat quart-sized bowls of seafood gumbo was not an education. But it was. I learned a lot."

The bench gave a crack when I shifted my weight but it held.

"Yeah? What did you learn at Tony's?" I'd been there. Once. Thirty-four dollars for a Philly cheesesteak. I don't care if it is Kobe beef.

"Ha! For one thing, putting a drink in a martini glass doesn't make it a martini, there's no such thing as a chocolate martini, and only girls drink vodka martinis. How's that for an education?"

"You could write a Chelsea Handler book with that kind of education. I think I'm with your dad on this one."

"Who is Chelsea Handler?"

"Never mind." My sister-in-law, Stacy, loves those books. I read a chapter of *Chelsea Chelsea Bang Bang*. I don't think I'm the target audience.

Baby Bear rolled over and offered up his

belly for Alex's ministrations. Alex started a slow tickle over the expanse that made Baby Bear wriggle and groan with pleasure.

"HD got Jenasy a Mini Cooper when she turned sixteen. He bought me that truck last birthday. Dad hates it. Dad was okay with HD getting Jenasy the Mini, but he wants me to drive a used Volvo. I mean, he wanted —"

"I know what you mean, son."

"Jenasy was always Dad's princess." He blew through his nose. "But after HD said what he wanted to give me for my birthday, Dad gave me this big talk about how much gas was going to cost me, and how he was afraid I would wipe out an entire trailer of immigrants with that truck, and all about conspicuous consumption and all, so I said, okay, whatever he wanted, and then on my birthhday, HD comes roaring up the front drive in that truck, big bow on it like in a car commercial, Fredrick following him in the Bentley, and HD hands me the keys and a gas card. Not one of those twenty-five-dollar gas cards, either. A credit card in HD's name. I've got a bottomless gas tank."

He put his sneakers against Baby Bear's back and shoved. "That's enough, Baby."

Baby Bear got up and ambled over to me. He laid that huge, heavy head on my lap

221

and sent up his pathetic look. That was meant to convey that he hadn't had any affection all day long and there was this place behind his left ear that really needed some attention. Normally, he would have gotten to me with those eyes, but I was feeling sore about the secrets he'd been keeping from me. When he saw I wasn't going to come through, he wandered off to gnaw on a young sapling that would have liked to grow up to be a tree, if only there weren't random tree-eating Newfoundlands in the neighborhood.

"What was I going to do? I mean, HD had already bought the thing. He'd driven it off the lot. I really couldn't say no."

I couldn't have said no to that monster truck at sixteen. Even at my age, I'd find it hard to say no to limitless free gas.

"But this 'master of the universe' thing he's been doing lately? I don't know where that comes from. It's weird. It's like he's channeling Jett Rink."

"You've seen *Giant*?"

"Like fifty times. It's HD's favorite movie. It's practically his only movie. 'Money isn't everything, Jett.' 'Not when you've got it.' "

He had the voices down and I gave a laugh.

"HD, he wasn't always all about the

money and what he could make happen with it. That stuff was cool, but . . . he's got a cabin over in Johnson City. Have you been to Johnson City?"

"I've gone through on my way to Pedernales Falls."

"I love that place. That's my favorite Texas park. That's why HD bought the Johnson City place, a long time ago when my mom was young, because it's so close to Pedernales Falls. Two bedrooms and then one room that's kitchen and living room all together. It's nothing fancy. Window unit air conditioners. It looks like he furnished it out of the Salvation Army. In one room there's four sets of bunk beds — one on each wall. My cousins are all a lot older than me, and when HD took them out to the cabin, he would fill every bunk. By the time I was old enough, it was just me and him. My cousins were in college or off and married. I didn't mind. HD would tell stories about the tricks my cousins would play on him, and what it was like in Texas when he was growing up. The house HD grew up in? Didn't have any air-conditioning. Imagine Texas in the summer with no air-conditioning."

There are lots of people in Texas who live through our monstrous summers with no air-conditioning. Not by choice.

Alex lay back in the grass, his knees up.

"Jenasy hated the place. She said it smelled. She and Beanie would go shopping when HD took me on trips."

"Last time I went to the cabin, it was me and Dad. Right before Christmas. Johnson City isn't much, but they do a big deal over Christmas lights. We hiked the State Park all day. Each night we had dinner at the Friendly Bar Bistro. Live entertainment, and on Sunday night, all these cool old people get together and play every instrument you can think of. Keyboard and fiddle and steel guitar, mandolin, and ukulele. I swear, one old dude was playing the ukulele. And they were *good*. It's not Dad's kind of thing at all, but he *loved* it. He had such a great freaking time. He was happy. He acted like everything was okay. Like he wasn't — my dad is almost never happy. Not with me."

Silence. Alex's knees went up to his chest and he rolled over on his side and wrapped his arms around his head. His shoulders shook. Baby Bear stopped chewing on the tree and loped over. He pawed at Alex's arms and snaked his tongue over the kid's face, making a worried rumble. I stood over the kid, not happy with him, either, feeling his heartbreak, and not wanting to. I gave his shoulder a squeeze.

"Hey. Alex. I know you miss him."

"I don't know if I do."

"What?"

"I don't think I knew my dad. Not really. I don't think any of us did." He shook his head.

"Alex, it's natural to have some confused feelings —"

He sat up and looked at me. One arm holding Baby Bear, the other fending off the dog tongue.

"Are you going to tell me you understand?"

I stopped.

"Because you don't. You don't understand anything. You don't know enough to understand."

Fair enough. I squatted down. My running shorts didn't give me as much protection from the prickles and burrs as Alex's jeans, so I balanced on the balls of my feet.

"I'm off track," I said. "I did see HD today, but it was Dr. Garcia who came to see me."

Alex didn't change position, but he got a sort of listening intensity about him. "Yeah? What did Granddad want?"

"He's worried about you."

Alex gave a snort and threw his hands out.

"Yeah? Well, this would be a good time to be worried about me. I'm worried about me, too. I've never even had a traffic ticket before. What do you think; is there a spin I can put on all this? Work it as some kind of 'life experience,' use it as an edge to get into UT?"

He crossed his legs in the grass and started picking at the rubber on his shoes. The full moon was high now and shining on his straight, fair hair. Baby Bear laid his heavy head on the boy's lap. Alex massaged the silky black ears. Seeing as good as he was with Baby Bear, he couldn't be all bad, even if he was a murderer.

"You know what?" he said. "I'm worried about him, too — not for the same reason he's worried about me, I mean, I don't think he killed Dad or anything —"

I interrupted. "Your grandfather does not think there's any chance whatsoever of your having killed your dad."

"No?" He lifted his head up to look at me. "Well, that's good to hear. He got pretty exercised last night when he talked to me after the police let me go and gave me my truck back. Truck is cleaner than it has been since the day HD gave it to me. And my lighter is gone and someone took the twenty dollars I had in the console."

Alex made a fist and stretched one of Baby's great ears over the closed hand. He stroked the ear while Baby Bear pushed into his hand, moaning with gratitude.

"Granddad is an old man, you know. I don't think about that most of the time. He's still working at the free clinics, you know, couple a days a month, and he still skis, if you can believe that. He's good, too. He taught me when I was three. He shouldn't ski. It's crazy for an old guy to go flying down a mountain."

He paused. Those had been better times for the Garcia family.

"Last night, though, he looked old. His hands were trembling. This has been a terrible shock for him." There was a pause. "Shit."

He tilted his face up and pinched the bridge of his nose, trying to keep the tears in. He was as fair as his grandfather was dark, but at the moment, Alex reminded me of Dr. Garcia, of his father, the three men, their gestures so alike. He didn't look a bit like HD.

I said, "Alex, I'm real sorry about your dad. I know I told you all that at the house, but I really am, for you and your mom and your granddad. For Jenasy. I'm even more sorry that you've been drawn into all this. And . . . Alex, was Jo with you that night?"

His fine-boned face shot up and he stared at me like he meant to stare me into consternation. It didn't work.

"Was she?" I asked.

Another snort and he shook his head, not in denial but over the unreasonableness of adults in persisting to butt in where they didn't have any business.

"The reason I'm asking, Alex, it's not that I think I have the right to know everything Jo does, everywhere Jo goes, who she's with. I do have that right, but we won't go there right now."

This time he made the sound that used to be written as "pshaw" and plucked a long grass and nibbled its root. I wanted to remind him that people walk their dogs on the levee.

"The reason I'm asking is because Detective Wanderley is going to want to question her. I hope you don't think she'd lie for you —"

"In a heartbeat," he shot back.

Just more and more good news.

I said, "Would you want her to?"

Silence, a long one this time, but I let it drag on. I wanted the answer to my question. It would tell me a lot about the young man sitting in front of me.

When he broke the silence, it wasn't to answer my question. He asked one of his own.

Alex said, "If I tell you something, and it's not about the" — he stumbled over the word — "the murder, it didn't have anything to do with Dad dying, would you swear not to tell anyone? Not the police, not Mom, and never, ever Granddad. Most of all, you can't tell Jo. Could you swear that? On the Bible?"

It was my turn to be quiet. I don't make promises lightly. They matter to me.

I said, "Alex, you know we don't operate like the Catholic Church. I'm not a priest, and if you confess —"

"It's nothing I did."

"My not telling, that's not going to put anyone in any danger?"

"I'm trying to keep someone safe."

So, I mean, this was a sticky situation I could be letting myself in for. Whatever Alex wanted to tell me could be dangerous information, dangerous to someone anyway. I don't think a sixteen-year-old is the best judge of . . . anything. But if the kid told me, at least he'd have a grown-up on his side to help him.

And I might be able to talk him into telling the right person, once I knew what the problem was. There was Jo, too, another reason to make this promise. Whatever it was, if Jo was involved, I wanted to be in a position to help.

I silently asked God to guide me but I didn't feel anything more specific than a strong urge to know what it was Alex was hiding and that was as likely to be coming from me as from Him. More likely.

Alex was waiting, his eyes intent on mine.

"All right," I said, reluctant to let the binding words out of my mouth, "I promise."

He kept staring at me, trying to decide if he could trust me or not, and I didn't look away. Either my word was good enough for the boy or it wasn't. After a minute, he nodded and stood up to take his cell phone out. Again, he made no attempt to keep me from hearing what he was saying.

"Jo." His voice was soft and gruff when he said her name. "Yeah, everything's fine. I mean I'm okay, everything isn't fine but nothing you don't know about. No, I'm not at the truck, that's why I'm calling, I'll be a little longer than I said. Yeah, he's here" — he flicked a look at me, and pushed his thick hair back — "but it's okay. Listen, I have to go. No, I'll tell you later. I'll call you soon. I love you, Jo, and listen, I am so freaking proud of you. Don't worry about anything. It's all going to work out, no matter what" — another look at me — "bye."

He snapped the phone shut, contemplated the toes of his shoes for a second or two, and then said, "Could we walk instead of sitting in the weeds out here?"

I said sure and Baby Bear was more than agreeable to the idea. We continued the way I had started out, away from my house and toward Elkins Road. I was thinking about how he had called Jo, not forgetting his promise, and I liked him for that but I was also thinking about his saying, "I love you," which sounded way too intimate and possessive for my tastes. I wondered if Jo was saying it back.

By night, the backyards we were passing were as different as they were by day. We passed a yard where the homeowners had lined their flower beds in dimly glowing solar lamps. I've been tempted to try those. They don't give off much light, but they're easy to install and not too expensive. Solar lamps are nowhere near as effective as the kind electricians put up. You can get a lighting specialist to come out to your home and get lights put up in the branches of your trees, highlighting the pool and I don't know what all. The Garcias' yard is lit like that, front and back, and it's real pretty when they give a party at night.

I was maundering on about these things as Alex and I walked, giving him time to get his thoughts together, and that's what I was talking about when we got to the gate that keeps unauthorized vehicles off the levee. I say a gate — there are two posts with a chain between them. You find a gate everywhere a road cuts through the levee — to keep teenagers from driving out onto the unpaved levee surface.

We had come out of the trees to Elkins Road. To the right was the Avalon Community Center parking lot, where Alex's truck had been parked the night his father died. Where it was parked now. Ahead and to the left was the corner of the golf course where Graham Garcia's body had been found.

I stopped talking. I had exhausted the topic of outdoor lighting, which neither of us had any real interest in. I'd been filling up the silence before I found out something I might not want to know. We crossed to the other side of Elkins and stood on the sidewalk under the streetlight. To maintain the levee system, the road is raised here, so we walked up through the thick, overgrown grass until we were sheltered in the belt of trees rimming the seventh hole. We looked down through the trees into the golf course. It was quiet, and in an unimaginative but well-groomed, lush, green way, it was pretty. There were lights on in the custom houses backing up to the golf course. Cars went by every now and then. From where we were standing, up close to the trunk of a fallen log, we were shielded by the trees, and you couldn't have seen us from the golf course unless you'd really been looking.

"You swear on your honor?"

I said I did.

Alex said, "I was sitting on the log."

"What time was this?"

"It was late." He cut his eyes at me. "It was seriously late."

He sat down on the log.

"I wanted Jo to meet me that night but she said she couldn't. I came over anyway. To be closer to her. Maybe she would change her mind if I was already here. And she did. She said she could give me half an hour. It wasn't much, but it was better than nothing. We sat in the truck and talked. Then she said she had to go. She had a test next morning. So I walked her home" — he cut his eyes at me — "the back way."

Meaning the levee to the back gate to the

garage roof, to her bedroom window . . .

"And then I came back. I wasn't ready to go home. So I sat here, just quiet, you know?"

"Alex, I don't much want you calling Jo after —"

"So I sat here, thinking about Jo, and I see this guy come walking out on the golf course, and you know, it's late and dark, so already he has my attention, and when he gets closer, I can see it's Dad. Which was totally random — it's o-dark-thirty on the golf course, and he comes walking out like it's Saturday afternoon and it's his turn at the tee."

"Where had he come from?" I asked. "Where was he parked?"

Alex didn't answer directly. He stretched his arm out to point where the golf course cart path veered down to tunnel under Alcorn Oaks and continue on to the other side of the golf course. He pointed.

"That's where I saw them."

"Them?"

"Dad and Jo."

"*What?*"

"It wasn't actually Jo."

"You just this second said —"

"It couldn't have been Jo. She went back home to study. And anyway, I picked her up from school on Monday. She said it wasn't her." Alex's mouth twisted.

"You actually asked Jo if she had —"

"It made her mad."

"You *think*?"

"Listen! It looked like Jo, okay? I'm telling you, it freaking looked like her!" Alex's voice was shaky.

"You're saying your dad was with a girl? Not a woman, but a *girl*?"

He plowed on, not acknowledging my questions. "He was standing there under the trees, acting like he was practicing his putting, which he wasn't." He gave a snort of derision. "You don't practice putting in the rough. And you don't practice swings that late at night on an unlit course. And you don't putt with a Big Bertha." He glanced at me. "A Big Bertha is a driver."

I didn't give a hoot about practice swings.

"So that was different. I mean, he was out there in the middle of the night, on the golf course, in the rough. Then the whole putting charade. And then she came out of the tunnel, her long hair all down her back, and Dad ran up to her and he put his arms around her and they kissed."

He turned his burning eyes on me.

"No," I said.

His eyes didn't waver. "He bent her over

235

backward. If I'd had a gun, I would have shot him." He leaned over and spit on the ground, then turned his back on the golf course and started walking to his truck, Baby Bear ambling at his side. "Then I left. I didn't need to see any more. I didn't want to see any more."

When he got to the Ford, he beeped the locks and climbed inside. It's a big truck for a kid that age. He unrolled the window and I put my hands on it, trying to keep him in place so I could tell him it wasn't Jo, it couldn't have been Jo. Because, you know, two hundred plus pounds can keep an F-150 in place.

"Could she have been older, Alex? Like, thirty?" Thirty would be better. Thirty would be much better.

"I told you. I thought it was Jo. She was Jo's age."

"Alex, Jo is fourteen."

He looked at me.

I had to step back quick to keep my arms from getting torn off when he reversed and peeled out of the parking lot. When he topped Elkins, I could see the cell phone at his ear. I knew he was calling Jo. The way he'd promised to.

Baby Bear must have thought he was jogging back to the house with an old man. That's how I felt. Old and shocked and sick at heart. Not believing what I'd heard. Graham Garcia with a child. Because a fourteen-year-old is a child.

Alex was mistaken. His father couldn't have been with someone that young. Alex had said it was late, it was dark; the kid would have been tired, and he'd had Jo on his mind. The mind can play tricks on you.

It couldn't have been a girl that young.

The idea of a man Graham Garcia's age touching one of my daughters . . . If Graham Garcia had touched my child, if he had so much as laid his little finger on her, I would have killed him myself. I would have killed that man. I would — someone else had killed Graham Garcia.

I wasn't the only man who loved his daughters. I wouldn't be the only man who would feel murderous at the violation of his child.

Baby Bear gave a yelp and I stopped, my body soaked and my knees trembling. Somewhere along the way, I'd started running and I'd outrun Baby Bear. I didn't think I could do that. Baby Bear didn't, either. He caught up, reproach in his eyes. I dropped to the grass and lay on my back, my blood pounding in my ears.

The black sky was sprinkled with stars — there's too much light in Sugar Land to see the whole panoply.

My God made that sky. My God was holding this world in His hands. He held me and He held Jo and He held the someone else. The fourteen-year-old someone who had met Graham Garcia on the golf course the night he died.

My heart slowed. I got to my feet and stumbled home, Baby Bear staying close and muttering in concern. The weight of my promise bowed my shoulders.

# SEVENTEEN

Annie had been waiting for me when I got back from walking Baby Bear. She knew something had happened with Alex; Annie had overheard Jo's side of those phone conversations. Not unreasonably, she wanted to know what Alex and I had talked about.

I told her about the promise. She said I never should have made the promise, which was true enough, but the advice was too late to do me any good. She wanted to know what I was going to do with whatever information I now had, and I couldn't give her a satisfactory answer to that question, either, because I didn't have a clue what I was going to do. Annie pushed harder and I bit her head off.

I hadn't slept. I'd stood under the shower until the hot water ran out, stood there until it turned tepid, stood there till it turned cold.

I had lain down next to my Annie Laurie, who wasn't speaking to me and was tossing and turning herself. When she finally fell into fitful sleep, I got up and prowled the house.

I climbed the stairs and rested my cheek against Jo's door. My child, my baby, my little girl. God protect her. Oh, if someone, some man had wheedled his way into my Jo's life, I would want that man dead. I would. I could understand that kind of murder. That's not saying it's right.

That's not saying it's wrong.

I don't know. I don't know. But I could understand. That's all I'm saying. I could understand.

Baby Bear heard me and snuffled at the door, asking me to open it. I opened the door as quietly as I could and Baby Bear pushed against my legs, his tail beating the air. I crossed to Jo's bed and looked down at my sleeping daughter.

Light spilled in through the window. The life-sized plastic goose with a five-watt bulb in its belly glowed from a corner. That goose had been in Jo's nursery and she's never turned loose of it.

Jo lay on her back, her dark hair in a braid lying across her pillowcase. Her lashes were so long they brushed her cheeks. She breathed with her mouth open like a child. She looked about ten.

Thank God it wasn't Jo.

Baby Bear and I padded out of Jo's room and down to the kitchen, where I studied Annie's collection of wine bottles for a long time before I pulled a box of Alpha-Bits out of the pantry and poured myself and Baby Bear each a bowl. I had mine with milk.

After a while, Annie Laurie appeared in her nightshirt, her hair tousled, and watched us from the door. She got herself a coffee cup and poured out some cereal into it, added a splash of milk, and joined us. When Annie was done eating, she put her cup on the floor and Baby Bear danced it over to the cabinets trying to get the last bit of sugary milk onto his tongue. She got out of her chair and put her hands on my shoulders. I covered one of her hands with my own. She kissed the back of my bowed head and went back to our bedroom.

It was a long night.

I woke up in an easy chair. Jo had left for school and Annie Laurie was off, too. She'd left me a note to remind me of the building committee meeting.

So I had to meet with the church building committee at ten o'clock and be at Honey

241

Garcia's side at eleven thirty while she made the final decisions concerning Graham's funeral. I wasn't sure which I dreaded most.

# EIGHTEEN

**From**: Walker Wells
**To**: Merrie Wells
**Subject**: Jo

Hey, Sweetheart — Do me a favor. Call your sister.

**From**: Merrie Wells
**To**: Walker Wells
**Subject**: Re: Jo

What's up?

**From**: Walker Wells
**To**: Merrie Wells
**Subject**: Re: Jo

Could you just call her? I'm asking.

**From**: Merrie Wells
**To**: Walker Wells

**Subject**: Re: Jo

A little information would be good. But okay.
I'll call.

# NINETEEN

By ten fifteen, there was no question. The building committee meeting was going to be the worst ordeal of the day.

Our church family is about three-quarters through a six-part building plan. The way we do it is we don't start building on the next phase until the phase we started before is completely finished and we have the money in hand for the next. Not pledged, mind you, but cash in the bank.

There's good sense in that policy. It means we don't get tangled in interest rates, and it doesn't send us into a tailspin if some member has a sudden reversal of fortune (or of conscience) and can no longer fulfill their pledge. We know what we have to work with before we get started.

On the downside (of course, there is always a downside, and sometimes it feels like there are always three or four down-sides, no matter which side I choose) — on the downside, building the way we do, piecemeal, ends up costing significantly more than if we just committed to the whole project at once.

I mean, the contractor has to shut down operations until we get all the money together. Then he has to gather his crew again, restart his supply lines, deal with the headache of finding brick and tile and what all to exactly match what we've already installed, because we wouldn't give him enough funds to have it reserved in the first place, and oh, I don't know.

Michael Edwin serves as our general contractor. He's a member and he gives us his time for free, which is a big deal — he normally oversees projects like sports stadiums and high-rise condos in far-off places. And he gets understandably chapped about what seems to him to be an amateurish and wasteful way of doing business. Michael is regularly on the line for millions; it's part of doing business as far as he's concerned. And when I talk to him, and he explains it all, I'm utterly convinced that we should go ahead and make the leap of faith and just build the dang thing.

Then Carl Shelby, who handles the accounting business for the church, also at no cost, gets hold of me and sits me down and scares me half to death with stories of churches who have bitten off more than they could gulp down and consequently lost hundreds of members who got tired of the constant pleas for money, so that even more funds dried up until finally the church was foreclosed on and sold to be a bar or a brothel or something else I don't want to contemplate, though the only Church of Christ I ever knew to be foreclosed on is now a public library and a very decent little pub.

They were both wasting their time telling *me* these things, though, and they should know that, because I'm not a voting member of the building committee. And thank you, God, for that.

But I still have to be at the meetings.

Today Bob Carmichael suggested a big cross on the steeple. Jim Brightwell thought that's too Baptist for words. Carmichael said, apropos of the Baptist comment, that what he really wanted was a cross that would rise higher than the Baptist cross that stands on the other side of Highway 59 from us.

Dr. Fallon, who usually has plenty to say at the building committee, was silent and ill looking — he seemed preoccupied. How he made it on this committee, I don't know, because usually it's members who (1) have some special expertise, like Edwin, or (2) have been with us for years, or (3) have a ton of expendable money and they're willing to spend it on the church. I know, I know. I'm not saying that's the way it should be. I'm just telling you how it is.

Brightwell said why don't we install stained glass windows and go all Catholic and have done with it. Sam Pearce said there's nothing in the Bible against stained glass, and for his part, he has never understood why all the Churches of Christ look like a cross between a basketball stadium and an upside-down swimming pool, and is there some reason we don't want our churches to look like churches?

Fallon roused himself, glowered a few inches over my head, and said why wasn't there more preaching on the Ten Commandments?

I sat up straighter and stopped playing Words with Friends on my cell phone.

Brightwell ignored Fallon and said, fine, let's put up some big, garish, neon, blinking-light cross; let's put up thirty, and plaster our windows with pictures of writhing bloody saints, and let's have a little incense while we're at it, only first, first let's take the name "Church of Christ" off the front of the building, because . . .

At that point I excused myself to meet with Honey Garcia. I was just about looking forward to funeral planning at this point.

Settegast-Koph Funeral Home was handling the funeral. They have a location less than ten minutes from the church, so I didn't really need the half hour I'd allowed for drive time, but I needed to get out of that meeting. Usually I use extra minutes to return phone calls, and that's what I should have done; my cell was showing two voice mails and three text messages. But I had hamster wheels spinning in my head and I couldn't settle to it.

I sat in the funeral home parking lot running the air conditioner like I had access to HD's bottomless gas card and tried to think about what I should do about what Alex had told me. The hamster wheels spun on without producing one single idea. I'd gotten out of the car and headed for the door when I saw Honey's Escalade pull in.

Cruz got out of the driver's seat. I'd never seen her drive Honey's car, and it was a little bit funny watching her clamber out of the high-set SUV. Short women should not drive SUVs.

Honey slipped out of the passenger side

and leaned her head against the edge of the opened door for a minute before she took a step away from the Escalade and slammed the door. Honey was wearing a crumpled black linen suit that bleached her of color, and one wing of her auburn hair stood up wonky-like. An unsteady step confirmed my suspicions about why Cruz was driving.

Jenasy Garcia got out of the backseat and slammed the door so hard it made my teeth hurt.

She looked like a taller, slimmer, and angrier version of Honey. Oh, and Jenasy was sober, so that was different, too. Her auburn hair was pulled into a loop and her face was somber and swollen from crying. In contrast to her mother's tailored suit, Jenasy was wearing jeans, flat sandals, and a Southwestern University tee. She had her arms crossed tightly below her breasts. She didn't look at me or her mother, and when Cruz said something to her in Spanish, Jenasy shot back in staccato Spanish that didn't sound particularly reconciliatory. My Spanish CDs evidently had limits, because I couldn't follow any of it except that I'm pretty sure Jenasy called her mother a cow's head. Or the mother of a cow's head, which sounds less likely, because that would make Jenasy the cow's head . . .

I got out to meet them.

Honey said, "Thanks for being here, Bear. Jenasy, you remember Mr. Wells, don't you?"

Jenasy looked up at me and nodded and offered me a cool, slim hand.

She said, "You're Merrie's dad."

I said I was and I offered my condolences.

Jenasy gave me another nod and a twist of her mouth.

She asked, "Is Father Nat already here?"

Her voice was rough and thick with the tears she was holding back.

I didn't know. We walked in together with Cruz leading the way and waited in the dim foyer for someone to come out and give us some direction. Honey sat on the edge of the sofa and hugged her purse.

"Where's Alex?" I said.

Jenasy was bent over a glossy casket catalog laid out on a side table, flipping through the pages without any real show of interest.

"The little shit didn't want to come." She said it without looking up.

Honey flapped her hands ineffectually. "Oh, now, Jen, it's not that he didn't want to come —"

"Glad you aren't contesting that the spoiled brat is a little shit."

Honey leaned over and slapped her hand down on the table next to the catalog Jenasy was looking through. Jenasy jumped. Honey looked at Jenasy hard until the girl dropped her eyes. I think it's interesting what can come through the alcohol haze when there's a real need.

Jenasy pressed her lips together and rolled her eyes without looking up. "Let me be more accurate. We told him last night about this appointment. We woke him up this morning in plenty of time to get ready and go. He didn't get up and he didn't come. I think it's safe to assume that means he didn't want to come, but if Mother —"

Before Jenasy could continue, as she seemed prepared to, Cruz interrupted.

"Jenasy," Cruz said, "you will speak to your mama, and of your mama, with respect. Don't be shaming the family. Time like this."

Jenasy flushed. We were all relieved when a young woman opened a staff door and walked in. Everything about her, from the center part in her dark hair down to her sensible black pumps, was understated. She closed the door behind her so softly I barely heard the click, and then she walked over to Honey and held out her hand. She had the low, even voice I've noticed funeral directors cultivate.

"Mrs. Garcia? My name is Margaret Butler. On behalf of all of us at Settegast-Koph, I'd like to express our sympathy for your terrible loss."

After Honey had given the offered hand a squeeze, the woman sat down across from her, her knees angled toward Honey and her hands folded quietly on her lap. The move was so practiced it looked natural. I'd seen it done often, and I knew it was, in fact, practiced and deliberate. Not that I had a problem with that. These people know their business, and in spite of what you see on television and the movies, I've never seen it done with anything but compassion and dignity.

Margaret Butler said, "It's our job to make this part of the process just as easy and painless as we possibly can. Please feel free to ask any questions, and to make these decisions without feeling pressured. Is this your priest?" She looked up at me.

That's when Nat Fontana came through the door, and his clerical collar alerted Margaret that she had the wrong guy.

It's a testament to Graham's involvement with his church that Nat was here instead of a lay volunteer from the St. Laurence Funeral Ministry. With over five thousand registered families in his parish, Nat can't be everywhere for everybody, and with masses of volunteers mustered for every call from Friday fish fries to visitation of the sick, he doesn't have to be. That he was, was an indication that Nat had a personal relationship with Graham or, possibly, with Dr. Garcia.

Nat is almost as big as I am — and big coincidence, he played ball for Notre Dame. The little local weekly, the *Fort Bend Sun*, once did a story on us, "Defending the Line — From the Stadium to the Sanctuary." The photographer wanted us to pose in a three-point stand, but we politely declined.

Nat is at least ten years older than me, but he once offered to arm wrestle. I told him "no." Mainly because it sounded like something out of a John Huston film, a Catholic priest arm wrestling a Protestant minister, but also because I thought he might beat me — Nat is one tough booger. I know for a fact he's still lifting.

Nat saw me first and gave me a head nod. "Bear." He bent down to give Cruz a hug and kissed both her cheeks.

"Thanks again for those tamales, Cruz. Those fresh corn tamales? Be still, my heart. I think I ate six at one sitting and I didn't even add salt. You cannot improve perfection."

Cruz gave Nat a smile she has never given me. I've never gotten those fresh corn tamales, either.

Then Nat crossed straight over to Jenasy, who had abandoned the selection of custom coffins. Nat took her in his arms and gave her a hug that lifted her to the tips of her sandaled toes. It surprised me for a second that he hadn't greeted Honey first, but then, Jenasy was a member of his parish; I don't know how well he even knew Honey.

Nat put Jenasy back down on her feet and, with his arm around her shoulders, guided her to the sofa where her mother sat. Jenasy sat down, but she left two feet or so between herself and Honey. Nat took Honey's hand in both of his, murmured something consoling, and then covered up whatever message Jenasy was trying to send her mother by squeezing himself in that two-foot space. After introducing himself to Margaret, Nat took his phone out, checked the time, and reholstered it.

"Honey, I can only be with you for a few minutes; I've got another commitment."

I admired the way Nat left it at that — he didn't feel any need to explain what the commitment was, why he couldn't get out of it — I am forever getting trapped into endless explanations.

Nat went on, "I've spoken to Detective Wanderley and my understanding is that there won't be any problem with holding the funeral on Friday afternoon, so with your permission, we'll schedule it for one o'clock at the church. Then there's the hour drive to Mount Olivet, the interment, an hour back . . . the parish ladies will have a dinner set up for the family at, say, six, six thirty, and that can be done at the church or at your home, whichever works best for you, Honey."

Cruz answered for Honey, "We'll be having the dinner at the house; we got plenty room." Then, as an afterthought, "That's right, Honey?"

Honey didn't look like she was taking all this in but she nodded and said, "About the service, I've written out a list of who all should speak and the songs and Graham always liked the poem, that Rudyard Kipling one, you know which one I mean? That . . . 'You'll be a man, my son . . .' "

" 'If,' " said Jenasy.

"If what?"

Jenasy blew air out her nose. " 'If'! That's the name of the poem, Mom, 'If.' Are you re—"

"Jenasy!" Cruz's voice cracked like a whip.

Nat shook his head before Cruz could take it further. "Honey, why don't you leave the service to me? We don't have eulogies at a Catholic funeral, that's usually saved for the wake, and the Catholic Church is pretty strict about the songs we allow, too."

"I told her, but she won't listen," Cruz said.

Honey rummaged in her purse. "I brought this CD that Graham really —"

Again Nat shook his head; he put a hand over Honey's. "No, Honey, no recorded music, no secular music, and no Kipling. It doesn't matter how special it was to Graham. I promise you the service will be exactly what Graham would be comfortable with. You save those other things for when your friends and family gather together for the visitation." He gave Honey's hands a final pat.

"I told her," Cruz said.

"Got to go," said Nat. "Jenasy, walk me to the car, will you?"

Jenasy stood obediently and followed Nat out the door.

Honey gave me a sad smile. She said, "Looks like I won't need your help planning the service, Bear, and I guess I can choose a casket by myself. I'm sorry to have taken your time. You go on. I'll be fine."

Cruz sat down next to Honey and nodded up at me.

"I'll see to things," Cruz said.

You know what Wanderley said about brown-skinned people taking care of the poor white people? Okay, forget all the brown skin–white skin part of it. I'm telling you I really believe God is using Cruz to minister to the Garcias. Jenasy obviously minds Cruz in a way she doesn't mind her mother, Cruz is keeping an eye on Honey's drinking, and I didn't miss the fact that when Alex got home on Monday, it was Cruz he spoke to, not his mom. That speaks of relationship, doesn't it? So, sure, Cruz gets paid to do her job. I get paid to do mine; I'm still a minister. And so is Cruz.

I left the building confident that Honey was in good hands.

I walked through the door and saw Jenasy and Nat in the parking lot, deep in conversation. Jenasy was talking fast with her mouth and her hands and Nat leaned against his white Taurus, arms folded across his chest, his mouth frowning. He looked up and gestured me over. Jenasy glanced back and, I think, protested at my being brought into the conversation, but Nat waved me over again.

"Jenasy, your dad talked to Bear last Friday; maybe he told Bear about this. Tell Bear what you started to tell me," he said.

Jenasy stepped in front of Nat, effectively cutting me out of the circle, and said, "Maybe he didn't."

"You tell Bear anyway. I want his take on this, and he's not going to go blabbing it all over Sugar Land. I know Bear."

Jenasy stood hands on hips, staring at Nat.

"Jenasy." Nat's voice was soft but confident in his authority, and a little impatient.

Jenasy threw her hands up in exasperation and then dropped them. She stared back at Nat, held the stare, then dropped her gaze. Her hands went to her hair. She pulled the elastic band out, let her hair fall, and then gathered it together again and twisted it up in the band. It's a delaying tactic I've seen my girls use. She tilted her head back and squinted at the pale blue sky, blew a breath out.

"All right, then. You know I'm pre-law?"

I'd heard something about it. Mainly it meant you could do your undergrad work in anything at all. If you had good grades, and did well on the LSAT, you could get into law school with nearly any degree — linguistics, art history, whatever.

"Last summer I clerked for Dad. Not a real clerkship; you have to be in law school for that. Mainly I filed papers, delivered papers, and typed papers. I got to do some research. Dad wanted me to see what it would be like to work in a law office before I made my mind up about law school, right?

"I've already made up my mind. You know anything else that can earn you more than a hundred and sixty thousand straight out of grad school? Tell you what, a master's in social work isn't going to bring that in."

No, it wasn't. But I'm really glad there are people who master in social work, because there are too many lawyers and not enough social workers. I couldn't see it in her looks, but HD's genes were coming through on this grandchild at least.

"I thought I'd get to see a ton of Dad, but he didn't spend much time in the office, and when he did, he was usually with clients. Still, we'd have lunch together at least once a week. He'd answer my questions. He'd tell me things.

"There was this one guy, a partner. He was real friendly with me, always stopping by my cubicle, asking how things were, did I need any help, which I didn't, and did I want to come with him to such and such a meeting, he could introduce me to this client or that judge, which I didn't want to do, either. You know, real helpful. Tooooooo helpful."

Jenasy gave Nat a look, then turned and focused her gaze on me to make sure we'd gotten her point, which we had since we're neither of us morons.

"None of the other partners were any-where near that attentive — not the associates, either, and they were a lot closer to my age. I thought he was maybe hitting on me, right? And then I thought maybe he wasn't, because I wasn't getting any vibe or any-thing. I mean, he was uber-tense and every-thing? But it wasn't like sexual tension. You know what I mean?"

Jenasy shot an uncomfortable look at Nat, but he nodded and put a big hand on her shoulder.

She went on, reassured, "It was confusing. So I told Dad about it at lunch."

She stopped and pulled her hair out of the band again and shook her hair out, then held the navy band in her hands, stretching it and twining it between her fingers as she went on. Cat's Cradle.

"Dad gets all grim and quiet and I'm thinking that maybe I pissed him off or something, I don't know, telling tales and all. He's like that for a while, and I'm completely wishing I hadn't brought it up, and then Dad shakes his head and says no, he doesn't think the guy is hitting on me."

She took a shaky breath. "And then Dad told me to never tell another living soul what he was about to tell me, right?"

There was a long pause, and then in a rush Jenasy said, "So you know what? I'm not going to. I'm sorry, Father Nat, but this was a bad idea. I promised Dad."

She took a couple of steps backward, away from us. Nat shot out his hand and took Jenasy's elbow and pulled her gently back.

He said, "Sweetheart, let's hold on there a minute. What your dad told you, do you think — and you are a smart girl, Jenasy, so I'm going to accept your judgment on this — do you think that what your dad told you might conceivably be a motive for murder? Could somebody want your daddy dead over whatever this is?"

Now the tears came.

"I don't know, do I, Father? I don't know! All I know is that I promised Dad, and . . . and that's all I know!"

"Uh-huh. I understand."

Nat pulled Jenasy in close and hugged her. I wanted to shake her. She could have information that would get her own brother out of the police scrutiny, didn't she see

262

that? I stayed quiet and rocked back and forth on my feet. The hug would probably work better than a shake would anyway.

"Here's what I think, Jenasy. Your dad, he would be so proud of you . . ."

Fresh tears at that.

"You are trying to honor your dad by keeping his secret. And that's good. The thing is, Jenasy, when your dad asked you to promise, he was never thinking he could end up dead over this problem, am I right?"

Jenasy nodded her head against Nat's shirt and left a smear of mascara. She held him tight around the waist.

"What I think is, if there is even the slightest chance that the information you have might lead the police to the person who killed your dad, I think you have to tell. Your dad will understand, Jenasy, and I am giving you permission to break your promise. Sometimes promises have to be broken."

I filed that away to think about later.

"You understand, Jenasy?"

A long shuddery breath, and Jenasy nodded. So Nat had made the right call between the hug and the shake.

Jenasy wiped her eyes with the back of her hand and once again gathered up her tumble of hair and twisted it into the elastic band. It beat smoking for keeping your hands busy.

"Right. Well, Dad, he starts talking so low I had to lean across the table to hear him and he says, 'You know what perjury is, Jenasy?' Which is a total duh, yeah, I know what perjury is. Dad says, 'If your witness perjures himself, and you know about it, you must withdraw from the case. You can't say why you're withdrawing. You file a Motion to Withdraw with the court.' I said, 'Wouldn't everyone know your witness lied? I mean, why else would you quit in the middle of a trial?' But Dad says that there are lots of legitimate reasons to withdraw, and anyway, it's the law. You have to withdraw, and if you don't, and the info gets out, you get disbarred. You can't ever practice law again. Which means you're going to be deadbeat poor, right? But it's worse than that."

Jenasy said "worse than that" as if the idea of anything being worse than "deadbeat" poor was mind-boggling.

"If the court's decision is affected by that lie, then the whole partnership could get sued. Dad's law firm is old-school — they're a pure partnership. That's like all for one and one for all — if one is screwed, they're all screwed. This man? The one who was paying me too much attention? He did that."

"He perjured himself?" I asked. I was getting lost.

Jenasy gave me an impatient look.

"His client perjured himself. The lawyer knew it and he didn't withdraw. When it was all over, the guy who lied won a multimillion-dollar settlement."

Nat and I came out with our questions at the same time.

"How did your dad know about this?"

"But if your dad knew about this, isn't he in the same boat as the first lawyer?"

"Just a sec," Jenasy said. "Give me a minute. The client, he came to Dad first; he wanted Dad to be his lawyer. And Dad talked to him, took some notes, and recorded the meeting, which is good CYA."

I said, "CYA?"

Nat said, "Cover Your Ass. We're having to do it all the time down at the Catholic Church now." He gave a weary sigh.

"So, somewhere in the meeting, Dad discovers that he has a conflict of interest with this case. You know what a conflict of interest is?"

We both nodded yes, but of course, Jenasy explained it to us anyway.

"That means, maybe one of the involved

parties is another client of yours, right? Or maybe you've invested money in one of the involved parties' business or something, right?"

We both said yes, we truly did understand what a conflict of interest was.

"But that doesn't mean someone else in the firm can't handle the case. Dad passed the case, with copies of his notes and recordings, on to the creep who kept hanging around me."

"What's his name?" I asked.

She ignored me and continued, "After the case, everyone at the firm is all happy because it was a contingency case, and the firm was going to get a huge payoff. You know what a contingency case is?"

I said, "Oh, my gosh, Jenasy, yes, we know what a contingency case is. Old people watch TV, too."

Jenasy looked miffed but kept on talking. "A contingency case means you only get paid if the client wins the case, and if he wins, you get a percentage of the judgment. Because the lawyer is taking on the risk of not getting paid for his time, that percentage has to be good or there isn't any incentive to take the case, right? Lawyers have retired off what they got from one contingency case. It can happen."

Yeah, Miss Jenasy was going to be a fine lawyer. Already thought she was getting paid by the word.

"So everyone was all, 'Wooo, wooo!' Right? Champagne popping, backslapping — the works. The lawyer telling his big triumph story, everybody all, 'You the man!' and Dad hears something that makes him think. Once he's in his office, he gets the transcript to the case, and reads it, then he gets out his original notes, and he reads those, and then he knows."

I needed to go. This was the loooongest story.

"This lawyer's client perjured himself. The lawyer had to know — he had Dad's notes and all, no way would he have left them unread."

Got it. Got it.

"Dad goes to this guy's office —"

"What's his name?" I asked again.

Again she ignored me. "Dad wants to think there's an honest mistake, because normally, Dad wouldn't rat out a fellow partner. I mean, he'd never do something like this himself, but you don't take down a partner without some pretty serious thought about it. Dad spells it out to the guy and the lawyer, a total dumb ass, he leans back in his chair and says that those are pretty serious allegations, and that in the first place, any little discrepancy wouldn't have made any difference to the outcome of the case, and secondly, he unfortunately can't prove to Dad how untrue the allegations are, because he doesn't happen to have those notes and recordings anymore. They were in his briefcase, the one he left in a cab in New York. And he smiles at Dad.

"Dad tells the man that, of course, he had passed on copies; he would never have passed on the originals. And then Dad walked out of the office."

"Is that all?" I asked. "End of story?"

Jenasy turned so that she was facing Nat directly, kind of edging me out.

"Dad goes to Bradford Williams," she says, looking only at Nat. "He's the managing partner, and Dad tells Williams what he knows. Dad said Williams was seriously pissed. Pissed that one of their lawyers would have pulled such a trick in a court of law, but Dad said it was pretty clear that Williams was even more upset that Dad had brought it to his attention. Williams didn't come right out and say it or anything, but the feeling Dad got was that Williams thought Dad should have just kept his mouth shut and forgotten about it. That Dad had dumped it all on Williams's shoulders and Williams was not happy."

"And?" I said.

"So Williams said there would have to be a confidential meeting with all the partners there, and that's like, halfway impossible because everybody is traveling and there's never a time when all the partners are in the office, and each time Dad asked Williams about it, Williams got snottier and snottier.

"Dad told me he thought he was going to have to report it himself. And that would mean he would have to leave the law firm, because he would not be the most popular partner on the seventeenth floor, right? Everyone was going to be hurt bad. It could even bring the law firm down, but if Dad couldn't get the firm to take action, he didn't know what else to do. He said he was not going to be a party to a lie; his father hadn't raised him that way, and it counted less than nothing that this sleaze lawyer was sucking up to me."

Now Jenasy's eyes teared up and she tilted her head back to keep the tears from spilling out.

"You know what I'm wondering, right? I'm wondering did this perjury guy decide to make sure Dad never reported it?"

Or that Bradford Williams guy, or another

partner who got wind of the story and didn't want to see a twenty-year investment turned to ashes for a mistake someone else had made, and for someone else's conscience. Seemed to me the circle of suspects had just increased by however many partners Graham had.

And who had gone to the Garcias' the very day Graham was killed and tried to collect Graham's laptop and papers?

# TWENTY

How could you fit together all the pieces of
Graham Garcia's personality? Baby Bear
and I had a short run on the levee, then
took a break right about where Alex told
me he'd seen his dad the night Graham had
been killed.

Graham Garcia had not been a simple
man, whether or not he was, as his son
suspected, a Humbert Humbert. But not
with Jo. With some other young girl with
long dark hair. Who was Jo's size.

My own meeting with Graham had left
me puzzled. Graham came off as a distant,
hard man, determined to end his marriage
on his own terms. He hadn't once mentioned his children by name, or the effect a
divorce might have on them. There were no
questions as to how to do as little damage
as possible to the wife he would be leaving
behind. On the other hand, he hadn't tried
to justify himself, or explain why Honey was

the real reason the marriage had failed. He hadn't told me it was all her fault.

Garcia had said his adopted son would not have wanted to shame his father. From Dr. Garcia's description, he had been driven even as a child, a boy who had to become a man way too soon. A twelve-year-old rescuing his mother.

When I was that age, my greatest worry was whether or not I'd get to play first string for my junior high football team. Graham, once he escaped his terrible home, had worked like a demon to fit into a world he hadn't been prepared for. And he had succeeded. He'd fit in beautifully. He'd made serious money. He'd married the beautiful daughter of a rich man. He'd had two beautiful children.

Father Nat told me that Graham had been a deeply committed Christian, a regular at the seven-thirty mass Sunday mornings and a generous giver. Once Jenasy had left, I'd asked if Graham had ever said anything about an affair — Nat had replied, "You know we Catholics hold ourselves to a higher standard; the confessional really is sacred, Bear." Then he'd given me a slap on the back that I felt clean through to my sternum.

I felt sure that if Graham had confessed

to the affair, he hadn't mentioned that it had been with a young teenager — no way Nat would've been so blithe.

The story Jenasy recounted showed her father as a man who would accept great personal sacrifice rather than compromise his integrity. But somehow, sleeping with a teenager wasn't a challenge to that integrity?

In spite of what Dr. Garcia said, I didn't see him as the reason why Graham didn't initiate divorce proceedings himself. Graham's stepbrother had divorced and there had been no rift in the father-son relationship. Sooooo . . .

I couldn't make it work. I don't know what a pedophile looks like, but still, Garcia didn't look like one. And wouldn't a pedophile want to hang on to a background like Graham's? Wouldn't his family offer the perfect cover? What would he have to gain from a divorce? I mean, it's not as though he could marry a child. There's no way such an affair, if it can even be called an affair, could be anything more than a dalliance.

Twenty years ago, when I started preaching, I was expected to have a fresh sermon Sunday morning, Sunday night, and Wednesday night. It doesn't matter how good a preacher you are, you're going to run dry if you keep to that schedule. Thank you, God, most churches handle things differently now.

Unlike Tuesday nights, when you have a number of more secular and social classes to choose from, Wednesday night is worship and Bible study. You could choose from four or five adult Bible studies on Wednesday nights, and all our youth classes met then, too. Usually, this was time I enjoyed. I love my job, but it's good to hear someone else's take on the Christian walk.

Last night, the idea of sitting in any of the classes for an hour made me feel itchy all over. Like I ought to be someplace else, doing something else. I didn't know what I could do, and that made it worse.

Worse yet was going out to my car with Annie Laurie at eight thirty — the soonest I could leave on Wednesday nights after all the meeting and greeting — neither of us having seen Jo anywhere in the halls. We thought she might be visiting in a friend's car. She was. Alex's.

Once we were all in our car (the wayward daughter, too), with the windows rolled up, I put the car into drive and said, "I thought I had made it plain that you weren't to have anything to do with Alex until this whole mess was straightened out."

Jo said, "Yes."

I said, "Yes, what?" and squeezed past Mrs. Farmer, who will wait for an engraved invitation before she'll venture into oncoming traffic.

She said, "Yes, sir."

I said, "Jo, you know what I mean."

Jo said, "Dad. Yes. You made it plain you didn't want me to see or talk to Alex. You've been clear how you feel about me seeing Alex. What I don't know is how your feelings fit in with your Christianity."

If we hadn't already been so close to home, I would have pulled the car over. Annie Laurie put a hand on my knee.

"Okay, explain that, please. The bit about my feelings and my Christianity."

"All right. But just so you know, you are asking me a question, and I'm going to answer it honestly, and if you ground me for answering honestly, then you're a Nazi."

I said, taking a deep breath first (it didn't help), "In the first place, Jo, you're already grounded until your wisdom teeth come in, and that's going to be when you're around twenty-five —"

Annie Laurie said, "Actually Bear, Jo's are coming in early. She's going to have to have them out; I meant to tell you —"

"And in the second place," I said, ignoring Annie Laurie's helpful comment on Jo's upcoming dental expenses, "we need to go over our World War Two history again if you think I'm being a Nazi —"

We pulled into the garage and Annie Laurie jumped out of the car saying, "I'm going to go walk Baby Bear while you two refight World War Two."

I grabbed a bottle of water from the garage refrigerator on the way into the house. Jo, making a huge business of it, got a glass out of the cabinet, filled it with ice and tap water, and sat down in the easy chair Baby Bear favors. The tap water was her way of letting me know I was destroying the planet by way of disposable plastic bottles.

Jo said, "If you sit down instead of glowering over me, I'll answer your question."

Where does my girl get words like "glowering"? I can't remember the last time she picked up a book that wasn't required reading.

I sat down on the hassock in front of the fireplace. That put me eye to eye with Jo. She didn't flinch.

Jo said, "Dad, will you please not interrupt —"

I said, "I never interrupt —"

"Like you just did? I'll tell you when I'm

done, okay? If you have a question, hold up two fingers. If I don't stop, that means your question has to wait until I'm done."

What she was doing was she was being snotty. Back when I read to Merrie and Jo, I used the two-finger method. If I hadn't, we'd never have made it through a book.

Jo said, "And I'm not being snotty, either. I think your two-finger trick worked. So is that okay?"

I looked at my Jo, face like a heart, dark waves of hair falling halfway to her waist, her jeans too snug on her frail, slim body.

I said, "How am I not living up to my faith, Jo?" I really wanted her to tell me. I needed to know.

She said, "Okay, so you know how you used to read to us? Remember you read that book about how some German people fought back against the Nazis? How some people hid Jewish children, even though hiding them put their own children at risk? How the Nazis discovered some families that had hid Jewish children, and to make an example of them, the Nazis took away the Jewish children, and hung the family's own children right in front of their eyes? Do you remember reading that to us?"

I did remember. Thinking back on it now, it seems like reading *Foxe's Book of Martyrs* to children, but I thought it was a good idea at the time.

Jo said, "I remember Merrie asking you if you thought those parents had done the right thing, because parents are supposed to protect their children, and you said yes, the German parents had done the right thing, even though their children died, and they died, too. You said a Christian had to love God more than anyone else, more than your father or your mother or your children, and that the way you show God that you love Him is to 'trust and obey.' You remember?"

What I didn't remember was Jo paying attention during all this reading and discussing. In my memory, she was always dressing and undressing Barbie dolls or messing with the hair on her My Little Pony while I read at bedtime. Merrie was the one who was listening. I finished my bottle of water and crushed it in my hands.

"So, Dad. You don't want me to spend time with Alex because even though you know it's not true, some tiny little weasel part of your brain thinks, 'Oh my gosh, what if he's a murderer.' " Jo used a deep "dad" voice.

"See, you're trying to protect me. You're mad at me all the time, but it's still your job to protect me."

The "weasel brain" didn't hurt, but the "it's your job" did. It really did.

"But, Dad, that's like being a bad German parent. Alex is my friend. This is the worst time in his entire life."

All sixteen years of it. I noticed that Alex was Jo's "friend." I wasn't hearing anything about love from Jo. That was good. Unless it was bad. Unless Jo wasn't saying she loved Alex because she thought she loved someone else. Someone older.

"His dad is dead and he's dead in a horrible way because dying from murder is way worse than dying from cancer or something normal. And Alex was already upset about his dad before the murder so things weren't good between them and they can't be fixed now."

Echoes of Honey's grief, that now things could never be put right.

"The police are all over Alex's case because of . . . stuff. His mom is a wreck and Jenasy is being a complete" — a look at me — "witch. And this is when you want me to stay away from Alex? When he needs me most of all? And you know what? Even if Alex was a murderer — Dad, sit back down, he's not a murderer; he didn't kill his father, but even if he did — you know what the Bible says? You have to forgive him. You have to. Because if you don't, God won't forgive you. That's what it says, Dad. You know what you say from the pulpit, 'Hard truths.' "

I held up two fingers.

Jo considered, and then nodded. "Go ahead, I'm not done, but you can ask a question." She lifted her planet-friendly ice water to her mouth, drank, and set her glass on the floor near her feet.

The kitchen door opened. Annie and the dog were back. Baby Bear leapt into the room, did a fast circuit of the family room, kitchen, dining room, and hall bath, then ran back to the family room and jumped up into Jo's lap. He outweighs her by nearly a hundred pounds, but Baby Bear can't stop longing for the three or so months of his life when he could be called a lapdog. Jo pushed him to the floor and he settled between her Doc Martens, got up, sucked down half of Jo's water, secured an ice cube, and settled back down to make a mess. Jo always wore those heavy black Doc Martens on her delicate little feet because if someone stepped on her foot and she was wearing sandals, it could mean an injury. If someone stepped on the Doc Martens, Jo wouldn't even notice. And no matter how hard Baby Bear tried, he couldn't get them off her feet.

He'd pretty much given up trying.

I heard Annie take a glass from the cabinet, and then the glug of wine being poured. On a Wednesday night. She came in and sat on the arm of Jo's easy chair, her wine-free hand automatically stroking and twining through Jo's dark hair.

I said, "Jo, what about 'Obey your parents'?"

Jo threw her hands out; the poor child was dealing with density.

"Dad, shit, that's it."

I started to say something.

Jo said, " 'Shit' is a vulgarity, not a profanity. Nana says you're very vulgar."

I let it pass.

Jo said, "Dad, I'm sorry I said 'shit.' But don't you get it? That's what Jesus was saying when he said that 'Love me more' thing. It's seriously wrong to abandon a friend; to abandon Alex when he needs me more than he ever did before, that's like, that's going-to-hell wrong. And even if it wasn't wrong, Dad, I will never leave Alex, Dad, he loves me, he believes in me."

And then the tears, and the rush upstairs, and the slammed bedroom door, and there I sat, two fingers up. "Jo, do you know I believe in you? Do you know I love you?"

# TWENTY-ONE

The phone rang at six seventeen. In the morning. That's too early for calls. I haven't had my coffee at six seventeen.

Honey's voice was strangled with tears. I couldn't understand a single word except, "Bear, Bear!" and that wasn't helpful.

I took the phone with me into the bathroom and began brushing my teeth while I waited for Honey to calm herself enough to become articulate.

When she finally did, I felt like a toad for being so callous.

"They've arrested HD. They've arrested my daddy for murdering Graham."

Annie Laurie said she wanted a larger share of our household income as she was doing triple duty as a wife and mother, an educational program developer, and a preacher's wife, which, she insists, is a whole different job from being a regular wife.

I gratefully accepted the mega-mug of coffee, milk, and dash of vanilla syrup, and the peanut butter and banana sandwich she was handing over, and said she was welcome to whatever she could squeeze out of the household books; since she kept them, she would know best how much that would be. Baby Bear begged to be taken along, and I promised him a ride as soon as I could manage it.

The police station isn't but a ten-minute drive. The sandwich was finished and I drank as much from my mega-mug as I could before I got out of the car. HD's Bentley was parked in a corner of the lot. Someone, Fredrick, I guess, had parked in such a way as to take up two parking spaces. Honey nearly ran into me as the station door swung open.

She wore no makeup and her red hair was pulled straight back from her face. She was wearing yoga capris, a sports top, and sneakers. She had a light jacket tied around her waist. My guess was the call had caught her right before her morning workout.

"Oh, Bear. I can't stop. Daddy won't say a word until he's had his breakfast. I'm off to get him some. Could you sit with him until I get back? Mom couldn't come. She's home with a sick headache."

I said I would. But when I got inside, no one I asked seemed to think it was a good idea for me to go past the public area of the police station. Finally, I called Wanderley on my cell and he had me buzzed in.

In the movies and on TV, police stations are loud, cluttered messy places. Not here. The large room I found myself in was clean and bright and ordered. It was quiet, too. Soft phone conversations and the hum of electronics.

Wanderley poked his head out of an office, acknowledged me, and ducked back in for more hurried words. Neatly uniformed men and women moved in and out of the room doing whatever it was they were doing, quietly and without much drama. The pretty officer with the ponytail recognized me from the Garcia house and gave me a wave. There wasn't any sign of HD.

Wanderley emerged from the side office with a sheaf of papers in his hands and a grim expression on his face. His grin was gone. His shirt was rumpled and his sleeves were rolled up. There was dried mud on his boots. He didn't offer to shake hands and he raised an eyebrow inquiringly.

"Honey asked me to sit with HD."

"You can't do that, Bear. He'll sit alone until I can be in there with him, and I don't have time to waste if he won't talk."

"Look, Wanderley —" I started.

He put a hand on my wrist.

"Bear? It's Detective. It's always Detective Wanderley in here. Understand?"

"Look, I don't want to second-guess you —"

"You're going to anyway, right?"

"I'm —"

"You don't want to second-guess me, but you're going to. You're going to ask me why I have that frail old man locked up in an interrogation room. Right?"

"I'm having trouble picturing that poor old man —"

"You are too quick to judge. With the leverage a golf club would give him, Parker isn't too feeble to brain a man. If he had adequate motive."

"And, Detective, what motive do you suppose HD could have had to kill his son-in-law?"

"I don't know." That came out quick and flat. Wanderley was waiting for me to ask that next question.

"Well, then, why did you go off and arrest an old man with no motive? An old guy so feeble he has a chauffeur to get him around?"

Wanderley turned his back and dropped

the stack of papers on a desk.

"He drove himself down here this morning. There's no chauffeur I've noticed. You want to take a look at him?" He looked at me over his shoulder and took off down a hall.

"At HD? Yeah." I followed. *Take a look at* — that sounded objectifying. I don't use that word but I know what it means. Also: HD drove here alone?

Wanderley stopped in front of a closed door. He looked through the wired glass of the window, and gestured me forward.

"Can't I go in? I don't want to stare at him through —"

"You can't go in. You want to see him or not? He can't see you. The glass is one-way."

I saw a clean, bare room. It held a conference table and six chairs and a vending machine. HD sat in profile at one of the tables. It wasn't yet eight in the morning. HD was cleanly shaven, dressed in a tailored, dark suit with a blue shirt and a bright red power tie. His cropped white hair was slicked back close to his scalp. HD's hands were spread out on the table. His index finger was tapping a slow measure; otherwise he was still. He didn't look around. He didn't look worried. He looked prepared.

Wanderley touched my shoulder and I stepped back from the window.

"You wanted to know why I arrested an old man with no motive, Bear? I arrested HD Parker because he walked into the station this morning and confessed to the murder of Graham Garcia."

"No," I said, "he did not." But I already believed it. Walking in and confessing like that seemed just like something HD would do, from what I'd seen.

Wanderley looked at me.

"You're not taking him seriously, are you?" I said. "Wanderley, Detective, from what I've seen, HD isn't entirely —"

"He referenced Ash Robinson."

I took another step back. Oh no. No, no, no, no.

Ash Robinson was the father of Joan Robinson Hill, a Houston socialite who died under mysterious circumstances in 1969. What is pertinent about the reference is that Ash Robinson, a rich oil baron, believed his son-in-law, Dr. John Hill, was responsible for Joan's death. He tried to have his son-in-law convicted of murder by omission — failing to provide Joan with proper medical care — but a mistrial was declared. Robinson had also set a detective on his son-in-law, and had discovered that Dr. Hill was having an affair. Shortly thereafter, Dr. Hill was gunned down in the front door of his River Oaks home. Rumors were rife that Robinson had contracted the murder, though he was never charged. It's a complicated story, and none of the major characters come out of it well. In 1976, Thomas Thompson wrote a book about the case, *Blood and Money*, and it sold four million copies.

I looked through the window again. HD had crossed his arms on the table and was resting his head upon them. He looked calm and tired but he didn't look crazy. Still . . .

"Wanderley, I'm not sure HD is all there."

"I'm not, either. But I'm not a mental health expert. Neither are you. And crazy people do sometimes kill people. Or pay to have them killed."

Wanderley's eyes were steady on my own.

Honey took forever. I couldn't imagine where she had gone for that breakfast. There are half a dozen restaurants five minutes from the station.

Sitting outside the interrogation room was the closest I could come to keeping my promise to Honey. I loped out to my car to fetch a paperback, and then sat on the hall floor, my back against the door. L. C. Tyler's snarky British wit was doing a lot to distract me when Honey finally got back, an hour and thirty-five minutes later.

The bag she clutched was grease-stained and smelled of breakfast sausage.

"Did you drive to Luckenbach for those sausage biscuits?"

"To the Breakfast Klub." She set the bag on the floor, slipped on her jacket, dropped her car keys in a pocket, and zipped the pocket closed.

"Why aren't you in there with Daddy?" she asked.

"To the Breakfast Klub downtown? In rush-hour traffic?"

She retrieved her warm, greasy, fragrant bag and leveled a look at me.

"That's what Daddy wanted, Bear, so that's what I got. If I tried to make some substitute, we'd be sitting here until tomorrow or until I did get what Daddy wanted, so I skipped all the pleas and arguments and suggestions and drove all the way downtown, asked for Daddy's special order, which isn't on the menu, and got back here as fast as I could. Why aren't you sitting with him?"

L. C. Tyler got put away and I stood up and peeked in the window. It looked like HD was sleeping, head cradled on his arms.

His mouth was open.

"Detective Wanderley wouldn't let me in. Does he know you're here?"

"I'm sure he does by now. My bag of breakfast got more interested looks than a busty blonde. Someone will have told him." She tried the door handle but it didn't open. HD didn't look up. "Do you know what he's been saying?"

"He said he killed Graham."

Big sigh. "That is plain crazy. That's all it is. Daddy is a good two inches shorter than me. You knew Graham. Could any right thinking person imagine my daddy over-powering Graham? And exactly why would Daddy want Graham dead?"

I said, "Detective Wanderley told me that HD mentioned something about Ash Robinson."

That hit Honey the way it hit me. Her eyes widened. All the expression and color flowed out of Honey's face until I was look-ing through her eyes into anguish and ter-ror.

Wanderley rounded the corner. He had a young man and a woman in her thirties with him. He introduced the woman, who wore plain black slacks and flats, and had her sleeves rolled up, as Detective Cat Dortch. On asking, I found out the Cat was for Caterina. That's a pretty name but she wasn't in a pretty business and it was clear that Cat would serve her better as a police detective than her parents' choice. The man was dressed in a suit and he addressed Honey, his hand outstretched.

"Mrs. Garcia, I'm Jonathon Blake. Mr. Mathis got your message. He's out of town and won't be back until tomorrow, maybe the day after, but he sent me to represent your father. I assure you I'm experienced and competent to counsel."

Honey left his hand out there too long. She was staring into a possibility the young lawyer couldn't see.

"Walker Wells," I said, and shook his abandoned hand.

Wanderley gave Honey and me an assessing look and unlocked the door. HD's head popped up at the sound and he drew a sleeve across his mouth. I started to follow into the room but Wanderley and Dortch both gave me inquiring looks.

"Oh, right," I said. "Honey, you'll be fine?"

"No, I won't," Honey said. "I want you here with me."

Dortch shook her head and Wanderley held the door for my exit.

"Daddy." Honey hadn't gone to her father.

She stood apart, clutching her bag of sausage biscuits. "Daddy, I want Bear here with me," she said.

HD waved me in.

"I'm not saying a word unless Honey can have her preacher boy."

Blake broke in. "Mr. Parker, I'm Jonathon Blake, I work for Mr. Mathis. He can't be here to advise today, so I'm standing in for him and I'd like for the two of us to have a private conference before another word is said."

HD gave Blake a once-over and a chin jut. "Nobody asked you to be here. I didn't call Mathis."

"Uh, no. Mrs. Garcia called the Mathis home quite early this morning, and I —"

"I guess you're working for my daughter, then. You want to *advise* Honey, go right on. If I was looking for advice, I'd've made the call myself."

There ensued a thirty-minute argument, Honey and HD against Dortch and Wanderley, Blake trying to be lawyerly with a client who wasn't looking for his services. I kept my mouth closed and started thinking like Annie Laurie — this was more than I was getting paid for.

HD emptied the bag Honey finally passed over out on the table, found eight Styrofoam containers of sausage biscuits and three tubs of cream gravy. HD countered arguments as he uncapped the gravy tubs and slid sandwiches, plastic forks, and napkins to each of us at the table. Dortch and Wanderley stood behind their chairs, literally talking down to HD. I wasn't using my mouth for talking so I ate my sausage biscuit and it was good. HD ate two, flooded with gravy, in between stating his position.

"Honey wants him here. That's all I'm saying."

Wanderley pinched his eyebrows together and gave his chair a shove. He picked up his sandwich container, poked the biscuit, closed it, and dropped it on the table. He fell in his chair and gave me his attention. Dortch took that as a signal and pulled her own chair out.

"Not one word, Wells." Wanderley wasn't happy with me. I wasn't all that happy with me. I knew I didn't have any business in that room. I had plenty of my own obligations to attend to. I had things of my own I wanted to talk to Wanderley about, though it looked like those would have to wait until our appointment. However, Honey felt like she needed me and I didn't like to walk out on her request.

"Got it," I said.

"That was two more words than you are allowed. I don't even want to see body language."

I wiped my mouth with a napkin and held my palms up in concurrence.

"That's the sort of thing I'm talking about. Sit on your hands if you have to. I don't want so much as an eyebrow twitch. Understand?"

I didn't look at him. I didn't respond in any way.

"Good. Keep it that way."

There were four of us facing Wanderley and Dortch. HD sat directly across from Wanderley, Blake was on HD's left, Honey on his right. I sat next to Honey. Wanderley and Dortch looked like they could take us even with the two-on-one odds. Dortch was a good-looking woman, especially if you liked your women on the tough side. She played down her handsome looks and I thought that was a pity, that to get along in some professions, some women had to distract from their attractiveness and . . .

Dortch let me know she had noticed my scrutiny and I moved my eyes somewhere neutral.

There ensued a long, boring schmoo while Wanderley and Dortch went through the digital camera and recording business and all the establishing who was who business — they cut most of that stuff out for the television shows. When I was asked to name myself for the record, I looked to Wanderley for permission to speak and got an eye roll worthy of Jo.

Wanderley finally got around to the reason we were all gathered around a conference table watching Breakfast Klub sausage biscuit sandwiches grow cold.

"Mr. Parker, tell us why you came to the station this morning."

Blake did some whispering in HD's inattentive ear. HD jerked his head away and ignored Blake, who picked up his iPhone and did some frantic thumbing until he caught Dortch's eye on him.

"My name is HD Parker."

We'd already established that.

"I am eighty-eight years old next month."

That, too. Honey was staring fixedly at the pile of food and detritus in the middle of the table. She was waiting for HD to say the words.

"And I'm the reason Graham Garcia is dead."

Honey swung around on HD and took him by the lapels, forcing him to look at her. Honey's face, free of cosmetics, was

295

fierce and bleak. "Daddy — you look at me now."

Dortch sprang up to intervene, but Wanderley put a hand on her arm and she sank back into her chair.

"I want my old daddy here, not whatever phony HD you've been putting on for the last couple of years," Honey demanded.

HD took his daughter's forearms in a gentle grasp.

"It's always only me here for you, Honey. It's the way it's always been. No different."

She shook her head.

"You tell me, forget the rest in the room" — she made an encompassing gesture — "you tell me, Daddy, did you have Graham killed?"

Everything I'd seen of HD so far gave me the impression that he was a crazy old coot. Not now. In this craziest of moments, HD's voice was tender and his eyes were full of love. HD squeezed Honey's arms.

"See this, Honey? How skinny you've gotten? You're almost all gone. You've eaten yourself up trying to make that cold stick love you."

Tears poured down Honey's cheeks. She shook her head.

"Tell me, Daddy."

"Your mama and me, we come over to

dinner now and then and you keep his house so fine. You give him Jenasy, pretty and smart, and Alex, a fine, fine boy. And that man can't even look at you. You think we haven't noticed that? The harder you try to get his attention, the more we see him turn his face, give you the cold shoulder. I tell you, your mama and me, we have cried in our beds after a night at your house. Graham sits there in the house I gave you, talking about clients I sent his way, and he gives Cruz more attention and respect than he can muster for his own wife. In front of her daddy. You sail on as if everything is fine and you get skinnier and your eyes get bigger and your mouth is getting bitter, Honey. You're getting that bitter face women get when they've been hoping, and not getting, for too long a time."

"Daddy, please."

"We tried talking to him, your mother and me, both. Not ugly talk, either. I know a man can be tempted. I didn't hold myself righteous over him. I wanted to know what the problem was, how maybe me and Beanie could help. He told us to mind our own business. That's exactly what he said to me, word for word. 'HD, mind your own business.' Right out, he said it."

"Daddy."

"And, Honey, we both talked to you, too. You know we did. Told you to leave his sorry ass, let him have the damn house and come on with the children and live with us. We're rattling around like two peas in that house. You wouldn't budge."

"Graham was going to come back to me. He was going to love me again."

"No, Honey, he was not. He didn't have it in him. You were going to walk the heartbreak mile all the way to your grave."

"Please tell me, Daddy. Please just say it."

"Honey, my precious one, I am eighty-eight years old. It was the last big gift I could give you. I set you free."

Honey cried out and curled over in her chair.

"Daddy, I loved him, I loved him!" She was sobbing as if she and HD were the only people in the room.

HD had tears in his own eyes. He smoothed her back with the palm of his hand.

"I know you did, Honey. And now you're free to love someone else. Someone who can love you back. There's going to be lots of good men for you to choose from."

Honey staggered from her chair. HD reached out a hand to steady her but she pushed him away. Her glance swept across the table — she didn't seem to see us. The door sighed closed behind her.

HD pulled out a linen handkerchief and sniffed into it.

He said to the table, "She'll be okay. She's gonna be all right. It's all for the best."

Blake leaned over to Wanderley. "I'd like you to note down that Mr. Parker has not confessed to any crime here. His words were 'I set you free,' which cannot be construed as —"

"Oh, I had Graham killed," HD said. He tucked the handkerchief in a pocket and ran a hand over the top of his head. He looked bemused. "The golf club was a surprise."

Jonathon Blake slapped his forehead and stood up.

"Mr. Parker, I'm going to tell Mr. Mathis that you have unequivocally declined the services of the firm. Is that what you want?"

HD gave the guy a tight grin.

"Why don't you take that bee out of your butt and scamper on out of here? I know what I'm doing."

Blake blew air and stopped next to Wanderley's chair. "We'll see you Friday, then?"

"I'll get word to you. We'll see," Wanderley said. Blake touched his shoulder and walked out of the room. I filed the exchange away to ask about later.

"Would you start from the beginning, Mr. Parker?" Dortch's voice was smooth and low, a little husky.

It brought to mind Kathleen Turner. I love that woman's voice. Not only the *Body Heat* and Jessica Rabbit voice, I liked her in *Romancing the Stone* and *Undercover* . . .

I glanced up to find Wanderley's eyes on me.

"I should leave," I said.

"Stay." HD reached over Honey's empty chair and patted the back of my hand. "Honey will want someone she trusts to report back to her. She likes you, I don't know why."

Wanderley's eyes went heavenward.

Dortch made a business of straightening the papers in front of her to get everybody's attention again.

"From the beginning, Mr. Parker?"

"Oh. Okay. Well, I wasn't going to let Honey live her life the way it had been going there, you heard, how Graham had been treating her, and you can bet there was a lot worse, because that was only when he was in front of me and Beanie."

She asked, "Beanie?"

"Belinda. Honey's mama. That's Beanie."

Her voice sharpened.

"Did Mrs. Parker know about your plan

300

to have Graham Garcia killed?"

HD slapped his hands down on the table. "Lord, no! Why would I tell Beanie?" He was really asking the question.

Dortch said, "You didn't think this was a decision that would involve her?"

HD tilted his head at Dortch, the way a dog does when he doesn't understand what you're saying.

"Goodness, no. She would only worry and fret. It's just best not to tell Beanie a thing. She's happiest that way. Anyway, old Beanie has been getting a little" — he tapped his temple — "you know. She's getting loose in her moorings."

Belinda Parker was at least fifteen years younger than HD.

"She's been losing stuff lately. Misplaces things. I was looking for one of my guns the other day and found the whole gun cabinet was cleaned out. When I asked Beanie about it, she got all flustered and said she couldn't say where they were. If I hadn't happened upstairs when Juana was changing out the hall air filter, I likely would never have found them. Juana never says a word about Beanie's spells. But there the guns were, lying on the floor of the air vent all higgledy-piggledy, and thick with dust — took me several hours to get them cleaned and oiled again.

"Poor Beanie was so embarrassed, she took herself off to La Madeline for a quiche and a carafe of wine. I wanted Fredrick to take her, I don't like Beanie driving when she's had a tipple, but she said no, she wanted Fredrick to stay right by me and give me a hand."

A significant look was passed around the table. Dortch had her pen woven between her fingers and she paddled it up and down, making irritated tapping noises on the table.

Wanderley produced a guitar pick from somewhere and slipped it in his mouth. He rested his elbows on the table and clasped his hands, calm and relaxed except for the sound of that pick making its way over his pretty orthodonticized teeth.

"Now then. Mrs. Parker didn't know about your plans. How did you put these plans into effect?"

"Okay, I got myself a hired gun —"

"Who was this person?"

"We never exchanged any names."

"You didn't?"

"I had to give him Graham's name, of course."

Dortch took over again.

"How did you find this hired gun?"

"I got him from the classifieds."

"The classifieds?"

"From the *Houston Press*."

Everybody sat up straighter.

"For real?" I said. The *Houston Press* is Houston's alternative weekly paper. If it had a slant, it would be a left-leaning slant. I've seen some interesting classifieds in the back of the *Houston Press*, but they tend to be of the peculiar-people-looking-for-peculiar-partners nature. If the *Houston Press* was printing classifieds for assassins, that was a departure.

"Bear." Wanderley worked his eyebrow at me and turned back to HD.

"Really, Mr. Parker? You found an advertisement for a gun for hire in the *Houston Press*?"

I said, "I've heard of such things in *Soldier of Fortune*, but the —"

Wanderley said, "Wells!" and HD said, "That's it!" at exactly the same time as I remembered why Wanderley wanted me to keep my mouth shut.

Dortch put her pen down with a hard clack and gave me a look that was intended to wither my organs, and I did feel some shrinkage. I picked up a cold sausage biscuit and rolled some bread pills.

"It was that *Shoulder of Fortune* magazine.

I mixed it up with the *Houston Press* because their covers are so similar."

They are not. They aren't even the same format. *Soldier of Fortune* is a magazine and the *Houston Press* is a tabloid. Nothing at all alike. And you wouldn't find the two publications at the same place, either. The *Houston Press* is free — you can pick it up at restaurants and stores. I don't know for sure, but *Soldier of Fortune* probably comes to your home in a brown paper wrapper.

Dortch and Wanderley must have had the same misgiving. There was a long, thoughtful pause.

Wanderley exchanged a look with his comrade and got back to HD, who was sitting there straight-backed, looking mildly discomfited, but steady-eyed and holding his own.

"Riiiight. So you contacted someone out of the *'Shoulder' of Fortune* Magazine, and you got lucky and didn't happen to call one of the ringers the FBI and CIA plant. Could we please see the number you called?"

"I lost it."

"Of course you did. How much money did you pay?"

"Around five thousand."

"Around five thousand? What, five thousand five hundred? Five thousand twenty-six dollars? What's 'around' five thousand, specifically, if you can."

HD looked at the ceiling and pulled on a thumb joint. There was a pop and he did the same to his other thumb.

"I don't remember exactly."

"But when we check your bank accounts, we're going to find a recent withdrawal of around five thousand dollars."

"Yes, you will."

Wanderley and Dortch got more focused.

"Unless I took cash from the house. I might have done that. I don't remember."

Dortch said, "You keep five thousand dollars in cash around the house?"

"I do. For emergencies."

"If we drive over to your house right now, can you show us five thousand dollars in cash?"

"Yes, I can. Unless I haven't replaced that five thousand yet. I'm not sure I've been to the bank since we, uh, me and the fellow, met."

"HD," I said, knowing I was going to be in trouble for butting in, "why did you decide to come forward today and confess? It doesn't seem to be a case of conscience. You aren't expressing any remorse."

Wanderley had started to cut me off, but now he watched HD, the guitar pick peeking out between his teeth.

"I'm not sorry." He dipped his head emphatically. "Graham Garcia took and took and took from Honey and didn't give her a thing back."

"So why confess?"

He scootched his chair closer to the table.

"Because Alex has got to get out of that place, that's why. I know what goes on in these places to young men. I don't believe for a second you're keeping that boy safe. And he's missing school."

He took in our surprise.

"What?"

"Mr. Parker." Wanderley was almost kind. "We aren't keeping Alex Garcia. We didn't even keep him overnight. He's in school right now, unless he cut classes again. Didn't your daughter tell you?"

HD turned to me and I nodded.

"I saw him night before last, HD. I know Honey would have called you. What made you think Alex was still in custody?"

He puzzled on this.

"Where's Fredrick?" HD looked to the door, patted his pockets for his phone.

"Is that why you confessed? Because you were afraid for Alex?"

"Are you telling me Alex isn't a suspect anymore?" HD addressed this to Wanderley and Dortch.

"We think he can help us with more information than he's been willing to supply so far, but —"

HD cut him off.

"Uh-huh. Doesn't matter. I did it and it was the right thing to do." He crossed his arms. "Let's get on with it."

It was an hour later before I left that room and I hadn't learned anything more.

# TWENTY-TWO

Rebecca gave me two messages that sent me halfway across the city for something that could and should have been handled over the phone, but I went. Afterward, I stopped at one of the rolling trailer taquerias that cater to the construction crowd and got three pork tacos on soft corn tortillas and an icy bottle of Mexican Coke. Cost me a total of six dollars. And I got all the fresh pico de gallo and homemade hot sauce I asked for, too.

Loooooove taquerias. It was Annie Laurie who first introduced me to the pleasures of what my high school friends had dismissed as "roach mobiles." Annie and I were taking Highway 6 to Galveston, and when we passed one on the road, she demanded I U-turn and get her some tacos. I thought she was joking. She wasn't, and when I saw the *abuelita* cooking in there and, oh mercy, *smelled* what the little grandmother was cooking, I was a convert. Annie Laurie doesn't have a snobby bone in her. Good is good and she doesn't care where she finds it. I love that about the girl.

Along with some men in hard hats, I sat in the shade at the nearby picnic table, bowed my head for a brief prayer, and enjoyed my lunch. The hard hats noticed my Blue Bonnet Bowl ring and started up a conversation I could only half participate in — my Spanish is too slow. I was sorry when they piled into a pickup and headed back to work. They had been keeping my mind off Jenasy's story.

Nat had thought it would be a good idea for me to tell Jenasy's story to Detective Wanderley. He'd gotten Jenasy's permission. I wanted to know why it wasn't a good idea for Nat to tell Wanderley. Nat hemmed and hawed. He said that while, technically, it wouldn't be a problem — there was a long-ish pause — he'd be much more comfortable if I did the telling.

We stood there looking at each other until it hit me that Graham might have told Nat this story; Graham might have told him in the confessional. So though Nat had the story from Jenasy, too, and her story didn't bind him, Nat didn't want to disclose the story himself and violate Graham's confession. That's paring the apple pretty finely, but I won't criticize a man for trying too hard to do the right thing.

After this morning, I was unsure about telling Wanderley about the work angle — it seemed like HD's confession made the work connection moot.

Finally I decided that it was bad enough not telling Wanderley what Alex had seen between his father and the girl who wasn't Jo. I could at least give him Jenasy's story, and Wanderley could do what he would with it. I would keep my appointment.

They were pretty heavy feet, the ones that took me back into that police station.

Wanderley didn't have an office. I should have known that from all the cop shows I've watched. He had a desk in a room full of desks; his was neither messier nor neater than the ones around him. He had four or five framed pictures on his desk, all of them of Molly. The earliest was an ultrasound. I hate those ultrasound pictures. The babies always look like aliens. Wanderley had his fine, old cowboy boots on his desk, and he didn't bother to take them down when he saw me. Sometime in the hours I'd been gone, Wanderley had found time to clean the mud off those boots and buff them up.

He grinned when I walked over.

"Long time, preacher. I'm wondering if you have a crush on me. Or was it Detective Dortch you were hoping to see?"

"I made an appointment."

"I know you did. I'm giving you a tough time. Sorry you had to make the extra trip — I had to shoot out as soon as we were done in there this morning."

I sat down in the chair he indicated next to his desk and asked a personal question of my own.

"Where did you get those boots? They don't make them like that anymore."

Wanderley's eyebrows went up and he swung his feet down. He pulled a pant leg up so I could admire the stitching.

"You know boots? These are Lucchese's. Custom. Nineteen fifty-four."

" 'Fifty-four?" I whistled. "How do you keep the leather from cracking?"

"Lanolin. Pure lanolin. Every week I rub lanolin over every inch of leather, that's whether I wear them or not; I've got four more pairs made between '54 and '99. All custom and all original, except the heels and soles, those have been replaced. It's the shafts that matter. The boots were my granddad's. I wear exactly the same size. He was going to have a pair made for me when he was sure my feet had stopped growing."

"Are you sure they have?" I asked. The guy had remarkably small feet, especially for such a tall lanky fellow.

He didn't take offense. He grinned.

"Nine-and-a-halfs. And uh . . . that whole thing about the size of your feet correlating with the size of your . . ." He waggled his eyebrows at me suggestively. "That's a no-go. Check it out on Snopes.com. You can bet my brothers did."

I assured Wanderley I was not trying to cast any aspersions on his male member and chanced another question.

"How many brothers?"

"Two. One plays baseball for TCU and the other is raking in cash with some kind of computer operation. They're both younger."

"How about that," I said. "I'm the oldest of three brothers, too. You your dad's favorite, oldest son and all?"

Wanderley smiled again; it was a thin smile.

"Oh, no sir, I am not my father's favorite." He swung his boots back onto the desk and looked away from me. "Not that I give a crap what my dad thinks. I was my grand-father's favorite, and he was the better man."

Alrighty then. I'd put my foot into it, and I wear a size twelve.

"What do you have to tell me, preacher? We need a private room or are you okay here?"

I said I'd rather tell my story to him privately, and he led the way to a small conference room or interrogation room, I don't know which. It was smaller than the room we'd been in this morning, and not as bleak. It had a vending machine in it, too, and Wanderley offered me a Coke. I said no thank you, and he got one for himself and sat across from me at the wood laminate table. He snapped off the aluminum tab on the Coke and immediately put it in his mouth, which gave me visions of doing the Heimlich maneuver on a cop. It was worse than the guitar pick.

I asked him about HD, and he told me that HD had thrown a fit when he'd been asked to change into the orange jumpsuit and had complained ceaselessly about how cold it was.

I asked if it was cold in the holding cell or was that HD's thin blood.

"We keep it cold. We don't want you getting comfortable. We don't want repeat guests, so I'm afraid we do our best to make sure nobody wants to come back."

He told me it wasn't easy checking up on a story that couldn't be verified, no matter which direction they moved in.

"We did get to meet Beanie," he said.

"Oh? What did you think of her?"

"She looks a lot like Honey Garcia will in twenty-five years. The whole confession was news to her and she says it can't be true, that HD has been leaving his marbles here and there for the last two years and he's lost most all of them now."

He smiled. "She's got a colorful way of talking. I'd say she is teetering at the edge of the very end of her patience with HD. I noticed the empty gun cabinet and she told me that, this time, she took all the guns over to HD's oldest son's house and made him promise not to tell."

"What do you think? Is she right? Is HD gaga?"

"He could be coasting downhill and still be a murderer, Bear. He is clear as a bell most of the time."

That was true.

"So what did you come here to tell me?" Wanderley asked.

As accurately as I could, I told him Jenasy's story, leaving her name out of it. Wanderley listened intently without expression until I'd finished. He opened his mouth over his hand and the tab dropped out. Since he had been drinking his Coke all the time I was talking, I was real glad to see the tab again.

He said, "Is that all?"

I said it was.

He said, "I know all that."

I said, "Why in heck didn't you say so instead of having me go through the whole dang story?"

Wanderley shook his head slowly, that sneaky grin back on his face.

"Bear," he said in this compassionate sort of voice, "it's 'hell.' Nobody says 'why in heck?' — they say 'why in hell?' And it's 'damn,' not 'dang,' even for preachers. I promise. I'm an officer of the law and I officially give you permission to say 'hell' and 'damn.' But not the F word, okay? Don't get crazy with your permission." He chuckled and I held my temper.

"The reason I didn't tell you I knew your whole story already was because I didn't know I knew everything you were going to say until you'd said it all. I might have stopped you, said 'Old news; heard it already,' and missed some vital piece of information that you were about to say, right? I might have missed out on that one crucial piece of the puzzle that would make everything fall into place. Not that that happens anywhere except in novels. After you told me your story, *then* I knew I'd heard it all. How did you know all this anyway?"

"How did you know?" I asked.

That's when I discovered that my chair had four sturdy legs on the ground, but Wanderley was in a pivoting office chair. He started that back-and-forth thing again.

"No, Bear, you know it doesn't work that way. You tell me, and maybe I'll tell you if I don't see a reason not to. You understand this isn't 'quid pro quo'; you tell me no matter what."

Since Nat *had* gotten Jenasy's permission, I went ahead and gave Wanderley her name and told him how she knew the story.

I said, "Are you going to have to talk to her?"

Wanderley shook his head "no." "Probably not. Our Mr. Garcia was a very, very careful man. You know what lawyers say? First rule of law is CYA. That means 'cover your ass.' "

Yeah, I'd heard that one.

"Garcia has reams of notes." Wanderley put the tab back in his mouth. I could hear it "scritch, scritching" over his perfect white teeth. I wanted to ask him to trade the metal tab for the plastic guitar pick and stop wreaking such havoc on all that expensive orthodontia his parents had paid for.

"The notes on that little story were hard-copied. When we delve into his computer, I expect to find lots more interesting information."

I nodded my head, determining to go home and delete everything on my computer I wouldn't be comfortable with the whole world reading in their Sunday papers.

"It's not as if that would be much of a motive for murder anyway . . ." I said. I was reluctant to give up a possible motive for someone else; I felt ready to seize on anything that might clear HD and, more especially, Alex. Who said he was in love with my daughter.

Wanderley guffawed. Really.

"Bear! I've known men murdered because they wouldn't give up their place in a taxi line! We had a guy in here a year ago who shot his wife because she wouldn't iron their bedroom sheets — he was still indignant when we snapped the cuffs on him. Shoot, two high school kids from Clements took a girl from their school, a friend of theirs as far as we can tell, took her out to one of the new home construction sites in Commonwealth and shot her, and even they don't know why! People get murdered all the

317

time, Bear, and for some pretty whacked reasons."

"Do you think this guy did it then?"

Wanderley shook his head and looked wistful.

"God knows I'd like to pin it on a lawyer. Someone has sure been eager to get hold of Garcia's work-related shit, briefcase, laptop, papers. Did you hear we found his car?"

I said I hadn't and wondered why I hadn't thought about Graham's car before this. Maybe because I'm a preacher and not a detective.

"Yeah. Parked on a residential street a block from where he was killed. His driver's side window was bashed in."

"That's great!" I blurted out.

One of Wanderley's eyebrows dove toward the bridge of his nose.

"It's great that his car window was bashed in?"

"It's kind of suspicious, don't you think? Seems to me like somebody was looking for something."

"Well, yeah, probably cash, or ganja, or something to pawn. The stereo. That's why most cars get broken into."

"I wouldn't think cars get broken into out here in the suburbs."

"You'd think wrong, then. Park an expensive car on any street overnight and it can happen."

"Does it happen a lot?"

"Bear, it happens, okay? It happens more often than the lawyer stuff that goes on in Grisham's novels, okay? So that's the first thing we're going to think. But we're considering everything. The stereo wasn't stolen. So maybe the thief got interrupted, or maybe he wasn't after the stereo system. And, well, it looks like the car was wiped. Not seriously wiped, but the door handle, the console . . . things the guy touched. That's a little sophisticated for most smash-and-grabs."

"Could the partners have hired a hit guy?" I asked, not with any real hope. "Killed Graham and then searched his car? They could have been following him and —"

Another chuckle from Wanderley, and he finally plucked the metal tab out of his mouth and pitched it into a wastebasket that stood against the wall. It made a "ting" against the side of the basket.

"Could have but I don't believe I've ever heard of a professional hit man using a Big Bertha; that would be . . . unconventional. If HD hadn't walked right in and forced us to arrest him, he'd be sitting in his La-Z-Boy, keeping busy making Beanie nervous.

We were not thinking pro. From my own experience, and truly vast reading of thrillers" — he worked his eyebrows up and down — "hit men use guns and use them well. Maybe a knife. They get fancy in books and movies, but not in the world we walk in. Oh, wait. Russians get fancy. Polonium." Wanderley laced his fingers and rested his chin on the tops of them. That stopped him rocking the chair.

"But no, Bear, we don't think we're looking for a professional hit man. We think this was a very personal crime."

My heart clenched up at that.

"I mean, picture it, Bear — Garcia is on the country club golf course in the middle of the night. There are no major streets near this corner of the golf course; there's Elkins and Alcorn Oaks, quiet, residential streets. No businesses. Lots of expensive homes that back up to the golf course and every one of them has expanses of plate glass windows that look out onto the golf course. Well, sure, they paid extra for acreage on the fairway. If you like green grass, it's a great view.

"If you were planning a murder, Bear, you think you'd plan to do it with a weapon the victim provided himself, a Big Bertha? Would you choose an incredibly exposed location right out in the open in the middle of affluent suburbia? In a neighborhood where the citizens get outraged and form committees when someone eggs the Silverado their kid parked on the street?

"I don't think this murder was planned at all. I think someone lost it and hit Garcia. The murderer may have already had the driver in his hand; if he did, it's not going to be as bad as it would be if he picked it up for the purpose of hitting Garcia — or if he took it away from Garcia. So you're asking me could it have been one of Garcia's partners? Sure. There's not many things as personal to a man as his livelihood and reputation. If HD claimed that he killed Graham himself, I'd take it more seriously. He's an old bird, but a tough one. Could Alex Garcia have killed his father? You bet. If Jessica Min didn't have an airtight alibi, I would take a look at her. She's fit. She could have done it."

"Jessica Min?"

"That's the thirteen-year-old middle schooler who found Garcia."

Jessica Min was close to Jo's age. Likely to have dark hair, might have long dark hair . . .

He laughed at my expression. "It was a joke, Bear. She's thirteen."

Wanderley slapped the table top with both

321

hands and pushed himself up, sending his chair spinning back on its casters. I stood up as well.

"I thank you for the information, Bear, and I will let you get back to your work. You don't have anything else you want to tell me, do you?"

He said this over his shoulder as he was escorting me out of the building. I let out a breath of air I hadn't known I was holding. I could answer the man honestly.

"No sir, I don't." I'm pretty sure it wasn't a lie. I did not want to tell Detective James Wanderley that Alex Garcia had seen his father in a passionate embrace with a young girl who surely, surely couldn't have been Jo.

"Listen," I said, "I'd be grateful if you'd keep me up to date . . ."

Wanderley held the door open, leaning out to see me off. His extraordinary eyebrows went way up.

"Uh, noooooo, we don't do that, update private citizens. You check the paper. Or our website. Anything we want you to know, it'll be there."

Nice distinction, that. "Anything we want." Nothing about what you want to know.

I was headed out when Wanderley grabbed

322

my shirtsleeve. I turned. Wanderley hesitated a moment, the wicked grin gone.

"Were you?" he said.

"Was I what?"

Again the smallest hesitation.

"Your father's favorite. Oldest son and all."

My turn to hesitate, to nearly answer that my father hadn't played favorites, he loved us all, and both my brothers had their own successes. That's all true. My dad had been an evenhanded, fair man.

But face it. This is Texas. I'd been a high school football star. I'd played first string for The University of Texas, and I had enjoyed all the attendant social glory that Texas awards her football players. All the achievements that had been denied my bookish, intellectual father who had taught high school calculus and trigonometry at Foster for years, and still taught at the nearest Houston Community College campus.

I said, "Yeah. I'm his favorite."

His eyes stayed steady a second longer, and the easy smile was back. He punched my arm.

"Ah, yes, the indomitable Bear. I knew it." And he swung back into the air-conditioning.

# Twenty-Three

**From**: Walker Wells
**To**: Merrie Wells
**Subject**: Did you call Jo?

Did you?

# TWENTY-FOUR

After I left the police station, I made a showing at the Garcia visitation at six thirty, spent some time with the family, and signed my name in the guest book, but didn't stay long. That's usual at a Protestant visitation; at a Catholic visitation, after a period of meeting and greeting, there are often formal eulogies, and impromptu ones — that can go on late into the evening. I needed to get back home and repair some bridges.

Thursday night is one of my free nights, and normally we would spend it as a family. Tonight Jo and I were on our own. Annie Laurie had a meeting with a new publisher she was trying to sell some of her programs to, and she was meeting with them on the University of Houston campus. She promised me she would park in the garage and get someone to walk her to her car afterward. It's a great school, a beautiful campus, but stuff happens.

Annie Laurie is the only person with any sense who will willingly cook for my picky daughter — I sure didn't plan to try.

Dinner together, the two of us. It would be a good time to talk. Get Jo to open up to me. Please God.

I pulled up outside of Jo's ballet class and watched through the plate glass windows for her to come out. I have never, ever once in my life picked Jo up from dance class and found her ready and waiting for me outside. This time she was showered and changed; lots of times I've arrived to find her still working on the barre. Jo was in line to speak to her instructor, Madame Laney (in spite of the "Madame" business, Laney talks like a Georgia Peach), who was giving instructions to an assistant. When she gave her attention to Jo, she listened, then threw her arms about Jo and spun her around. There was a big hug session before Jo grabbed her tote bag (she still used a silly pink bag with an appliquéd ballerina teddy bear — my mom made it when Jo was five or six) and flew out the door.

"What was that all about?" I asked.

"What?" Jo said, still flushed and happy. She did not look like a girl who had been mixed up with a married man more than three times her age. She did not look like a

326

girl who had been mixed up in a murder. My heart eased.

"The big kissy fest in there?"

I got the look.

"We didn't kiss, Dad. Don't be a homophobe."

"What? No, I —"

"Or a lesbophobe."

"A what?"

"Whatever."

So the evening was starting off well, and that was good.

We settled for Pho Saigon, our favorite Sugar Land noodle restaurant.

One of Jo's friends had introduced her to Vietnamese noodle soup, *pho*, and Jo had introduced it to the rest of us. Pho Saigon became a regular; everybody had a favorite dish there and it didn't cost much — the same as fast food, and nowhere near the health hazard; pho is light and low calorie, certainly when compared to burgers and fries.

When Jo became a vegetarian, she had fewer dishes to choose from at Pho Saigon, but she still had choices. So we don't argue over the food there, which is a relief. We come here once a week or so. There's not a lot of atmosphere; it's in a strip center dominated by Asian diners, nail salons, boutiques, and dentists. It's anchored with a Wellfarm, an Asian grocery store, and the only one in Sugar Land that sells pig uteri in the meat department. Really. I've seen them there.

We were waiting for our orders, both of us preparing piles of the extras we like to add to our soup — bean sprouts, cilantro leaves, basil, lime juice, and minced jalapeños. Jo stood up to pull a paper from her jeans pocket. Her jeans were so tight, there was no way she could get anything out of her pockets sitting down. She sat back down and pushed the folded paper over to me.

Before I could look at the paper, our soup came. I always get a large number eleven — that's spicy beef broth with slivers of eye round roast and lots of thin rice noodles and shaved onion slices. Jo had her veggie soup, a small. It looks tasteless, but Jo made me try it once and it's good. Very spicy. She adds Sriracha and fresh-squeezed lime juice. We were busy for a minute adding our extras, me lifting up my noodles and putting the bean sprouts underneath so they would soften some, Jo keeping them on top so they stayed crisp. Then I reached for the paper and took a look.

Jo's progress report. I don't think Jo had willingly showed me her progress reports since she started middle school, so I was surprised before I even looked at the grades. I glanced up at her — she had her porcelain soup spoon up to her mouth and was softly blowing the soup to cool it. Her eyes were watching me.

I was even more surprised when I saw her grades. This was an improvement over her last progress report. An improvement over her last several progress reports.

"Well, all right, then, Jo. Not too shabby. You see what you can do when you apply yourself? Those study techniques we went over must have really helped."

Her eyes fell and she let the cooled spoonful of soup drop back into her bowl. Soup splashed onto her T-shirt.

I said, "What?"

Nothing from across the table. She stirred her soup and reached into the bowl with her fingers to pull out a bean sprout. She nibbled the bean sprout with tiny, deliberate bites.

We ate in silence for a while before I tried again.

"You know, if you can keep up this math grade, and if you go to summer school, you could be on grade level in math next year." I was trying to be encouraging. Annie says I should be more encouraging with Jo.

Evidently encouragement was not what was needed because Jo set her spoon down on the table with a loud "clack" and pushed back from the table. Phuong, one of the waitresses, stopped at the table.

"Everything okay here? You want something? What's matter, Jo, your soup no good?"

Jo gave Phuong a smile that didn't include me. "It's always good. You know I love it here."

Phuong smiled back and patted Jo's arm.

"You not getting mad at Daddy. You two always fight, fight, fight." She laughed, gave Jo another pat, and moved off.

Maybe we were getting too regular at Pho Saigon.

My bowl was nearly empty; Jo's barely touched. Jo still sat back from the table, her arms crossed. In spite of her reassurance to Phuong, Jo didn't look like she was going to finish her soup.

I picked up my bowl and drank off the last of my soup — perfectly acceptable manners in a pho restaurant. I put my bowl down, wiped my hands with a towelette, and tried to take Jo's hand; she pushed her chair back another three inches.

"You want some hot tea?" I asked.

"Dad, I'm on class level in math. I'm on

class level in all my courses. You don't have to send me to summer school. I wanted to talk to you about this summer."

"Well, sweetie," I said, "I just meant . . . what math class was Merrie taking in ninth grade?"

Jo stood up and snatched her purse with one hand and her progress report with the other.

She said, practically in a hiss, "Dad, why would I give a shit what math class Merrie was taking in ninth grade? Merrie wants to be an accountant."

Jo said "accountant" the way you might say "extortioner."

"I would rather roast in Dante's hell than be an accountant. I am going to be a dancer. I am going to dance for the New York City Ballet for ten years while I study choreography, and when my body gives out at thirty or so, I'm going to be a choreographer, and if I need algebra once, even once, in all those years, then I will take off my pointe shoes and eat them, laces and all. So I am already waaaay overeducated in the math department. And" — this she delivered with the tone of one who knows they are turning the knife — "I have never, ever, not once, ever used one of your lame-ass 'study techniques.' You want to know why my grades are up? It's Alex. Alex helps me. And he's a much better teacher than you are."

She flounced out of the restaurant, totally spoiling the grand exit when she got yanked off her feet after the shoulder strap of her purse caught on the door handle.

Both my brothers have sons. So does my sister-in-law, Stacy. Not a daughter among them. They are forever telling me how lucky I am to have two girls. Girls are so easy. That's what they all say.

Jo didn't walk home. It's a five-mile walk and Jo saves her energy for the ballet studio. She tries to tell me that jogging and hiking develop her muscles in the "wrong way." Please. She's also very careful of those tiny feet she's so proud of. So she didn't walk home, she went and leaned against the car, but she didn't talk to me, either.

Jo went straight to her room when we got home, and I went straight to mine. Baby Bear was undecided. My room or Jo's? He prefers Jo's company, but he didn't want to miss the chance of a run with me, so I won out.

I wanted a run. Annie wasn't back yet. I felt irritated and anxious. A week ago, I wouldn't have wasted brain space over leaving Jo in the house by herself while I went

332

for a run; now I was uncomfortable with the idea.

There is no way I could keep a teenage girl a prisoner until she's too old to worry about. I still worry about Merrie, and she's in college. So I changed into my running clothes and remembered to put my dry cleaning into the dry cleaning bag and not just on the dry cleaning bag. It makes Annie Laurie crazy when I drop them on top.

The stairway is lined with portraits of Merrie and Jo. We started having them done when Merrie was eight months or so, and we've had them done every year since then. It costs a fortune — Annie's parents picked up the tab for the first five years, then, when we were more settled, Annie and I paid for them. Annie's mom said I would never regret the investment, and I don't. Most times I pass by without a pause; tonight I took the stairs slowly, Baby Bear at my heels.

In the youngest baby pictures, the girls are wearing ruffled white panties over their diapers and nothing else. My mother-in-law's idea, and it was a good one. Merrie looks directly at the camera. Her plump hands clutch at her round, peachy belly, and her face is creased with merriment. In Jo's eighth-month portrait, the photographer has caught her in profile; a soap bubble floats in the corner of the frame, and Jo's hands are stretched out, her eyes wide and wondering.

There was no answer when I tapped at the door. It was locked when I tried the handle.

"Jo?" I called.

No answer.

"I'm going to take Baby Bear for a run. Will you be okay while I'm gone?"

No answer.

I sighed.

"Um, Jo, you can answer politely, or I'm going to go get a screwdriver and hammer, open the door, take it off the hinges, and then you can answer politely."

Jo sighed. "I'll be fine, Dad."

"Will you please stay in the house while I'm gone?"

"I'll stay in the house while you're gone."

"And not let anyone in while I'm gone?"

"And not let anyone in while you're gone."

"So help you, God?"

"Dad!"

"I'm joking, Jo. Kind of."

She sighed again.

There are three or four routes I take to jog. I regularly run past the corner of Alcorn Oaks and Elkins, close to the golf cart tunnel where Graham Garcia died, and I'd been drawn back along this route since the murder.

Baby Bear and I left the high point of the levee and were jogging on the sidewalk that curved around the ninth hole. At tenish it was dark, but the suburbs are never truly dark — part of what you're paying for when you buy a house out here is the plethora of streetlights.

Baby Bear and I had rounded the corner so that I could look down at the golf course tunnel that ran under the street. It was there that Graham had lain dying.

And that's where I saw her, standing with her back to me, hands on her hips, looking down at the ground. Her shoulders were heaving, as if she were trying to catch her breath, or as if she were crying.

I stopped running and put a hand on Baby Bear's head to keep him still. For two or three seconds, I thought it was somehow Jo. But Jo was back in her room.

There was the long dark hair, small body, something in the turn of her head. But this girl's hair was a straight sheet of blackness, not the tumbled wisps and waves Jo's hair was. And even if she was as short as Jo, her body was more muscular — a runner's, not a ballet dancer's. She was wearing those brief split-leg running shorts and an exercise bra, and I was thinking her daddy was crazy to let his little girl jog this late at night by herself, and the skimpy outfit was a bad idea, too.

But when I first saw her, I thought it was Jo. I really, really did. My head knew my daughter was back in her room, that short of transporting, she could not have gotten to this spot before me. But for a fraction of a second, I saw the girl and thought, *Jo*.

And I've known Jo for all her life. And I was seeing this girl standing on a rise, bathed in the streetlight, not in the dark hollow of the cart tunnel. And I was not a lovesick adolescent seeing my dad with someone other than my mother.

A starburst of relief went off in my chest. That's when I knew that, for all my self-assurances, I'd been very much afraid Alex truly had seen my Jo with his father. But it wasn't Jo he'd seen. It really wasn't.

The name "Jessica Min" floated up and I started to move forward, and that's when the girl turned and looked over her shoulder and I saw her face.

A fresh startle. A new relief.

Thank you, God.

Because the tear-soaked face I was looking upon was not a girl's, not a teenager's, not, I thought, even a young woman's. This was a mature woman. A trim, slim, adult Asian woman. I couldn't be sure at this distance, but I would guess she was over forty.

If this woman was who Alex had seen late Sunday night — and I had been fooled myself for a second — then Graham Garcia was not a pedophile, and his son was not going to have to carry that dark secret in his heart for the rest of his life.

I'm not saying that cheating on your wife is ever okay, but whoa, it is surely better to cheat on her with a woman than a child. If this was the woman with Graham that night. If.

She looked up at me so I dropped my hands to my knees in the "winded but recovering" pose. By the time I'd straightened, she was crossing the golf course, not making any attempt to stay on the path, a golf course no-no. I started jogging slowly forward, keeping my eyes on her back. I marked the spot where she went through a cast-iron gate that opened onto the golf course. I heard the soft "clash" as the gate swung closed behind her. I counted the houses. The sixth house from the corner. She hadn't taken the sidewalk around to a parked car. She had gone through a back-

yard gate without any hesitation.
She had gone home.

# TWENTY-FIVE

**From**: Merrie Wells
**To**: Walker Wells
**Subject**: Re: Jo

Dad, I did. Yes. You need to talk to Jo. No, you need to let Jo talk to you. And try to chill.

# TWENTY-SIX

Friday morning I woke so buoyant I needed a tether to keep my feet on the ground. Annie Laurie was sitting at the table with a cup of coffee and so, wonder of wonders, was Jo. Sitting, that is. No coffee for Jo. She sat with her feet on the rung of the chair, her fingers laced through the mane on Baby Bear's scruff. Annie and Jo and Baby Bear, expectant looks on all faces, smooth and furry, were angled away from the table so they could watch my entrance and I knew something was up. Yeah, nearly psychic.

"You having breakfast, Jo?" There wasn't anything consumable in front of her. Jo never ate breakfast.

Jo had her hair tied back and wore her every-day-but-Sunday uniform of too-tight jeans, too-tight tee, and heavy black Doc Martens.

Annie Laurie gave Jo's arm a push.

Jo said, "Remember last night I said I

needed to talk to you?"

"No," I said. "Mainly I remember that you didn't want to talk to me last night. There was lots of not talking last night." I walked over to the coffeemaker and sniffed to see how fresh it was.

Jo looked at her mom.

Annie said, "Get some coffee, Bear. There's something Jo wants to tell you."

Just like that, my heart went from helium to lead and sank down to somewhere in my left heel.

I'm thinking, *Oh God, pleeease don't let her be pregnant, pleeease.*

I got my coffee in my bathtub-sized mug that nobody else is supposed to use even though I still sometimes see it on the floor, half-filled with Rice Krispies or Frosted Flakes for Baby Bear.

"Aren't you due at school in, what? Ten minutes?" I said. I did not want to have this conversation. Two percent milk, three sugars, a teaspoon for stirring, skip the toast, *please, please don't let my little girl be pregnant.* I sat down at the table, not looking anyone in the eye, and stirred my coffee over-vigorously.

Jo's eyes were glistening with tears. She rubbed at Baby Bear's neck until he shook her hands off. Her hands were trembling.

She had to be pregnant. *Let the words of my mouth and the meditation of my heart . . .*

"Daddy . . ."

Oh, I was dead. I was so dead. Jo never ever calls me "Daddy." She hasn't since she turned ten.

"Last Saturday Alex took me downtown —"

*Oh, pleeease God, not an abortion. Oh, please, oh please . . .*

"— to the Ben Stevenson —"

*I'm going to kill the doctor who . . .*

" — Academy, to audition for the American School of Ballet for —"

Half my coffee sloshed onto the table. I stood. Coffee stains khaki. Annie Laurie leaned over and grabbed a stack of paper napkins to catch the spill before it rolled off onto the floor.

Annie said, "Bear?"

"I'm fine, I'm fine," I said and now my own hands were shaking. I sat down and Baby Bear laid his head on my shoe. Tethering me.

"— their summer program, and Tuesday I got a call, and Daddy, I'm in!"

So what were the serious faces for? It still wasn't clear what was so great about yet another ballet class, but no pregnancy, no abortion, no Graham Garcia. Jubilation!

342

Thank you, God.

I got out of my chair and gave Jo a hug. Her shoulders felt like bird bones.

"That's great, Jo, that's terrific." I gave her another big hug and put her back on her feet. My heart was sick with relief. All this adrenaline up and downing couldn't be good for my system.

Annie didn't seem to be joining in the celebratory mood.

She dropped the sodden napkins in the trash in an emphatic sort of way and stood next to my chair.

"Bear, what do you know about the American School of Ballet?" Annie asked. She put her hand on my shoulder. That meant something. I don't know what it meant, but something.

I said, "It's downtown? Ben Stevenson runs it?"

Jo said, "Dad!"

"It is downtown, Bear," Annie said, giving my shoulder a final squeeze. She sat down again and looked like she had a headache. "In downtown Manhattan."

Jo said, "Daddy! It's only the very best in the world, Daddy, and *I* got in, and almost nobody gets in and they have dorms and everything and it's chaperoned and all and there will be girls from Russia there, Dad, girls from all the world over because this is the best in the world, and *I* got in and —"

"And it's six thousand dollars for five weeks. If you include the airfare." Annie said this with her face in her coffee mug.

I drank some of the coffee still left in my cup.

Jo was up, Doc Martens planted, ready to do battle. She said, "Grandmother says she'll pay half, and Nana says she and Poppy will pay for the airline ticket, so it would only cost, maybe, twenty-six hundred, and I have almost three hundred in my bank account."

"Wait a minute, you told Nana and Poppy before you told me? You told Grandmother?" I turned on Annie Laurie. "When did you find out?"

"Half an hour ago."

I sat there. Now I understood why Jo's hands were trembling. I was grateful that she wasn't pregnant, but six thousand dollars for summer camp?

"Jo, before we go any further," I said, "Nana and Poppy aren't paying for any plane ticket. And we are not going to allow Grandmother and Grandpa to shell out three thousand dollars, either. And if I ever find out that you've asked your grandparents for money again, you're looking at serious trouble."

That was a rebuke. Jo took it like a benediction.

"Oh, Daddy! Then you'll pay for it?"

Great.

I said, "Jo, this isn't a two-minute decision. When do you have to let them know?"

"Today! I have to let them know by four o'clock today!"

"Jo, why did you wait so late to tell us?"

"I tried to tell you Tuesday night after youth group, but you got all over me about why I left the house, and then I tried to tell you Wednesday night, but you got all over me about seeing Alex, and then last night over noodles, I brought my progress report so you could see how good I'm doing and then I was going to tell you and all you could say was" — and here she did her "Bear" imitation, hands on her hips, her head thrown back, her voice a cartoon villain's — " 'Josephine, why can't you be just like Merrie? Josephine, why don't you take calculus so no one will think you're retarded?' "

Annie looked up at me.

"I did not call her retarded. And I don't sound like that," I said. "The thing is, Jo, six thousand dollars! Baby, that's a lot of money . . ."

She came back like a whippet.

"How much did you spend on Merrie this year?"

"Merrie's in college; that money comes out of her college fund. You have a college fund, too, and —"

"Then take the six thousand dollars out of my college fund!" She threw her hands up. Funny how I could be so simpleminded when the solution was perfectly clear. All she wanted me to do was rob her college fund for a fancy-pants dance camp.

"A little help?" I looked at Annie Laurie, but she decided that now was the time to get more coffee.

I tried to get things a little calmer.

"Jo, I can't take the money out of your college fund. If I do, it won't be there for college."

Her hands went to her hair and she gripped it at the roots.

"Oh, Daddy, I'm not going to college! I am not going to college! I'm going to the American School of Ballet Summer Program, and they're going to see how good I am, and at the end of the five weeks they're going to invite me to stay on for their winter term. The website says a 'select few' will be invited to stay on for the winter term. And almost every single dancer in the New York

City Ballet is drawn from the American School of Ballet! So that's what I'll be doing instead of college!"

My poor baby girl.

I said, as gently as I could, "And what if you aren't among the 'select few' who are invited to stay for the winter term?"

"I will be! Oh, Daddy, please, please, Daddy, it's the only thing I've ever wanted and this is my only chance ever."

And she was in my arms, crying her heart into shreds, her tears dripping down the back of my shirt. I smoothed her hair out of her face and rocked her in my lap.

There was no way this was a good investment. The way to be successful was to study hard and work hard and get as much education as you could, at least up to a point. Jo was nowhere near that point, and I didn't have six thousand dollars to throw after a dream that didn't have a chance and probably wasn't worth pursuing.

I looked down at my child's raven hair, the nape of her white neck showing through the dark.

"Jo, Jo, we'll work it out, Jo. I promise."

The face Jo lifted to mine was worth the six thousand dollars.

This is what we decided. I would send my

fourteen-year-old daughter to the American School of Ballet this summer. In New York. City. Four thousand dollars of the expense would come from her college fund. I would pay two thousand — that's how much we'd paid to send Merrie on that Summer-in-Europe program she'd done at nearly the same age as Jo.

If Jo didn't get invited to stay on for the winter term, she would buckle down to her academics and plan on going to college. Because her college fund would be reduced, she might be looking at a year or two of junior college.

Does this sound harsh? Let me tell you something. Do you know how many ballet dancers can support themselves on what they make dancing? Four. Okay, not four, but not many. I looked it up.

If you go all the way through the American School of Ballet, that's a twenty-thousand-dollars-a-year proposition if you need the room and board program. Then, if you are accepted into the New York City Ballet Corps de Ballet (those are what I would call the "chorus" — the background dancers), then maybe, only maybe, you can afford to live in a tiny walk-up studio, about the size of my bedroom and bathroom put together, if you waitress on the side, too. You'd probably have to get a roommate.

And you can do that maybe, *maybe* ten years. If. If you're incredibly lucky and you don't come down on your ankle wrong and sustain a career-ending injury. If your tendons don't wear out. If you don't need to eat on a fairly regular basis.

Being a professional ballet dancer is not a career; it's a vocation. You're going to spend your heart, soul, and body down to the last penny, and have nothing to show for it except memories and bad feet. It's like deciding to be a nun, only the retirement program isn't as good and the clothes don't keep you as warm.

That's not the life I want for one of my girls.

Annie Laurie and I agreed that she would call her parents and I would call mine to undo the financial tangle. There is never a good time to call my mother, so as soon as I got into the office, I decided to go ahead and eat the frog and get it over with.

It went like this:

"Hey, Mom, it's Bear."

"Yes, I know it is. What's the problem?"

Once a week I call my mother, and there is almost never a problem. Maybe three times ever, and two of those times I was in high school, and one of those times it wasn't me driving and I'd only had one, maybe two, beers. But every time I call her, it's "What's the problem?"

"Uh, there's no problem, Mom, only I understand Jo asked you for some money and I —"

There was a tongue-clicking sound that means disapproval even in Namibia.

"She did not ask me for money," Mom said.

"Yeah? Well, Jo said —" I didn't get to finish my sentence.

"When I heard she had this incredible opportunity to hone her God-given talents, I offered her the money. I consider it an investment."

"Mom, it's only an investment if you get a return on your money; you don't get a return on a ballet dancer because they don't make any money."

"Bear, *you* invest for money. *I* invest for the future."

What that means I don't have any clue. What I do know is that my mom was staking her claim to a higher moral ground than she thought I had my marker on.

"Right. Well, in any case, please don't do it again. It encouraged Jo to call her grandmother Gaither and ask her for money, too, and —" She cut me off again.

"She most certainly did not. Naturally, when I heard that Jo had been accepted into the most prestigious ballet program in the country, in the *world*, I knew Gaither would want to help her out —"

This time I interrupted.

"Oh, my gosh, Mother! You cannot call people and suggest to them how they should spend their money! I can't believe you called Gaither."

"How much did she say she would contribute?"

"It doesn't matter and I am not going to tell you. Jo is not going to accept the money."

"Bear! Hold on a minute — let me sit down before I pass out right here on this cold, hard tile floor."

The phone clunked onto the counter and then there was the sound of a chair being dragged across the kitchen floor. She was huffing when she got back on the phone.

"Now, you listen here, Bear, Jo is going to be a prima ballerina, and if you don't have enough faith in your own child to —"

This was rich.

"Mom? Did you have faith in me?"

"Why, you know I did —"

"What kind of chance did you think I had

to play for the NFL?"

"Your coach said you weren't big enough or fast enough to go pro —"

"The reason I'm asking is, statistically speaking, I had a way, way better chance of playing pro ball than Jo has of being a prima ballerina. See, there are maybe twenty-five prima ballerinas in the world and there are more than three hundred linemen in the NFL. And Mom, if I had made it into the NFL, they would have paid me a truckload of money. Ballerinas make squat. They get paid by the job. I looked it up."

There was a brief regrouping silence. When my mother started speaking again, she allowed herself the smallest tremor. It's been an effective tactic for her in the past. Not with me, of course, but as my mother will tell you, I'm a Philistine.

"Bear, I know you won't be able to understand this, but your youngest daughter is an artist." I could actually *hear* the dramatic hand-at-her-throat gesture, à la Blanche DuBois.

I sighed. How had I let myself get derailed? I guess the same way I always let myself get derailed with my mom. No matter what I do, she is never happy with me. I tried to get back on topic.

"Jo's going to New York this summer."

"She is?! Praise God, Bear, I knew you'd do the right thing!"

No, she did not, either, or she wouldn't have been scrambling to get other people to pay for it.

"And Jo will not be accepting 'contributions' from her grandparents or anyone else. Jo and I have worked out the finances."

"Well, now, that's fine, but Gaither and Kenneth have more money than they know what to do with, and it would be a positive blessing to them if you and Annie would —"

"That's out," I said. It took enormous self-control not to whack the telephone on my desk three or four times. I've done it before, and the phones never work right after that.

There was an offended silence on the other end of the phone.

"Mom?"

"I understand, Bear, and I won't offer Jo money anymore. Incidentally, Jo tells me you have taken her locket away from her and won't give it back. Would you mind explaining why you have taken my gift from my grandchild?"

That's right. I get tattled on by my own child.

"Did Jo tell you she had given the locket

to a boy to wear?"

Now there was a considering silence.

"That is a valuable locket and chain, Bear, and I don't just mean sentimental value."

"I know it is," I said.

My mother sighed.

"If I get Jo to promise that she won't let anyone else have it until she's a grand-mother, will you please give it back to her so she can wear it around her lovely neck the way I intended when I gave it to her?"

I hate being backed into corners.

"Mom, I'll think about it."

"One more question, Bear, satisfy my curiosity. How much did Gaither say she would give Jo?"

"Gotta go, Mom." I disconnected.

It wasn't a satisfying conversation for either of us. It never is.

# TWENTY-SEVEN

Scheduling conflicts meant that Annie Laurie and I would meet at Graham Garcia's funeral instead of riding together. I wanted to get there early. I wanted to see if the woman who I'd seen at the golf course would come.

No way was I going to call Alex and give him the good news that his father's mistress was a woman, not a child; I didn't know for a fact that I was right. All I knew was that I first mistook this woman for Jo, and that she'd been standing right there where Garcia had been killed, and yes, she had been crying. It was suspicious; I was suspicious . . .

What I wanted to know was, could a woman that small have dealt the blow that killed Garcia? If what you see on the forensic television shows is true, then you can darn near tell the color of a person's eyes by the way a gun was shot or a club was swung.

Wanderley had said that even the little girl who found Graham could have killed him, but surely he was joking.

The St. Laurence foyer was cool and dim and empty except for Detective James Wanderley. Of course he would be here; I should have thought of that.

Wanderley wore a dark suit — it looked new, not something he had inherited from his grandfather's closet. Though he had paired the suit with envy-worthy black cherry boots, which, judging by the styling, were older than he was.

I found the whole boot thing interesting. It's not all that unusual for a grieving person to wear a piece of jewelry or an article of clothing that belonged to the deceased, but a boot is especially intimate; a well-made boot will mold itself to the owner's foot. Could be Wanderley was symbolically molding himself after his grandfather. Total psychobabble, of course. I gave a laugh and that eyebrow rose up.

"You're here early," Wanderley said and extended his hand.

"You are, too. Guess we both wanted to, uh, greet the guests. Nice suit." I gave exactly the same pressure with my hand.

Wanderley ignored the suit comment.

"Greet the guests? You aren't here early to

356

scope out possible suspects, right? Bear, you do know that I'm the detective and you're the guy who stands up front on Sundays and asks for money, don't you?"

Yeah, Wanderley was going to need to put a little more effort into those "people skills."

He went on, "Crime-solving preachers, or rabbis, or housewives — that's make-believe. You know that, right?"

"Don't be a patronizing ass, Wanderley."

"Good. I'm reassured. Sometimes playing football can cause severe head injuries — the effects don't show up for years. I heard that on NPR. The Sugar Land Police Department does not need you running around thinking you're Father Brown."

"Wanderley! You read books?"

It was gratifying to see him flush.

"I read —"

"And Chesterton, at that! For someone of your generation, that's —"

"My grandfather read Chesterton to me."

Ah. The grandfather again. Where was the father while this boy was growing up?

There was a soft cough. I turned, and saw Dr. Alejandro Garcia.

He was standing between two distinguished-looking men — presumably William and David, the stepbrothers Graham had been so anxious to equal.

Grief had eaten at Dr. Garcia. He looked thinner and his face was shadowed. His elegant dark suit looked as if it had been tailored for a bigger man. I thought there was a tremor in the hand he held out to me, and I took his hand in both of mine. I wanted to hug him, but it would probably have made him uncomfortable, and anyway, his two sons flanked him like bodyguards.

Dr. Garcia introduced his sons to Detective Wanderley and they swelled, their faces solemn and protective. Wanderley shook Dr. Garcia's hand. He had the good sense not to offer his hand to the brothers Garcia.

Dr. Garcia said, "Detective Wanderley, Honey tells me you've cleared Alex? He is no longer a suspect? I am so grateful. Of course, I knew you could never really have thought the boy could . . . that he could . . ." His eyes brimmed over and he fumbled for a handkerchief.

The older of the two men, William, took his father's elbow.

"Come on, Pops. Let's sit down. David, get Dad a glass of water."

Wanderley said, "Dr. Garcia, after the funeral, if you could give me a few minutes, I wanted to clear up . . ."

William hurried Dr. Garcia off.

David lingered long enough to give Wanderley a warning look. He leaned in to him and said, dropping his voice so Dr. Garcia wouldn't overhear, "Listen. You want information, you come to me or Will. Dad's not doing so well. This has been too much for him. He's an old guy, you know? Graham was his 'Joseph.' But we're not the jealous brothers, so don't go in that direction. Graham was good to Dad. He was good *for* Dad. You find out who did this. If it wasn't the crazy old man. Which I doubt."

David thrust two business cards into Wanderley's hand.

The man strode off.

I said, "You cleared Alex?"

Wanderley reached into his pocket and pulled out a black plastic guitar pick. He popped it into his mouth.

"Nope," he said.

"Then why would Honey —"

He shook his head. "Bear, the waters run deep here. The waters run deep."

A door off the foyer opened. Margaret Butler from the funeral home walked out, and at the same time three or four cars pulled into the parking lot. Wanderley and I shook hands with Butler, signed the book she held out for us, and positioned ourselves near the front doors.

A ten-year-old Continental pulled in

behind Honey's Escalade. An old man got carefully out of the Lincoln and walked around to open the passenger door of the Continental.

Wanderley leaned over to tell me. "That's Honey's Uncle Ralph. Doing HD's job for him. Since HD is still wearing an orange jumpsuit."

Ralph reached a hand into the car and drew out a tall, frail woman. Beanie. Or Belinda, rather. Honey's mother looked like a Belinda — I don't know how HD could ever have called such a gracious woman "Beanie." She took a minute gathering her purse and sweater and a Bible, took the old man's arm, and began walking slowly with him over to the church.

The doors to the Escalade were still shut. Honey was probably still sitting in the car, taking the time to touch up her makeup, I thought.

Finally, the Escalade's side door opened and Jenasy got out and joined the old couple. They both embraced her. The man took Jenasy's face in his hands, bent her head down, and kissed the top of her head as though he were bestowing a benediction on his best loved. Cruz opened the driver's door and clambered out. She smoothed down a navy suit and settled a navy pillbox firmly on her head. She leaned back into the car and said something.

Another minute passed before Honey Garcia opened the front seat passenger door and stepped down from the SUV. Black chiff on drapery and an overelaborate hair arrangement made her look like a Hollywood widow from a dated movie. Ralph took Belinda's arm, and escorted her, along with Honey, toward the door. Jenasy walked with her arm hooked into Cruz's. The group was stopped by a couple who had arrived at the same time and had been patiently waiting by the door.

"Wanderley," I said, snatching my chance, "how tall was the person who struck Garcia? Do you know? Could they have been as short as, say, Jo?"

He swung back to me. "Bear! That's what I was talking about! You're Father Browning it!"

"No, no, I only —"

Wanderley turned to the door and studied the group outside.

"I don't know how tall the murderer was. That's mainly TV stuff, knowing the murderer's height, weight, and the color of the eyes, all from the angle of the blow," he said without looking. "I haven't had any word that would tell me someone Jo's height

361

could not have delivered the blow that killed Garcia, but forgive me, Bear, you're a sick puppy to even think that. Your own daughter —"

"Wait," I said. "No, I mean, I never thought Jo —"

"So why did you ask me? If you didn't think it was Jo? Do you have something to tell me?" He studied me.

"I . . . no! I was wondering, that's all. You see things on TV . . ."

But he had dismissed me. Honey and her group were coming through the doors, and more people were pulling up and getting out of their cars. Wanderley pulled back to a corner of the room where he could watch unobtrusively. I started the handshaking, back-patting thing.

Belinda and Ralph were looking grieved and a little puzzled at Honey's manner — she was over-enunciating everything she said and walking with a care that her three-inch heels couldn't account for. Honey had evidently fortified herself for the occasion with some more of her doctored lemonade.

If Honey didn't already have a full-scale drinking problem, she soon would if she kept up like this. I would have to find someone to have a talk with her.

The room was filling up. Lots of people

from our church were there, lots of other people who I assumed were from the Catholic church, and a group of about twenty men and women with good haircuts and even better dark suits, who I thought must be from Graham's law firm; something about the way they kept surreptitiously checking their phones and texting.

I wondered which of the dark-suited crew was the lying dog. I wondered if all of them were. Then I made a mental mea culpa for that kind of prejudice.

I was greeting Honey's Uncle Ralph, saying all the expected things. I didn't see Annie Laurie come in, but suddenly she was by my side, breathless and tugging at my arm.

"Bear . . ."

Ralph was talking, I had no idea what he was saying, but of course, I was pretending to listen, giving every appearance that he had my full attention, and patting Annie Laurie's hand to let her know I'd be with her in a moment.

"Bear . . ." she said again. But then I saw them.

Alex Garcia stood in the door of the building. He had on dark Ray-Ban sunglasses. I don't know if they were real Ray-Bans; they could have been Walgreen's five-dollar knockoff. They looked like Ray-Bans. He wore a black jacket and charcoal slacks and his thick blond hair was tied into a nub of a ponytail at the nape of his neck. I took all that in, which surprises me, because all I really remember seeing was the woman on his arm. Not a woman, a girl. She only looked like a woman. My Jo.

Jo was wearing one of Annie Laurie's dresses, a black jersey wrap that Jo had pulled tight enough to fit her slimmer frame. When Annie Laurie wore the dress, it hit right at the knee; it fell to midcalf on Jo. She wore black pumps on her feet and small pearl earrings dangling from her earlobes — the earrings were another present from my mom — and had wrapped her long dark hair into some kind of loose updo. I don't have any idea what you'd call such a hairstyle, but the sum total effect was that Jo looked like a twenty-eight-year-old woman, not a fourteen-year-old girl.

Am I making it sound like Jo was tarted up? She wasn't. She had on almost no makeup, and except for those pearl earrings, no jewelry. I hadn't given her back her locket.

She didn't look like a little girl playing dress-up in her mother's clothes, either. She looked like a mature woman of twenty-something and she looked . . . heart-crashingly beautiful.

I felt a terrible fear. I can't tell you why. Why am I so frightened for this child of mine? Why does Jo tear at my heart in a way my lovely Merrie never has? I cannot catch hold of her. I am so afraid of losing her.

Annie Laurie picked up the conversation I had let fall, and linked her arm through mine — short of physically shaking her off, I couldn't free myself to go confront Jo. Exactly Annie's intent, of course.

And what was I going to say anyway? I had laid down the law that Jo couldn't see Alex; Jo had been clear that she wouldn't stop. I had no idea what to do. I had never openly defied my father when I was a kid. Naturally, I had disobeyed him on a number of occasions, but I had taken precautions to keep that from him. See, I think that's a sign of respect, not being open about it.

Had I known what to do, there wouldn't have been time anyway. Before I could catch Jo's eye, I saw the Asian woman from the golf course.

She passed right by me, a light, bright citrus scent trailing her. Up close I could see that she was closer to forty-five than thirty-five. The black sheet of hair I had seen hanging to her waist the night she was at the golf course was now knotted in a sleek chignon at the back of her slim neck. She was wearing a fitted black-skirted suit — the only soft touch was a pink and gray silk scarf tucked into the neckline. Three-inch-high heels put her at all of five-two, five-three. Barefoot, she would stand an inch shorter than Jo.

The woman wasn't beautiful. Handsome, yes. And definitely attractive. But she was no stunner. I glanced over at Honey. This woman was Honey's physical opposite. In my experience, men who have affairs often choose younger, prettier versions of their wives. You know, the John Derek marriage model.

Honey was tall, full-bosomed, and round-hipped even at her reduced weight. She was naturally soft and pillowy. The woman who was making her unobtrusive way through the crowd had the body of an athlete, lean and toned and tiny. Honey's touched-up red hair and blue eyes could not have contrasted more with this woman's dark eyes and inky hair, slightly silvered at the temples. Honey's face was flushed with emotion and cosmetics. And drink. This woman was pale under her darker skin, and her makeup was muted.

If Graham Garcia had gone in search of a woman who was as dissimilar from his wife as nature allowed, he couldn't have done better than the woman who slipped into the aisle seat of the last row.

"You all right?" my wife asked.

I brought myself back.

"I'm fine. Where's Jo?" People were moving toward the auditorium and we followed.

"She's with Alex. She's sitting with the family."

"For crying out loud, Annie Laurie, what is she, his fiancée? Do you think that's appropriate, Jo sitting with the family? I can't think that's going to go down well with Honey. I don't like this one iota."

Annie Laurie stopped short of the sanctuary door, veered to the right down an adjacent corridor, and kept walking. I waited a second but she didn't come back. I had to trot after her and take her arm before she stopped.

"What?" I said. I could hear soft organ music. Annie didn't say anything. She didn't turn around. I pulled her around to face me.

"What is it?" I couldn't understand her behavior, and if we didn't hurry, we were going to be Standing Room Only. The auditorium was filling fast. A crowd had turned out for Garcia's funeral.

Annie took a big breath. She pushed my hand off her arm and smoothed her sleeve. I hadn't crumpled the fabric.

"You're hurting me."

"I didn't mean to."

Annie shook her head at me and I reached out to smooth back a stray strand of her soft, blond hair but she caught me by the wrist.

"You never mean to, Bear. You tromp all over people's feelings, brush aside anything that doesn't fit in with your way of thinking, and if anyone gets in the way and gets hurt, well, you didn't mean to. You know what, Bear? You're too big. You take up more than your fair share of oxygen."

"Annie, all I said was —"

"I heard what you said. I heard what you said because I listen to you. You said you didn't like Jo sitting with Alex and his family.

"Bear, today isn't about you or what you like. We are here to pay our respects to Graham Garcia and to comfort his family. Jo is a comfort to Alex. That is the beginning and the end of the story and you aren't in this story."

"Sweetheart, I didn't want Honey to —"

"Honey is two drinks away from falling

flat on her fanny. Whatever clear-thinking part of her there is will be grateful as hell that her boy can take comfort somewhere, anywhere at all today." Annie had tears in her eyes and she dug in her purse for a tissue.

"Well, all right then, let's go on in —"

"No!" Annie blew her nose and sniffed and shut her purse with an emphatic click. "I want to know why everything Jo does is wrong! Did you see our daughter walk into this church? How you can keep from perishing with pride every time you look at her is a dark mystery to me, Bear. What the hell more do you want from her?"

"Annie!"

"Bear, you are the only adult in the whole state of Texas who thinks it's a sin to say 'hell.' It's not a curse; it's not even a vulgarity, and I'm your wife, not your child, so don't you dare correct my speech."

"All right, then, fine. Can we please settle down and go —"

"Bear! Don't you *ever* tell me to settle down, not after some of the fits I've seen you throw. And no, we can't go in, not until you've answered me." She had her hands on her hips now, and that is not ever a good sign in a woman even if the hips in question are Annie's very comely ones.

I looked around for someplace to sit but there weren't any benches down this hall and I don't know the Catholic church well enough to go trying doorknobs.

I said, "First off, you're entirely wrong about everything. Didn't I say she could go to New York? Didn't I say I'd pay the six thousand dollars?"

"No, you said it would come out of her college fund. Which my parents have generously contributed to and I put almost as much money into those accounts as you do."

"Are you saying that we should have taken six thousand dollars out of our savings so Jo could go to a fancy-pants rich-kid summer camp?"

"If Merrie had been good enough at volleyball for the Olympics, you wouldn't have thought twice about spending that money. About spending twice that much money."

I would have, too, because twelve thousand dollars is a lot of money, and in any case . . . "This isn't the Olympics."

"It *is* the Olympics, Bear. For a classical ballerina, the American School of Ballet is the goddamn Olympics!"

I had no clue what had gotten into my women, but this new thing with the language was not going to fly. "Okay, now, Annie, you're out of line here. I'm not going to discuss this with you right now; it's neither the time nor the place. Let's quiet down, and go take our seats."

Annie started to say something; she closed her mouth. I put my hand on her waist and we walked back toward the door of the sanctuary. When we got there, she kept walking across the lobby. She went over to the guest book, signed her name, and then walked out of the church. I watched her get into her car and drive away.

# TWENTY-EIGHT

It wasn't my finest moment, letting Annie Laurie drive off; I know that. I should have gotten in my car and followed her and made things right, even if I wasn't in the wrong. That's what I should have done. Or maybe not, the way things turned out. Or maybe so, the way things turned out.

While I stood there debating whether to go into the sanctuary for the rest of the funeral, or go after Annie Laurie and mend what needed mending, the sanctuary door swung open and the mystery woman slipped out. If she saw me, and I'm hard to miss, I didn't register on her. She had a hand in her glossy leather purse and she pulled out a pair of oversized sunglasses and a crystal key ring shaped like a Nike running shoe. The glasses went on before she stepped outside, tears streaming from under the lenses; she had her key at the ready. If my stride weren't twice as long as hers, I would have had to trot to catch up. I was doing that a lot today.

"Miss, miss!" I sounded like an importunate waiter.

She glanced over her shoulder, saw me, scanned the rest of the parking lot, which was full of cars and empty of people, and decided that, yes, the big man lumbering after her was calling her. She stopped.

If women still wore gloves, and if the mystery woman had conveniently dropped one in the foyer, well, that would have given me an opening. But women don't wear gloves anymore unless they're golfing or gardening.

Instead I said, "I saw you at the golf course last night. Near where Graham was killed. You're a friend of Graham's, aren't you?" Clear, direct, to the point.

She spun around, sprinted away on those high heels, and held her key fob out to a cream-colored BMW sedan. The locks popped open. Stilettos are not good sprinting shoes. I outpaced her easily and put my hand on her door before she could open it.

I looked down at her and tried hard not to look menacing — that's tricky when you weigh more than twice what the woman does and you are blocking her from her car.

"His son saw you. That night. With Graham. Alex misunderstood the situation and he's in a lot of pain about it. I really need to talk to you."

There it was. I'd done it. Without a thought, I'd broken my promise. The moment I realized it, I slapped my head. Shame rose up in me like a flash flood.

If I was wrong, and this woman was not Graham Garcia's lover, then I had just let a total stranger in on a very, very personal secret, and I would need to be taken out and shot.

When I opened my eyes, she was studying me.

"You okay?"

I flushed again.

"Yes." If a promise-breaking idiot can be said to be okay, then yes, I was fine. For a fat-mouthed jackass, I was triple peachy keen.

Big breath.

"I want to clarify things for Alex," I said. It was too late to wish I hadn't followed her out of the church. Too late to wish I'd kept my jaws clamped shut. I kept one hand on her car door and fished a business card out of my jacket. She quit tugging at the door handle and took the card from me.

She looked up at me. "Would you back off a little? Take two steps back, do you mind? You're crowding me."

She spoke distinctly, but with a strong Asian accent.

I took two steps backward.

"Two giant steps."

I took two giant steps back.

She opened her car door and slid behind the wheel. I thought she would be off, and if I tried to stop her, I'd end up like that cheating dentist in Clear Lake who got run over four or five times by a very unhappy woman. A fitting punishment for the promise breaker I was.

The mystery woman started her car. Music blasted from the speakers so loudly I had trouble identifying it. She smacked the dashboard and silenced it. I waited while she sat there in the idling car.

I said, "I know where you live."

She gave a yip of laughter and wiped her face with her sleeve. She left a tan smear on the black jacket.

"You sound like a stalker, you know that, Mr., ah" — she held my card arm's length from her eyes and peered at it — "Mr. Wells."

"Okay, that's fair, I only —"

"Do you know where the Vineyard is?" she said.

"In Towne Center? Right next to City

Hall? Yeah, I —"

"I'm going to the Vineyard. We can talk there if you want to." She shut her door and rolled the window down. She tilted her head inquiringly.

"Oh, sure, or we could meet in my office at the church and —"

"I'm going to the Vineyard. You go wherever you want."

She backed out and wheeled onto Sweetwater in a manner that indicated she wasn't thinking "school zone." Which it was.

This wasn't going to be any kind of car chase. On Sweetwater Boulevard, you pass through four school zones and five lights in the four miles between St. Laurence Catholic Church and Towne Center, and at two o'clock on a Friday, the SUVs are already lining the boulevard, all the patient mothers waiting to transport their gifted and talented progeny from the award-winning public schools to the afterschool enhancement classes of piano, or gymnastics, or Mandarin, or yoga. Nobody was going anywhere fast.

The mystery woman would have done better to have taken Austen Parkway, two and a half miles, one school zone, and two lights if you go that way, but whatever.

I'm two cars behind her, keeping her in

sight, so I see her doing the whole "woman in a car" thing. Her visor comes down and she's driving with one eye in the mirror, one on the road. She does powder, lipstick, something over the lipstick that she applies with her pinky, mascara. She pulls pins from her hair and it tumbles down. She brushes it with a brush the size of two fingers. At the next light, she pulls that mass of hair up to the top of her head and twists it through a band into one of those messy knots the high school girls wear. By the time she gets out of her car, she's lost the suit jacket; she's wearing a low-cut tank top with her suit skirt and she's taken the scarf off her neck and tied it around the knot of hair on the top of her head. Women don't wear scarves that way anymore. They should — it was eye-catching. The stiletto pumps had been switched for high-heeled sandals. I would have been impressed, but I know for a fact that Annie Laurie has exchanged torn panty hose for new ones while she was driving — no mean trick.

The mystery lady set off like a woman who knows the man is going to follow, and I did. She had that quick, purposeful stride I associate with lawyers and CEOs.

The Vineyard is an indoor-outdoor wine bar with tables on the terrace that fronts the Sugar Land City Hall. I've heard the city hall's architecture referred to as Neo-Brutalistic. Don't ask. I kind of like the thing.

One of the guys Merrie dated in high school had pointed out to me that there was a Freemasons' Square and Compass carved into the façade.

I said, "And that means?"

He shook his head in disbelief at my base ignorance, and said, dropping his voice as if the KGB might be listening, "What it means, Mr. Wells, is that Sugar Land is run by the Illuminati."

I didn't ask. I had asked this fellow for clarification once before and I had gotten way more information than I had been looking for. Instead, I wikied "Illuminati" and, well, I know the kid is spooky smart, but the world he lives in is evidently much more interesting, and dangerous, than the one I live in. I still see him occasionally when Merrie is back from school, but she isn't dating him anymore and that's a relief.

At a few minutes after two on a Friday afternoon, only two or three of the Vineyard's outdoor tables were occupied. A couple of young mothers were sipping chardonnay while their assorted preschoolers lapped up Ben and Jerry's and teetered on the edge of the cowboy fountain. Some business travelers from the Marriot were enjoying Sugar Land's mild spring, drinking and texting and shedding layers of clothes.

Graham's mystery lady laid claim to an empty table by flinging her big black purse on it. I have packed for long weekends in bags smaller than that purse. She picked the menu up and held it out to me.

"I'm having the BV Tapestry, what do you want?"

"Do they have iced tea?"

Her forehead puckered. "You're going to drink iced tea at a wine bar?"

"I'll have a pinot grigio. And ice water."

"Pinot grigio? Any pinot grigio?"

"You choose. I'll pay." I reached for my wallet.

"Sit down. I'll be right back."

I put my jacket across the back of the chair and looked around the square. I didn't see anybody I knew. There's nothing wrong with having a glass of wine with an attractive woman who isn't your wife. But.

I sat down at the heavy wrought-iron table and tried not to feel self-conscious. Mystery woman emerged from the bar, empty-handed, and sat down before I could stand up and pull her chair out for her.

"I got you the Graffigna. From Argentina," she said.

She could have gotten me the Wobblies from Australia; I wouldn't know the difference.

I held my hand out to her.

"Walker Wells."

She left my hand out there too long for comfort. Finally she took it. Her grip was firm and dry and warm.

"Mai Dinh."

It sounded like "My Din."

"Spell it for me." She did.

The door to the Vineyard swung open and a young man with an abbreviated Kewpie's curl brought a tray to our table. With a flourish he put two coasters on the table. In front of Mai he set down a crystal globe filled nearly to the top with a dark ruby wine. The stem of the glass looked impossibly long and thin. The glass of wheat-colored wine he set down in front of me. He put a basket of sliced French bread; a plate with six cracker-sized slices of blue, Brie, and Swiss cheese; a pronged cheese knife; and a cheese cleaver in the center of the table. He murmured, "Enjoy!" and left. No ice water.

Mai dropped her sunglasses into the purse and held the wine up to see the color with the afternoon sun behind it.

"So." She drank from her glass. "Alex saw us." Her eyes filled and she tilted her head back to keep the tears from spilling out. Mai rummaged inside her oversized handbag, pulled out her sunglasses again, and put them back on. She tipped the glasses up and pressed a tissue to the corners of her eyes and then to her nose. "That wasn't supposed to happen. When did he see us? Where did he see us?"

I asked, "How long have you known Graham?"

She gave a grimace of a smile. "All of my life. For a thousand years. One year two months. It's not what you think."

"What do I think?"

"What anyone would think. He wasn't trawling. We weren't 'looking for love in all the wrong places.' That song."

The man at the table next to us lit up a cigar. A small aromatic cloud of smoke drifted over.

Mai looked over at him crossly.

"Jesus!" she said. "Grab the wineglasses, would you?"

I picked the glasses up. Mai stood, seized the wrought-iron table edge in both hands, and yanked. Teetering backward in the heeled sandals, she dragged the table five feet, out of the cigar's draft zone. The plate of cheese traveled to the edge of the table during the trip.

I was impressed. Mai's biceps and thigh muscles were taut and defined with the effort. She got the table where she wanted it, grabbed the back of her chair, and dragged it to the new location, taking her glass of wine from my hand. She sat down, crossed her elegant legs, and shoved the cheese plate to the center of the table. As I pulled my own chair over to join her, I looked back at the smoker. He was hastily stubbing his cigar out.

I was thinking that any woman who could haul a wrought-iron table several feet over cobblestones had to be strong enough to swing a golf club with enough force to kill a man.

"I can't stand smokers. I'm a runner. I run marathons. That's how I met Graham."

"I didn't know he was a runner." I tasted my wine. I liked it. It was cold and clean-tasting, faintly sweet.

Mai shook her head and smiled. "He wasn't. Graham liked to do his sweating in an air-conditioned gym." She slid her glasses down to the tip of her small nose and looked at me over the frames. "You a friend of Graham's?"

"No. Not really. I knew him and we were friendly, but I didn't know him well enough to call him a friend."

She nodded. "Umm. He never mentioned you. I would have remembered. He never mentioned any friends much. I'm not sure he had close friends. Acquaintances, colleagues, but not friends. Only me. Graham . . . he was close to me. *I* knew him well enough to call him 'friend.' "

"What about Honey?" I asked. "Didn't Honey know Graham?" I hate it when the spouse is completely left out of the equation. It's another betrayal.

Mai didn't miss the challenge. She set her glass down and leaned way over the table toward me, even rising a few inches from her chair. She looked me full in the eyes. I looked back into the lenses of those sunglasses.

"No. Honey did not know Graham. She never knew him at all. She never wanted to."

She held my eyes an uncomfortable while longer, and then slowly settled back into her chair.

"You want me to feel guilty, Mr. Wells? I'm the 'other' woman, right?" She gave a snort. "I feel guilty for a lot of things, so don't you worry. The kids, yeah, about them, I feel guilty."

Mai rolled her glass of wine on its base, the red liquid rising nearly to the lip of the glass. She pressed her lips together and her smooth forehead furrowed. No Botox there.

"Mostly, I feel guilty that Graham is dead, that we could have had our life together, and I put up these . . . I made him . . . we could have been happy."

A drop of wine escaped from the glass, fell through the wrought-iron lattice top, and made a star-shaped red splash on Mai's exposed thigh. "If I had let us." She took a big breath. The drop of wine on her leg looked like a small birthmark. My hand wanted to reach out and wipe the wine off her tanned leg. I didn't. It was the sort of impulse you learn to quell if you want to be a happily married man.

"Just so you know, Mr. Wells, life isn't perfect. Not in the real world. Your stained-glass world, everything all rosy in there, all the happy families. Bad things happen to bad people, good things happen to good people. That's what you believe, right? You get what you deserve?"

See, I get that all the time. Why do people assume that preachers have the mental outlook of a twelve-year-old? A sheltered twelve-year-old? People tell us things they

wouldn't share with their dog. Grand-
mothers have shared secrets that gave me
nightmares. I know of obsessions that I can't
find a name for in Wikipedia. I have seen,
and shared, suffering.

I said, "You think I believe the world is
righteous and free of pain? That good
people don't suffer? Do you know the book
of Job? Heard of Father Damien or read
Dietrich Bonhoeffer?"

Mai thrust her chin out. "Yeah, preacher,
I have." That surprised me. Assuming she
was telling the truth — preachers hear more
than their share of lies, too.

I said, "Me, too."

The chin stayed out there a second longer,
then Mai relaxed.

"I got nothing against Honey Garcia. Graham married her when he was, what?
Twenty-five, I think. Right after law school.
What do you know at twenty-five?" Mai
recrossed her lean legs, shook her head, rue-
ful, and the sway of her hair, and the waft
of that light, bright scent, those lean, lithe
legs, made me do a spiritual girding. "Here's
the thing, preacher . . ."

I said, "Could you call me Walker? Or
Bear?"

She looked up at me, her mouth pursed
in amusement.

"You want me to call you 'Bear'?"

"It's . . . Walker would be fine."

Mai snatched her glasses off. "Honey didn't love Graham. She couldn't love Graham because she didn't *know* Graham, you understand? Honey loved her *vision* of Graham, the Graham she thought he should be. You get that? She didn't love the man. She loved a figment of her own imagination. What she had created in her mind. That's what she loved. Me? I loved the man. I loved Graham."

I said, "How do you know?"

"That I loved him?" Mai wiped a ruby-stained mouth with the back of her hand.

"That Honey didn't love the real Graham? That she loved an illusion?" I asked.

"Because he told me so, Walker, that's how I know. Graham told me so."

"Maybe Graham didn't know Honey. Maybe Honey knew exactly who Graham was, and she loved him, as best a human woman can love a human man."

She stopped on that, her hand against her mouth, her eyes on mine. I could see her mind whirling behind those large, dark eyes, sooty with mascara and grief. Just as clearly, I saw the moment of rejection.

"No. A man knows when he is loved. And anyway, it doesn't matter. Graham loved *me.*"

That's what it comes down to so often. Dante's second circle. When "love" is your god, you can justify whatever it is you want. You did it for "love."

"Do you think Graham loved Honey when he married her?"

At that, Mai gave me the stink eye and took a long swallow of her wine. Mai Dinh hadn't come to me for counseling, or moral direction, or even advice. I'd forced my company on her because I wanted information. "I apologize," I said.

"You should."

"Well, I just did."

"You're married, right?"

"I am."

"How long?"

"More than twenty years."

"And you love her?" One delicate eyebrow rose, volumes spoken.

"Oh, yes. I do. Absolutely and completely. Annie Laurie is, I mean, she's my soul mate. If there is such a thing. I'm tied to her, body and soul. We fight sometimes, of course" — like within the past hour, and I didn't have a clue what about unless it was a hormonal thing; Annie's, not mine — "but yes. I love Annie."

Deliberately, Mai put her elbows on the

table, one hand steadying her goblet, and leaned forward.

"And what would you do, Walker, if you met your Annie today?"

"What?"

"Twenty years ago, you meet and marry a nice woman, everything pretty much okay, or maybe not-so-okay, then all these years later, you meet Annie Laurie, your 'soul mate.' What happens then?"

I took a piece of bread and tore it into bite-sized pieces.

It could have happened like that. Before I met Annie, there was a girl — well, there were lots of girls. When you play football for the University of Texas, girls are part of the perks package, or seemed like it anyway. There was this one girl, though, Serena, and man, she had me skinned and gutted. Turned me inside out, Serena did. I even took her home to meet my folks and I had never, ever done that before. My mother was taken with Serena. My brothers thought she was way too hot for me.

My dad asked me to walk our dog Ladybird with him before Serena and I drove back to Austin through the cool, dark, fall evening.

Ladybird had done her selective spot choosing and had finished her business before Dad had gotten around to what he wanted to say.

He said, "Serena is a beautiful woman, Bear, and you aren't going to be able to hear me, son, but try to keep this in the back of your mind. How many times did that girl put you down in front of your mom and me?"

"What?"

"You know, the digs about your car, no awards during the football banquet — that bit about Tucker getting all the family good looks."

"Well, he did. Even Mom says Tucker is the best looking."

"I don't think I'd want the woman I love telling me my brother was better looking."

"Mom tells you all the time that Uncle Richard got all the looks and you got the brains."

There was a pause.

"Yes, she does."

Which left me nothing to say at all.

Serena and I said our good-byes, and when I pulled out of the driveway, I was every bit as much in love with Serena as I had been when I pulled in.

But my ears were primed. All the ride home, and the days to come, I began to be aware of the teaspoons of diminishment Serena dosed out, all flavored with her sugar to take the bitterness away.

We broke up before Christmas.

Mai leaned closer in, allowing me a glimpse of cleavage.

"Graham was my soul mate. I was his."

Getting a tad too close over this table. I leaned back in my chair and pushed away from the table, making a show of stretching out my legs.

Mai watched my show and settled back in her chair. She smirked.

"Don't worry, preacher, you're safe with me. I'm not going to eat you." Another smirk.

There wasn't any point in denials. I was already feeling nibbled on by those small white teeth.

"You were going to tell me how you met Graham."

"Yeah. I was. Now, I don't think so." She drank down half her glass at one go.

I wanted some ice water. And some peanuts or Chex Mix or something. I broke off a piece of the cheese that looked like cheddar and popped it in my mouth. It wasn't cheddar — the texture was different and the flavor only got as far as cheddarish.

"You were saying it wasn't what I thought," I reminded her.

"That's right! It wasn't. Not some bar thing, Internet chat room. Not like that."

The waiter breezed by but missed my signal.

"So how was it?"

So she told me.

## TWENTY-NINE

"I was training for a marathon — this was late January last year. I had already run, oh, maybe fifteen miles. I was tired. I had another three, four miles to home. I was running on the shoulder of Highway 6, okay, not smart, but my route had me on 6 only, what, a half mile? It was getting dark, and this, this truck, not a pickup, you know, a big van, like they use for a business, he's driving too fast and he, swoosh! Right past me, so close, and it startled me, you know; I stumbled and fomp! I'm slipping and right over the edge I go into the ditch. Oh, my God. I'm all scraped up, my elbows and my knees, all down my leg here." She ran a hand down a perfectly toned, caramel-colored leg. Mai was short, but a lot of her height was in those nicely shaped legs.

"And, oh my God, you know, that nasty water in the bottom of a ditch? That's all over me, and mud. The stink! The truck didn't stop. He probably never saw me. So I crawl out of that stinking ditch and I'm bleeding, no broken bones, thank God, and all wet . . . what a mess."

Mai ran her finger around the rim of her glass and then took a sip. That's all that was left.

She hadn't touched the bread or cheese.

I said, "And then?"

Mai picked up the menu and did some perusing, pulled a pair of jeweled reading glasses out of her purse and perched them on the end of her tiny nose, and perused some more.

Without looking up, she said, "A minister? Huh. You look more like a bouncer."

"So then what happened?" I wasn't insulted by the "bouncer" comment. I thought it was sort of cool.

She slapped the menu closed and whacked it down on the table. She did the neck-craning thing people do when they want a waiter. There was a total dearth of waiters. Mai sighed.

"So my legs are trembling — it shook me up, you know? That truck passing so closely. My running shoes are soaked . . . and I pull my phone out to call my dad, but it's soaking, too, so . . . I'm on Highway 6, I'm hurting all over, and now I'm cold, because I'm wet, and I'm not running anymore . . . Graham pulls up behind me. I mean, I don't know it's Graham. This black Mercedes pulls up behind me and Graham gets out. He's standing one foot out of the car, one foot in, and he yells, 'Are you all right? Do you need any help?' and I say, 'No, I'm fine.' So stupid because, you know, I am not fine. I am shaking all over now. You should eat some cheese. That's an Emmenthaler. You'll like it."

It looked like Swiss cheese. I cut a slice, put it on a piece of French bread, and laid it on the napkin next to her glass. I took a slice for myself, too. Tasted like Swiss cheese to me.

Mai took a bite of the bread and cheese and chewed. Our waiter made an appearance and she waved him down like she was warning an oncoming train of rail damage. She pointed to her empty glass and tapped an entry on the menu. He nodded and smiled and swanned off. Not a word spoken and I'd forgotten to ask for that ice water.

"So anyway. I'm telling you this because it's not what you're thinking."

I nodded. She put her sunglasses back on, took them off, and dropped them in her purse. Her dark eyes were red-rimmed and smudged with makeup, but the tears were gone.

"So. Graham hears me, 'Oh, no thank you, sir, I'm fine.' " She mimicked a high, little girl voice.

"But Graham is looking at me. He is really looking at me; he sees *me*, you know? Graham was someone who could really see what he was looking at."

She shook her head. "That sounds stupid, 'He could really see.' " Mai folded her tissue and put the corner under her eyes, catching new tears without wrecking the mascara that still clung to her lashes. Then she gave a great, unladylike blow of her nose, wadded the tissue up, and put it in her purse and withdrew a clean one. Glasses, cell phones, and purses have taken care of the current "what to do with your hands" problem. A generation ago, it was cigarettes. Before that, I have no idea. Maybe knitting.

"I don't know how to say it better. It's like . . . he wasn't, 'Here I am, Good Samaritan, poor lady. Oh? You fine? You don't need my help? Okay, that's good, I got places to go, but yeah, I did a good thing.' No. Graham stands there, half in, half out of his car, looking at me, and I'm thinking, 'Go, then,' because I'm about to cry, and, you know, crying, that's charming on a young woman, not so good on an old one." She gave that wry smile again.

I said, "You're not old."

She did that up and down thing with her eyebrows that women do to say, "Well, you're a liar, but thanks for making the effort."

"Graham gets out of his car and comes over and looks me over, taking everything in; I'm shaking hard now. Jesus, I was so cold, and maybe in shock some, too. I'm wearing running shorts and a singlet, that's all. He says, 'I think I'd better take you to the hospital.' I say, 'Could you drive me home instead? It's not far. My dad will take care of me.' And he says sure and opens the passenger door for me and then I stop, because, his nice leather seats, and I'm not only muddy, but I ran at least fifteen miles, so, you know, I've been sweating."

She laughed a full, throaty, unselfconscious laugh. It was very attractive.

"I do not smell like a lady! He sees what I'm thinking and he gives my shoulder a push. 'Don't worry about the seats. They'll come clean.' "

Her second glass of wine arrived. She held her hand up to detain the waiter; did a sniff, sip, and swirl; nodded her approval; and handed him the empty glass, adding, "Go ahead and bring me another one of these. I like this better than that." A finger pointing at the empty the waiter held. So I'm guessing she really liked that second wine because she'd polished off the first without a quibble.

"On the way home, Graham reaches across me, and I'm thinking, 'Oh my God, he's going to grope me,' but no, he pushes the seater-heater button on my door and then he turns the heat up high, and oh, God, in a minute I'm starting to warm up. It feels so good, that heat pouring over my legs, and the hot seat warming my back and my butt. And the new car smell. I like that, you know? He doesn't ask any questions, only, 'Turn here? How far down?' and then we're at my house, my dad's house. I'm all 'thank you' and 'send me the bill when you get your car cleaned,' getting out of the car. Graham turns the car off and he gets out, too. I say, 'No need, my dad, blah, blah blah.' But he comes to the door and I reach inside my waistband, very ladylike, right? And I unpin my key and open the door and I'm calling, 'Dad! Dad?' and there's no answer because he's not there. My dad."

I ask, "You live with your mom and dad?" She had to be over forty.

"For now. My mom died a few years ago, and I got divorced. My dad needed me. So. Anyway Graham follows me into the house and he turns the lights on, it's full dark now, and he leads me over to sit on the stairs and he kneels down and holds my ankle and turns my leg this way and that, looking at the scrapes and saying, 'Does this hurt?' and rotates my ankle, 'Does this hurt?' I asked if he was a doctor and he smiles and shakes his head no, he's not a doctor, he's a lawyer.

"He says, 'Why don't you call your dad and let him know what's happened. Then you take a hot shower. I don't like that ditch water over all these open wounds.' Then he wants to know where the kitchen is, he's going to make me some hot tea."

She hunched her shoulders and spread her hands, palms up.

"Sounds crazy, I know. It's like, I'm waiting for my 'uh-oh' alarm to go off. There's this strange guy making himself at home, and I'm all alone. He's nice looking, sure, but Ted Bundy wasn't bad looking, either.

"I never got it. That 'uh-oh, bad idea' feeling — it never came. I call my dad and leave a message on his phone. I take a hot shower. Okay, sure, I locked the bathroom door. I take a long time, I wash my hair, I wash all the scraped places, get the gravel and the dirt out. I dress in shorts and a T-shirt because so many places are all bloody. My wet hair twisted in a towel. When I go downstairs, it's very quiet. I wonder if he left — I took such a long time in the shower.

"You want another glass?" Mai pointed to my glass. I'd barely touched it. "No? I'm having one more." She waved at the waiter to remind him and he nodded. He was being more than attentive. Mai was over forty, but she was a striking woman.

"Graham is in the kitchen, sitting at the table, reading the paper. I walked in and he jumped up and pulled a chair out for me. On the table is a teapot, a carton of milk, the sugar bowl, a mug. And bandages, cotton swabs, antiseptic, and tape."

She laughed. "You know, I should have been scared. He had to do a lot of looking around to find all this stuff. Well, the kitchen stuff, that was easy, but, you know, he had to go in my dad's bedroom and bathroom to find the first aid creams and bandages. I would never do that. Maybe in one of my brothers' houses, but a stranger's? No way.

"He pours me a mug of tea. 'Milk?' he says, 'Sugar?' I don't want to hurt his feelings, tell him, it's green tea, you don't put milk or sugar in green tea. And then he gets down on his knees, right? This handsome blond man in his expensive car, in his expensive suit, he gets down on his knees . . ."

Mai stopped. This was a mythopoeic moment in her life. She had to regain control of her voice.

"And he starts to dress all the scraped places. He was soooo careful, so gentle. And when I am all bandaged up, looking like a brown and white patchwork quilt, then he takes the towel off my head." She pantomimed this. "And this is the really weird, this part, but it didn't feel weird. Not when it was happening. Graham, he brushed my hair out, slowly, gently, he works out the tangles and he brushes my hair until it is all smooth and silky around me. He takes my hairbrush, and he brushes my hair, softly, softly, in the warm kitchen until my hair is all glossy, shiny, dry."

In a dreamy kind of way, Mai reached up and pulled the scarf and band off her hair. She shook her hair out, and ran her fingers through the silken weight of it. It fell below the seat of her chair, quite a sight, that mass of rippling black satin. The waiter stood stock-still, watching, before he reverently placed the third brimful glass in front of Mai.

I'm not attracted to small women. I feel big and clumsy around them, and I look silly when they stand next to me. But I didn't have any trouble understanding why Graham found this exotic woman, with her big eyes and her athletic body, and that lovely, self-deprecating smile, very appealing. She leaned her forehead on her hand and stared into her glass, her third glass. That's a lot to drink for a tiny woman.

"Why am I telling you?" she said. "So you won't think bad of Graham? Of us? You're a preacher; you think bad about everybody."

She drew out the "everybody."

That surprised me.

"Why would I think bad about everybody?"

"You said Alex saw us. Where did he see us?"

"Were you and Graham going to marry?"

"Oh, my God. Were we going to get married? I don't know. We wanted to, but my God, Graham has two children! Graham says, 'My marriage is over, we were never suited for each other, I can't make her happy, the kids — they're nearly grown up.' I say, 'Okay, she's so unhappy? She will divorce you. Then we're okay. Then we didn't break . . . then *I* didn't break up this family.' Months pass, and his wife . . . Gra-

401

ham says, 'I will tell her about us; she has a right to know, it will help her make the decision.' But I am not having it. It's all on me then, you know? 'Oh, this evil dragon woman, she comes and steals our daddy away.' Yeah, then his kids hate me forever. I tell Graham, 'No. If you tell your wife about us, you are forcing her to divorce you. If you tell her, then I am gone. I am not going to be the reason why your marriage fails.' I meant it, too. My husband? He left me for someone else. I didn't love him the way I should have, so it shouldn't have hurt, but it did. I was humiliated. I . . . that took something away from me, that he chose someone else. And my daddy. God, I thought he would kill Jonathon when he found out, he was so angry. I was glad we lived two thousand miles away."

Mai gave a laugh when she saw my face.

"No, Mr. Wells, I didn't mean my daddy would really kill my husband just because I was sad at being left. My dad is a good man. A real hero." She leaned over and tapped her third wineglass against my still-full glass. A tiny tribute to her dad.

"I told Graham I was not going to do that to another woman. What Jonathon did to me." Mai shook her head with the deliberation of the slightly intoxicated.

My Friday meeting with Graham came clear. He had to have a divorce from Honey so he could live with Mai, but if *he* initiated the divorce with Honey, Graham would assuredly have lost Mai. Graham was well and truly trapped; only Honey could release him — and Mai had forbidden Graham to give Honey the one piece of the puzzle that would have enabled Honey to let Graham go.

Mai put her pink tongue to the tip of a finger and drew it around the rim of her glass. It rang with a sweet, low note.

"Graham said, 'Maybe you don't love me the way I love you. Maybe you want me to leave.' "

The waiter passed our table with a laden tray. Mai flapped her hand at him and seesawed her wineglass, showering drops down through the open metalwork of the cast-iron table. He hesitated and caught my eye. I shook my head. No more wine. I mouthed, "Ice water." He nodded.

Mai's hand suddenly flew to her mouth; her eyes were squeezed shut on the tears that were welling. Her left hand held the stem of her wineglass so tightly that I thought she might snap it. She was breathing raggedly, trying to control sobs. She drank off the rest of her wine as if it were water. It took her three attempts before she could speak without choking.

"I was so screwed! I couldn't keep Graham, but I could not lose Graham. Not one more. I could not lose one more."

The strong, competent, striding woman who had met me at the Vineyard melted away. She wasn't looking at me anymore, or talking to me. Her gaze and her speech were directed inward. Her voice was a whisper and her accent had thickened. Her forehead was creased and she looked older.

"If I had said, 'Yes, tell her, leave her, come to me, *viens à moi, viens à moi*. Graham would be alive. He would be here, *avec moi*." She brought her fist to her heart and thumped her chest twice. "Instead of with the others. *Tous les autres. Mon père, ma mère, ma soeur, mes frères. Mon grand-père, mes tantes, et mes oncles- tous, tous*."

I put my hand over her trembling fingers and held them still. I don't know where Mai was at that moment, I didn't know where the French came from, but she wasn't sitting in a suburban wine bar on a sunny, mild March afternoon.

Mai recovered herself slowly. The waiter brought a glass of water and I set it in front of her. She drank from it, took a tissue from her purse, and moistened it on the perspiring side of the glass. She patted her face with the cool, damp tissue.

"Oh, my God," Mai said, her voice back under control. "What time is it?" She lifted her wrist and looked at a nonexistent watch. "So late! I gotta go."

She pushed her chair back and stood, one hand on the chair back. She laid a couple of twenties on the table but I folded them up and put them back in her purse. She didn't notice.

"Are you sure you're all right?" I asked. She didn't look all that steady. She dug in her purse and withdrew her sunglasses and keys, perched the glasses on the tip of her nose.

"Mr. Wells, you didn't ask me what you came here to ask me." She took a step to the side and stepped off one high-heeled sandal; she nearly tumbled over but she caught herself with the back of the chair, adjusted the sandal, and looked at me; with her standing and me sitting, we were just about on eye level.

I hesitated.

"Did you kill Graham Garcia, Mai?"

She tilted her head back and laughed that rich, full laugh again and it ended in a long descending sigh. She looked me straight in the eyes.

"Oh, my God, Mr. Wells, I would gladly have laid down my life for Graham Garcia."

Mai hefted her purse under her arm, and walked back toward the parking garage. She was unsteady at first, but as she got farther away from me, her gait grew longer and more confident.

She hadn't answered the question.

# THIRTY

After the waiter brought the bill for the wine and cheese — sixty-four dollars, not including the tip — I drank the rest of my wine and ate every last bit of bread and cheese, even the runny one. It was the principle.

The first thing I needed to do was find Alex Garcia and reassure him, now that I knew for certain, that what he had seen had been bad, but nowhere near as bad as he thought. His father had been an adulterer, but he wasn't a pedophile.

I calculated the family would be home from the interment around seven, seven thirty. If I gave Alex time to greet the people who would be at the house preparing a meal for the family, I could speak with him at eight thirty or so. The day of your father's funeral is a terrible time to have news dumped on you, but I didn't want Alex thinking what he was thinking a second longer than he had to.

Once Alex understood, I also had to persuade him to go with me to speak to Detective Wanderley. Wanderley hadn't met Mai, and didn't have any idea what kind of strength her little body held. And with those stilettos, Mai would be at least, well, five-three. Maybe. Not that women wear stilettos on golf courses, even in Sugar Land. What her motive could be, I couldn't guess, but she was clearly unstable — her motive might not be rational.

That left me plenty of time now to go home and make peace with Annie Laurie.

I would have, too, if her sister hadn't been there.

Stacy occupied all the counter space in our kitchen with her Williams-Sonoma bags. Annie Laurie was taking a bowl of steamed edamame out of the microwave. Stacy was at the table pouring out two glasses of white wine, something from a bottle with a starfish on the label. Baby Bear had been locked out on the back porch because Stacy doesn't like to get dog hair on her clothes.

Stacy and Annie Laurie look like sisters, and they don't. Seeing Stacy with Annie Laurie is like hearing a familiar folk song covered by an avant-garde rock band. Stacy is two years older than Annie and dresses like she's two decades younger. Their features are shaped the same except that Stacy's are stretched, exaggerated. Her mouth is wider, her nose is longer, her eyes are bigger and rounder. Stacy is taller, thinner, and her boobs are bigger. Given the angularity of her hips, my bet is the boobs have been enhanced, but Annie won't tell me.

Right now Stacy's hair was the same honey-gold as Annie's — their natural color. But I've seen Stacy's hair a flaming red, platinum blond, deep mahogany. To make up for wearing her hair in its natural, and conventional, shade, Stacy had cropped it in a short, blunt, Cleopatra cut. Annie had changed from the dress she had worn to the funeral and was now wearing jeans, white Keds, and a button-down shirt. Stacy had on spike-heeled Gladiator sandals that laced nearly to her knees, and a formless shift of coarse fabric that made me think of sackcloth. Her earrings looked like a fold of chain mail and they brushed her shoulders.

"Bear!" Stacy cried when I walked in. "We were just talking about you! Hold on a sec, I'll get you a glass."

"No thanks," I said and crossed over to peck Annie's unresponsive cheek. "It's barely five."

Annie lifted her eyebrows and took the

glass from Stacy.

"Hmmm. You smell like you've had a glass already, Bear," Annie said.

"Oh! Yeah, I had a meeting . . . ah, at the Vineyard."

Stacy slapped my shoulder, her faux ivory bangles clacking. "You dog. Elders' meetings at wine bars — strange times coming to the Church of Christ."

"No, I, uh . . ." Stacy talks too fast.

"Bear, we don't care. Here." Stacy grabbed another wineglass out of the dishwasher. "Tell me what you think of this." She sloshed wine into the glass, filling it three-quarters full. "This is a New Zealand sauvignon blanc — Starborough — screwoff top, but don't let that mislead you. All the New Zealand wineries are using screwoffs. It's earth-friendly or some such garbage, but it doesn't hurt the wine, only the presentation."

"Listen, Stacy, if I could borrow Annie Laurie for a moment . . ."

"Oh, she's not still mad at you. Or she won't be after we've had a couple of glasses of wine and talked over all your bad qualities, and taken a second to list down your good ones," Stacy said. "Drink that wine and tell me what you think of it. Go on, sit down, Bear, I want to show ya'll my steals."

Stacy doesn't buy "deals." Stacy buys "steals." Shopping is a cross between a blood sport and an art form for Stacy. I didn't need to see her purchases itemized to know that she had gotten at least seventy-five percent off on all of them — she won't slow down for less than seventy-five percent off. Now, whether or not Stacy needed another pure linen, banquet-size, brocade tablecloth, which, even at seventy-five percent off, had cost two hundred dollars — that was between her and my long-suffering brother-in-law, Chester.

Annie was resolutely refusing to meet my eye, which seemed to me to mean that she might, indeed, need a couple of glasses of wine before she was ready to hear me out.

It's hard enough talking to an unhappy woman without doing it when she is both unhappy with you, and unwilling to hear you. I decided it could keep and it turned out I was painfully correct.

It felt good to take off the suit I'd worn for the funeral. I shut the bedroom door so I could let Baby Bear in from the backyard, and he took a long, sloppy drink from the water bowl Annie keeps under the bathroom sink. He shook the water from his hairy cheeks and pushed his nose into my knees, muttering complaints about having been shut out of the kitchen when something like a party had been going on. I pulled his ears gently and explained that I, too, wasn't welcome in the kitchen right now.

After I'd changed into jeans and a T-shirt and slipped on my sneakers sockless, I had a great idea.

Baby Bear loves to ride in the car. I'd take Baby Bear with me to the Garcias'; I could leave him in the car while I talked to Alex, or if Jo was still there, she could give Baby Bear a romp in the Garcias' spacious yard while Alex and I talked. After I'd given Alex the news, and persuaded him to fill Wanderley in, I'd drop Jo and Baby Bear off at the house and swing by Wanderley's office. Baby Bear is good company; he doesn't go all hormonal on me.

I clicked a lead on Baby Bear's collar to make sure no dog hair got on Stacy's dress, which, come to think of it, looked like it could have been woven out of dog hair *and* sackcloth, told Annie Laurie my plan and that I expected to be back for dinner. She said why didn't I pick up dinner since she didn't think she would be cooking. I said fine and gave her another unreturned kiss.

I guarantee you that at any given time, Stacy knows more about the state of my marriage than I do. Stacy and Annie Laurie

412

speak the same language — it's a shorthand code that calls on years of history from before I was in Annie's life. It doesn't bother me. Stacy is good people and she likes me because, once a year or so, I can get her three heathen sons to sit down and listen. Most of the time she's working on my behalf.

As I headed out to the garage, Baby Bear in tow, I said, "Stacy, if ya'll are already on the second glass, please feel free to open another bottle. It looks like it's going to take a third glass before Annie's ready to stop being mad at me."

Stacy said, "Shoot. I knew we should have made it martinis. I can convince Annie of anything once she's had two martinis."

I paused at the door. I may be the only Church of Christ minister who has to keep jalapeño-stuffed olives in the fridge for martinis, not cheese plates. For my sister-in-law.

"No martinis. You staying for dinner?"

Stacy shook her head.

"Nope," she said. "Not unless you want Chester and the boys, too?"

I like Chester, and I love Stacy's three sons, but having the boys over is like having three Jack Russell terriers on fast-forward. I was not up to it.

"Sometime soon," I said, and shut the door. I grabbed two bottles of water from the garage fridge and Baby Bear and I were off.

# THIRTY-ONE

Dogs are pure. Everything is on the surface — their feelings, their needs, their likes and dislikes. Baby Bear leaned his head out the open window and let his velvet ears flap in the wind. His joy was so infectious that I couldn't help catching it. A good dog is a great help in mood control. I mean, I'm not moody, but everyone gets a little blue sometimes.

The Garcias' capacious front yard gravel drive and gravel parking spaces can hold twenty or more cars. I had to park on the road. As I did, another car slid in behind me and a couple slipped out — the guy was in slacks, his tie loosened and his jacket folded over his arm. The woman wore a dress you'd either wear to church or a secretarial job. I looked down at my faded Gap jeans and sneakers and mentally slapped my forehead. Right. Honey would assume I was coming straight from the interment. So I would be dressed in jeans and a tee why?

There was nothing for it. I rolled the windows all the way down. Even in this mild weather, a closed car can heat up fast. With the windows well open, Baby Bear would stay plenty comfortable. I pulled out the foldable pet bowl I keep in the console, filled it with cold water from one of the bottles I'd grabbed, and set the bowl on the floor of the passenger side. Since Baby Bear was too big to fit in the passenger foot space, he had to hang his head down from the seat to drink, but he'd never found that to be a problem.

Because, at 180 pounds, Baby Bear was a large, a very large, ungainly fellow, I could leave the windows down without fear that someone would snatch him, and because he's an obedient dog, in a general kind of way, I could say "Stay," and know that he would. Now, Baby Bear had sense enough to get out of the car if it caught on fire, or started rolling down the street, or if a meteor hit me and he ran out of water. That's why I could never bear to lock him up without an escape.

The gathering had spilled out onto the lawn and I shook lots of hands as I maneuvered through the stands of blooming azaleas. Found myself murmuring "Ran home to change" to a few faces that raised eyebrows over my informal dress.

The front door was open to the early evening air, and the clinking of glass and cutlery mingled with the rumble of many voices flowing out onto the porch.

The ladies of St. Laurence and the Church of Christ had plied the Garcias with casseroles and cakes, and had I been hungry, I could have helped myself to Gina Redman's airy white rolls or Irene Hayden's spectacular lemon chiffon pie. Nothing should taste that good. I decided to take a couple of Gina's rolls before I left. I'd have taken a piece of the pie, too, if I could have wrapped it up in a paper towel.

Cruz was wearing the skirt and white blouse of her navy suit and, in place of the pillbox hat, had a square of white lace bobby-pinned to her hair. She held a tray filled with cups of coffee and she handed me a cup of coffee I didn't want, looked me up and down, and said, "I didn't see you at the cemetery."

I nodded, and asked where I could find Alex and Jo.

She thought about pushing her question, decided against it, and said, "They're in his room." She gestured down a hall with her chin and said, "Third door on the left."

There was a twenty-minute delay, with all the conversations I got pulled into, before I could head down the hall to Alex's room. I passed the study and noticed the door was cracked. I don't know why I did it, but I pushed the door open.

A large dark-haired man was sitting at Graham's desk, going through his drawers. One of the suits from the funeral. He was intent and didn't notice me.

I said, "Hey."

Guy jumped like I'd touched him with a cattle prod.

"Looking for something?" I said, no smiles.

The guy looked wary.

"Honey said . . . I'm looking for some business papers; Graham was working on something for me. Honey said I could . . ."

I came all the way into the study and kind of squared myself out, the way you do on the line.

"Graham didn't work for you. He may have worked *with* you. I don't care what Honey said. Get out of Graham's study."

"Listen . . ." He put on some bluster but he didn't wear it well. "Honey said —"

"Five seconds and I'm going to help you out."

"Who the hell are you?" he said, slamming a drawer shut, grabbing a handful of papers and standing up.

I blocked him at the door. The guy went all puffer fish.

"I want to see your driver's license," I said.

"What are you, security? Honey hired security?"

In the space of a day, I'd been told I looked like a bouncer and mistaken for security. All that working out was worth it.

I reached behind him and plucked his wallet out of his pants pocket. He yipped like I'd goosed him, which I most assuredly had not. The name on his driver's license was Bradford Williams. I thought about keeping the license but Wanderley might see that as Father Browning it.

The guy was getting himself worked up. I leaned into him. Only a little bit.

I said, "Walk down that hall and tell Honey you have to go. Don't come back to this room. Don't even think about coming back to this house. Not ever. And you should be expecting a call from Detective Wanderley."

The guy's red face paled.

"I don't know who you —" he began, but I snatched the papers out of his hand and gave him a push to help him out the door.

He took a few steps backward, giving me the stink eye and thinking about carrying this further, but he was not stupid — lawyers never are, in my experience — and he thought better about it. Williams turned around and hurried down the hall.

I walked over and dropped the papers on Graham's desk. A framed photo caught my eye and I picked it up. The picture showed the Garcia family on a sailboat. A gap-toothed Alex looked about six years old, wearing white swim shorts, his skin tanned brown and his hair sun-bleached. Graham had his arm around Honey. She had on a navy Bettie Page swimsuit, her red hair flying in the wind. Honey looked like a 1940s movie star. Jenasy was grinning up at the camera. I studied Graham. He had that Great Gatsby look that Ralph Lauren favors in his models. His smile was wide and easy. But the eyes. Was there a shadow there? Something unconnected, distant? Or was I getting all airy-fairy?

I looked at the glowing family a long time and then put the photo carefully back on the desk and locked the study door behind me.

Alex's door was closed — Merrie and Jo are strictly forbidden to be in a guy's bedroom with the door shut — so I knocked. I'm big on not putting myself in the way of seeing something I know for sure I don't want to see.

No one answered and I knocked harder, and Alex yelled, "It's open!" which it wasn't, but it was unlocked and I walked in.

Alex was sitting on the floor, his back against the bed's footboard, headphones the size of traffic controllers' strapped to his ears. No Jo.

I said, "Where's Jo?"

Alex looked up at me in surprise. He took the headphones off and pushed a button on a complicated-looking control panel. He stood up. He had changed his clothes, too. Like me, he was wearing jeans and sneakers; he still had the dress shirt on, but the neck was unbuttoned and the tail was out. His hair was loose around his neck.

"She left with Cara. They were going to Cara's to change, then your house, I think. They're planning to be back here later. I'll have her home on time."

"Well, all right," I said. "It was you I wanted to talk to, Alex. You got a minute?"

He grimaced. "I'm not going anywhere."

I looked around for a place to sit and settled in an easy chair covered in a flag print fabric. His bedspread was out of the

421

same fabric and there were framed antique flags on the walls. The room was unbelievably tidy for an adolescent boy, but I assumed that was due more to Cruz's ministrations than Alex's.

"You collect flags?" I asked, gathering a pile of books from the seat of the chair.

Alex shook his head and sat down on his bed, one hand clasping the wrist of the other around his drawn-up knees.

"Nope," he said. "The designer probably thought it was a nice, masculine theme I could grow into. Those flags" — he waved a hand at the tattered flags that were matted and framed around the room — "they aren't really old or anything. They make the flags look that way on purpose."

"Does that bother you?" Having this artificial décor chosen for him. I sat down on the flag chair.

He looked surprised again.

"What? No. What do I care what's on the walls? I'm not some emo, get all bent out of shape over furniture. Are we going to talk about Jo?" His face was wary.

I was looking at one of the books I'd picked up.

"Huh. *Ender's Game*. Jo has to read this, too."

Alex smiled. "I know. That's her book. I'm

reading it to her."

I snapped the book shut. "You're what?" I'd heard what he said.

"I'm reading it to her. That's why her English grade has gone up. That's why all her grades have gone up. Because of me." His smile wasn't smug. It was beatific — the smile of a man who loves his job and is good at it.

"Why are you reading it to her? Why doesn't she just read the book herself? Is that so hard?" I slapped the book shut and dropped it on top of the pile of books at my feet.

He looked at me like I'd asked for a cup of mouse droppings.

"Uh, yeah. It's that hard if you're freaking dyslexic."

"Jo's not dyslexic." With my toe, I spread the pile of books out. They were all Jo's.

"Yes, Mr. Wells, Jo is dyslexic."

"I don't believe it."

He grinned at me and jumped off the bed to gather Jo's books back into a neat pile.

"Just because you don't believe, doesn't mean it isn't true, Mr. Wells. Didn't I hear you say something like that from the pulpit?"

I hate it when people quote me to myself.

"All right, then, define dyslexia. The way

the term is used today, it's too broad to mean anything."

"Ummhumm, okay, that's fair. What is agreed is that the term covers people who process information differently from most of us. 'Dyslexia' " — Alex made quote marks with his fingers — "pretty much applies to people who are smart, who've had every opportunity to learn, but still have trouble reading. Does that fit Jo?"

"What fits Jo is that it's easier for her to use her pretty face to get a boy to do her homework for her than it is for Jo to do it herself." My hands were kneading the arms of the easy chair. I forced myself to relax.

Alex looked up at me with his arms full of my daughter's books. I decided I'd be taking those books home with me when I went.

"Did you just call Jo a whore?" Alex said. His face was rigid.

"Did I what!?"

"And a cheat. Think about what you just said, Mr. Wells. You said Jo trades on her looks for favors, and you said I was doing her work for her. A whore and a cheat."

"I never —"

"You need to be careful how you talk about Jo. You need to be careful how you talk *to* Jo. She's dyslexic. She is not stupid. She hears everything you say and she hears what you don't say, what's underneath your words. She hears it, Mr. Wells, and you are sowing the wind and you will reap the whirlwind."

It's encouraging that young people can quote scripture. I'm not all that thrilled with the way they've been quoting it to *me*.

I spread my hand out and touched my index finger.

"In the first place, Alex —"

"Don't do the finger thing."

"What?"

"You aren't counting off sermon points. Talk to me. Don't preach at me. I hate that finger thing even when you do it from the pulpit. It makes you sound like you're talking to a first grade class."

Big breath as I tucked that away to consider later. I put my hands on my knees.

"Not in one million years would I call Jo a whore or a cheat or allow a man to continue to stand if *he* did."

Alex opened his mouth and I held my hand up.

"However, I take your point about being more careful about my words. I'll do that. I'll try, okay?"

He nodded.

"If Jo let's you do her work for her —"

"I don't do her work for her! Excuse me,

Mr. Wells, but get a freaking clue!" Alex slammed the pile of books down on his desk. "I read her assignments to her; I do a lot of her writing. I mean like, I take dictation. All the thoughts, all the words, those are Jo's."

"Then what does she need you for?"

"She can't read the books! Can't you get that? She's dyslexic! Do you think Jo's stupid? Because if she's not dyslexic, if there isn't something different about the way her brain works, then why can't your kid read?"

"She can read!"

"Have you *heard* her? When's the last time you heard Jo read? She sounds like a fourth grader — like a slooooow fourth grader. How do you think that makes her feel at school? Especially with Miss Merrie Hotshit and her straight A's blazing trails through Clements ahead of her."

I felt my face grow hot.

"If Jo needed some extra help with her schoolwork, she could get that at home. For crying out loud, her mom designs lessons," I said.

Alex turned his desk chair around and sat on it backward, straddling the back, his arms crossed over the top of the chair back.

"Oh, yeah?" he said. "Jo said the last time she got her mom to read to her, you came bursting into her room and told Mrs. Wells to stop treating Jo like a baby, and 'let her get on with it.' "

I spread my fingers across my knees again, trying to keep my voice level.

"Alex, Jo's not going to be able to get through college if she has to have someone do all her reading for her."

"You think?" Alex's tone implied that I had made a miraculous observation. "Mr. Wells," he continued, "Jo's not going to get through *high school* unless someone does all her reading for her, and if that someone is me, then I'm screwed. Because there's no way she's going to stay with me if she can't break up with me."

"Okay, I think I missed something . . . run that by me again?"

Alex waved off my objection. "It's like, if Jo was blind, you'd get her Braille books or audio books or you would read all her school stuff to her, you and her mom. But because you can't see what's wrong with Jo, you don't believe anything is, so you don't help her and you won't let Mrs. Wells, either. Or you know what I think? Maybe if you've got a kid who's not perfect, maybe that means God's favorite quarterback isn't perfect, either. What do you think?"

"I was a lineman," I said.

"What-freaking-ever. You know what? I start reading to her, not that much at first, but it makes this huge difference in her grades — you've noticed that, right? The more I read to her, the better her grades get, and Jo loooooves that. You think she doesn't care about her grades? That is so wrong. You completely don't know your own kid. Jo is mortified . . ." Alex stopped and checked the word in his head. "No, I'm right, 'mortified' is not too strong a word. Jo is mortified when she gets lousy grades. She acts like it's no big deal, but damn, she is red from here" — Alex touched his hairline — "to here." He put a hand at the neck of his shirt. "Even her ears go all red.

"So I'm reading to her and she gets better grades and that makes Jo all happy, so I'm happy, too, because, I'm in love with her, man, I really, really am. But we'll have a fight over something stupid, just nothing, and in the middle of the fight, Jo will go all still and get quiet and then she'll apologize, even when I know she's not sorry, even when I know I'm the one who's in the wrong.

"And I finally figured it out. Jo is afraid to make me mad because she needs me to read to her." Alex shook his head, exasperated. "Well, I don't want her to need me that way.

I want Jo to love me back; I don't want her to be grateful to me."

He said "grateful" as if it were a curse. There will be a day in his future when he'll be looking for gratitude from the women in his life, but I got his point. I think I did.

I said, "Son, don't you think you and Jo are a little young to be tossing around a word like 'love'?"

Alex gave me a hard stare and then dropped his head to his folded forearms — very dramatically, I thought. Had some of his mother's genes.

"Uh, Mr. Wells? Did you hear anything I said?"

I shifted in the chair. Baby Bear was doing more waiting than I had expected him to have to.

"Alex, I heard you. But I don't want to talk to you about Jo right now. Or maybe ever. I do promise I'll discuss with her mother what you've shared with me. That will have to do for now, right?"

He gave an eloquent shrug.

"Alex, remember what you told me about your dad meeting a young girl? A girl you thought was Jo?" I said.

Alex shot his head up.

"I want to tell you what I've found out."

And then I told him. I didn't give him

names, and I didn't tell him how the affair had started; mainly I wanted to communicate that he had seen a woman with his dad, not a girl, not Jo.

Alex listened stone-faced until I'd finished. Once I had, he covered his stricken face with his hands and wept silently, his shoulders shaking. I got up and went to the bathroom that opened off his bedroom, found a clean washcloth (with a flag appliquéd to a corner), wet it, wrung it out, and then went back and handed it to the kid. He scrubbed his face violently. I laid my hand on the back of his neck for a moment, and then I sat on the end of his bed.

"This is what I want to do now, Alex," I said. "Tomorrow I'd like you to tell Detective Wanderley what you saw the night your father was killed."

Alex jerked.

"Not that I'm saying I think this woman had anything to do with his death" — I didn't want the kid getting all vigilante on me — "but she may well have been one of the last people to see your dad, and I think Wanderley needs that information."

"No freaking way," Alex said. His words were measured and decisive.

"What?" I said.

"You're doing that a lot, 'What?' You heard

me. No. I mean, yeah, it's better than if Dad was having an affair with a girl, and . . ." Alex teared up again. He swallowed, his throat making a clicking sound, and he took some time to control himself. "But Mom doesn't know anything was going on at all, and that's how I want it to stay. It's not as if this is going to be good news to her. And what about Jenasy? We're not real close — she can be a total ass. But she's my sister. She doesn't even know Mom and Dad have been fighting! She's been at school!"

Alex stood suddenly and his desk chair went over backward. He leaned over me, his fists clenched tightly by his side. His eyes were slits and he was talking through his teeth.

"You think my mom needs to deal with something like that right now? My dad having an affair with another woman? Your promise still stands, man; you gave me your word." The cords on the kid's neck were as prominent as a weight lifter's.

I stood up from my chair and Alex took a step back. If he hadn't, the top of my head would have cracked his chin — that's how close he was standing to me.

I haven't felt physically intimidated since I gave up football; I'm a big man, and I spent years getting pounded by some of the best.

431

A good number of the guys I came up against went on to play pro ball. That this half-a-glass of skim milk thought he could loom over me was a joke. The expression on his face, however, was not funny. It was creepy.

I kept my voice gentle.

"Sit your butt back down, Alex, and that little bit of business you just tried? You want to wait four or five years and fifty-plus pounds before you even think to work that one again, you hear me?"

Alex backed into his easy chair — the intensity in his face and muscles releasing at once. He looked flustered and embarrassed.

"I'm only telling you —" he started.

"You'll find most people can hear what you're telling them without you pulling that psycho-on-the-edge crap. You don't have to remind me of my promise. I'm over here talking to you, right? I didn't go all 911 on you, did I?"

"No, sir." Alex sounded like a different kid.

"Here's the thing, Alex. This business with another woman? That's going to come out. Detective Wanderley isn't a fool. The only reason I know about this before he does is because I fell into it, understand? Wanderley is going to find out, and so are your mom and Jenasy. You have to release me from my promise, Alex. It's time."

He wouldn't, though. He was just as set as ever. I wasted another half an hour trying to argue him out of his position. He wasn't having it.

Irene Hayden's lemon chiffon pie was long-past history before I gave up on getting Alex to do the right thing. Cruz had tucked away a few of Gina Redman's white rolls for me and had filled them with slices of honey-baked ham, ubiquitous at Texas funerals. I thanked her, made my good-byes, and left, frustrated in spite of the ham-filled rolls.

Baby Bear sat in the driver's seat, front paws against the dash on either side of the steering wheel. He looked like a large black bear in a circus act. He was terrifically glad to see me. He would have acted the same if I'd been gone ten minutes instead of over an hour. The dog has no sense of time. But twilight had turned to evening while I was in the Garcias' home, and Baby Bear doesn't like being left alone in the dark. I let him out to water the azaleas, which he did with the professional ardor he always gives to the task. After Baby Bear finished his business and I finished wiping the pool of drool off my seat, I gave him one of the ham-filled rolls. I ate the other two.

I was uneasy. The Jekyll and Hyde turn Alex had done had thrown me. I mean, the kid needs to put some weight on, but he's tall enough and strong enough to swing a Big Bertha, no question.

Alex had seen his father passionately kissing a strange woman. Alex thought it was Jo, and he thought he was in love with Jo. He was protective of his mother and Jenasy, even though Jenasy seemed to think he was useless. Could such a sight push a tightly strung teen over the edge? If you watch the news, you know a lot less can undo some people. According to Wanderley, unironed sheets could do the trick. Who the heck irons sheets anyway?

I had given my word to Alex that I wouldn't disclose what he had told me. Now I'd gotten the information from another source, but it was, essentially, still the information Alex had given me. I was tied by my promise.

One of my lawyer friends told me to never, ever make a promise without having a lawyer look at it — that verbal contracts were binding in Texas unless they involved real property. I don't know why I hardly ever take lawyers' advice. Almost all the lawyers I know are good and intelligent people and they are always right.

But what was I supposed to have done at the time — tell Alex to wait a minute while I got my lawyer on the phone so the lawyer could explain the possible ramifications of my promise?

There wasn't any escaping that Wanderley needed the information I had. It might be possible to convince Mai to speak to Wanderley on her own. If I explained that Alex was under suspicion, she might tell Wanderley that she had been with Graham after Alex left — but since she never knew Alex was there, it didn't make sense to hope she could clear the kid. The very fact that Mai was still keeping their affair a secret after Graham had been murdered seemed suspicious to me.

On impulse I turned left off Alcorn Oaks, toward Mai's house.

## THIRTY-TWO

The sixth house from the corner was a large redbrick vaguely traditional something. By which I mean that, as with almost every house in First Colony, it was not any specific architectural style. Early-Executive, maybe.

The yard was perfectly groomed by one of the many companies owned by second-generation Mexicans, operated by their college-educated sons and labored at by newly arrived Mexicans. The house had elaborate landscape lighting, which made it glow like a theater set in the early evening. I parked in front of the house, rolled the Volvo's windows down, and refilled Baby Bear's water bowl. I left a console light on to keep Baby Bear company.

The porch had one of those carriage lanterns with a flickering electric bulb that is supposed to simulate a gas lamp. There wasn't a doorbell next to the door. Instead, on the door, there was a well-polished brass knocker in the shape of a pineapple. The pineapple is a symbol of hospitality — who knows why. Pineapple sets my teeth on edge.

The door knocker gave a nice, resounding "Bang!" when I whacked it, and before long, I could hear someone making their way to the door, their shoes shloping across the floor. The door was opened by Dr. Malcolm Fallon, pages of the *Houston Chronicle* clasped in one hand, backless black leather slippers on his feet. His eyebrows went up and I'm pretty sure I looked surprised, too. I tried not to look like a salesman or a Jehovah's Witness. How had I gotten the house wrong? Sixth house from the corner . . . wasn't this the sixth house from the corner?

I said, "Well, hey, Dr. Fallon!"

I stepped back from the porch far enough so that I could count the houses to the end of the street. This was the sixth house. I looked back at Dr. Fallon, who stood, unsmiling, in his doorway.

I said, pretty sure I was looking as foolish as I felt, "Uh, hey! Do you know a Mai Dinh?"

Something flickered over Fallon's face. The man stood there for a long, uncomfortable moment, taking me in, and then stepped to the side.

"Come in," he said, and I stepped into the two-story foyer (every two-story house in First Colony has a two-story foyer — they may look grand, but they're a waste of space and makes it impossible to heat or cool these houses with any kind of efficiency).

The man shut the front door and I followed him through a dimly lit hall back to a masculine study, all hardwoods and leather upholstery and sepia prints of golf courses on the walls. He clicked on lamps with amber shades that gave the room a soft, golden glow. The large plate glass window looked out on a postage stamp pool surrounded by a terrazzo patio, and beyond, the ninth hole of the Bridgewater Country Club golf course.

The man said, "Have a seat, Mr. Wells."

I sat on one of his overstuffed leather chairs near the big window, and then, still not answering my question, the man took the seat across from me.

Fallon's head of thick, wavy hair reminded me of meringue it was so white and shiny. Like I've said, Fallon was trim and conditioned for an old guy, on the rangy side, nearly as tall as me, but looking gray and old and ill. He wore expensive-looking dress slacks, a white business shirt with the sleeves rolled up, and those soft-looking leather slippers. Even his old feet looked frail.

Fallon said, "I'm Mai's father." He leaned back in his chair, his hands resting loosely on the arms of the chair.

I said, "Is that right?" trying to hide my surprise. I mean, I'd been picturing a short, slim, dark-skinned, a, well . . . someone who looked Asian. I tried to recover. "I've never seen her at church. She's come to live with you then? Left California for good?"

I was trying to put all the puzzle pieces together: Fallon's California daughter who had finally gotten him running; Mai telling Graham, "My dad will take care of me," because her dad was, in fact, a doctor.

"How long have you and Mai known each other?" Fallon asked without responding to my question.

"Oh! We met today. We, uh, we shared a glass of wine at the Vineyard." I couldn't mention that Mai had been at the funeral — I didn't know if her father knew about her and Graham, and I didn't have to be sworn to secrecy to know that it wasn't my place to be telling the old gent that story.

He nodded his head. "A glass of wine, I think you said?" He put special emphasis on the "A."

I colored. "I had a glass of wine. Mai may

have had, ah . . ."

He nodded in a confirming sort of way. "Yes," he said, "she may have. I presume you bought the wine?"

I nodded. This is Texas. Men still pay. At least, guys my age do.

"Tell me, Mr. Wells, is that a wedding ring you're wearing on your finger?"

I looked down at what was obviously a gold wedding band on the ring finger of my left hand.

I said stupidly, "Yeah."

I did not see where this was going, which means that the college IQ test I took may have been seriously skewed in favor of big dumb linemen. I mean, Fallon knew Annie Laurie; everyone knows Annie Laurie . . .

"So you're still a married man? I haven't missed an announcement in the church bulletin?"

"Oh! No, I'm married, I —"

"But I suppose, in this day and time, it's archaic of me to expect that ring, or that marriage, to mean anything to you?"

"Gosh, no! I —"

"Mr. Wells." Dr. Fallon steepled his fingers in a way my UT coach would when he was sitting across his desk from you, preparing to give you one of his "The game of football is like the game of life" speeches. "Mr. Wells,

I'd like to tell you a story. May I tell you a story?"

The situation I found myself in was ludicrous; we're going to have a good laugh over this, me and Dr. Fallon, I thought. Might could work it into a sermon, kind of a funny preacher story. People would get a kick out of it, seeing their preacher so wrong-footed.

"Dr. Fallon," I began, smiling at him so he wouldn't think he had offended me. I hated to embarrass the old guy. I thought his being so fatherly with a woman around my age was kind of touching. "Let me explain . . ."

He held his hand up to stop me and his face grew severe.

"If you don't mind, it's my house. I'll do the explaining."

I leaned closer to him and held my palms up. "It's just that you've misunderstood —"

He stood and leaned over me, his finger pointing at my face, his voice harsh. "That's what the other one said, 'You misunderstand me, Dr. Fallon.' " His voice took on a mocking, wheedling tone.

"But *he* was the one who misunderstood. Not me. Not me. Now" — his voice went back to his normal range — "are you going to let me tell you my story? It didn't make any difference to him, but maybe, just maybe, there is some shred of character left in the men of your generation."

I was leaning my head back, looking up into this furious old man's face. My head had gone still and quiet. *That's what the other one said . . .*

I said, "Yes, sir, I'd like for you to tell me your story."

He stood a moment longer, finger inches from my nose. Then he tucked his finger under his thumb and stood straight.

"Right. That's good," he said. He stepped back a pace and folded himself back into his chair. "Mai is in bed asleep. I don't know how much you managed to make her drink . . ."

I started to interrupt; again he held his hand up to stop me.

"But it was enough to make her ill when she got home. I've given her something for the nausea, and something to help her sleep."

"Are you sure that was wise?" I said — the combination of alcohol and sedatives . . .

His lip curled. "Excuse me, Mr. Wells, I am a doctor. Now then. Am I to be allowed to tell my story, or not?"

I nodded.

"Yes. Good," he said. He seemed to relax a little.

"I don't suppose you ever served your country?" he said. Oh, good. This question again. I shook my head.

"No, that's right. I've already asked you that, haven't I? After that memorable Memorial Day sermon. You told me you had 'missed the draft.'

"I chose to serve my country. I enlisted. And I didn't enlist to pay for my medical school bills, either. I left a budding practice, and a family, in San Rafael to become a doctor with the Air Force in Vietnam," Fallon said. "Men who don't serve don't have a clue about the sacrifice. You reap the benefits of freedom without ever understanding the price that's paid, much less paying part of that price."

I hoped that "you" was a generic and all-inclusive "you" and not a personal statement about my own patriotism, but that seemed overly optimistic. My fingers had found a button in the upholstery and I realized I had been worrying at it. I clasped my hands to keep them still. I once pulled a button off the family room couch after worrying it, and that had made Annie Laurie really mad. I don't think Fallon had noticed the slightly loosened button. Might even have been loose before I started on it.

"I worked alongside Mai's father, and her

grandfather — they were doctors, too, fine men, good doctors. My wife and children were back in the States, and I didn't have much in common with most of the servicemen. For one thing, I was a lot older than the others; even the other doctors were mainly in their twenties. I was on my own a good deal, missing my family. I was lonely. Trung, Mai's father, often had me in his home. His wife, well, his whole family, they were lovely people.

"Americans, when Americans think of the Vietnamese, they picture peasants in coolie hats and Mao pajamas. The Dinhs were an educated, cosmopolitan family. They lived in a big, old French town house — the whole extended family together. Grandparents, parents, aunt and uncle, Mai's two brothers, and little sister. Mai was twelve, Trung's oldest. She was in a Catholic boarding school in Paris — both Mai's parents and three of her grandparents had attended the same school — it's the Stanislas College. I can't ever get the pronunciation right.

"So Mai was in France the whole time I was in Vietnam and I never saw her there. In Vietnam."

Fallon got up and walked over to his desk. There was a carafe of water on his desk, one of those where the lid to the carafe is an upside-down glass. He took the glass off, and I heard the clinking of glass against glass. He filled the tumbler with water, drank it all, and then upended the glass on the carafe again. Fallon came back to the sitting area and sat down heavily. He hadn't offered me any water. Not that I wanted some — it was interesting, that's all.

What I wanted was for Fallon to get to the part of his story that included "the other one." He might have been talking about Mai's first husband, Jonathon; but again, he might have been talking about Graham Garcia. Fallon could have known about Graham. Knowing what I did about Fallon, he wouldn't have been at all happy about the affair. I sure as heck wouldn't be happy if one of my daughters let herself get caught up in such a situation.

There wouldn't be any use in trying to hurry the old man. An old soldier has earned the right to tell his story.

Fallon fiddled with the angle of a crook-neck floor lamp until he had adjusted it to his satisfaction — I couldn't tell that the fiddling had made a difference.

He said, "Skip to 1975. How old were you in '75?"

"I'd have been in junior high," I said.

445

Fallon frowned as if being born too early for the draft was just what should be expected of a slacker like me.

"Did you read the papers back then?"

I said, apologetically, that I had not. I had discovered football and girls and those two subjects had occupied my mind to the exclusion of nearly everything else, war or no war. I didn't say that last part out loud.

Fallon sighed at my ignorance.

"In brief, then. In 1975, without ever having made a full-out effort to win the war, the U.S. government no longer finds it politically expedient to support the South Vietnamese, regardless of promises made. We are packing up and moving out. I get Trung Dinh and his entire family secure seats on a transport plane. I mean everybody: his parents and in-laws, his brother and his sister-in-law, the kids, everybody who lived in that house and more than a dozen who didn't but were closely related. I called in every favor I was owed and pulled strings I didn't have any business pulling. I was determined that at least one God-damned American was going to be true to his promise."

I had no idea where this story was going. It didn't appear to be going anywhere near the Bridgewater golf course last Sunday evening, but Fallon had my complete attention.

"Trung called the Stanislas College and arranged for Mai to be flown to California to meet them. He wanted the family to make this new start together. Mai's flight was, I think, three days before the evacuation transport. There is a Catholic boarding school in Monterey, the Santa Catalina, and it was arranged that a nun would pick Mai up from the airport and she would stay at the school until Trung and his wife came to get her.

"I was at the house while he made the call. All around me the women were rushing, trying to decide what to pack. They had to leave almost everything, all that gorgeous antique furniture, the rugs. Trung's dad was walking through the house cutting paintings from their frames, layering the paintings in silk and wrapping them into scrolls. Family pictures and jewelry, that's about all they were able to take with them.

"Trung has Mai on the phone, he's speaking Vietnamese — Mai didn't speak English, she spoke Vietnamese and French — but I'd been in Vietnam for three years and I could understand him a little. He was saying, 'Mai, we're all going to go live in California near my friend Malcolm. Malcolm says you will love California; it's always sunny, and there are fruit trees in every yard.' He explains about the Sister from Santa Catalina who will pick her up from the airport. Trung says, 'Two nights you will go to bed in Santa Catalina, and then you will wake up and Mommy and Daddy will be there to take you to your new home. Be brave for a little while only. Daddy is coming. I promise.' "

Fallon put a fist to his mouth to still his lips. I knew enough to realize this story wasn't going to have a happy ending.

He cleared his throat roughly. "We get to the airport. Marines are clearing the way for us, there are desperate people clawing to get through, screaming for help. You know, these people were our allies, they had helped us, risked their lives for the American forces, and now, now we were leaving them behind to face the enemy alone. I couldn't save them all, but I'd made a promise to Trung and I was doing everything I can.

"I've got a duffle slung over my shoulder, and a little girl by each hand. We're all there, Trung's entire family, his wife's family, too. And oh, about a hundred and thirty orphans who will also be starting new lives in America, the little mixed-blood boys and girls whose American fathers had never claimed them. It is flat chaos. The C-5 stretches in front, looking like an airport hangar with wings — it's huge.

"Trung's family is getting counted in, one by one. I hand over the two little girls, they feel like puppies, they're so light and warm; they get checked off, and then, there's one too many. We count again and Trung's nephew has a young woman by the arm, his fiancée, he's not leaving without her, oh, Dr. Fallon, she weighs nothing, if you can't take her, let her have my seat, I'll stay behind.

"The kid is pleading, the girl is the size of my thumb, eyes dark and still — not begging, only waiting for my answer. She never says a word. Trung's sister starts crying, no, no he has to go, I'll give up my seat, only let my baby have a chance for life. I said, 'Give her my seat.' I'm not being a hero — there's no chance a U.S. doctor is getting left behind, I'll catch another plane, no fear.

"But, my God, they think I'm a hero, they're crying, embracing me, kisses, hugs. I'm yelling, 'Go, go, go!' " Dr. Fallon passed a hand over his face.

"Trung, very solemn, shakes my hand. He says, '*Bạn là một người đã đứng của mình hứa hẹn.*' 'You are a man who stands by his promise.' " Fallon's voice broke in a sob.

He took a moment to gather himself back together, rotating his head, working out the strain, then giving me a stern look.

"Trung got on the plane. He had his entire family with him, everyone except Mai. Also on that plane were a number of young American nurses, and some of my fellow doctors, who had served selflessly and stayed until the end. There were three hundred and twenty-eight people on that plane. I was supposed to be one of them."

Dr. Fallon fell silent. He took a long gasping breath as though he had forgotten to breathe for a minute.

"The C-5 is in the air twelve minutes and there is an explosion. The Air Force still doesn't know for sure whether it was shot down, or sabotaged, or if there was a systems malfunction. It doesn't matter. The plane goes down in a rice paddy, hits a dike. A hundred and fifty-three people died. Almost all the orphans, three of those pretty, young nurses, and every last member of Mai's family."

There was a quiet "pop" and I felt that chair button come free in my hand. I tried to palm it back into place.

Fallon's hands were trembling. I stood and went to his desk and poured him another glass of water and handed it to him.

He drank it and nodded his thanks. It took him a while before he could go on.

"Oh, my Lord. I had sent them to their death." He waved off my protest. "No, I don't take responsibility — I really had done what I could, but . . .

"Then I had to get out myself. There wasn't any time to mourn, to see to the funerals. The North Vietnamese were only miles away. Five days later, I'm out of the mud and the heat and the blood and in the sweet, cool arms of my beautiful, blond Faye. I am in a different world from the one I left behind.

"For the first couple of weeks, I was working at fitting back in with Faye, and getting to know my boys again. Not that I had forgotten Mai, but I needed to choose the right time to ask Faye . . . She never hesitated, not one second. It doesn't matter that she was already raising four sons; of course we would adopt Mai.

"Faye says, 'Malcolm, you know I have always wanted a little girl.' "

Abruptly Fallon stood up and took a framed picture from his desk. He handed it to me. I looked into the soft, blue eyes of a pretty blond woman. She wore her hair in the full, puffy, pageboy style I associate with airline hostesses. Her smile was warm.

451

Fallon tapped the face.

"That's Faye," he said.

"She's lovely," I said. That's the only thing you can say when a man shows you a picture of his wife, but Fallon's Faye was a truly lovely woman. She looked gentle and kind and calm — which is quite an achievement for a woman raising four sons and somebody else's emotionally wounded daughter. My sister-in-law Stacy has only three sons, and I once saw her pull her shoe off and fling it at a kid. Not that I blamed her. I just wished I'd thought of it first — my shoes are bigger and heavier and I've got a better aim.

"But first we have to find Mai. Because I couldn't remember where she is! When Trung was on the phone telling Mai about the school, he was speaking Vietnamese, very fast, and everybody was bustling around me, talking a hundred miles an hour, and mainly it didn't occur to me that I was going to need the information. It wasn't like now when you can get on the Internet and search and ten minutes later you have your information. All I really remembered was that a nun was going to pick Mai up at the airport.

"Faye and I are going through the Yellow Pages calling every Catholic parish listed.

Meanwhile, Mai is in Santa Catalina. She doesn't speak English, and none of the little girls speak French. A couple of the Sisters do. Three days pass and there's no daddy there to get her. Of course, the American withdrawal from Saigon is all over the television, the crash, too, and it's very frightening, but Mai doesn't have any reason to believe her family was on that plane, except that her dad said he would come and get her and he hasn't.

"I don't know who finally called the school. Trung had told someone in Vietnam where Mai was going to be sent, I guess. One of the Sisters who can speak French takes Mai out to the garden, and she tells her. Her father, her mother, her little sister, and her brothers, grandparents, aunts, uncles . . . everybody is gone.

"Mai finds herself in a strange country, with a strange language. There is no one on earth who knows her and loves her. She is alone in a way you and I can never imagine. She has lost everyone.

"She stops eating. At night she thrashes around in her bed until she throws herself on the floor. The Sisters start constraining Mai to her bed at night. They're afraid she's going to hurt herself.

"So a month or so into Mai's stay at Santa

Catalina, at last we know where she is. Now we have to get permission to see her, and before that we have to get permission to adopt her, because the school is concerned about Mai's mental health — they don't want us coming into Mai's life and then disappearing. Mai can't have any more people disappearing. We go through all the interviews, the home visits — the boys were troopers — they want all our financial information . . . it took forever.

"Mai can't wait forever. One day Mai is sitting in front of a dinner she won't touch, with a bunch of American girls she can't talk to. One of the Sisters touches her shoulder and says, 'Mai? Will you walk with me outside?' The Sister takes Mai out to the gardens, and on a sudden impulse, the Sister told me she'd had a message from God, but on this impulse, she kneels down next to Mai and says, 'Mai, run. Run as hard as you can. Run until it stops hurting. And then run back here to me.' Mai stares up at her for a long time, and then she turns and runs. Mai runs for more than an hour. She's running in her woolen school jumper and cloggy, leather-soled Oxfords.

"That night, Mai sleeps without the nightmares. The next morning, Mai dresses in her uniform but puts her sneakers on. She

454

won't eat her breakfast, but she does drink some juice and that is a great relief to the Sisters. Instead of going to class, Mai goes out to the garden and she runs. She really never stopped running. 'Run till it stops hurting.' It never did.

"Do you know what Mai does most Saturdays? She runs to the Galleria, eats lunch at the Cheesecake Factory, and runs back. That's a thirty-mile round trip."

I made appropriate noises of amazement.

"It was soon after Mai discovered running as a pain management tool that Faye and I qualified for the adoption process. Faye asked the nuns not to pack for Mai. She didn't want Mai to feel she was being shipped around like a parcel. The nuns did tell Mai that I was a friend of her daddy's, and that we wanted to meet her. We left the boys at home with my mom and dad; four brothers at once, well.

"We talked it over beforehand, Faye and I, what would be the best way to handle this. So, as we had planned, I waited out in the garden. This school is gorgeous, you should see the pictures. While I'm outside waiting, my Faye goes to the parlor with Sister I-can't-remember-her-name. Mai is sitting as still as a china doll on a shelf. She is a Thumbelina, you could blow her away like flower thistle.

"Faye gets down on her knees in front of Mai, and with the Sister translating, Faye says, 'Mai, it broke Malcolm's heart when he heard about the plane accident. Ever since then, we have been searching and searching for you. We can't bring back your family. But if you will let us, we will be your new family, and I will be a mother to you.' And my Faye opens her arms, and after four heartbeats, Mai slides down from the chair and into Faye's arms and into our lives."

Fallon's eyes were swimming. He groped at his pockets and pulled out a handkerchief. A real cotton handkerchief, not a Kleenex.

I had to blink myself. I waited until I was sure he had finished his story. It was a story he had told many times, I thought, the way someone keeps a stone in his pocket and rubs and rubs it until it is polished and perfect.

I said, "What a grace that you and Faye were there for Mai, Dr. Fallon. You saved that little girl. I can't bear to think of her growing up without a family to love her. You really are a man who stands by his promise. You have walked the walk." I reached over and touched his knee. "But, Dr. Fallon, why did you tell me that story?"

"Why?" Fallon was aghast. "How can you not know why? Because Mai can't have you in her life; she's not strong enough. You think she's a pretty face, a diversion from a stale marriage, but she's a *person*. I thought she was going to die when her worthless husband walked out on her! I really thought she might die! She stopped eating again — she ran herself to the bone!"

I'd never had the slightest interest in Mai, not as a woman, not to act on.

I stood up and turned off the lamps. With the lamps off, I could see the green, groomed golf course, even in the dark. I could see the flag at the ninth hole.

"Did you tell Mai's story to Graham Garcia?"

"I . . . what? Did I . . . who?" His voice sounded frightened in the dark room.

"Did you sit here in the dark and see Mai leave through the back gate to meet her lover? Did you see them embrace? Did you go out there to confront them together?"

I tried to picture the scene in my mind.

"No," I said. "You wouldn't have done that because Mai isn't strong enough for confrontation, is she? And you were trying to protect her. You were trying to keep your promise."

Fallon stumbled to his desk and poured

himself water. The glass rattled against the carafe, and I heard the glass click against his teeth when Fallon lifted it to drink. He fell back into the chair behind his desk.

I stood before Fallon at his desk.

"You waited until she came back in, didn't you? Then you went to find the man."

"Not to kill him. I didn't go out there to kill him." Fallon whispered the words.

Fallon's face glowed white in the dark room. He had his hands braced against his desk as if he needed the barrier between us.

I said, "You didn't go out there to kill Graham Garcia, but you killed him all the same, didn't you?"

Now Fallon yelled at me, roaring, "I told him the story! I knew if I explained, if I could make him understand what Mai had been through . . . why he had to leave her alone. I told him everything I told you!" Fallon shouted.

He started shoving stuff around on his desk, yanking drawers open and knocking papers to the floor, as if somewhere on his desk he could find the proof that he had acted in good faith, the certificate that would vindicate him. I was afraid he would work himself into a heart attack.

I held my hands wide and took a step toward him in the darkened room.

"Take it easy, Dr. Fallon, take it easy." My words had no effect.

"He wouldn't listen to me. He said it was too late. He had a family, did you know that? Just like you do, but here you are, sniffing for another woman!"

"No, Dr. Fallon."

"You deny it! You deny it just like him! You take my daughter to a bar in the middle of the afternoon —"

"No!"

I could not get through to this guy; he kept on as if he couldn't hear me.

"You pour liquor down her throat, you play on her weaknesses —"

"I did not!"

I pulled my phone from my pocket and scrolled for Wanderley's number, grateful for the lighted screen.

"Because you're the same as he was . . . you want what you want and . . ."

I looked up from my phone.

"You killed him." I said it quietly, and somehow through his mental static, he heard me.

"No. No. I didn't." His voice was calm and quiet, rational, and for a second, I thought I had gotten it wrong.

Then Fallon went on, "I didn't mean to. It was an accident. We were sitting out on the golf course, and I was explaining. I was telling him Mai's story and he was listening and asking good questions and nodding his head and I thought he understood, I thought we were on the same page, two gentlemen."

Fallon's dark profile was turned up to mine. I couldn't see his expression, but there was pleading in his voice.

"I used his golf club to help me stand up," Fallon said. "Sitting out there in the damp, I'd gotten stiff, and I said, I said, 'Then, Graham, we agree and you won't see Mai anymore, I'll let her know, you don't need to . . .' and there he was, shaking his head no, and he said, 'Dr. Fallon, I'm sorry, but I can't do that. You don't understand, it's too late for that, what you're asking is impossible.' So then I hit him."

Fallon sounded stunned; he still couldn't believe he had done what he was telling me.

"I didn't mean to." His voice broke. "It happened. I had the club in my hand and I hit him and he fell down."

I said, "You left him there."

"He was dead!"

"No, he wasn't," I said. "He didn't die for some time. I don't know if he could have been saved if you had called for help, but I know you didn't make that call."

"He was dead!" Fallon roared.

"Dr. Fallon," I said, "you are a medical doctor. You had wartime experience. You knew very well that Graham Garcia was not dead, yet you left him to die. Hitting him might have been an accident, but you *chose* to walk away."

There was silence from the form hunched behind the desk.

I said, "I'm going to turn on the light."

He said, "No!" and I heard a click and I absolutely knew, and could not believe, what that click meant.

I said, "Dr. Fallon, if you shoot me, is that going to be an accident?"

There was a banging of the knocker on the front door, and I felt my knees go weak with relief. Wanderley to the rescue. Someone to the rescue. I took a step back.

Fallon said, "Don't you dare move. You came to my house, looking to violate a woman you had made helpless with alcohol —"

I yelled, "No!"

The front door opened and I was expecting to hear an authoritative voice say, "Freeze!" but instead I heard the worst thing on earth:

"Daddy?" The voice was thin and frightened, and quavered up a scale on the one

461

word spoken.

And it was Jo's.

I heard Baby Bear's deep rumble.

Jo said, "Hush, Baby."

Baby Bear's tags rattled as if Jo's grip on his collar was unsteady.

I said, making my voice as firm as I could, "Josephine, sweetheart, I want you to turn around and go out of this house right this second. I'm busy, Jo; this is private. It's church business. Go home, sweetie. Obey me, Jo."

Praying she would, just this once, obey me. Please, God, please, God, please, God.

Baby Bear growled and his toenails scrabbled on the marble floor. I heard Jo's tentative steps toward the study.

"Daddy?" Jo's voice trembled.

I said, "Jo. Please." And it was a prayer.

From upstairs Mai's sleepy voice called, "Dad? Daddy?"

I saw Fallon's face tilt up in the dark, and I threw myself across the desk at him. There was a shot and I heard Jo screaming as I had never heard my baby, my baby, my baby girl screaming and screaming and screaming and screaming.

# THIRTY-THREE

Graham Garcia was teeing off at the ninth hole, and I was explaining to him that he couldn't see Jo anymore, it wasn't right, she was too young, and he shook his head sadly and said, "I'm sorry, Bear, but it's too late. I promised."

Jo sat next to me in Alex Garcia's bedroom, her hair a dark tent around her. She was holding a book upside down and reading to me backward and I said, "I don't understand, Jo, read it again." She said, "If you'd only try," and she slammed the book shut. Then Jo looked down at her hands and they were filled with blood and she screamed and screamed.

I was walking down the hospital hall on my way to see Miss Lily. I was humming, *"Can you count the stars of evening . . ."* Wanderley walked next to me, holding my hand, saying, "Well, Father Brown, do you have anything to tell me? Do you have anything to tell me?"

When I awoke, Annie Laurie sat next to my bed with *Sing Them Home* on her lap, her reading glasses askew on the end of her elegant nose. She was asleep, her head back against one of those awful vinyl upholstered hospital chairs. In back of her were banks of flowers. Banks of them. Balloons, too. Nearly blocked the window; I couldn't see a thing out of it.

What a waste of money. Annie Laurie should have told everyone to donate to the Fort Bend Women's Shelter or the church's food pantry. Or something.

I felt like hell. I can say that. A law officer gave me permission.

There was a tube down my throat and it hurt. I was thirsty. I wanted Jo. I wanted to cry. I never cry.

It was morning or afternoon. I don't know. Merrie sat in the corner, working a sudoku. In ink. The sun was shining over her fair hair and through all those flowers. It was kind of nice having people think of you, send you flowers. They were pretty. They smelled good. Wait. No, they didn't smell that good. One of those vases needed a water change.

The tube was gone. Annie Laurie was bending over me. I could see the tender round tops of her breasts. Her breath smelled like coffee and mints. Her skin smelled like Annie. A good smell.

Annie Laurie said, "Bear?"

I asked, "Jo?"

It didn't sound like me. I sounded like an old beach ball, deflated and crusty with salt and sand. I sounded like a geriatric.

Annie smiled. It was the best smile. It was a warm, safe, happy smile; it touched her whole face. Annie's smile.

Annie said, "Hon, your baby girl saved your life, you know that?"

I felt myself seal over in coldness and stubbornness.

"No, she didn't," I croaked. "What she did was nearly get herself killed."

My heart tightened at the words.

"Because she wouldn't obey me," I said. "I told her to leave, Annie Laurie, I told her to take Baby Bear and get out of that damn house, and I couldn't make her go. She wouldn't —"

I couldn't speak. I didn't dare try to say another word.

"Oh, Bear." Annie stroked the hair behind

my ears with her cool, smooth fingertips. "Would you have left? Other way around, would you have left Jo in there by herself?"

I held it for a while, trying to hold my place. But I couldn't. I shook my head, "No," and the cold flooded out of me.

"She's her daddy's girl, Bear," Annie said, her lips inches from my ear. "She's your girl, all over."

There was a tickle on my ear. I jerked my head away. The tickle came again. I opened my eyes and Jo was standing over me, a twist of her dark, fragrant hair brushing my ear. She smelled like fruity shampoo and salt.

I said, "Jo," and I tried to hug her but I couldn't. My arms were taped to the railings of the bed and to tubes and bells and whistles, and when I tried to move, my arm hair got yanked. Jo put her silky arms around me and I cried for a long time, Jo saying, "Daddy, don't, Daddy, don't."

I woke up and Detective James Wanderley was standing at the foot of my bed.

Wanderley said, " 'Lucy, you got some 'splaining to do.' "

I said, "Could you get me a drink?"

Wanderley patted his jacket pockets.

"I got nothing, Bear; I haven't reached that stage yet."

"Water, Wanderley, would be fine."

"Oh! Right."

Wanderley fumbled about till he found a tan plastic pitcher encased in Styrofoam and filled with ice water. He held a glass with a straw to my lips and I drank cold, stale hospital water and it was mango-cherry — Heaven's own nectar. It was delicious.

Wanderley was wearing one of his good forty-year-old tweed blazers. I couldn't see his feet, so I don't know whether he had on those cool boots.

I said, "How does your grandmother feel about you wearing your dead grandfather's clothes?"

Wanderley smiled and took a purple guitar pick out of his mouth.

"She can't decide if it's sweet or disturbing," he said.

"What about your dad? What does he think, seeing you dressed in his dad's clothes?"

Wanderley's smile broadened. "It pisses him off good and proper, preacher."

I thought that answered lots of questions.

I said, "Am I in trouble?"

"You are with me," Wanderley said. "Everybody else thinks you're a cross between

Lassie and the Coast Guard. I can't decide whether you saved Jo's life or nearly got her killed."

"What happened?" I said.

Wanderley said, "We got a call about a possible gunshot."

"I called you," I interrupted.

Wanderley rubbed the base of his nose vigorously. "Yeah. Sorry. I didn't get that call. Molly dropped my phone in the toilet."

Okay, I could see that. I've wanted to drown mine a time or two.

"So, anyway, some neighbor calls about a possible gunshot. Then we got a nearly incoherent call from a frantic and slightly drugged Mai Dinh saying there was a dead man and a crazy girl and a wild dog in her house.

"When the officers arrived, just ahead of the fire engine and the ambulance, they found a small Asian woman trying to pull a teenage girl off a recumbent old white man who was in the process of having his ankle worried off by a giant, black hell-hound. The old man had a gun in his hand, which cooled the officers' sympathies precipitately. Good thing or they would have shot your dog. You were in a back room trying to bleed to death. You nearly succeeded. That's what happens when amateurs play pro."

"About that, Wanderley, see, I had promised —"

Wanderley shook his head. "No, Bear. Don't give me that promise crap." He made quote marks with his fingers when he said "promise." "It won't do," he said. "You didn't have any right to make that promise and you sure as hell didn't have the right to keep it."

I opened my mouth to explain but Wanderley shook his head.

"Don't worry. I'm not going to ask you to tell it to me now. Mainly because I think I've put it together from what Annie Laurie told me and what I got out of Mai Dinh. And also because Annie Laurie made me swear on my grandfather's grave that I wouldn't bring it up with you until you were out of here. You make sure she knows you brought it up, not me, okay? You live with some fierce women, Bear, you know that?"

Ah, yes, I did know that. Fierce women. I really liked that. Fierce women.

"You ready for the rest of the story?"

I nodded and crunched ice.

Wanderley glanced around and found the chair hidden under a couple of flower arrangements. He moved the flowers to the floor and took a second to look over all the flowers and balloons and cards.

He said, "Jeez, what a waste," sotto voce, and dragged the chair closer to my bed and planted himself.

"When I got there," he said, "I found a hysterical Jo in the front yard being constrained by an officer who was anxious not to have any charges of sexual harassment or undue violence placed on his record, which made constraining your Jo quite a task indeed. Fortunately for all of us, Jo recognized me as the detective who had been with her dad Tuesday night and I was able to get her to calm down. I had her call your wife. Then I had her tell me her story.

"Seems she was walking home from a friend's house, a . . ." He shifted his butt and pulled a notepad out of his back pocket, flipped through some pages.

I said, "Cara Phelps."

Wanderley found the name and nodded. "Cara Phelps, and she sees your car, Jo, I mean, Jo sees your car, dash light on, parked in front of an unfamiliar house and your car windows are down. But Baby Bear — did you name that dog after yourself, Bear? Because that's seriously bent if you did — isn't in the car as she would expect him to be, he's standing on the front porch and he's growling and pawing the door.

"Evidently your namesake isn't known for

growling and that puts Jo on alert. The dog won't come when Jo calls him and that spooks her, too. She goes to the front door to get the dog and she can hear raised voices and she recognizes yours.

"She said she knocked, but no one came so she tried the door and it wasn't locked. She walked in, and that in itself was pretty ballsy, if you ask me, and you told her to leave and then there was a shot."

Wanderley put a foot on my bed to shove his chair back and stood up again. There wasn't enough space in the room for him to pace, but he did this sort of rocking stand, one foot to the other, back and forth. Wanderley was as jittery as a cat with wayward kittens — the boy was never going to get fat.

"If I understand Ms. Dinh's account, she came downstairs to find the Hound of the Baskervilles and a strange girl trying to kill a Dr. Malcolm Fallon, Dinh's father. All teeth and nails, from what I hear, and I'm not at all certain it wasn't Jo using her teeth. All the while, Fallon was holding a loaded gun, which, interestingly, and most fortunately, he did not use."

"Again," I said.

"What?" Wanderley said; and used the break to take the pick out of his mouth and turn it in and out of his fingers like a cardsharp.

"He didn't use the gun *again*. He used it once anyway."

There was Wanderley's easy grin. That grin gave you a glimpse of the kid he had once been, smart, maybe too smart, all cool confidence on top, uncertainty underneath. Of course, I was on drugs, so I could have been reading too much into it.

"Right," he said, "I wasn't counting that." The pick went into the breast pocket of his shirt and I could see the purple through the thin white cloth — I could see a blue pick in there, too, and maybe a yellow one, if that wasn't a slip of paper.

"Imagine my surprise," I said. "You know what I want? I want some real food. I'm thinking Goode Company Barbeque, their sliced link sandwich. Extra sauce, jalapeños, and onions. And a great big piece of their pecan pie, better make it two pieces."

"Yeah, that sounds good. Nearest Goode Company is on Kirby, and the Sugar Land Police don't do deliveries. So you want to hear the rest or what?" Wanderley asked, his eyebrow doing Groucho tricks. I nodded.

"So we've got firemen and cops littering the sidewalk, neighbors torn between being offended at this clear violation of neighborhood restrictions and being titillated by an honest-to-God Human Drama right on their own overpriced turf lined up three deep in the street, and every teenager from a mile's diameter trying to get video footage for YouTube while medics do their best to stuff you in the back of their ambulance, and all the while your horse-sized mutt is running circles as if someone put menthol oil on his bung hole."

"Take a breath," I said. He did, then continued.

"When I can get Jo calmed down to the point where she stops repeating over and over, 'He killed my daddy, he killed my daddy . . .' "

I sniffed.

Wanderley looked surprised.

"Bear, don't go soft on me, you're not dead yet, old man."

"Allergies," I said.

"Better be," Wanderley answered. "As I was saying, when I can get Jo to speak like the intelligent and thoughtful girl she is, I learn that when she hears the gunshot, instead of running like hell the way I would expect an intelligent and thoughtful girl to, she rushes in the direction of the gunshot and physically attacks the man with the gun. Didn't you teach your daughters about 'stranger danger,' Bear?" Wanderley sounded outraged.

I sighed. "I did. Waste of breath, but I did."

Wanderley shakes his head in disapproval. "I gotta hope I do a better job with Molly."

I suppressed a snort and felt a wicked delight curl up in my insides. "May God be as good to you as He has been to me."

I get a kick out of young people. I really do.

"Bear, your changeling daughter did a number on poor old Dr. Fallon. I think I have now officially encountered the kind of girl who was once labeled a 'spitfire' and a 'firebrand.' "

This day was full of revelations!

I grinned. "Oh, my gosh, Wanderley, you're a closet romance reader."

Wanderley blushed.

"So did you arrest that old man?" I asked.

"For shooting you? No, we gave him the keys to the city. I always carry a spare pair."

I wasn't amused. I was still hurting.

"Yes, we arrested him. He's in jail. HD is out, by the way. He isn't being charged with obstruction because we're not sure if he was trying to take a bullet for Alex, or if he was so confused and jumbled that he thought he really had killed Garcia. I incline to the latter. So I only have one old man in jail right now and he's not talking. I mean, Fallon's not talking at *all*. I haven't heard the man say a word. I don't even know if he's talking to his lawyer."

"I'm not sure I can press charges," I said. "The man is a member of my church."

Wanderley did a mock double-take. "Are you crazy? Is this some 'turn the other cheek' business?" He gave a laugh and shook his head. "It doesn't matter whether you press charges or not, Bear. It's against the law to shoot people, even really annoying crazy people, who went off and did exactly what they'd been told not to do. There were a few minutes there, Bear, when I felt like shooting you myself. Damn, you're a glory hound."

I tried to explain, but Wanderley cut me off.

"His lawyer is already making noises about 'self-defense,' and since you were in the man's house, big no-no in Texas, Bear . . ."

"He invited me in," I said.

"Your say-so. And since it does look as though you tried to launch yourself over his desk, that might get the guy off, but going on what you said while you were taking happy pills, we decided to compare Dr. Fallon's prints and DNA to what was found on the Big Bertha that killed Garcia. I think we'll find a match." Wanderley nodded in satisfaction.

I said, "Why don't you sit down again? You're giving me an ache in my neck, looking up at you."

"That's a new one for you, huh, Bear? Looking up to other people?"

"I said I'm looking up *at* you."

"Same thing."

It's not. But Wanderley sat down.

"What about Mai?" I said. "How is she? She didn't know, about her dad, I mean. I don't think she knew."

"In less than twenty-four hours, that woman had four brothers and a slew of sisters-in-law, nieces, and nephews running opposition for her. I had a five-year-old try to stare me down when I went to Fallon's house to talk to her. Kid was a tough little bugger. He didn't come right out and say so, but he was doing his best to communicate that he could take me down if it came to that. I think there's a strain of pit bull in that family."

I said, "I think that family protects its own, Wanderley. I think that's all Dr. Fallon was trying to do. I don't believe he meant to kill Graham Garcia."

"It's not up to you to decide, Bear. That's

going to be in the hands of twelve Fort Bend citizens, all honest and true. As for Mai, even after talking to her, I don't know if she knew her father had killed Garcia, but I think she suspected.

"Mai swears her dad couldn't have killed Garcia, but not with a whole lot of conviction. More like it's an article of faith, not like she's a true believer. Mai can't bring herself to believe that her hero, her savior, killed the man she loved best in the world. She can't make the pieces fit. Anyway, I don't think it's likely the prosecutor will try to pull her into this."

I had a thought.

"What about that lawyer fellow? Did I tell you I found a lawyer guy, what's his name, in Graham's study? Day of the funeral. Guy was going through Graham's desk. Is that guy in jail, too?"

Wanderley blew air out his nose.

"No, he didn't kill anybody. Not that I know of."

"Yeah, but there was some serious malfeasance —"

"If there was, that's a civil case. And there's not going to be any case. Any evidence there might be is in Honey Garcia's hands, and I don't think she's going to be making any noise about it."

"What do you mean, she won't —"

"Bear, her husband was a partner in that law firm. That partnership is worth a lot of money. When a partner dies, his share of the partnership goes to his estate, goes to Honey. If that partnership goes bust, Honey gets nothing. Worse, if there are claims against the partnership, the plaintiff could and would go after Garcia's estate, along with the rest of the partners. Honey could owe money she doesn't have. She's got a girl in college and a boy still at home and a very, very sweet life. What with insurance and her share of the partnership, not to mention HD Parker's money, Honey is not ever going to go hungry. You hear me?"

I grunted.

"Before you get all judgmental, see this from Honey's view. It was Dr. Fallon who killed her husband, not one of Garcia's law partners. I doubt she even understands the ins and outs of the so-called malfeasance, and for all she knows, even without the perjury, the trial could have gone the way it did. And if she makes a fuss, she could be destroying not only her own life and livelihood, but those of other men and women, and their husbands and wives and kids, people Honey has known for years. Partnerships are close, Bear. And only one of those

478

people did anything wrong. You get that, Bear? So don't be laying down heartache on Honey when you see her. Hear me? I don't know the Bible the way you do, but I know right from wrong, and I'm telling you that would be wrong. It's none of your business, so back off. You listen to me this time."

I said I would.

"You, to get back on track, you're going to be a star. Talk about a primo witness. A local Church of Christ minister — you're already a media darling, Bear. Get this, your daughter Merrie tells me that Amazon is showing an increase in sales of that boring book you wrote."

I said, "Yeah? Which one?" That was good news. Sales had settled down to a slow trickle. "Listen, Wanderley, I had a reviewer call my third book 'lively.' "

"For a theological tome, Bear. It might be 'lively' for a theological tome. Your book is probably required reading for some poor seminarians, but that's not a real fast crowd we're talking about. You're no Stephanie Meyer."

"Stephanie Meyer?"

Wanderley shifted in his chair and looked away from me.

"Vampire books. Never mind. Anyway. I gotta go. You have to rest."

He stood up and sent the chair spinning back to knock over a potted palm that had been looking dejected among all the tropical blossoms.

I said, not feeling real comfortable with it, but feeling like I needed to ask, "You want to pray with me, Wanderley?"

Wanderley stopped with his hand on the door and his amazing eyebrow did its most amazing trick to date.

"Uh, that's going to be a no, Bear."

He opened the door and stepped out, then stuck his head back in and gave me a hard look.

"And don't be praying for me behind my back, either, preacher. That's seriously not kosher." He left.

I prayed for Wanderley anyway. It's all kosher to me.

Before they wheeled me out of the hospital, I asked them to take me to see Miss Lily. Annie Laurie said, "Bear, Miss Lily's gone. But before she died, one of her visitors told her about the shooting. She cried and said, 'Tell Bear I'm going to pray him all the way home.' "

I said, "Did she mean Heaven or Sugar Land?"

"Where will I be driving you to?" Annie asked.

"Sugar Land," I said.

"Well, all right, then," Annie answered.

I was on the levee with Baby Bear, walking home in the warm, moist twilight. We weren't jogging. It would be some time before I'd be up to jogging again.

Merrie was home for the weekend and she had promised me a game of chess. I told Jo I would read her the first four chapters of *The Jungle Book*. It's required reading. I like that book. It wouldn't be too bad. Then I would read her a chapter out of *Hurlbut's Story of the Bible*. Miss Lily left me her copy.

And Irene Hayden had baked me an entire lemon chiffon pie, all for myself, and that's what I was going to have for dinner. Jo said she would have a small piece if I could be persuaded to share. Madame Laney says she's going to have to build up some muscle mass if she's going to make it through the American School of Ballet program — so my Jo is actually eating. No meat. But still. Imagine. Pie for Jo.

I looked down into the lit houses that backed onto the levee. There was happiness and heartbreak going on in those houses that I would never know about. It wasn't on me. And that was good.

# ACKNOWLEDGMENTS

My family is a family of storytellers. As a child, my parents gave me and my sister Lisa more books than toys, and more cautionary tales than lectures. We were allowed to read anything, age-appropriate or not, if it was well written. I'm grateful for that. I am grateful for the faith my parents shared, and for how they taught me to make my own.

Ten or so years ago, Niti Nguyen told me a remarkable story. I asked her if I could use it if I ever managed to get a book written, and she said I could. A fictionalized version of that story is in *Faithful Unto Death* — I thank her.

Author and editor Sarah Cortez was my first writing mentor — a gentle and encouraging teacher.

Roger Paulding and the entire Houston Writer's Guild — good readers and good listeners, all of them.

Dr. Mary McIntire conceived of the Rice University Master of Liberal Studies program. Thanks to Dr. John Freeman, I was accepted as a member of their first class. The first version of *Faithful Unto Death* was my capstone project for the program — Drs. Dennis Huston and David Schneider were my mentors, and they couldn't have been more generous with their time and their helpful, pointed, funny, and frequently snarky comments. Every professor I ever had at Rice University was the best professor I've ever had. I am profoundly grateful to my professors and classmates at Rice, who didn't change just my life, they changed me.

My sister and brother-in-law, Lisa and Michael Nicholls, have believed from the beginning. They have been relentlessly supportive — in addition to the celebrations at each milestone, they bought me my first laptop so I would not have to write in seclusion, they gave me my Rice class ring — engraved "It's never too late" inside so I would never forget. I never will.

Friends and neighbors Dr. Tim Sitter and Dr. Fae Garden helped me kill Graham Garcia in such a way that I would not forever scar little Jessica Min. They tell me they are keeping the phone messages that begin, "Okay, can you help me out? I want to kill a guy . . ." Thank you.

Michelle and Kathi and Terri and Audrey and Lisa listened to interminable book questions and took them all seriously — unless it was time not to, and then they helped me laugh it off.

Michelle Pinkerton wrote my French for me. Online translators have their limitations. Michelle doesn't.

In March 2010, Harriette Sackler of Malice Domestic called to say that I had won a William F. Deeck — Malice Domestic Grant for Unpublished Writers. Thanks to Malice Domestic, and the magic train of events they started, I arrived at the convention a year later with a book deal. Harriette Sackler and Arlene Trundy of the grants committee, wise, witty, and wonderful women, have continued to be friends and mentors, and if you are an aspiring mystery writer, you cannot have better.

At the 2010 Malice Domestic Convention, I met the inimitable Janet Reid, of Fine-Print Literary Management. She is my fairy godmother who made all my dreams come true when I clicked my heels three . . . no. That's not right. There was no heel clicking. There was a good deal of rewriting and reworking and very strict instructions to be followed. At a very low period, Janet wrote me a short e-mail that so heartened me, that I would have the entirety of that e-mail tattooed on my body if I weren't so worried about what my sons would think of their mom. But at the end of the road, there was a book deal, just as Janet had said there would be. She tries to come off sharky (and she can be) but she is true-blue, the right stuff, and thank you, God, for bringing me to her attention. What a gift.

And then Janet brought me to my editor, Shannon Jamieson Vazquez of the Berkley Publishing Group, who is beautiful and very scary and the most careful reader in the entire world, and no, I am not excepting the scrupulous people who compile the *Oxford English Dictionary*. Shannon's comments, cuts, and changes have made this a richer, deeper book — and also saved me from a timeline error that would have haunted me for as long as the book is read.

Glenn Pinkerton, Winn Carter, and Walter Cicack answered legal questions on a host of topics. ("Did your murderer *bring* the golf club, or find it there?") I thank them for their advice.

My meticulous copyeditor, Joan Matthews, went out of her way to assist me and provide useful information. Cover designer

Judith Lagerman captured Sugar Land for me.

W.J., Evans, and Charlie Cicack, my three sons, answered my questions about current vernacular, and football and architecture and technology and trucks, and high school and murder and the Norman French and . . . who needs Wikipedia. But mostly, they have supplied me with a host of unbelievable-but-true boy stories to use in future books. It was my sons who taught me that if I hadn't specifically forbidden them to shoot off fireworks in the bathtub, well, then.

The biggest thank-you of all is for my spooky-smart husband, Richard Box. He kept my writing schedule on a spreadsheet, fended off visitors and phone calls, proofed and edited one thousand versions of the novel, brought me flowers and wine and a gold locket like Jo's. He believed in the book. More important, it was Richard who made me believe. Faithful unto death, Richard.